Summer's Lease

CARRIE ELKS

pıatkus

PIATKUS

First published in Great Britain in 2017 by Piatkus

1 3 5 7 9 10 8 6 4 2

A CIP catalogue record for this book
is available from the British Library.

ISBN 978-0-349-41550-5

Typeset in Caslon by M Rules

Printed and bound in Great Britain by
Clays Ltd, St Ives plc

Papers used by Piatkus are from well-managed forests
and other responsible sources.

MIX
Paper from
responsible sources
FSC® C104740

Piatkus
An imprint of
Little, Brown Book Group
Carmelite House
50 Victoria Embankment
London EC4Y 0DZ

An Hachette UK Company
www.hachette.co.uk

www.littlebrown.co.uk

Carrie Elks lives near London, England and writes contemporary romance with a dash of intrigue. She loves to travel and meet new people, and has lived in the USA and Switzerland as well as the UK. An avid social networker, she tries to limit her Facebook and Twitter time to stolen moments between writing chapters. When she isn't reading or writing, she can usually be found baking, drinking wine or working out how to combine the two.

Visit her website at www.carrieelks.com and follow her on Twitter at @CarrieElks

To my friends who are more like sisters.

1

There's beggary in the love that can be reckoned

– Antony and Cleopatra

'You're fired.'

It wasn't the first time Cesca Shakespeare had heard those words. It wasn't even the sixth time, but it was the only time they'd been said to her inside the ridiculousness that was Cleopatra's Cat Café, London's premiere fine-dining establishment for lovers of the feline species.

It was a crazy idea, Cesca thought, combining afternoon tea with furry cats who seemed to take pleasure moulting their hair all over the food and drink. Yet since she'd begun working here two weeks ago it had been completely booked out, full of cooing, selfie-stick-clutching tourists, who loved the way the cats curled up on their laps while they sipped lapsang souchong out of fine bone china cups.

The people, not the cats. The kitties preferred licking cream out of the hand-painted jugs.

'I'm sorry?' If it wasn't for the fact she needed this job – or at least the way it paid her rent – she'd be laughing in the owner's face right now. You couldn't really describe it as her dream job, carrying trays of sandwiches while trying not to trip over cats as they seemed to deliberately jump in her way. More than once they'd sent her flying, launching plates full of cakes over the unsuspecting clientele.

'You obviously aren't cut out for working here,' Philomena, the owner, told her. 'In your résumé it said you were a cat lover, but you've done nothing but shout at Tootsie, Simba and the others. And what you just said to Mr Tibbles, well that was unforgivable.'

'He'd just peed on a whole tray of afternoon tea,' Cesca protested.

'If you'd have picked up the tray as soon as I called service there wouldn't have been a problem. These cats are highly strung, they need to mark their territory. It's our job to give them boundaries. You told me you had experience of rare breeds like Mr Tibbles.'

From the corner of her eye, Cesca saw him prowl along the floor towards them. Mr Tibbles was a Sphynx, a hairless breed that made him look as though he'd taken all his clothes off and was prancing around the café in the buff.

'I do have some experience. There were lots of cats around when I was growing up ... ' Cesca trailed off weakly, knowing she'd lied through her teeth to get this job. Not that the job was a catch, but by the time she'd seen the advert in the window, she was desperate. Enough to take a job surrounded by hissing cats who seemed to want nothing more than make her life a misery.

'Well it isn't working out. Customers have complained about the way you've been treating the animals. You can't just drop-kick them whenever they misbehave.'

'I didn't drop-kick them, I swiped them off the table. And

it was my first day, I didn't know the customers liked sharing their food.'

'That's the point.' Philomena sighed. 'A real cat lover wouldn't think twice. You're clearly an imposter.' She lowered her voice, brushing her hair away from her sweaty face. 'Do you even like cats?'

Torn between a natural urge to be truthful, and her need for a job, Cesca hesitated. As if he could sense the drama, Mr Tibbles wandered over, weaving his way between Cesca's legs. Looking up at her through his watery blue eyes, he narrowed them as if in challenge.

'I ... um ... I'm not that fond of them. But I needed the job and I've never had a problem with animals. I used to spend every weekend playing with our neighbour's dog.'

Philomena shuddered. 'Dog lovers aren't welcome here,' she hissed, sounding almost cat-like herself. 'Now get your things and leave before you upset Mr Tibbles with your nasty words.'

'Can I at least have my wages?' It had come to something when Cesca had to beg for money, but with this week's rent looming ominously above her, there was nothing to do but embarrass herself. Too many times she'd had to make up excuses for paying late, or sometimes not paying at all. Living hand-to-mouth in London wasn't for the faint-hearted.

What choice did she have though? At the age of twenty-four she was on a downward spiral when her friends were all on the up. While they'd been studying hard at university, and getting professional positions that paid them a good salary, Cesca had been rebounding from job to job like a pinball, not staying still long enough to really take a good look at herself.

She'd become good at that avoidance, too. Six years of pretending she was happy, she was OK, that she actually liked a bohemian lifestyle of drifting between flats, making her friends double over in laughter every time she lost another dead-end job, or told them about yet another failed relationship. But when she was lying in bed at night, trying to ignore the pervasive smell of damp and mould that seemed to permeate the walls, she wasn't laughing at all. She wasn't even smiling. That was when the monsters seemed to crawl out from their hiding place in the bottom of her brain, whispering in her ear, reminding her she was a failure, a loser, and she would never amount to anything.

That she'd had her big chance and she'd blown it.

'Here, take this.' Philomena shoved a thick envelope into her hand. She'd not bothered to close it, and Cesca could see the curled up corners of bank notes through the opening. 'Please don't ask me for a reference,' her boss continued. 'I won't be able to say anything nice.'

Cesca wouldn't dare. There weren't many of her previous employers who had agreed to say anything pleasant about her, which was so unfair because she was genuinely a nice person. She simply wasn't very good at holding down a job.

Stuffing the envelope full of cash in her bag, Cesca shrugged on her summer jacket, zipping it up to the neck. It might have been June outside, but nobody had bothered to tell the weather that, and a cold wind had decided to make its home in the city, whipping through the streets like an angry ghost.

'Goodbye.' Cesca walked across the kitchen floor, heading for the back door that led to the small, paved yard full of rubbish bins and cardboard boxes. Just before she reached out to open it, Philomena yelled again.

'And close the door behind you, we don't want the cats escaping.'

Resisting the urge to slam the door, Cesca stepped into the yard and took a deep breath, immediately regretting it when the pungent aroma of used cat litter filled her nostrils.

Maybe getting fired wasn't the end of the world, after all.

On Friday afternoons London took on a life of its own, full of wandering tourists who barrelled into suited city workers in search of their first drink of the weekend. Even the cars seemed noisier, engines roaring a little louder, their honking horns full of fury. The streets were full of people on a mission, with places to go, things to do, and that didn't include being polite to anybody else.

Cesca barely noticed. She was too busy trying to push her way through the crowds while she mentally calculated how much money she had left. Over the years she'd learned how to eke out her wages to the last penny, coming up with experimental recipes that combined the strangest of ingredients. There was even a time when she was a skip-diver, running around with a gang of rich kids who thought it was subversive to eat a sandwich two days after its sell-by date. They'd been playing at being poor, finding the same exhilaration in living in a squat that most people got at the top of a roller coaster, holding their breaths before going down, down, down. But while for them it was a choice, for Cesca it had already become a way of life.

It was hard to pinpoint the exact moment she realised how far she'd fallen. By the time she looked around and discovered the hole she'd found herself in, it was already too late. She was too proud to ask for help, too afraid to admit to her family and friends what a state her life was in.

There was a big crowd of Japanese tourists trying to push their way into the Underground station, spilling out onto the pavement where the lobby wouldn't hold them all. Cesca walked around them, shooting them an envious glance, knowing she couldn't afford to take the Tube train home. The money in her purse wasn't quite enough to pay this week's rent, and it definitely wasn't enough to stretch into next week. Luxuries like train journeys and dinner would have to wait until she found another job, or got her jobseeker's allowance, or somehow managed to swallow her pride and ask for help.

The crowds thinned out as she crossed the Thames, heading towards the darker, dingier part of town where she shared a flat. The shops, so bright and full of pretty things north of the river, became less salubrious, offering overripe fruit and unwanted cuts of meat, the aroma wafting out into the smoky air. This was the part of London Cesca had come to know in the past few years, so far removed from her childhood in Hampstead, where her father still lived. Growing up in north London, the second youngest of four sisters, had been something of a fairy tale compared with the life she now lived.

Not that her childhood had been idyllic. Her mother's death, when Cesca was eleven, had been enough to see to that.

The flat Cesca shared with another girl – Susie Latham – was on the top floor of a tall, crooked building. The red brick walls had long since turned black, coated with hundreds of years of soot and fumes, with patches eaten away by the wind and rain. The ground floor housed an old newspaper shop, the sort that sold cigarettes by the stick to children who weren't anywhere near the legal age of eighteen years old. Stepping over the pile of empty soft-drink cans and screwed-up sweet wrappers, Cesca opened the door leading into the stair lobby, kicking the pile of unclaimed mail to the side. Like the rest of the building, the steps had seen better days, the carpet worn to shreds by years of trampling feet.

Susie was in the bathroom, using a set of tiny tweezers to apply false eyelashes with glue. She stuck them on strand by strand, cursing every time she dropped a tiny hair into the crusty blue sink. Hearing Cesca's footfall in the hallway, she looked up, flashing a closed-mouth smile.

'All right?'

Cesca nodded. She'd been living with Susie for almost half a year, yet they were still only on polite terms. That was the weird thing about life in London; a flatmate could be a virtual stranger, yet you could instantly click with somebody you met on the street. Cesca found the situation uncomfortable, enough to spend most of her time in the cramped bedroom she'd claimed as hers.

'Dave rang this afternoon, he's coming for the rent tomorrow.' Susie glued the final lash to her right lid. 'You've got the money this time, haven't you?'

'Of course.'

'Good, because it's too bloody cold to be out on our arses.' Susie tipped her head to the side, scrutinising her reflection. 'Oh, and Jamie's coming over tonight.'

'I thought you two had broken up.'

'He came crawling back, they always do. He's taking me dancing first, then maybe for something to eat.'

'Is his wife going?' Cesca asked pointedly.

'No she isn't! Anyway, he's explained all that, he's planning on getting a divorce, but she's making things difficult for him. She needs to get a bloody life.'

Cesca rolled her eyes. 'What time will you be back?' She walked into the kitchen and switched the kettle on. Pulling open the fridge, she looked inside, grabbing a small carton of milk that was languishing at the back of the shelf. Shaking it, she saw the telltale signs of yellow gunge sticking to the plastic sides. Black coffee it was, then.

'Probably after midnight,' Susie shouted from the bathroom. 'Will you be up?'

It was funny how people asked the wrong questions all the time. Susie didn't really want to know if Cesca would be awake – she wanted to know if she'd hide in her bedroom like she always did, letting Susie and her married-man-of-the-week have some space.

'I might go and visit my Uncle Hugh,' Cesca called back. 'He's offered for me to stay over. So don't wait up.'

Her godfather hadn't offered anything of the sort, though Cesca knew he would in a heartbeat. Hugh was like a second father to her, and her confidant since her mother died.

'Oh!' Susie's response held a whole range of emotions in a single syllable. 'Well, enjoy yourself.'

That was that, then. Cesca was jobless, cashless and even the person she lived with couldn't wait to see the back of her.

Was this rock bottom? She hoped so. If she sank any lower she wasn't sure she'd ever be able to climb back up.

2

*Love is like a child
that longs for everything it can come by*

– The Two Gentlemen of Verona

'Well I can't say I'm surprised.' Hugh walked into his living room, balancing a tray of cups, saucers and cakes. 'It's hard to picture you enjoying a job surrounded by cats. You never were one for animals. I can remember taking you and Kitty to the zoo one year, you both screamed whenever we went near the enclosures.'

'That's not true,' Cesca protested. 'Kitty's scared of everything, I'll give you that. But I loved the zoo. I've got lots of good memories of you taking me there.' She smiled at the mention of her youngest sister. 'She said hi, by the way.'

'Oh, have you spoken to her?'

'We still Skype every week. Lucy's orders.' Cesca rolled her eyes.

'Good old Lucy, she has you all under control. That's what oldest sisters are for, isn't it?' He smiled gently.

'It's like a military operation,' she agreed. 'With Kitty in LA and Juliet in Maryland, Lucy and I are the only two in the same time zone. Trying to get us all on the call at the same time is like herding cats.' And even then, Lucy was three hundred miles away in Edinburgh. The Shakespeare sisters were like flowers scattered in the wind.

Hugh placed the tray on the polished coffee table, leaning over to pour Earl Grey from the ornate Chinese teapot into the cups. Passing one to Cesca, he took the other with him to the winged chair by the fireplace. Closing his eyes, he inhaled the aroma before taking a tiny sip. 'Ah, bliss.'

Cesca took a drink of her own tea, appreciating the mild, flowery perfume. Like so many other things, it was Hugh who had introduced her to the intricacies of tea, forcing her to learn the many variations of leaves at a time when her friends were downing cans of Coke. From those first few tastings she'd developed a love of the hot drink, appreciating the luxury of a well-brewed leaf, able to tell the difference between a lapsang souchong and a da hong pao with her eyes shut. For Hugh, tea was a ritual, something to be savoured. He winced every time he saw somebody simply dunking a bag in a mug filled with hot water and milk.

Placing her cup down, Cesca sat back on the sofa, curling her feet beneath her. 'You'd think that if I love tea this much, working in a café would be simple.'

'Two completely different things, my dear,' Hugh told her. 'It's like enjoying a good steak and then comparing it to working in an abattoir.'

'That might be my next job,' Cesca said grimly. 'Except they probably wouldn't even give me a chance. Not with my history.'

She sat back and took a look around Hugh's beautiful apartment. The red brick building in Mayfair couldn't be further from Cesca's dismal flat, although only a few miles separated them. In lifestyle, though, they were oceans apart. Hugh came from old money, and his late mother had willed this apartment to him when he was in his twenties. The furnishings inside were family heirlooms. The chairs ranged from the Regency to the Victorian period, and despite their age all the tables looked almost new, their wood polished and shiny. Even the walls held evidence of his ancestry, with his long-dead great-great-grandfather staring down at them from a painting above the fireplace.

'This has to stop. You know that, don't you?'

She whipped her head around to look at Hugh. 'What do you mean?'

He looked pained, but resolved. 'You know exactly what I mean. I've watched you hop from job to job for too long. It's not right. I promised your mother I'd look after you. I hate breaking promises.'

'You do look after me,' Cesca told him. 'By being here, by listening to me moan. Most people would have given up on me.'

Hugh topped up their cups, holding the china pot carefully. 'You need help, poppet, not a listening ear. If I were an American I'd have staged an intervention by now.'

For the first time since she'd walked into his apartment, Cesca smiled. 'You'd hate an intervention. All that talking about feelings and making me cry. The only thing you like staging is a play at the theatre.'

He looked up and caught her eye, and Cesca realised she wasn't going to get out of this conversation easily. 'That's the only thing you should be thinking about, too. You have the theatre in your blood, yet you've been running away from it for six years.'

She felt her chest constrict. 'I don't want to talk about that.'

'And I thought I was the one with a stiff upper lip. That's your whole problem, don't you see? Maybe if you talked about it, and really worked things through, you'd have got over it by now. Instead here you are getting sacked from dead-end jobs, and squandering your talent.'

Her mouth felt dry, in spite of the tea. 'Shit happens, and it happened to me. I had my chance and I'm not good enough for it to happen again.'

Hugh slammed his cup down, causing tea to spill over the sides. 'I don't want to hear you say that! You were eighteen years old; the world was at your feet. And yes, "shit happened", as you so elegantly describe it. But that doesn't make you any less talented.'

'My play bombed.' It still hurt to say it, even after all these years. 'They closed it down after a week. The producers lost all that money.'

'Damn it, Cesca, it wasn't your fault. The play was good, you know that.'

'It doesn't matter. If nobody wants to come to see it, if everybody returns their tickets, then I may as well not have bothered.'

'They returned the tickets because the leading man disappeared. And that wasn't your fault either.'

No, it wasn't her fault at all. It was Sam Carlton's fault, the good-looking, talented bastard. 'I should've known it was all too good to be true. I mean, what kind of man leaves town after press night? Before the play even opens?'

Hugh shrugged. 'I know he left at the wrong moment, but it wasn't personal.'

She slammed her hand on the table next to her. 'Of course it was personal.' Tears stung her eyes. 'Everything about that play was personal. I *bled* those words out. And he just left, Hugh, without saying a word. He left us all in the lurch the day before we were supposed to open. So don't tell me it wasn't personal, because it was.'

'You're being irrational.'

She took a deep breath. 'I know I am. You must think I'm an idiot. And I know it's not his fault the understudy sucked, or that the play closed. But look at him, he's disgustingly successful, and I'm ... well, I'm *me*.'

Leaning back against the cushions, she closed her eyes. The tears pooled behind her lids. 'The play meant everything to me,' she said quietly. 'It was meant to be my memorial to Mum. It was supposed to show everybody how wonderful she was, how much we missed her.'

'There will be more plays. You have a talent.'

'It doesn't matter whether I have a talent or not,' Cesca replied. 'I haven't been able to write a single word since.'

Hugh winced. 'You have a gift, Cesca. That isn't something to be squandered.'

'Don't you think I've tried?' she said, remembering all those days spent in front of her computer, a blank screen sneering back at her as her thoughts turned to dust. It wasn't so much a writer's block as a writer's mountain. 'Every time I try to type, nothing comes out. It killed me.'

'You know, Winston Churchill said that success is jumping from failure to failure without losing enthusiasm. Well, something like that. Where's your enthusiasm?' Hugh demanded.

Cesca sighed. 'I managed the failures all right. It's the success that's elusive.'

'You're not going to bloody find it in a cat café, are you?' He shuddered. 'All that hair, and people drinking coffee. Disgusting.'

She wasn't sure whether he was referring to the cats or the coffee. In Hugh's opinion both were unseemly, but coffee usually got the biggest rant.

'I haven't found it anywhere, Uncle Hugh. I've looked and looked and it's gone. In the end there's only one conclusion to make: I was a one-hit wonder. And that hit wasn't even any good.'

'That's a load of poppycock and you know it. My God, Cesca, you won a national competition at the age of eighteen, with a play the judges described as brilliant. You don't get those sort of accolades unless you're hugely talented, you know that.'

She didn't want to think of those days. For a few brief months she'd been riding a wave of excitement, only to have it come tumbling down around her. Cesca had been in her final year at school when she'd entered the competition, absolutely certain that her play would end up at the bottom of the pile. To have it win Novice Play of the Year and then get picked up for production had been a dream come true.

'Talent means nothing.'

'So you're just going to give up?'

'I have to accept that I'm not meant for writing. So I'll keep trying these jobs until something sticks.'

'Nothing's going to stick.' Hugh stood up, striding over to the fireplace. He lifted a photograph, holding the silver frame between his fingers. Cesca recognised the portrait of her mother, standing on stage, holding bunches of roses after a spectacular first night. 'Look at your mother. The theatre is in your blood, it flowed from her to you. And you can pretend it isn't there all you like, because it won't go away. Your mother was born to act, and she did it wonderfully. You were born to write, and when you wrote your first play it was amazing. Prize-winning. Don't let the actions of an immature pretty-boy stop you from fulfilling your potential.'

There was a truth in his words that brought the tears back to Cesca's eyes. Of all the sisters, it was Cesca who had loved the theatre from the moment she was born. Cesca who had begged as a toddler to sit in the wings and watch her mother as she acted on the stage. She'd been hooked from the moment she'd smelled the greasepaint and musty old costumes.

'I can't do it. I promise I've tried. But every time I do, I hear these voices telling me I'm useless, that I'm lying to myself. That Sam Carlton leaving for Hollywood was a blessing, because I'm not meant to be a writer.'

Hugh sat down beside her, his knees clicking as they bent. 'We both know that's not true. You just need to give yourself a bit of time and space. Somewhere to think, to breathe, to let the words flow.'

She laughed. 'Not really possible in London.' At least not the part of London she lived in, surrounded by Susie and her married boyfriends. It was hard enough to breathe, let alone process her thoughts.

'Maybe you should get away.'

Cesca smiled at him fondly. 'Where to? I can't afford to pay next week's rent, there's no way I can find the money for a holiday.'

'I'd give you the money.'

There it was again. She instantly tensed. 'No. No thank

15

you. I know you want the best for me, but I'll pay my own way.'

'What if there was another way?' Hugh asked, looking suddenly crafty. 'What if there was something cheap you could do? I could lend you the cash and you could pay me back.'

'Unless it was exceedingly cheap, I'd never be able to pay you back. And as my namesake said, "never a borrower nor a lender be".'

Hugh smiled at her Shakespearean reference. 'Then we'll make it exceedingly cheap. Plus with the lovely writing you'll be able to do, you can pay me back in no time.' He leaned back and rubbed his chin for a moment, deep in thought. Then he sat straight up, clicking his fingers. 'I've got it!'

'What?'

He ignored her question. 'Stay there, I just need to make a phone call.' He stood, putting his cup on the table beside him.

'I haven't exactly got anywhere to go,' she pointed out, as he walked out into the kitchen.

Five minutes later he was back, a big smile on his face.

'You look like the cat who got the cream,' she told him, wincing at her own joke.

He laughed loudly. 'I just spoke to some old friends. I'd heard on the grapevine they were having trouble finding a house-sitter for their villa in Italy.'

Cesca raised an eyebrow. 'Well that's convenient.'

'Don't look at me like that,' Hugh chided. 'I'm not stretching the truth or making anything up, it's simple serendipity. They have a live-in couple that takes care of the place, but they want to go away for a few weeks, and need somebody they can trust to stay in the house. You won't have to do very much, apart from keep an eye on the place, so there'll be plenty of time to write. Plus if you agree to it, they'll pay for your flights and food while you're there.'

Sceptical didn't even cover it. 'And where is this villa that needs a messed up failure to take care of it?' she asked.

'It's on Lake Como, just outside a pretty little village called Varenna. Villa Palladino – that's where you'll be staying – has been in their family for centuries. I've been there myself, it's absolutely beautiful. What's more, it's secluded and quiet, and nobody will interrupt you there. You can breathe in the lake air, take lots of walks, you can even lie on the beach if you want to.' He paused, glancing up at her again. 'Or you can write.'

She was so torn it almost hurt. Part of her wanted to get up and jump up and down, show some excitement and thank her uncle for saving her life. The other bit – the Cesca who had been running the show for the past six years – was telling her it was too good to be true, that things like this didn't happen to her. She was being set up for a fall, and was going to let her godfather down once again.

'I can't hold down a job,' Cesca whispered, 'so what makes you think I can do this one?'

'I know you can do it,' Hugh replied, 'because there's nothing to do but write and get your head straight. It's what you should have done all those years ago after the play folded. I should have insisted upon it. Instead you got yourself into this downward spiral, and you're spinning so fast that nobody can catch you.'

It was impossible to ignore the truth in his words, and Cesca didn't bother to try.

'If I do go,' she said hesitantly, still not quite able to bring herself to agree, 'then I'll need to sort some things out. Like a passport, and clothes. Plus I need to work out what the hell I'm going to write.'

Hugh gave her a beaming smile. 'Those are the easy things, we can get them arranged tout de suite. Getting you to agree to it is the tricky one.'

'Do you have a photograph of the villa?' Cesca asked. 'How big is it?'

Hugh shrugged, glancing away. 'Oh, it's medium-sized. I don't think I have a photo, they're very private people. There's enough rooms for you not to bump into the couple who look after the house while they're there, but it's not so big that you'll be overwhelmed after they leave.' Sensing her reluctance, he reached out for her arm. 'Just give it a try. Do it for me, for your dad – goodness, do it for your mother if you have to, but get on a plane and go to Italy. If you hate it, I'll talk to my friends and we can think again.'

'I don't know . . .'

'Stop thinking and just say yes,' Hugh told her. 'Look at this as rock bottom, and now you have a chance to start climbing back up.'

He was right, she knew he was. It was crazy how little she had left to lose. There came a point in everybody's life where you either accepted that things were never going to improve, or you took hold of the wheel and actually started thinking about where you were going. Sitting there, in that London flat, Cesca realised this was the moment for her.

Could she ignore it? Could she bear to walk away and only look back with regrets? She already had enough of those to last a lifetime.

'OK, I'll do it,' she said, causing Hugh to let out a relieved sigh. 'I'll go to Italy and I'll look after that damn house and I'll try to make some changes in my life.'

Hugh pulled her up into an uncharacteristic hug. Stunned, Cesca returned the embrace, her hands on his back, feeling the bones pressing through his thin frame.

'Good girl,' he whispered, 'I'm so proud of you.'

His words touched her, and made her feel wistful. There was a time she was proud of herself, too. If only she could feel that way again.

'When do you leave?' her father asked, looking at her over the rim of his mug.

'Tomorrow,' Cesca told him. 'I catch a flight from Heathrow in the morning.' She glanced around the kitchen. The walls were shabby, paint peeling away from the plaster. The sink was piled up with dirty dishes. It was crazy, really. The house itself was worth a lot of money, but Oliver had neglected it for years, more interested in studying insects than the interior decor.

She felt a twinge of anxiety about leaving her father behind. Though he was still a good-looking man, sitting across the kitchen table from her he looked frailer than she remembered. Older.

'Have you told your sisters you're going?' he asked.

'I spoke to them this morning. On Skype.'

'On that video phone thing?' Oliver questioned, shaking his head. 'It's amazing how you can all see each other, even though you girls are scattered far and wide.'

She smiled softly. She'd never get used to sitting in this kitchen without them. It held so many memories for her.

Lucy desperately trying to make their packed lunches for school, Juliet painting a picture on the old wooden table. Kitty glued to the ancient television perched on the kitchen counter. It felt so quiet now, in comparison. As a child, this house had been full of life. The Shakespeare sisters had been vibrant and noisy. But now all that was left were the ghosts of their past.

She could almost see her mother in here, too. Looking as glamorous as ever, leaning down to kiss each one of them before leaving for the theatre. She'd always smelled delicious, like a bouquet of flowers. Sometimes, Cesca caught a whiff of that same perfume and it brought everything back.

'Will you be OK while I'm gone?' she asked her father.

'Of course I will. I've got my work to keep me busy. Plus Hugh called to invite me to dinner. Oh, and Lucy will probably pop down from Edinburgh at some point.'

Thank goodness for Lucy. Their oldest sister always seemed to have everything under control. 'I'll try to call you,' she told him.

He waved his hand. 'I probably won't pick up. And I still can't work that damned answering machine. Why don't you send me a postcard instead?'

'I can do that.'

He was looking down at his crossword, tapping his pen against his mouth. She'd lost his attention again. 'Dad, you will take care of yourself, won't you?' she asked, aware of the irony of her words. 'Make sure you eat properly.'

Pulling his pen from his mouth, he scribbled an answer. 'I always eat properly,' he said. 'Though not as well as you, I expect. Italy has some wonderful food.' Finally, he looked up at her. 'What are you going to do over there anyway?'

She sighed. 'Like I told you, I'm going to look after a villa. And I'm going to try to write again.'

For the first time, his face lit up with interest. 'A play?' he asked.

'If I can. I'm a bit rusty though.' Understatement of the year.

'That's wonderful news. Your mother would be so proud if she was alive. She always dreamed that one of her daughters would follow her into the theatre.'

'I know.' Cesca looked down. 'I don't think she'd be proud though. I've turned out to be a disappointment.'

'Of course you haven't.' Oliver shook his head. 'All you girls, you've done so well. It wasn't easy for any of you after Milly . . . ' He faded out, tears springing to his eyes. 'Well, anyway, do your best. That's all you can do.'

For a moment there she'd thought he was going to open up to her. But she could see him withdrawing in front of her eyes. He carried on filling in his crossword puzzle, as she finished her mug of tea.

He was right, though. Her best was all she could do. But would it be good enough?

3

I was in a better place;
but travellers must be content
— As You Like It

The Italian sun was beating through the huge glass windows of the airport, as if to welcome her. She basked in the radiated warmth, trying to work out which group of people to follow, attempting to understand the foreign words on the signs overhead.

Everything sounded better in Italian. Words such as *Imbarchi*, *Attenzione* and *Partenza* seemed to drip off the tongue like honey. Sadly she didn't understand any of them, not even when she finally located her guidebook and started to leaf through it, hoping there might be a map of the airport somewhere. It was only when she looked again that she saw each sign had an English translation. Stupid? Her?

By the time she got to baggage reclaim, Cesca's was the only bag left. A battered red leather case that was going round in circles, forlorn in its seclusion. Cesca hefted it from the belt and onto a trolley, cursing the fact it was so old it didn't have the handle and wheels that most modern luggage had.

Her stomach contracted with anxiety as she walked into the arrivals hall. It was full of people, all waiting for their loved ones, and drivers holding cardboard signs with names on. Milan was one of Italy's busiest airports, serving the city as well as the tourist-oriented lakes, and today was testament to that. She came to a stop and looked around, wondering whether she should try to find a public telephone and call Hugh.

'Miss Shakespeare?' A deep voice came from her left. She turned to see a tall man standing next to her.

'That's me.' She offered him a smile. He looked to be in his thirties, maybe a little older. He also didn't look as though he was lost. That in itself was a minor miracle.

'My name is Alessandro, this is my wife, Gabriella. We're here to take you to Villa Palladino.'

A tiny brunette stepped forward, beaming. 'I'm Gabi, and you can call him Sandro. I'm so pleased you're here.' She enveloped Cesca in a tight embrace, knocking the wind out of her. For a petite woman, Gabi was very strong.

'It's lovely to meet you,' Cesca replied. 'And I'm so happy you speak English. My Italian is woeful, I'm sorry.'

Gabi waved off her apology. 'Not at all, you'll pick it up while you're here. And most of us around the lake speak English, it's our second language.'

'Still, I should at least try,' Cesca replied. 'When in Rome and all that.'

Gabi frowned. 'This isn't Rome. This is Milan.'

Cesca laughed. The woman must think she was crazy. 'No, it's an English saying. When in Rome, do as the Romans do. It means when you're in a different country, you should adopt their ways.'

'Well I would agree with that.' Sandro took the trolley

from Cesca. 'But we will give you a few days before we expect fluent Italian.'

Gabi hit his arm good-humouredly. 'Stop it, she's here to do us a favour. We should be nice to her.' She grabbed Cesca's hand and pulled her along, following Sandro to the exit. 'I'm so pleased you could come, you don't know what a relief it is to us. Sandro's sister is due to have a baby later this month, and she has nobody to help her. She and Sandro are orphans, you see. So we are travelling to Florence to look after her, but we couldn't leave the villa empty.'

Cesca wasn't used to hearing somebody sharing so much within moments of meeting them. Yet there was something so guileless about Gabi, so engaging, that she couldn't help but join in.

'A new baby, how wonderful,' she said, as they walked out of the airport and into the Milan air. 'Do you know if it's a boy or a girl?'

'A boy,' Sandro said, at the same time as Gabi replied, 'It's a girl.'

Cesca laughed at them both.

'It will be a boy, and she will name him after me.' Sandro looked proud.

'We don't know the sex,' Gabi whispered to Cesca. 'But both Sandro's sister and I think it will be a girl.'

'Then she'll have to be called Alessandra,' Cesca replied. 'Almost as good.'

They reached the car – a beautiful old Fiat 500, with bright blue paint and chrome trim. Sandro opened the trunk, squeezing her case into the tiny space.

'I'm afraid it's a tight fit in here,' he told her. 'It's a good car, very efficient, but not much room.'

Cesca shrugged. 'Not a problem, I'm only little.' She glanced down at her small frame. Like Gabi she was just over five feet, with a tiny waist and slender curves. Growing up, she'd felt like a dwarf next to her sisters.

The journey to Varenna took just over an hour, heading east on the main highway out of town, past luscious green fields and dusty brown construction sites. Occasionally they drove through pretty villages, with tall old buildings and verdant gardens. Gabi kept up a constant stream of conversation in almost-perfect English, telling Cesca about the history of the region, the beauty of Varenna, and how much she'd love the villa. By the time they reached the mountains surrounding Lake Como, Cesca couldn't wait to see all the sights Gabi had described. She stared out of the window at the tree-topped cliffs, and at the sparkling lake below, wondering what it would be like to wake up to a sight like that every day.

She was about to find out.

'Of course, the house is beautifully maintained. Signor and Signora Carlton visit every year and are always making renovations. But Signora Carlton, she likes to maintain the history of the place, too. It's very tasteful.'

'Who?' Cesca frowned.

'The owners, Signor and Signora Carlton,' Gabi replied, patiently. 'Our employers.'

'I thought the villa was owned by an old Italian family. Hugh, my godfather, told me it had been in the same family for generations.'

'Of course,' Gabi agreed. 'Signora Carlton, she was a Palladino before she married. She grew up in the villa. Theirs was a fairytale romance. She was studying in New York, and he was a Broadway producer. The two of them fell in love and married within a month. Now they have three beautiful children.'

'They do?' Cesca replied, faintly. A sense of doom was starting to descend. 'What are their names?'

'Well, their eldest son, Sam, you will have heard of, he's a famous actor. Then there's Sienna and Isabella, their daughters. Sienna is sixteen, and Izzy is eighteen.'

'Sam Carlton,' Cesca repeated, her chest tight. She was going to kill Hugh. 'I've heard of him,' she said. 'I think he's overrated.'

Gabi shot her a sharp look. 'He's not only talented, but very kind, too. He has a lot of time for us whenever he visits.'

'Not that he visits very often,' Sandro added, his eyes trained on the road. 'He's too busy with his movie career for that. Now Gabi has to settle for hero-worshipping him from afar.'

'I don't hero-worship him,' Gabi chided. 'I just think he's a good actor.'

'A handsome actor,' Sandro added, smiling wickedly. 'I know what's really going through your mind.'

Gabi launched back into Italian, letting out a stream of words that Cesca couldn't understand. Her sentences shot out like bullets. Cesca leaned back in the car, leaving Sandro and Gabi to their heated exchange. Even their argument sounded beautiful, thanks to the Italian language.

She closed her eyes, letting the afternoon sun bathe her face. As soon as they got to the villa she was going to find a way to call Hugh and arrange for a flight back home. There was no way she was going to sleep in a house owned by a Carlton. Plus she needed to get back to London so she could give Hugh a really good piece of her mind, face to face.

She glanced at her watch. It was two hours since she'd landed in Milan, and she wasn't planning to stay in the country any longer than she had to. If Cesca had her way, she'd be back on a plane within a few hours.

Some trip this was turning out to be.

As Sandro pulled the Fiat up to the gates, Cesca took a moment to take in the sumptuousness of Villa Palladino. The house itself was surrounded by tall, stucco walls, with bougainvillea tumbling over the top, as if it was trying to escape onto the road. Their way was blocked by wrought iron gates, which she could see led to a driveway flanked by Mediterranean cypress trees. Elegant in their height, the thin evergreens swayed softly in the wind, dancing to a silent tune.

It was breathtaking. For a moment, Cesca felt a pang of regret that she wouldn't be able to stay and enjoy the splendour. But then she remembered who owned it, or rather who their son was, and her resolve hardened.

'Is there a telephone I could use?' she asked. 'I haven't got any coverage on my mobile in Europe.' She hadn't been able to afford the roaming charges. Better to walk into town once a week and find an Internet café or public telephone. At least that way she could keep a control on her expenses.

Sandro shook his head. 'I'm afraid not. Signora Carlton insists on seclusion when the family visits. No telephone line, no Wi-Fi, and the networks barely stretch this far.' He pulled his own phone from his pocket. 'I have to walk into Varenna myself to get a signal. I'd be happy to lend you this.'

'It's fine, thank you, if I have to walk into town I can call from a phone box.' Probably best to have some privacy for the choice words she wanted to say to her godfather. 'But

I have to admit I'm surprised there's no connectivity here, what with Mr Carlton having such an important job.' Cesca frowned. Foster Carlton – Sam's father – had been the director of the National Theatre in London for years. It had rocked the acting community when the brash American had taken over such a prestigious role, but he'd taken the theatre from strength to strength.

'That's why his wife insists on complete seclusion when they visit. She's been known to throw his phone in the lake if he doesn't turn it off.' Gabi turned to her and smiled. 'She's as fiery as he is.'

Cesca's mouth turned dry. 'I'll need to walk into town this afternoon,' she told Gabi. 'I have a few telephone calls to make.' And plane tickets to buy. Somehow she was going to have to find the money to pay for them, too.

'Of course,' Gabi agreed, smiling. 'We can all go in together. It will be a pleasure to show you around.'

The interior of the villa was just as entrancing as the outside. The floor was laid with warm, polished wood, and the walls painted in the palest of creams. Dark beams crossed the ceiling, and the rooms were filled with lush, green plants and beautiful furniture, reflecting the impeccable taste of the owners. Gabi led Cesca from room to room, keeping up a stream of conversation, telling her about the cleaners, the gardeners, and where the main electrical fuses were, in case of emergency.

Cesca barely listened, overwhelmed by the beauty of the villa. What a contrast to her shared apartment in London, with its threadbare carpet and mismatched tables. She'd left there this morning, carrying a single suitcase, and somehow she'd ended up here. It was some kind of cruel joke that she couldn't stay. Who wouldn't be inspired by such beauty?

When they walked into the living room, Cesca could see that Gabi had saved the best until last. The space itself was impressive enough, with vaulted ceilings and arched glass doors that led to the garden, but it was the view that made her gasp. A paved terrace, flanked by beautifully tended topiary, led down to a well-maintained lawn, sloping down to the next level. Then there were the flowerbeds, filled with geraniums and pelargoniums, their colours a delight to the eye. A winding path from the lawn led down through a small box hedge maze, with the sparkling lake beyond. Though she couldn't see it, Cesca knew from Hugh's description there was a small beach between the garden and the lake. The thought of the sun warming the sand excited her.

'It's beautiful,' she whispered, to herself as much as to Gabi.

'It is,' Gabi agreed. 'Sandro and I are very lucky to have this job. We're very grateful to have such gracious employers in Signor and Signora Carlton. They've been so kind to us, especially now when Sandro's sister needs him.' She lowered her voice. 'Most employers wouldn't let us leave in the height of summer. But they have been kind enough to find us an angel – you – so that we can go and help Sandro's sister.'

It was almost impossible to ignore the way her stomach contracted. Cesca tried anyway. It would be fine, the Carltons could easily find somebody else to house-sit. It wasn't the most strenuous of jobs, being at Lake Como for free.

'It's been very hard for the Carltons since their son became famous,' Gabi continued. 'This is the only place they've been able to spend time with him without being surrounded by the paparazzi. They value their seclusion and privacy so much, it's hard for them to trust anybody. That's why they were so delighted to find you. They told me you were recommended by a dear friend. That means a lot to them, to know you're not here simply because of their fame.'

Tearing her eyes away from the beautiful vista, Cesca forced a smile onto her face. Just a few hours and she would be gone from here, and this would all be somebody else's problem.

It didn't stop her from feeling guilty, though.

'You lied to me.' She sounded petulant, she knew, but Cesca couldn't help it. She leaned her head on the glass door of the phone box, waiting for Hugh's reply. If only he'd hurry up, this call was costing a fortune.

'I simply omitted the truth, and it was for your own good. Face the past head on and all that, but I knew there was no way you'd go if you knew who owned the house.'

'Damn right I wouldn't have. And now I'm in the most awkward situation. Did you know the couple who run the house are leaving next week to help his sister have her baby? And that they think I'm an angel for coming over to rescue them?'

Hugh laughed, and it made Cesca want to throw the phone. She might have, too, if it wasn't connected to the box.

'That's because you *are* an angel. Can't you give it up to fate and simply let it be? Or look at it this way: the Carltons owe you after what their son did. Think of this as retribution.'

'Hugh! There's absolutely no way I can stay in that house. What if I have to talk to them? Oh my God, what if they come and stay while I'm here?'

'They're in Paris for the summer, I thought I told you

that. Foster is a visiting director at a theatre there, there's no opportunity for them to travel to Italy. That's why they needed a house-sitter.'

'All of them?' Cesca asked ominously.

'All of them,' Hugh confirmed. 'Lucia and the girls are spending the summer with him, and I think their son is filming in LA.' He was very careful not to say Sam's name, she noticed.

'I still can't stay here. You'll have to tell them I'm leaving. I'm planning to go into an Internet café and find a flight home.'

There was silence for a moment. Cesca stared out of the glass windows of the phone box, and into the piazza. Gabi and Sandro had taken a table in one of the cafés, and were chatting away to the waitress. Another pang of guilt shot through Cesca's body.

'What if I can guarantee no visitors?' Hugh asked. 'You've seen the place, it's completely secluded. It's beautiful. Perfect for you, dear girl.'

Cesca added ungrateful to her list of sins. 'It would be perfect,' she agreed, 'if it wasn't for the family who own it.'

'They've never done anything to you. Not Foster or Lucia. And maybe it's the best place to bury some of your demons. You can breathe, you can write, you can come to learn there is good and bad in everything, it all depends on your outlook.'

From her position in the piazza, Gabi caught her eye and waved madly, a huge smile on her face. Cesca had only met her a matter of hours ago, and yet they'd taken to each other right away. Almost like another sister – not that she needed any more. Now she was going to ruin their plans.

She hated this, so much.

As if he sensed a softening, Hugh went in for the kill. 'Why don't you give it a week and see how you feel then? Do it for me. Give yourself a bit of time to think about things, and then call me next Friday. I'll be ready to book you a ticket if you want me to.'

'Will that give the Carltons enough time to find a replacement for me?'

Hugh sighed. 'There *is* no replacement. If you aren't able to do it, their housekeepers will be staying at the villa. The only reason they agreed to let them go is because I suggested you could step in at the last minute. I'm sorry, but there it is. Give yourself a chance to sleep on it and think things through.'

There was no doubt about it, she was between a rock and a hard place, and it was getting more uncomfortable by the minute. Cesca stared out across the piazza again, torn between shouting louder at Hugh and hanging up to join her new friends for a coffee. The sun was slowly sinking down in the sky, casting orange rays across the paved ground, and there was nothing more she wanted to do than go out there and pretend to be a tourist for a few hours.

But could she do it for Gabi and Sandro? She wasn't sure if she could stay in that house and not feel constantly anxious.

Taking a deep breath, she closed her eyes. She couldn't be the one to spoil Gabi and Sandro's plans, not after they'd been so kind to her.

'OK,' she said, aware that she'd been agreeing to things outside her comfort zone ever since she spent the night at Hugh's. 'I'll stay. But you need to know I'm going to be cursing your name every night. I might even make a voodoo doll.'

He laughed again. 'I'll let you know when I feel the pain. And you've made the right choice. You're stronger than you think, just give yourself a chance. You'll be pleasantly surprised.'

Cesca shrugged, even though he couldn't see it. There were worse places to find yourself than in a secluded villa by the side of Lake Como, and worse situations to find yourself in than being given free run of the house for the summer. If she was going to have a nervous breakdown, at least she could do it in style.

That would be something to write home about.

4

Having nothing, nothing can he lose
– Henry VI Part III

Sam Carlton leaned back in his chair, rubbing his face with his palms. The bristles from three days' beard growth scratched at his skin. He hadn't bothered shaving since he'd first been contacted by the journalist, it hadn't seemed worth it.

'I don't understand,' he finally said. 'What possible reason would she have for selling her story?'

Charles Dewitt folded his arms across his chest, his head tilted to one side as he stared back at Sam. They'd known each other for six years, since Sam had moved to Hollywood and been referred to the Dewitt Artist Agency. With a movie offer already in hand, Charles had snapped him up as a client. Since that time, Sam's career had skyrocketed, first as part of the *Summer Breeze* movie franchise, then in the leading roles that had come flooding in after his initial success.

'Publicity.' Charles shrugged. 'Everybody wants it, even Serena Sloane. She's got a new release coming up, she needs to get her name out there.'

Sam could feel the agitation creeping through his bones.

'But this piece is full of lies. I didn't know she was married, she told me it was over. This article makes me out to be some kind of cheating asshole.'

Even the headline was enough to make him feel sick. Serena Sloane: *Hollywood's Mr Nice was Nasty in Bed. And I Loved It!*

'Can't we quash it?' Sam asked. 'Send a rebuttal or sue them or something? Maybe I should call my publicist?'

'I've already called Melissa. She's on the case right now. But tell me, Sam, why would you want to quash the rumours?'

Sam's mouth turned to ashes. 'Because it's fucking embarrassing. All those things she said we did. Half of it isn't true. And the other half I'd rather people didn't know about. Did you know they're all calling me "The Jackhammer"? What kind of nickname is that? It's all over TMZ already.'

Charles' mouth twitched. 'Jack Hammer, eh? That's a pretty good nickname, if you know what I mean?'

Sam closed his eyes, pinching the bridge of his nose between his thumb and forefinger. 'But it's completely exaggerated. Serena and I only went out on a few dates, and as far as I knew she was single. We were friends more than anything. The article is full of lies.' He sighed. His head was starting to pound. He hadn't slept at all last night, too busy reading all the websites he could find, Googling his own name to find out the worst. All the things Charles had told him he should never do.

'What part of it do you want us to refute?' Charles asked. 'The bit where she calls you an animal in bed, or her description of you as a "drill sergeant"?'

'Am I supposed to be flattered by that?' Sam rolled his eyes. 'The whole thing is embarrassing.'

Charles raised one silver-grey eyebrow. At twenty years Sam's senior, no doubt he'd seen it all. A seasoned Hollywood resident, where Sam was still a mere beginner, Charles was rarely fazed by anything. 'But you did know she was married. It's common knowledge around here.'

'I thought you were supposed to be on my side? As far as I knew, they were separated. I can't even leave my apartment without people laughing at me. I can't escape it. And when my parents find out, God, I don't want to see their faces.'

'Give it a few weeks and it'll blow over. Somebody else'll do something stupid, and you'll just be yesterday's news.'

'Well thanks for that.'

Charles shrugged. 'What do you want me to say? I'm your agent. As far as I'm concerned all publicity is good publicity. So you have to put up with a bit of ribbing, so what? This could be the making of you.'

Sam sighed loudly. 'Have you read the article? It's so explicit, she talks about *everything*. How would you feel if everybody knew the exact measurements of your anatomy? There's stuff in there that nobody needs to know, especially not my family.'

'You mean the kinky stuff? They'll get over it. Tell 'em not to read it.'

Sam shook his head. 'I'm not going to talk to them about it.' Even the thought of that made his blood run cold. His mother, he guessed, would let loose at him, in her dramatic Italian accent, berating him for being so stupid, for getting involved with a woman who didn't deserve him.

His father, well, that was a different matter. Not that he thought of him as a father any more. Foster Carlton didn't suffer fools gladly. No matter what Sam did, it was never enough to earn the man's respect, and this wasn't exactly going to change his mind.

'Look, Sam, I know this has all come as a shock, but you need to look at it from a different perspective. You've been telling me you're sick of the roles you're getting offered, that you want to break out of the nice-guy mould they've all put you in. Here's your chance, you need to capitalise on it. Come out, be honest, and let the public see a different side to you. I guarantee you'll get offered some meaty roles after this.'

'Or my career will die a slow, miserable death.'

'It's not gonna happen. You're too good for that. You don't get Oscar nominated unless you have something special, and you, Sam, have that thing. It's gold, you and I both know that. It's just time to take it in a new direction.'

Charles was strangely unperturbed by this whole chain of events. Sam stared at him, wondering why he was so nonchalant. After all, he'd built Sam's career on being a nice guy. Even if Sam did complain about the roles he was offered as a result.

'Did you know about this?' Sam asked, suspiciously. 'You're way too calm. Did the journalist call you about it?'

Charles shrugged. 'This is the first time I've seen the magazine.'

His response did nothing to allay Sam's misgivings. 'You knew, didn't you? You had to. You were the one who introduced me to Serena, after all.' They'd met six months earlier at one of Charles's parties in his Beverly Hills home. Hitting it off immediately, Sam had ended up taking Serena home, and the rest was history. The sort of history that everybody in LA would know about as soon as they read the headlines. Another thought hit Sam. 'You knew she wasn't separated?'

'Of course I did. She's my client, after all. But who am I to judge?'

'You could have told me!' Sam felt indignant. 'Given me a chance before I ended up splashed across the news stands. You must have known it would end up like this, with me looking like an asshole.'

'You're catastrophising,' Charles told him. 'It's only going to give you a bit of street cred. You'll be known as a stud. Girls are going to want to sleep with you, and guys are going to want to be you. Sam "The Jackhammer" Carlton. It has a ring to it, doesn't it?'

There was something so glib in his response that Sam immediately felt his back stiffen. 'Did Serena tell you she was selling her story?'

For the first time, Charles looked uncomfortable. He shifted in his chair, not meeting Sam's gaze. 'I can't discuss my other clients with you, you know that, Sam.'

'So you knew.' Sam swallowed, trying to get rid of the bad taste in his mouth. 'And you didn't warn me.'

'It isn't a big deal. I knew you'd be OK. This is going to be great for your career, Sam. Especially when the next issue comes out, that stuff about your father is dynamite.'

Sam froze at the mention of his father. 'What?' He shook his head, trying to slow the rush of blood through his ears. 'What about my father?'

Charles ignored his shocked expression. 'This is career changing, Sam. First we show you as a sex god, then we show your softer side. Women are going to be falling at their knees for you, the broken guy they all want to lay.'

'She told you I was broken?' Sam couldn't seem to get enough air into his lungs. 'Why did she say that?' He leaned forward, slamming his hand down on the desk. 'What the hell did she tell you?'

'It all makes sense now,' Charles continued. 'I never could work out why you didn't want to talk about your dad, or use his connections. But now I know ... Jeez, you should have told me this before. There's nothing like a scandal to send your career to the next level.'

It was almost impossible to think straight. He'd never imagined she'd use his secrets against him. 'I told her about my family in confidence. It's private, I don't want everybody knowing.'

'Well that's women for you.' Charles was still smiling, oblivious. 'They sleep with you, spend your money, and then when the chips are down they kick you in the teeth. Ask my three ex-wives.'

A vein twitched in his neck at the thought of his messed up family becoming common knowledge. 'She promised she wouldn't say anything.' He breathed in, but the air wouldn't get past the lump in his throat. 'Fuck, this is awful. The sex stuff was bad enough, but this ... '

'You're overreacting,' Charles said. 'Look, this is going to be great for you, and great for Serena. You asked me to work on your image, and that's what I'm doing. Relax, enjoy the ride.'

'How long have you known for?' Sam had the bit between his teeth now. He wasn't about to let go.

'What do you mean?'

He should have known it was going to end like this. Six years in Hollywood had taught him to watch his back. But Serena was a famous actress, and for some reason Sam had thought there was honour among thieves. They'd only dated a handful of times, and yes, some of those times they'd ended up in bed together. But as far as Sam was concerned they were good friends. Or at least, they had been.

'Did you set me up?'

Charles looked surprised. 'What makes you think that?'

Sam could feel the adrenalin building in his body. 'This is all a little too convenient. You and I had a meeting only a few days before your party, and we talked about ways to get some different roles. Some meatier ones. I can remember you telling me I needed to get rid of my wholesome image.' The more Sam talked, the more plausible it all was. 'Jesus, you did arrange it, didn't you?'

Charles smiled. 'Now come on, Sam—'

'Did you set me up?' Sam was almost out of his chair. 'I knew this town was rotten, but I didn't think you were, too.'

Charles threw his hands up in a gesture of surrender. 'All right! Yes, I did suggest to Serena that you might enjoy some more time together. That it could be good for both of your careers. She's desperately trying to get some publicity, and you're attempting to redefine yourself. Why not use this to both your advantages?'

'What the hell gives you the right to agree this without talking to me? You don't get to make these decisions without my go-ahead.'

'It's how this town works, you know that. I'm your agent, Sam, and in many ways I'm your manager, too. If you want to change direction you need to make some difficult choices and I'm wasn't sure you had it in you. I was doing you a favour. When the offers come rolling in I can guarantee you won't be so goddamn puritanical about it.'

Was Charles for real? Sam might have wanted to stop

playing the good guy all the time, but that didn't mean he wanted to be set up. He could guarantee by now that Sam Carlton's fall from grace was the topic-du-jour.

'You asshole. You're supposed to be working for me, I pay you pretty damn well for the privilege. I trusted you, Charles, and you've fucked me over.'

'That's not true, and you know it. I've just made your career for you. A juicy little scandal is box office magic.'

The pounding in Sam's head increased, until it felt like it was about to explode. There was no arguing with Charles. From his self-satisfied smile and smug demeanour, he felt he'd done a good job.

'That's not the career I want,' Sam said. 'And it's not the career I'm going to have. You'll be hearing from my lawyer. If that article about my family is printed, I'll sue you and Serena for everything you've got.' He straightened up. 'As far as I'm concerned, this conversation is over. And so is our working relationship.' He threw the magazine onto Charles's messy desk. 'You're fired.'

Sam managed to lose the paparazzi when he swung his Lexus hybrid through the entrance to the gated community. The security guard beckoned him through with a wave, used to the caravan of media that followed Sam around. He wasn't the only resident who attracted this kind of attention. The community was high-end, with twenty-four hour protection, and it sheltered the rich and famous.

Letting himself into the apartment he shared with his fellow actor and friend Will Allen, Sam threw his keys onto the marble side table and walked into the kitchen. Pulling the refrigerator open, he grabbed a beer from the otherwise-empty ice compartment. As the door closed, he got a glimpse of himself in the shiny chrome, and stepped back, squeezing his eyes shut.

It came to something when he couldn't even look himself in the face. The same face that had made his fame and fortune. But now it was plastered across every tabloid and gossip website, he couldn't stand the sight of it.

Slumping on the sofa, he looked out of the glass doors that led onto the steel balcony. The view from here was stunning, capturing the Hollywood Hills in their full glory. If he leaned to the left he could get a glimpse of the white 'D' that formed the end of the Hollywood sign.

It looked tarnished.

A mouthful of beer did nothing to calm his nerves. Nor did the incessant red flash of his landline voicemail, and the vibrating of his mobile phone in his pocket. No matter where he turned, his life was totally connected; he couldn't escape the enquiring journalists even if he tried. And the thought of what Serena might have said about his father . . .

'Hey! What are you doing home? I thought you would be in crisis meetings all day.' Will threw his jacket across the back of an easy chair, then leaned down to slide off his shoes. 'Did your agent have any bright ideas?'

'No.' Sam's answer was short and sweet. He didn't feel up to going through the details once again, he was too exhausted for that. Will had known him for long enough not to bother persisting, Sam would open up when he was ready.

The two of them had met on their first day at RADA. Sam had walked in nervously, feeling that he'd only been given a place on the acting course because of his father's influence. Out of his comfort zone, he'd hung around at the back of the class, an onlooker in a room full of extroverts. Their instructor had asked them to be flightless birds, staring with envy at their airborne counterparts.

'Well this is a load of old bollocks.' A deep voice had come from Sam's left. 'I thought we'd have to be weeping willows. I've been practising the arm movements all week.'

Since that morning in the drama theatre, the two had become fast friends, climbing through the ranks together, until in their final year they were fighting each other for all the leading roles. When it came to their showpiece play, they were both surrounded by admirers, though it was always Will who was tipped for the top. It had been a surprise to both of them that Sam had been the first to make it.

'Your, ah, folks called earlier.' Will looked hesitant when he said it. More than most, he was aware of Sam's fractured relationship with Foster. 'They left a message on the voicemail.'

The mention of his parents was enough to make Sam feel nauseous. Fuck Charles and Serena Sloane. The two of them were nothing more than snakes in the grass.

'Them and a hundred others.' Sam looked at the landline once again. 'It doesn't matter, anyway, it's not like I ever return Foster's calls.'

'It wasn't your dad. It was your mum. And Izzy called later, too.'

Sam groaned. His sisters idolised him, and he adored them right back. The last thing he wanted was for them to hear anything Serena Sloane had to say. It would tear the family apart.

'I can't talk to them, not right now. I need to get my head straight somehow. I can't even hear myself think here, surrounded by the damn paparazzi. I only have to leave the gates to find myself being stalked.'

Will grimaced. 'Yeah, the bloodsuckers were crowded around the gate when I came in. A few of them started shouting questions at me.'

'What did you say?' Sam leaned forward. 'Did you answer them?' His eyes shifted to his friend.

'Hell no. You know I wouldn't say anything. And anyway, it's not as if there's much to tell them. You went out with her a few times, hooked up, and that was it.'

'That's not what she's saying. Did you know they're all calling me "The Jackhammer"? They've made me out to be as kinky as fuck.' He couldn't mention the other stuff. It was personal, and painful as hell.

Will laughed, shaking his head. 'Oh man, it could be so much worse. What if she'd said you were a bad lay?'

But Sam wasn't smiling. 'I just wish she'd shut the hell up.'

'Well that's not going to happen, not while she's getting her fifteen minutes of fame. So you're going to have to learn to live with it, or go and hide under a rock somewhere. This is Hollywood, man, and you're famous. It's just how it works.'

Sam couldn't help but hear an echo of his ex-agent in Will's words.

'A rock to hide under sounds good right about now.'

'There isn't a rock in the world that you can hide behind, man. As far as the paparazzi are concerned, the Oscar-nominated Sam Carlton is fair game.'

Sam rubbed his face with the palm of his hand. 'I hate this damned town. Whatever happened to the place where dreams are made? It's a nightmare.'

'You're exaggerating. And anyway, we both know how this

industry works. We sold our soul to the devil for a piece of fame.' Will grinned. 'And it's worth it, isn't it?'

'I don't know if it is any more,' Sam said. 'All I know is I can't sit around here while people are reading all this crap about me. I need to get out of town for a while.'

'But where would you go?' Will frowned. 'The paps will just follow you. If you're thinking of going back to London, it's just as bad there.'

Sam shuddered. 'No, I'm definitely not going to London. But I could go to Italy,' he said, mulling the thought over in his head. 'To Varenna, I mean. The villa there is pretty much isolated from everything.'

Will raised his eyebrows. During their time at RADA he'd spent his summers with Sam's family at Villa Palladino. Lazy days hanging out by the pool, evenings wandering into the village for good food and wine. 'It's an option, I guess. But isn't your family there? I thought you were trying to avoid them.'

Sam shook his head. 'Not this year. Foster's directing a show in Paris, and Mom and the girls are spending the summer there with him. They've left the villa in the care of Sandro and Gabi, and we both know they'd leave me alone.'

Will didn't look convinced. 'What the hell will you do there? Lake Como is notorious for having celebrities, the paps will get you as soon as you leave the gates.'

'Then I won't leave the gates,' Sam told him. 'Gabi and Sandro will do the shopping, and I can get my head straight in the peace and quiet. I'll come back here when I'm ready.' It was all starting to take shape in his mind. A few weeks at the villa and he'd be yesterday's news.

'You'll go out of your mind,' Will warned him.

'I'm going out of my mind here. At least there I can do it surrounded by good wine and great food.'

'Ah, the food,' Will smiled. 'And the girls. Man, if I wasn't contracted for this movie I'd be joining you.'

Sam nodded at his offer, but didn't comment. He was too busy thinking about booking a flight to Milan. A few weeks in Italy, without the scrutiny of the press. Time to think things through, and work out how the hell things had ended up like this.

Time to put a few thousand miles between him and Serena Sloane.

And if that bitch really did print an article about his family – and he'd be doing everything possible to make sure she couldn't – he'd be able to lie low for a while. That could only be a good thing.

5

I do desire we may be better strangers

– As You Like It

'I think that's it.' Sandro tried to close the trunk of his Fiat 500, his face dropping as it bounced off the cases stuffed inside it. He prodded them back and then tried again, this time putting his weight into the effort.

'Are you sure you're only going for a few weeks?' Cesca bit away her smile. Shielding her eyes from the bright sun, she peered over at Gabi who was rifling through her bag, desperately trying to find something.

'Of course.' Gabi looked up from her search. 'We promised Signora Carlton, we will be back within a month. Enough time to support Sandro's poor sister through her birth and the homecoming.' She paused for a moment, then threw her hands up in exasperation. 'Sandro, I can't find my phone. It's not in my bag.'

Calmly, Sandro leaned forward, reaching for his wife's hip. He slid the phone out of her pocket, handing it to her without a word. Then he pressed his lips against Gabi's forehead, whispering a few words in Italian.

In the two weeks since she'd arrived in Varenna, Cesca had become fast friends with the Martinellis. They'd spent their days showing her the house and helping her to explore the village, pointing out where the best coffees were served, which was the best gelaterie, and who Cesca should call in case of an emergency. Their nights were more relaxed, with long, pasta-filled suppers complemented by warm red wine and a lot of laughter. Somehow, within the space of a few days, Cesca felt that she'd found a home from home, and had settled into the rhythm of life at Villa Palladino.

The contrast between her time here and her life in London was almost hard to believe.

'We'll keep in touch, I promise,' Gabi told her, grabbing Cesca's face as she kissed her on both cheeks. 'I will email you, it's the easiest way. Just remember to go to the Internet café a couple of times a week.'

'And you have all my contact numbers in case of an emergency,' Sandro added. 'Call any time of the day or night. And there's an old car in the garage that you can use if you need to get to a telephone box.'

Cesca made a face. 'I don't think I'll be driving. I can barely drive on the right side of the road in London, I'll end up in an accident here. I'll use your old bike instead.'

Gabi looked concerned.

'I'll be fine,' Cesca reassured her. 'You've shown me everything I need, and if there are any problems I promise to call you. The cleaners will be here every other day, and the gardeners three times a week. It's not as if I'll be short of people if I need to ask questions.'

Sandro opened the passenger-side door for Gabi. The hot sun reflected off the shiny blue paint, lending it a yellow tinge. 'We should go, my love, if we want to get there before evening arrives.'

Gabi hesitated, giving Cesca a worried look. 'If you're sure . . .'

Cesca enveloped her in an uncharacteristic hug, wrapping her arms around Gabi's torso. Gabi held her tightly, though who she was trying to reassure the most Cesca wasn't sure.

'Stay in touch, *cara mia*.'

'Of course I will. And I'll see you when you get back from Florence. I expect to see all the baby photos.'

Gabi finally smiled. 'Of course, and I can promise you will be bored before I am. Thank you again, you've saved our lives.'

Shooing her petite Italian friend into the car, Cesca didn't bother to reply that Gabi and Alessandro may just be saving her own life in return.

The evening was pleasantly balmy as Cesca walked out of the huge glass doors in the living room, making her way to the terrace overlooking the lake. She was carrying a glass of red wine in her right hand, while her left was curled around a notepad and a pen.

Placing everything down on the small glass table beside her chair, Cesca lifted her glass, inhaling the aroma. Since her arrival in Varenna, she'd fallen in love with the full-bodied Sassicaia wine, loving the silky way it slipped down her throat. Now that Gabi and Sandro were gone, she needed to make sure she didn't drink quite so much. Between the three of them, they'd managed to polish off a bottle most nights.

It was impossible not to be amazed by the view of the sun setting over the lake. The sky was tinged purple and orange by its impending disappearance. Silhouettes of boats bobbed in the middle of the expanse, their masts free of sails as they moored up for the night. Cesca took another sip of her wine, closing her eyes to savour the taste. It lingered on her tongue, the memory still warming her even as the liquid disappeared.

How different everything was. Two short weeks ago she had been in cold, windy London. Views like this were almost impossible to imagine. Not that everything had changed overnight. Nowhere near. But even Cesca had to admit that there was some truth to the old adage that a change was as good as a rest, and this break in the sun was giving her a perspective she'd sorely lacked for so long.

She put her feet up on the footstool, crossing her slender legs in front of her. The strange thing about visiting somewhere new was the way you formed attachments so much faster than you would in everyday life. She'd been living with the Martinellis for two weeks, and she already knew them better than she'd ever known her flatmate Susie, in spite of their five months together. Maybe that's why holiday romances felt more potent than their back-at-home counterparts. The sun seemed to distil everything until its true meaning rose to the surface.

She'd managed to do some writing, too. Nothing to call home about, and certainly nothing that resembled more than a few jotted sentences, but they were words and they were down on paper, and the sense of accomplishment it had given Cesca was beyond description.

Baby steps. That's what they were. But she was moving forward all the same, no matter how wobbly her legs felt. It was more than she'd managed in the past, and Cesca was grateful for that.

The sun finally disappeared behind the Grigna mountains, the sky turning a deeper, darker blue. The solar lights
strung in the bushes and trees started to blink on, their tiny
bulbs resembling fireflies resting within the greenery. Cesca
lit a candle, nestling into the sofa as she picked up her notepad, letting the light of the flame illuminate the paper in front
of her. That's where she sat and made notes until her eyes
began to droop.

Perhaps she would have fallen asleep there, letting the
cooling air caress her skin, if things had turned out to be
different. But instead, just as a yawn stole control of her jaw
muscles, a loud blast of a horn from the main gate made her
sit straight up in her chair.

What in the holy hell was that?

In spite of the evening warmth, goose pimples broke out
on her skin. The darkness, so pretty when she was overlooking the lake, became more ominous as she walked around the
back of the villa, her footsteps tentative when she approached
the driveway. The moonlight had stolen all colour from the
landscape, turning the trees black and the driveway a curious shade of purple grey. The gravel crunched beneath the
rubber soles of her flip-flops, tiny pebbles spilling over and
getting beneath her toes. She wriggled them wildly until the
discomfort disappeared.

A pair of headlamps suddenly blinded Cesca as she froze
halfway up the path. For the first time, the seclusion of
Villa Palladino seemed more of a curse than a blessing. She
was achingly aware of her isolation here. No telephone, no
Internet, no connectivity at all. It made her a walking target.

'Gabi?' a voice called from beyond the gates. 'Is that you?
I've been buzzing for hours, can you let me in?'

'I'm not Gabi,' Cesca shouted, shaking her head at the obvious. 'And I don't know how to override the gate. It has an automatic lock on it at night. It should be usable by morning.'

She was less than twenty yards from the gate. Beyond the shining headlamps she could make out the vague form of a car, and was that a man standing beside it? The voice was certainly masculine.

'Well I can't wait out here until morning. For a start I'm starving. And I've been travelling for God knows how many hours, I just want to go to bed. Come on, just open it, OK?'

He wanted to stay here? Cesca's eyebrows nearly shot off her head. She had half a mind to turn around and walk back down to the villa.

'Well you can't just come in here without the owners' permission,' she shouted. 'And they haven't let me know anybody is coming.'

'Where the hell are Gabi and Sandro? They can let me in.'

Cesca hesitated, unwilling to reveal she was here on her own. Why wouldn't he take no for an answer? This man had no right to turn up in the middle of the night and demand to be let into a private home. She could feel the anger rising, replacing the anxiety he'd first caused. She wasn't about to take any shit off this guy, whoever he was.

'They're not here right now, so they can't let you in.' There was the merest hint of a gloat in her voice. Not that she was proud of it.

His sigh was audible. 'Then *you'll* need to let me in, sweetheart. There's an override switch behind the post. You just have to key in the code, whatever the hell it is right now, and it should let you open the gate.'

Cesca stepped back, surprised. 'How do you know that?'

'Because I live here.'

The wind was well and truly knocked out of her sails. She could feel the embarrassment suffuse her. 'Mr Carlton?' No wonder he sounded like a mixture of English and American. The New York born producer had spent enough time in London to talk like a native.

'Bingo. Now can you please let me in before I die of thirst out here?' His voice softened, as if he was smiling.

'Of course!' Cesca began to run towards the gate, mortification fuelling her speed. What on earth must he think of her? She couldn't believe she'd left him standing outside for so long, waiting for her to let him into his own house. Though she'd never met Foster Carlton, she was well aware of his reputation in theatre circles. His short temper was legendary: he must think Cesca was a complete idiot.

She walked around the gatepost to the control box. Sandro had explained that it was there in case of emergency. Her fingers shook as she tried to tap in the code. 'I'm just opening it now. I'm so sorry about the mix-up, Mr Carlton.'

In her distress, she managed to key the wrong code in, a shrill beep from the control box informing her of her error. Taking a deep breath to calm down her nerves, she pressed the numbers again, feeling the rubber giving way beneath her pressure. Within moments the mechanism was whirring, making the metal gates creak as they slowly opened up. Cesca looked over, seeing the form of the man just behind the iron, and as a gap slowly emerged he stepped forward, his feet sinking into the gravelled drive.

'Mr Carlton . . .' Her words trailed off as he stepped into the halo of light, spilling from the headlamps. The man she'd expected – the portly, middle-aged man that had graced the pages of *Variety* and other entertainment magazines – was nowhere to be seen. Instead there was a man in his mid-twenties, his sculpted jaw and dark brown hair as familiar to her as a family member. A regular in her dreams, or rather her nightmares, for the past six years. And the bastard looked even better than she remembered.

'Sam?' Cesca felt the words leap from her tongue. She felt like spitting to get rid of their taste. 'What are you doing here?'

He smiled at her, his face a mask of confused interest. 'What am I doing here? This is my house. The more important question is who are you?'

6

Come what come may, time and the hour
runs through the roughest day

– Macbeth

Sam felt a wave of exhaustion wash over him. He'd been travelling since yesterday, catching a flight first to Heathrow and then connecting to Milan. On the first leg he'd been hounded by reporters, stalking him through the airport, taking pictures and shouting questions. By the time security had ushered him onto his final flight, he'd felt all the energy seep out of him. He wasn't sure he'd be able to face going through the circus again when he arrived in Italy, but a combination of good luck and the late hour allowed him to leave the airport without being spotted.

His PA had arranged for a car to be delivered to the airport. A zippy little Ferrari that cleared the distance between Milan and Varenna in the blink of an eye. Sam had put his foot down, enjoying the open roads, so different to the gridlock that always seemed to surround LA. He'd been in a great mood all the way up to the gate, when he'd keyed in his code but the damn thing had refused to open. In spite of buzzing the house, he'd had no response, having to resort to using the air horn to get some attention.

And now, finally, he had managed to step inside, only to find this girl staring at him accusingly, as if he'd committed a monstrous crime.

'You …' The girl hesitated, still frowning. 'You don't know me?' She sounded insulted.

He looked her up and down, trying to gauge her by the light of the moon and the headlamps. She was small, maybe five foot or so, with warm blonde hair she'd twisted into a knot at the top of her head. Wearing a short, floaty skirt and skimpy vest top, her skin was glistening and smooth. Her body might be gorgeous but currently her face was anything but. Her expression was twisted with anger.

What the hell was up with her?

'Why would I know you? I've never seen you before. I'm just here at my family's villa to spend a few days away from it all. I wasn't expecting a fan club.' He flashed her a smile again, hoping it would calm her down. 'Though fans are always welcome, of course.'

'Oh, you're still full of yourself as ever.' The girl gave a short laugh. 'They promised me you wouldn't be here, they expressly told me you were in Hollywood. I wouldn't have come if I'd known you'd be arriving.'

Sam narrowed his eyes. That wasn't exactly the response he'd been expecting, and it definitely wasn't what he was used to. He rarely met attractive women who weren't either interested or at least friendly to him. 'I've no idea what you're talking about. I'm not full of myself, I'm just trying to get into my house and get some sleep. If you want to shout at me for even existing, then fine, but could you at least save it for morning?'

From the corner of his eye he could see the girl curl her hands into fists. For the first time since he'd arrived on Italian soil, he began to feel anxious. What if she was some kind of deluded psycho fan that he'd somehow managed to piss off?

What was it with women this week? If they weren't betraying him, they were stalking him. Jesus.

'So you're not the guy who runs out and leaves everybody behind to clear up his messes, while he flounces off into the distance?'

Sam's back stiffened. Did she know what had happened between him and Serena Sloane? Christ, he couldn't escape it no matter where he went.

'Who are you anyway?' He repeated his question of a few minutes earlier. 'What's your name?'

'Why should I tell you?' She folded her arms across her chest. 'You clearly couldn't care less about who I am. I'm just a bit player in the Sam Carlton show, aren't I?'

He put his hands on his hips, scrutinising her. She was English, her London accent was enough to give that away. Maybe in her early twenties, though the light was bad and he couldn't quite pinpoint her age. Closer up, he could see her bronzed skin was pebbled with freckles, making a cute line across her nose and cheeks. She looked wholesome, pretty. Even attractive – if it weren't for the fact that she was clearly completely crazy.

'Have I done something to upset you?' he asked her, giving that smile a final go. Third time lucky, right?

Wrong.

She threw her hands up in the air. 'What do you think? I'm not some kind of crazy woman who shouts at every stranger that walks through the gate, you know.'

Sam bit his lip to swallow down a sharp retort. 'That's exactly what you sound like.'

'You really don't remember me?'

He stared at her again, trying to place her face. If he was honest, there was a tiny bit of familiarity that tugged at him, but for the life of him he couldn't place her. Had she been at his school, or was she an extra in a movie he'd made? Damned if he knew.

'I meet a lot of people and I'm useless with faces. I'm sorry, I don't know you at all.'

'Typical.' She rolled her eyes. 'Somebody ruins your life and they can't even be bothered to remember who you are.'

Wow, that was sharp. Sam's head snapped back at the force of her words. He couldn't remember the last time a girl had looked at him with such hatred.

'I ruined your life?' He was incredulous. 'Funnily enough I don't remember doing that. You'd think if I'd been a real asshole I'd be unable to forget it.' Was he being set up? He craned his head around, looking for signs of other people, of cameras. Maybe she was planning to sell her story, too.

'Unbelievable.' The girl blinked rapidly. 'I'm not sure what's worse. Having your life completely trounced by somebody, or have them forget all about it. Either way, you're an asshole, Sam Carlton, and I wish I'd never let you into your house.'

The bizarreness of the situation didn't escape his notice. It felt as though he'd taken a trip into crazy town.

'What's your name? And please feel free to explain what I've done to piss you off. Because I have absolutely no idea.'

'My name's Cesca Shakespeare.' She paused, as if to let the words sink in. 'And once upon a time I wrote a play. It was a good play, everybody said so. Even the dickwad we chose to take the leading role. And then that dickwad left town and my play folded and everything turned to crap.' Her face screwed up in anger. 'That's just the short version. If you have a few days I can give you the full, unexpurgated version. With all the gory details.'

Realisation dawned over him. 'You wrote *Out of the Black*?' It was the only play he'd been cast in, and he hadn't managed to do much more than the press previews. 'You're *that* Cesca Shakespeare?' Christ, she looked different. The girl who had written the play had been exactly that – a girl. But this angry, spitting creature in front of him couldn't be described as a girl. No, she was all woman.

'You think there's more than one?' she asked. 'Or maybe you've made it your business to leave a trail of miserable Cesca Shakespeares in your wake. One in every city.'

'Don't be silly.' He immediately regretted his words.

'Don't call me silly, not after everything you've done.'

'Look, I've no idea what to say right now. I've been travelling for almost twenty hours, I'd like to take a shower and get some sleep. Perhaps we can talk about this in the morning?'

Her eyes widened. 'You're expecting to sleep in the villa?'

Sam laughed awkwardly. 'Um, yes? Where else should I sleep?'

'How about a million miles away from me? You could sleep in your car, maybe we could find you a blanket or something?'

'I'm not sleeping in the goddamned car. It's a big house, I'll just head to my room and get out of your hair. Then we can decide what to do in the morning.'

'There's nothing to decide. You're not staying here.'

59

Oh boy, she knew how to hit all his buttons. 'You're kidding, right? This is my house, I can stay where I goddamn want to. What are you even doing here? Where are Gabi and Sandro anyway?'

'I'm looking after the villa while they take a vacation. They're visiting his sister while she has her baby. Your parents have employed me to look after the villa in the meantime. And while I'm in this house you aren't welcome.'

He let out a long sigh. What the hell were his parents thinking, letting this woman take care of the villa? 'You don't get a choice. I'm coming in.'

'Then I'll sleep in the car,' she shouted back. 'It's not as if you haven't screwed my life up before. What's one more night?'

'No! Don't sleep in the car.' He could feel the blood warming his cheeks. 'Jesus Christ, woman, just go to bed and I'll do the same. It's only one night.' And after that she could leave and he would be able to enjoy the splendid isolation, without worrying he'd wake up with a knife in his back.

Cesca stared at him silently, the atmosphere between them growing thick and dark. Then she spun on the soles of her flip-flops, letting out the biggest huff he'd ever heard.

'Whatever. But remember this, your parents have employed me to look after this house, and that's exactly what I intend to do. So in the morning you need to leave.'

With that she was stalking up the driveway, her hips swaying from side to side. Sam turned and walked back to his car, trying to ignore the growing urge to put his foot down on the pedal and run her over.

It was one of the most difficult things he'd ever done.

*

Fuming didn't begin to describe how angry she was. Cesca stomped into the kitchen and grabbed hold of the kettle, jamming it under the tap. There were some aches only hot chocolate could soothe, though in this case she didn't think it could even come close. But she needed to do something with her hands, to stop them smashing those perfectly white teeth out of his beautiful mouth, and this seemed as good a way as any.

'You're being irrational,' she muttered to herself. 'Calm down.'

She heard his car come to a stop and the engine switch off, the door slamming after he climbed out of the driver's seat. Then footsteps in the hallway, the familiar slam against the marble tiles, making her shoulders tense up as she felt him coming closer.

'Do you know if my room's made up?'

She had to grind her teeth together to prevent herself biting out a bitter answer. Unwilling to look at him, she put the kettle back onto its stand, flicking the switch to make it boil.

'I've no idea. I don't even know which room is yours.' A horrible thought stole into her mind, making her skin crawl. What if she'd been using his bedroom without knowing?

'It's the blue one on the top floor.'

Thank God, her room was all pale whites and creams. 'In that case, no it isn't ready for you.' She still wouldn't look at him, keeping her back resolutely turned.

'Do you, ah, know where Gabi keeps the bedding?'

Cesca whipped around, her eyes wide, her lips thin. 'What are you, twelve? How can you live in this place for all these years and not know where the linens are?'

Irrational or not, her fury was real, and impossible to ignore.

Sam's mouth dropped open at her outburst.

It was as though the past six years had never happened, and Cesca was back to being that eighteen-year-old girl, her first play script in her hand, mesmerised by the beautiful actor who was auditioning in front of the stage. After seeing Sam's take on Daniel Cramer, there was never any question of giving the role to anybody else. Everybody in the room had agreed, Sam *was* Daniel.

Maybe that was the worst thing of all, knowing that Sam Carlton had the talent to back up his fame. Somehow he'd managed to rise through the ranks and take Hollywood by storm, while Cesca could barely hold down a job. The way he was looking at her now, as if he was innocent as a child, made her mad as hell.

And he could stop batting his bloody eyelashes at her, too. She wanted to pull them out with a tweezer, one by one.

'I really don't know what your problem is,' Sam said, shaking his head. 'I've tried to be nice, I've even tried to compromise, but all you seem to do is spit venom at me. So I left your play, it was six years ago, for goodness sake. Get over it.'

Were there any worse words to say to a girl than that? Get. Over. It. Every syllable seemed to punch against Cesca's skin, making her whole body tense at his insensitivity.

'Get over it? Are you being serious? You left and the play closed. I was eighteen years old, I'd worked on that play for years, and everybody told me it was my big chance. Then you disappeared and I was suddenly persona non grata wherever I turned. Do you know how it feels to be shunned before you're even nineteen?'

'Shit happens. If that's the worst thing you've ever been through then you've been wrapped in cotton wool all your life. Hell, I get rejected all the time and you don't see me wailing and crying about it, do you? Have you ever thought that maybe you're making a mountain out of a molehill? That you're blaming me for your own inadequacies?'

'So now you're calling me inadequate?' She wondered if he insured that way too pretty face in case of accidents. Her hand was squeezed into a fist, aching for some release. How delicious it would be to feel the impact of his jaw.

No, she couldn't do that. Not even if her mind was begging for retribution.

Sam rolled his eyes to the ceiling. 'Stop putting words into my mouth. All I'm saying is that everybody in this industry has to suffer from rejection. So if your later plays haven't done well, that's hardly my fault, is it?'

'There haven't been any more plays.'

Sam frowned. 'What do you mean?'

Cesca hesitated, torn between wanting to throw the facts in his face, and not wanting to admit the truth. She wasn't sure she wanted to give him any more ammunition to use against her.

'Nothing,' she finally replied. Two syllables rarely held so much venom.

He shook his head. 'You can't start accusing me of something I didn't do, then close down when I call you out on it.'

'I can do what I like.' Now she felt like a petulant child. This conversation was nothing like she imagined it would be. During the past few years she'd fantasised about confronting him, with a righteous anger and a vengeful fury. But not once in those dark reveries had she ever imagined him dismissing her accusations with a few glib words. Where were her apologies? Where was her retribution? Surely she deserved more than this?

'Yes you can,' Sam replied. 'And luckily I don't have to listen to you do it. So I'm going to bed, and when I get up in the morning we can arrange for you to leave. You've made your dislike for me more than clear, and I'm pretty sure neither of us wants to stay in the same house together. So now I'm here, you can go.'

'Are you freaking kidding me? I'm employed by your parents. You have no right to dismiss me.' Why should she be the one to leave? After all, he was the one who had wronged her before, and she wasn't about to let him win again. Oh no, as much as she hated Sam bloody Carter, she wasn't going to walk away from this villa. It was a matter of her newly found pride.

'I'll call them in the morning. Maybe they can even organise for Gabi and Sandro to return. It's clear this isn't going to work with us both here. I'm sure you can find somewhere else to stay.'

'Don't you dare ask Gabi and Sandro to come back.' She could feel her hackles rise even higher. 'They've taken a well-earned break, and they shouldn't have to give it up for the likes of you.'

'The likes of me?' He raised his eyebrows, clearly trying to stifle a grin.

'Yes. The sort of man who thinks everybody owes him something. So self-absorbed he doesn't realise that maybe other people have needs, too. Like being with their sister, or finding a haven away from London.'

'You can hardly talk. Apparently everything's about you. I ruined your life, remember?'

Cesca took a deep breath, but it did nothing to calm her racing thoughts. 'How could I forget? And stop changing the subject: I'm not leaving. I've been employed to do a job and I'm going to bloody well do it. So you need to go back to Hollywood and leave me alone.'

'I'm not going back to Hollywood.'

'And I'm not going back to London.'

Sam stared at her silently for a moment. His hand was opening and closing around his car keys, the rental company key ring lying in his palm. 'Then we're at an impasse. And if I'm being perfectly frank, I can't be bothered to argue with you any more. I'm going to bed. Perhaps in the morning you'll see some sense.'

With that, he turned and walked out of the kitchen, stopping in the doorway to pick up his bags.

The stupid, insufferable, handsome actor had managed to completely ruin her day. Sticking her tongue out at his retreating form, she decided to head to bed herself.

Tomorrow she'd work out what the hell she was going to do.

7

The better part of valour is discretion
– Henry IV Part I

Cesca looked up as the waiter brought a cup full of steaming coffee, laying it gently on the table next to the computer. She smiled her thanks, then lifted the china to her lips, taking a moment to inhale the sweet, milky aroma. On her first day in Varenna, Gabi had explained that a cappuccino was only a breakfast drink in Italy. The natives would laugh at tourists who ordered the frothy drink later in the day.

Swallowing a mouthful, she thanked God she'd ordered an extra shot of espresso. It had been a long, wakeful night, and her sleeplessness was taking its toll now morning had arrived. She'd climbed out of bed just before seven, being careful to be quiet, not wanting to wake Sam up. As far as she was concerned she wanted to be out of the house before he even got out of bed. She wasn't sure she could take another confrontation like last night.

The café computer finally sprang to life. Cesca took another sip of her coffee, looking through the window at the main piazza. Laid with a series of circular stones, the square was surrounded on all sides by tall Italian buildings, their façades beautifully painted in pastels, and their black iron balconies filled with flowering plants. On the far end of the square, past the huge, knobbled trees planted in rows, was the impressive church of San Giovanni Battista. The sun was rising over its roof, finally filling the square with light. It bounced off the bricks where they'd been washed by the café workers that morning.

Grabbing the mouse, she clicked on her email account. The unread messages loaded; the usual marketing emails from shops and services, plus a few strange spams that had evaded detection. In the middle of them all was a message from her sister Juliet, asking how she was enjoying her time in Varenna. Cesca scanned the words quickly. Juliet was living in Maryland with her husband, Thomas, and their daughter, Poppy. Cesca wrinkled her nose – none of the Shakespeare sisters had really taken to their brother-in-law, in spite of the whirlwind romance between him and Juliet.

Her sister's description of Poppy's latest escapades made Cesca smile, though. At six years old, she was the spitting image of Juliet and was always getting into scrapes. This time she'd managed to fly over the handlebars of her bike as she was learning to ride it. Luckily she'd managed to sustain only a few scrapes and scabs.

A wave of homesickness passed over her. Though her sisters were scattered far and wide, there was something about living in London that made her feel close to them. Growing up, the four of them had been a team, taking care of each other. It was the Shakespeare sisters against the world.

Now, though, she was the only one left in London. And though they kept in contact, it wasn't the same. All three of her sisters seemed to have their lives sorted. Kitty was settled in LA, and Juliet was setting up her own business – a flower shop. As for Lucy, she was the most secure of them all, a high-flying solicitor living in the beautiful city of Edinburgh.

Cesca opened up a new window, intending to write an email to her godfather. She had considered calling him, but the likelihood was she'd either scream at him and make him upset, or he'd talk her around with his sugar-coated tongue, making her wonder why she thought she had a problem in the first place. Neither option seemed very palatable right now. Instead she typed his name into the recipient box, then moved her cursor down to the main body of the email, hesitating as she tried to work out what she wanted to say.

Should she ask him to buy her a ticket home? Cesca wrinkled her nose, remembering that she had nowhere to live when she went back. Giving up her flat share with Susie had seemed like a good idea at the time. So that would mean moving back in with her father – at least for a while – and that thought didn't feel very acceptable at all. Not that her father wasn't lovely, in his absent-minded way, but even he would notice there was something wrong with her, that she couldn't actually hold down a job or find money for little things like food and rent. No, there was no way she wanted to go home to that.

What were the alternatives, though? She knew her sisters or Hugh would take her in, but she wasn't a child any more. She had to stand on her own two feet. It was either go back to London, or stay here. She couldn't afford to move out of Villa Palladino; she didn't have enough money to pay the exorbitant rates charged by hotels here by Lake Como.

Ugh, what a choice. Cesca felt as though she was bobbing

somewhere in between the devil and the deep blue sea, desperately trying not to drown. Either she returned to London with her tail between her legs, or she stayed here in Varenna and put up with the existence of her nemesis, all while attempting to write a play for the first time in six years.

The café was starting to fill up, the rickety tables in front of the window becoming populated by a combination of tourists and locals. Not that Varenna contained the regular sort of tourist. Lake Como was well known for its rich visitors; a mixture of the wealthy and famous rented or owned the lakeside villas, and descended upon the village in the summer. Prosperity reigned here, the visitors wearing expensive clothes and designer sunglasses, their burnished skins revealing the effects of years of sun worshipping.

'Is this seat taken?' Cesca looked up to see a tall man standing next to the table. For a moment, with his dark hair and chiselled jaw, she thought it was Sam. She opened her mouth to tell him where to go before realising it was simply another stranger.

'No, please feel free.' Cesca gestured at the chair opposite. She switched off the computer screen and moved her notepad, attempting to make some space on the table for the man.

'Don't clear up on my account.' He shot her a smile. 'I'm only stopping for a quick coffee.'

Ah, he was a local. She could tell from the hint of an accent in his words, although his pronunciation was almost perfect. She let her eyes meet his, taking in the tanned skin covered with a hint of a beard, framing his full red lips and sharp cheekbones.

'I was leaving anyway,' Cesca replied, flustered at her reaction. 'I just need to get the bill.'

'Please don't go. Let me buy you another coffee, keep me company.'

His manners were as sophisticated as the rest of him. He was wearing dark trousers and a white shirt, open at the neck to reveal a smattering of hair across the very top of his chest.

'Um . . . ' Cesca hesitated. She'd had a few conversations with strangers since she'd come to Varenna, but none as good-looking as this.

'If I tell you I've seen you around, will that make you feel any better?' He leaned forward, as if to share a secret. 'I'm staying in the villa next to yours. When I saw you here this morning, I decided it was time to introduce myself.'

Knowing he was a neighbour made Cesca feel slightly less agitated.

'I didn't know there was anybody living there. I haven't seen you down at the beach.'

'I only arrived last week, and I've been busy exploring the area. I've rented it for the summer, an attempt to get away. To leave work behind for a while, or at least try to.' He leaned forward, conspiratorially. 'Though I've already arranged some meetings here. Everybody keeps telling me I'm a workaholic.'

Cesca smiled. She wondered what he'd say if she told him she was pretty much the opposite, barely able to hold down a job for more than a week. 'Then a break sounds exactly what you need.'

'I'm so sorry, let me introduce myself. My name is Gatto. Cristiano Gatto. I'm from Roma.'

'I'm Cesca. From London.' She reached out to take his proffered hand. 'What is it you do in Rome?'

'Cesca, that's a beautiful name.' He was still smiling. 'I'm in the hospitality business. I have a number of restaurants in the capital.'

She felt her eyes get wide. Probably best not to tell him she'd been in the hospitality industry herself for a few weeks, even if she had been mostly dealing with cats. 'And you were able to get away?'

He looked down at the table. 'It was difficult. I find it hard to let things go, you see. But now I've met my beautiful neighbour I'm glad I made the effort.'

Oh, he was a smooth talker. She couldn't help but smile back at his handsome face. 'It's a pleasure to meet you, Cristiano. I'm glad you made the effort, too.'

The waiter came over and took their orders, returning a few minutes later with two steaming cups. Cristiano continued to talk about his restaurants, about Rome, asking Cesca what she was doing here in Varenna.

'Tell me, Cesca, what are you doing drinking coffee all alone? Are your friends back at the villa?'

'I'm not staying with friends.' She shook her head, her voice cautious. She wasn't sure how much she should reveal about herself. After all, she was a single woman in a strange country. 'It's a working holiday.'

'No boyfriend either?' His eyes twinkled. She wasn't sure whether it was simply the reflection of the sun.

Damn, he was good looking though. In a delicious, dark Italian way. Flirtatious, too. It was almost impossible not to flirt back. 'Not at the moment.' She smiled at him. 'Though I'm falling in love with your beautiful country. I feel very lucky to be here.'

'A beautiful girl in a beautiful country. It's the perfect

combination.' He lowered his voice again. 'I'm very glad I found the courage to introduce myself.'

That made her laugh out loud. He didn't seem the type who was backwards at coming forwards. Still, she accepted his compliment with a smile. It had been a long time since somebody had flirted with her, and she had to admit it felt good.

By the time they finished their drinks, Cesca's bad mood had all but disappeared. She tried to take the bill as it arrived, but Cristiano insisted on paying, shaking his head vehemently when she offered some euros to cover her half. 'It's been a pleasure to meet you, Cesca. Perhaps we can meet for coffee again later this week? Or maybe I'll see you down by the beach some time.'

Cesca thought she'd like that, more than she was willing to admit. And as she agreed readily, she realised she'd already made her mind up about staying here in Varenna. There was no way she was going to let Sam Carlton chase her out of Villa Palladino. Not after everything he'd already done to her. If Sam wanted a fight, then that's what he would get.

She wasn't going to let him win this time.

The house was strangely quiet when Sam woke up. He was used to being in the villa, of course – he'd spent most of his childhood summers here, after all – but he was usually surrounded by noise. Today, though, everything in the building was silent. His stomach growled, reminding him that part of his body at least was still on US time. And he'd barely eaten for nearly forty-eight hours.

Emerging from his bedroom wearing fresh shorts and a T-shirt, he padded onto the marble landing, still listening to hear if Cesca was up. He tipped his head to the side, brows

72

dipped, but all he could hear was the faint birdsong drifting in from the gardens beyond. Maybe he was lucky, and she hadn't yet awoken.

'What the hell is her problem, anyway?' he murmured.

He pulled open the refrigerator, grabbing an almost-empty carton of juice from the shelf. Without bothering to pour it into a glass, he swallowed the dregs straight from the spout. Leaving the carton on the side, he went back to look for food. There was some fruit in there, along with some platters of uncooked meat. Tomatoes – of course – all luscious and ripe, and some fresh pasta, too.

No snacks, though. No beer either – not that he wanted any yet. But it was just occurring to him that he might want some later, and if there was none in the villa, he'd need to find some. Gabi and Sandro knew what he liked to eat and drink – hell, they knew all the habits of the Carltons – but of course they hadn't bothered stocking up for his arrival. Not when they'd known nothing about it.

Groaning, he raked a hand through his hair. Any other time and he'd either go out and buy some snacks himself, or at least find some mobile reception in Varenna and call his PA in Hollywood who could arrange for some sort of delivery. But if he left the villa, he risked exposing himself and letting people know he was here. Which was really against the point.

He supposed he could try going out in the evening, under the cloak of darkness, and hope for the best. But after everything he'd been through, he was unwilling to risk it right then. The fewer people who knew he was here the better. A phone call to his PA would almost certainly alert his ex-agent and possibly his parents to his whereabouts. As far as

Sam was concerned, that was almost as bad as the paparazzi finding out.

The front door slammed, and Sam lifted his head up, stepping away from the fridge. Footsteps approached, echoing against the marble floor, then Cesca walked in.

'So you're still here, I see,' she said.

'Last I looked, it was still my house.'

'Your parents' house.'

'Same difference.' Why did she manage to bring out the worst in him? He felt like a petulant child having a playground argument. 'And anyway, where else would I go? I came here to keep my head down and have some quiet time without always being followed by the paparazzi. I'm not exactly going to parade through Varenna, am I?'

'I thought you might have gone home.'

'This *is* home. At least for the next couple of months. I'm not going anywhere.'

'Nor am I.'

Sam sighed. It was last night all over again. She really was as stubborn as a mule.

'Look, you don't like me. I get it. And right now I'm not exactly fond of you. So the way I see it we have two choices: either you leave and find somewhere else to live, or we both stay here and be miserable.'

Her mouth was set in a straight line. He'd already seen enough of her to realise this meant she was settling in for a fight. He huffed again, feeling the frustration rise inside him.

'There's no way I'm leaving. I was given this job and I intend to do it to the best of my ability. And anyway, even if I could leave, I can't afford to go anywhere else. Not without a job.'

'I could pay—'

'Don't you dare offer to help me out,' she shouted. 'I don't want any of your money. I just want you to go away and leave me to my job, so I can start pretending you never existed.'

So there it was. Last night's impasse hadn't disappeared at all, in fact it looked like it had pulled up a chair, made itself cosy and was settling in. Some escape this was turning out to be.

He shook his head, a sense of doom pulling at his guts. He couldn't help but feel this was all going to end in tears. Almost certainly his.

'Then I guess we're both staying.'

'I guess we are.' She folded her arms across her chest. 'And if we're going to be living together we need some ground rules.'

This was going to be good. 'Such as?'

'Such as no coming near me unless invited first. And there will be no invitations.'

'Done.'

She glanced at the mess he'd left on the countertop. 'And you tidy up after yourself, and do your fair share of chores.' She eyed the empty juice carton meaningfully. 'And if you use something up, you go out and purchase a replacement.'

'I can't do that.'

'You can't do what? Tidy up after yourself? Figures, someone like you must have so many minions to do that for him.'

'Don't be stupid, I'm perfectly capable of clearing up. I meant I can't go out and buy replacements.'

'Why not?' Cesca frowned.

'Because I'm famous. Everybody will know me, and I'd like to keep my presence here quiet, you know? I've come to get away from all the tabloids and the gossip and the bloody paparazzi, not to invite them to come and stay with me. I won't be leaving the villa, and I certainly don't want anybody to know I'm here.'

Cesca bit her lip. 'Nobody knows you're here at all?'

'Why, are you planning to commit murder and hide my body in the cellar?' Sam laughed uneasily. 'My friend Will knows, but he's the only one. So I'm afraid you'll have to call off your dastardly plan.'

'I was thinking more that I've got some leverage,' she told him, flashing him a gloating smile. 'If you step out of line, I'll let everybody know you're here.'

'You wouldn't ...' He could feel his cheeks heating up. 'Why would you threaten that?'

She leaned forward, her voice almost a hiss. 'Because if you can stick to your side of the bargain and not bother me, then I'll pretend you don't exist. Maybe that way we can live together without wanting to kill each other.'

Sam wasn't sure they'd ever be able to do that. 'Maybe we both have something to lose. I've got leverage over you, too. If you tell anybody I'm here, then I'll call my parents and ask them to get rid of you, which will leave you with no money and no job.'

Her face paled, in spite of the tan of her skin. 'You wouldn't.'

He smiled. 'Try me.'

She shook her head, swallowing hard as she stared out into space. Finally she brought her eyes over to meet his. 'OK, it's a deal.'

'There's one more thing.'

'There is?' She looked surprised.

'If I give you some money, I'd like you to keep this refrigerator supplied.'

She stared at him, as if mulling his words over. As if to show some sort of concession Sam picked up the empty juice carton and put it into the recycling bin, taking care to collapse it first. Cesca watched him carefully, her face placid and still. This time she wasn't giving anything away.

'Please?' He used his sweetest tone, wanting this conversation to be over for once and all.

She swallowed, her delicate neck bobbing. Her chest rose and fell with a deep breath. 'OK.'

8

How many fond fools serve mad jealousy!
– The Comedy of Errors

Sam was everywhere she looked. Not the real-life, smooth-tongued person, oh no, he was wise enough to hide his face. But his likeness smiled out of every wall, with photographs documenting his growth from a grinning, messy-haired boy into awkward teenager. Then there was the man himself, complete with sharp jaw and white teeth, his hair flopping across his forehead artfully. How had she not noticed them before? All these photographs on side tables and affixed to the wall had been in the villa all along, but it was only since Sam had arrived in Varenna that they had made themselves known.

And now it felt as though they were taunting her. Reminding her that this was his home, and he could throw her out whenever he wanted. The arrogant bastard.

He'd been here for almost a week and she still couldn't stand the sight of him. Every time they talked it seemed to turn into an argument, heated and angry, leaving both of them breathless. It was exhausting.

Sighing, she picked up her notebook and her sunhat, deciding that a morning spent on the villa's private beach was preferable to being cooped up with Sam. It was just past eleven; Cesca's shadow was short as it followed her across the patio, her sandals clipping the old paving stones as she walked down towards the footpath. Around the corner she could hear the gardeners talking to each other in fast Italian, their voices loud as it pierced the relative silence of the garden. She smiled as she listened, not able to discern any words, but impressed nonetheless at just how beautiful they sounded. No doubt the gardeners would be old and rotund when she saw them, but their voices were anything but. They were deep and throaty, their sentences rising and falling like music, and Cesca let it wash over her as she approached.

'*Buona mattina, signorina*,' the eldest gardener called across to her. He was wearing long, dark trousers and a grey T-shirt, his belt so tight his stomach bulged over the top. His face was deeply tanned from a lifetime exposed to the sun, his cheeks speckled with smudges of dirt where he'd been digging in the soil. Cesca lifted her hand and gave him a wave, aware she should know his name, but not able to remember it. Sandro had introduced them on her second day there, explaining that the gardeners came to the house three times a week. Like locusts they arrived in a swarm, descending on the greenery, able to tidy the whole estate up in a matter of hours.

'Where are you off to?' It was only when the second man spoke that she realised it was Sam. Without waiting for an answer he turned and began to talk to the gardener again, Italian words dancing from his mouth as though it was his native tongue. He sounded so different, his voice even deeper, almost guttural. And though every part of her screamed not to acknowledge it, she couldn't help but admit it made him even more attractive than he already was.

'I'm going down to the beach. Then later I might go into town again. Because I can.' She wrinkled her nose at him. Once again, he made her feel like a twelve-year-old girl.

'Maybe you can pick up a few things for me?' he asked smoothly. 'I've nearly run out again.'

Her lips tightened. She wanted to tell him where to stick his things, and refuse to help him at all. Every time she saw him she acted like a child.

'I said I would, didn't I?' she said. 'Make a list and leave it in the kitchen, I'll pick it up on my way out.' There, she was keeping her end of the agreement, even if it made her want to stab her own eyes with toothpicks.

She walked through the formal gardens and out into the wilder, shrub-filled landscape beyond, reaching the steps that led down to the beach. The sun reflected off the lake and straight into her eyes, making her squint as she covered her forehead with her hand. The beach was small but beautiful, with a covering of tiny shale that disappeared into the water. The Carltons had erected a small covered deck here, with sun loungers and tables to sit at while marvelling at the view offered by the lake. It was here that Cesca decided to spend her day sketching out her play. And though she hadn't begun to write the scenes yet, it still felt like a huge achievement. Over the last week she'd somehow managed to come up with the skeleton of a story – only an outline and barely fleshed out at all – but it was more than she'd managed for the past six years.

Leaning back, she tried to imagine what it must have been

like to grow up here, spending sunburned summers splashing in the water, surrounded by family and friends. From what she'd seen in the photographs, Sam had two younger sisters, who tended to stare up at him adoringly in nearly every portrait. She expected they had followed him around the villa in much the same way, running down to the beach with their swimsuits on, trailing buckets and spades behind them, demanding that Sam threw them into the water one more time.

He seemed to have that effect on women. Most of them, anyway.

Her throat tightened. She'd never been abroad in her life until now. She and her sisters had spent their school holidays in their Hampstead home, bouncing like pinballs between the library and the garden, sometimes taking picnics up to the heath. Even if he could have afforded to take them away, her father would have almost certainly baulked at the idea of taking four young children abroad with him. Cesca couldn't blame him, really, they'd each been a handful in their own way.

A shot of jealousy at Sam's easy life shot through her body, straightening her back like a rod of iron. She should channel the feeling, put it into her writing. That was easier said than done, though, especially when the object of her envy was sharing the villa with her. Was she going to feel permanently on edge for the whole time they were together?

'So we meet again!' Cristiano Gatto was standing at the fence separating the Carltons' part of the beach from their neighbours'. He leaned on the wood, his white shirtsleeves rolled up to his elbows, revealing tanned arms and a thick silver wristband. Smiling warmly at her, his teeth were almost sparkling in the sun. The sight of him was enough to make her grin right back.

It was so easy to interact with Gatto. He was like a ray of sunshine standing there, so guileless and friendly.

'You don't look like you're ready to sunbathe,' Cesca called back. Standing up, she wrapped her sarong around her waist, aware of her almost-nudity compared to his fully dressed attire. Bikinis were great if everybody was wearing them. Otherwise they made you feel like a Playboy Bunny in a house full of Hugh Hefner-style smoking jackets.

'I'm still exploring.' Cristiano glanced at his silver watch. 'I have a meeting this afternoon, but I wanted to check out the beach. It's very beautiful.' His eyes were still on hers. The way he talked sent a welcome shiver down her back.

'It's even better in the evening,' she told him. 'All the lights on the boats come on, and the lake reflects them. There's such a peacefulness to it, sitting here and staring across the water.'

His smile grew. 'That does sound beautiful. Tell me, Cesca, why is a girl like you here alone? In a house big enough to accommodate a huge family?'

Her cheeks turned pink at his flirtation. 'It's not exactly a vacation. I'm taking care of the villa for the summer. It's my job.'

Cristiano tipped his head to the side. 'So we are both on a working vacation, then? That's something else we have in common. Maybe at the end of our busy days we should come down here and share a glass of wine, put our feet up and talk about our work.'

Her throat tightened. She wasn't sure he'd be that interested in how she'd instructed the gardeners, or dusted the library. It wasn't exactly a high-powered position she was filling here. 'That sounds interesting.'

There was that easy smile again. 'Then it's a date. I'll bring the red wine, you bring your beautiful self. Shall we say Friday at eight o'clock?'

'This Friday?' Cesca looked at him, surprised. She'd thought he was just being nice.

'Why not? Unless you don't want to, of course.'

'Friday at eight sounds perfect.' She felt breathless. 'I'll bring us some food. Otherwise I'll end up getting drunk and talking too much.'

The skin around his eyes crinkled. 'I like the sound of that.'

Her blush deepened. 'You wouldn't if you saw me tipsy. Some bread and cheese will be all that stands between you and the utter twaddle that escapes my mouth.'

'Utter twaddle?' Cristiano questioned. 'That's a new one on me.'

'It means I'll be talking drivel if I drink wine without eating something,' Cesca explained. 'Believe me, you don't want to hear that.'

'Believe me, I do.' He was still leaning on the dividing fence, but it felt as though he'd moved closer. Her body felt suddenly warm. 'And I look forward to hearing your, how do you say it, utter twaddle. But now I must go and have my boring meetings, and somehow get through the hours until Friday comes. *Ciao, bella.*' He winked, then turned around, his shiny black leather shoes crunching on the gravelled beach as he made his way towards the steps that led up to his villa. Cesca watched him go, still flushed and breathless, wondering what on earth she'd just agreed to.

83

It wasn't like her at all. But then, nothing right now was like the Cesca she'd been only a few weeks ago. From a waitress dodging cats, she'd somehow transformed into a girl who was asked on dates by gorgeous Italian men, who asked her to share a bottle of wine with her as the sun went down. Her sisters wouldn't recognise her if they could see her now. Hell, she barely recognised herself.

It wasn't an unpleasant feeling.

Sam pressed his head against the cool glass of the window, staring out at the dazzling blue sky. Letting his eyes close for a moment, the sun turning his lids orange, he let out a sigh. This was nothing like he'd expected. When he left Hollywood, the villa in Italy had seemed like a haven, a bright beam of light that he wanted to steer his ship towards. He hadn't considered what he'd do once he got here, in this house so full of history yet so empty of connections, with only his dark thoughts and a crazy girl to keep him company.

And, let's face it, even she had abandoned him.

He'd managed to corner Carlito, who had been tending their garden for years, asking him if he knew how to contact Gabi and Sandro. To his dismay, Carlito had only confirmed Cesca's story, explaining that Sandro's sister was days away from giving birth. Even at his lowest, there was no way Sam could bring himself to demand them back, not after the way they'd taken care of his family for the past few years. They were friends as well as employees, always happy to see him, delighted to make him comfortable, he couldn't take them away from their family.

The breeze wafting up from the lake brought the sound of voices. Carlito's team of workers had left half an hour ago, and the villa was empty of life apart from Sam. As weird as Cesca was, he couldn't believe she was laughing at nothing, not unless she'd finally lost her tenuous hold on sanity. His eyelids flew open and he blinked rapidly, having to get used to the glare of the sun once again. As his pupils dilated enough for him to be able to focus, he could see her distant form, standing out on the small beach that ran into the lake. She was facing something – or someone – her hands gesturing wildly.

On the other side of the dividing fence he saw the form of a man, leaning on the wood. It was impossible to tell much more from here, neither his age nor his appearance was discernible from Sam's position at the window. He narrowed his eyes anyway, dry lips pursing as he tried to make the man out, but could only see the outline of his clothes.

His first thought was that he'd been discovered. Sam's heart started to beat rapidly as he continued to watch. A gust of wind from the lake lifted Cesca's skirt, revealing her bikini-clad body and glowing skin. She was surprisingly lithe, even from this distance. He wondered what she looked like a little closer up.

The conversation between her and the stranger was coming to an end, as far as Sam could tell. She was half turned away from the man, her left leg poised to walk forward. From the split in her skirt Sam realised it was a sarong, tied around her waist in an attempt at modesty. A pang of envy scratched at his stomach; she was free to go where she wanted, to do whatever the hell she liked without the scrutiny of a million eyes following her. If he'd been out on the lake you could guarantee there'd be boats circling, with photographers leaning off the side, their cameras equipped with long-distance lenses. But Cesca could wander around half-naked, without a care in the world.

It irritated him that she was doing so in front of the unknown man by the lake.

Not wanting to watch any more, Sam pushed himself off the glass, turning to walk back into the library. This had normally been his father's domain, and whenever the family were here Foster would hole himself up in the room, reading play scripts and flicking through books. As well as the book-lined walls there were two large leather chesterfields in the centre of the room, facing each other with an old wooden coffee table in between. In the corner was Foster's computer desk, usually tidy, but currently littered with paper and books. Sam grabbed one of them – a Stanislavski – and opened it. Within minutes he was so absorbed by the famous actor's words, he didn't even hear the door open.

'What are you doing in here?' Cesca walked into the library, her head held high as if she was discovering a thief. She stalked past him, her arm bumping into his, as she laid her work down on the corner of the desk.

Sam put the book back where he'd found it. 'Last time I looked I still live here.'

She sighed. 'Not this again. I mean what are you doing in the library? I've been using it since I arrived. I'd like to be able to write here in peace, if you don't mind. It's hard enough trying to beat writer's block without having you standing in here putting me off.'

Sam frowned. 'Why would I put you off?'

Cesca's eyes rolled up to the ceiling. 'Because your mere existence is telling me the universe hates me. And it would be nice to be able to write my play without having to acknowledge that.'

For some reason her dramatics amused him. He could feel

his lips twitch as he watched her sigh again. It was simply the boredom that made her interesting, he told himself.

'Who were you talking to on the beach?' he asked.

She lifted her eyebrows, shocked. 'What do you mean?' Her arms wrapped around her waist. He'd noticed her do it a few times now as a defence mechanism, but this time her actions drew his scrutiny to her body. She was still wearing that bikini and her pink and black sarong. He tried not to look at the way the bikini top covered the swell of her breasts, or how tight and toned her stomach was as it disappeared beneath the knotted fabric.

He didn't know why her sexiness surprised him. Her body was curvy yet supple, and he found himself wanting to touch her.

'I'm up here you know.' Cesca gesticulated at her face. 'If you want to talk to me, I'd suggest you don't address my tits.'

'Are you changing the subject?'

'From what?' Cesca asked.

'From the man you were talking to earlier on the beach. I asked you who he was and you've not bothered answering.'

'I don't have to answer if I don't want to.'

It was Sam's turn to sigh. 'I know you don't have to answer, but I'm here for a reason, and that's to get some peace and quiet away from all the fans and the reporters. I want to know who he is and if you told him I was here.'

Her face took on an expression of disgust. 'Oh my God, could you be any more self-centred? Why on earth would Cristiano be interested in you? Have you thought about seeing a shrink?'

Sam didn't bother telling her he'd been seeing a shrink for years. 'His name's Cristiano?' he prompted. For some reason it annoyed him that Cesca and the man were on first-name terms.

'Yes it is, if you must know. It's Cristiano Gatto. He's renting the villa next door for the summer while he takes a break from Rome. He's a restaurateur.'

'You learned a lot from him in a few minutes.' Sam knew he was giving himself away, exposing his interest to her when he shouldn't.

She shook her head. 'Oh for goodness sake. It was the second time we've talked. I've met him before, at the café.' Her eyes narrowed. 'And for what it's worth I haven't even mentioned you. You're just not that interesting.'

Sam pretended to reel back at her words, noting her irritated expression with a dark amusement.

'I'm going out,' she told him. 'You know, out into the town where I can wander around and look in the shops. And maybe I'll stop at the gelaterie and buy an ice cream, and lick all the creamy goodness until I'm shaking from the cold.' She was taunting him now. 'If you're really lucky I might take a photo.'

'I don't need a photo of you. I know I'm going to see you in my nightmares every evening.'

She stuck her tongue out again, her face screwed up with disgust.

'And don't forget to buy the stuff I need,' he reminded her. 'I left the list in the kitchen.'

Cesca said nothing, but another roll of her eyes told him all he needed to know. He'd managed to annoy her thoroughly; they were like two kids in the playground, winding each other up until poised to pounce, in a fight to the death.

He should hate it, he knew, but there was part of him that tingled at the deliciousness of their constant sniping. Each time he made her eyes flash with anger it made him feel more alive. Boredom, that's all it was. Just as soon as he was back in Hollywood he wouldn't even think about her.

But for now, baiting Cesca was becoming his favourite kind of sport.

Cesca watched him leave the library, her teeth aching from being ground against each other in frustration. The man was insufferable. It was as though some scientist had sat in a laboratory, trying to work out the best combination of sarcasm and wit designed to make Cesca want to snap and snarl. And after much experimentation and honing of their work, they'd managed to come up with Sam Carlton. Her own, personal *bête noire*. Lucky her.

Unclenching her fists, she wiggled her fingers to get some blood back into the white flesh. How strange it was, in spite of all her dread and worry, that when she finally saw him again it made her feel more alive than she had in six years.

She couldn't deny she liked that feeling.

9

Love looks not with the eyes, but with the mind,
and therefore is wing'd Cupid painted blind
– A Midsummer Night's Dream

The supermarket in Varenna was one of her favourite places. Cesca marvelled at the cured meats that hung from the ceiling on ropes, and the cheeses that were stacked so high she could barely reach the ones at the top. Unlike in London, where a trip to buy food meant little more than trying to eke out whatever money she had left in her moth-eaten wallet, here in Italy Cesca let her stomach rule her purchases. She filled her basket with prosciutto and pancetta, and pastas of various shapes and colours. Then she added cheeses wrapped with pale waxed paper: dusty parmesan and rich blue gorgonzola, along with an amazing casorette that Gabi and Sandro had introduced her to. A still-warm loaf of floury bread was her final choice, the perfect accompaniment to the cheese tonight on the beach. Along with whatever wine Cristiano was planning to bring, the thought of the food was already making her stomach rumble.

Pulling Sam's crumpled shopping list from where she'd

shoved it into her pocket, she smoothed the wrinkled paper and began to look for his goods, taking much less care in selecting them than she had for her own food. He hadn't asked for a lot this time, just some beer, toiletries, some crisps and cookies. She passed the newspaper stand, wondering for a moment if she should pick him up a magazine to help him pass away his boredom, but then turned her back, deciding she wasn't going to buy him anything he hadn't specifically requested.

That way madness lay.

The walk back to the villa was decidedly less carefree than her walk to town had been. Perhaps it was the weight of her bags, with Sam's food in there as well as her own. Her muscles were cramping in complaint at the extra effort they had to expend. Or maybe it was the heat of the afternoon, as the sun beat down from her nook in the sky, causing rivulets of sweat to pour down Cesca's neck. Either way, by the time she reached the iron gates and keyed in the access code, she was breathless and exhausted, looking forward to putting her feet up for a while.

Luckily for her, Sam was nowhere to be seen when she carried the bags into the kitchen and unloaded them into the big, stainless steel refrigerator in the corner of the room. Grabbing an already chilled can from its depths, she pressed the misty metal against her forehead in an attempt to cool herself, before opening it and pouring it into a glass. Taking it into the living room, she sank down onto the sofa. Another wave of exhaustion washed over her as she drifted off to sleep.

Her muscles were still aching when a noise alerted her back to wakefulness, her eyes flickering as she attempted to open them. The evening had already arrived, the sky painted with dark blues and pinks as the sun made her long dusky slide into the lake. Across the water, lights twinkled from the lakeside houses.

Somebody cleared their throat. She blinked again, seeing a shadow standing in the corner of the room. For a short moment her heart began to race.

'Sam?'

'I see you're keeping busy,' he said. 'I must congratulate my parents on finding such a hard worker.'

'You know you're just as charming as all the gossip sites say you are. When did you graduate from charisma school?'

His face fell. In the gloom of the evening, he looked like the little boy who stared out of the photographs on the wall. Lost, hopeful, something she couldn't quite put her finger on. 'What have you been reading on there?' he asked, his voice low. 'What are they saying now?'

There was a tremor to his voice that made him sound almost human.

'Do I look like I've spent my afternoon Googling you?' she asked. 'Seriously, I have better things to do than read all the gossip about you. As scintillating as I'm sure it is.'

'Gossip's never scintillating,' he said quietly. 'It's wrong and it's embarrassing and it hurts people.'

Startled, Cesca stared over at him. Could there really be a chink in his armour? Something that exposed the human he actually was beneath?

'I'd agree with that,' she said slowly, not quite believing they could have anything in common. 'I've suffered from enough gossip in my time.' Especially after her play had folded. So many people took some sort of sick satisfaction at her fast demise.

'Me too.' Sam cleared his throat. 'Anyway, um, thanks for the food. It was just what I needed.'

She blinked again, unaccustomed to hearing him say a sentence without it dripping with sarcasm. Cesca wasn't quite sure how to respond.

Luckily Sam spoke for her, not noticing she was struck dumb with shock at his softer side. 'I was wondering if you'd like to join me for dinner. We could maybe cook some pasta, open a bottle of my parents' wine. I'll even let you do the dishes if you insist.' A half smile played around his lips.

Gah, he really was handsome when he smiled. Not for the first time she could see why he was plastered across so many magazines and posters, the Instagram darling of a million teenage girls. 'Wine does sound nice ... ' Her voice trailed off as her words struck a memory. 'Wait, what time is it?' She looked around in vain for a clock. 'I'm meant to be somewhere.'

Sam flicked his wrist up to look at his watch. 'It's just past eight.'

'I'm late!' Cesca sat up, panicking. She'd promised to meet Cristiano down at the beach at eight, along with warm, ripe cheese and a cut up loaf. She hadn't prepared any of it. With the best will in the world it would take her at least ten minutes to get down there. Would he wait for her? Cesca wasn't sure. She hadn't even been in Italy long enough to know what was acceptable here in terms of lateness.

'Whoa!' Sam stepped back as Cesca rushed past him. He reached out for her, to steady himself, she presumed. His fingers curled around her arm, but rather than regain his equilibrium, he managed to pull her against his chest.

Alarmed, Cesca put her hands against him, planning to

push herself away. Then she felt the warmth of his skin beneath her palms, and the steady pump of his heart against his ribcage. Surprised, she hesitated.

'I need to go,' she said again, not sure if she was talking to Sam or to herself.

Sam moved his hands down, his fingers now circling her wrists. When she tried to move away his hold stopped her progress. 'Where are you going?'

Her mouth was dry at their unexpected contact. She wasn't sure why it was affecting her so much. 'I'm meeting Cristiano at the beach for some supper. We have a . . . a date.'

Sam released her arms, stepping back. When she looked up at his face it had turned suddenly impassive, betraying no hint of the smile that had been on his lips moments before. 'You should go then,' he told her, turning around and walking across the living room. 'I've got things to do anyway.'

Cesca stared at him, her right hand rubbing at her left wrist where he'd held her only moments before. She frowned, her brows knitting together, as she tried to work out why she felt so completely disoriented.

'What the hell just happened?' she asked herself, shaking her head as she heard the library door slam.

Sam was on a hunt for phone reception. Carrying his iPhone in his outstretched hand, he kept his eyes glued to the bars on the screen as he climbed up the hill behind the villa, heading for the highest point of the estate. A week without being able to call anybody or – God forbid – check the Internet had been more than enough for him. It was now that he realised how reliant he was on the damn chunk of plastic and metal he carried everywhere.

He wanted to know if the worst had happened. Before leaving LA, his lawyer had assured him he had things covered. But Serena was slippery, and she'd shown herself to be an excellent liar. He didn't trust her as far as he could throw this phone.

If only he'd realised that a few months ago.

This part of the garden was overgrown and wild, with huge bushes and trees obscuring him as he climbed his way up the earthen hill. Reaching the highest point, a bar on his cell began to blink, and he held his breath as he waited to see if it connected with his carrier.

Sinking onto a rock, he sat down and looked out over the lake. He'd forgotten how beautiful it was here. As a child he'd taken his mother's ancestral home for granted, more interested in swimming and splashing in the water than anything else. But after years of being surrounded by concrete and artifice, Italy was like a balm to his soul.

It felt real.

A splash came from the lake, and he glanced over. It was too dark to be able to make much out from the private beach belonging to the villa. He knew Cesca was down there – with whatever his name was – maybe he should go down to make sure everything was OK. But then, he wasn't ready for anybody else to know he was here, not even a neighbour who was intent on spending time with his housekeeper. No, better to stay here, under the radar.

Growing up, Sam had learned to become a chameleon, able to change himself to fit in with any situation. He was a half-Italian, half-American boy living in London, and part of him felt like he didn't belong anywhere. Sam's relationship with his father didn't help. Foster had always been larger than life, his loud voice silencing all others around him, his charisma sucking everything in like a black hole. The younger Sam had been desperate to earn his attention, bringing home school prizes, swimming badges and A-grade papers, but nothing seemed to impress his father, at least nothing that Sam could do.

On a good day, Sam would grudgingly accept that a large proportion of his success came from his 'daddy issues' – or his 'Family of Origin' issues, as his shrink defined it. But even now, six years after he'd learned the truth about Foster, there was still a huge part of Sam that still wanted to win his respect. All the acclaim he'd earned through his acting, the SAG nominations, the critical success, none of that could replace the thing he'd yearned for the most.

His phone managed to pick up a signal, and started to vibrate wildly, concurrent pings ringing out as dozens of messages downloaded at once. After almost seven days without connecting, a deluge of apps were filling up as texts and emails, instant messages and Twitter all vied for his attention. His throat tightened as he looked at the screen again, his index finger hovering over the glass. Where should he start? The emails would be long, possibly ranty, the voicemails would be too difficult to listen to. The messages, though shorter, would still be enough to make him want to throw his phone away all over again. Avoidance was always his natural inclination.

Switching his phone off without reading the messages, he slipped it into the pocket of his shorts. He wasn't ready to read them yet, he didn't want to know if the story had broken. He stood up, stretching his legs to lengthen his muscles as they complained about his sudden movement. Running a hand through his hair he looked out across the lake again, questions shooting through his brain like dying stars.

How long was he going to stay here? He had no idea.

What was he going to do about Serena Sloane and her betrayal? He had no idea.

Why, if he was hiding from his family, had he chosen this place to run to? Especially when his past seemed to have caught up with him, in the form of a petite fireball who was making it her personal mission to make his life as uncomfortable as possible. Sam's lips twitched at that question. Cesca annoyed the hell out of him, that was for sure, but there was also something about her that amused him, drew him in. The adrenalin that shot through him after every confrontation was a reminder he was alive.

Reaching for the nearest tree trunk, he began his descent back to the villa, avoiding rocks and roots, the soles of his shoes kicking up the dirt. Nearing the formal part of the gardens, he could hear sounds drifting up from the lake, the occasional laugh and conversation carrying up on the wind.

He didn't like the idea of a stranger being so close. Maybe he should talk to Cesca, forbid her from meeting this neighbour again. After all, it was the Carltons who paid her wages, surely she should follow his wishes if he said them out loud?

Another splash, louder this time, followed by a tinkling giggle. Sam curled his hands into fists, a flash of anger unexpectedly shooting through him.

He was definitely going to have words with her.

10

We are such stuff as dreams are made on
– The Tempest

'You need to do it like this,' Cesca said, picking up another flat stone from the beach. Curling her arm towards her, she held the stone tightly for a moment, before flicking her forearm back out, watching the pebble skim across the surface of the lake six, seven, eight times.

Shaking his head, Cristiano picked another stone up, then attempted to mimic her movements. It disappeared beneath the lake with a loud splash, causing Cesca to collapse into a fit of laughter.

'There's no need to be rude.' Though his words were tight, his eyes flashed with amusement.

'I always thought it was girls who couldn't throw, not boys. I'm sure this little lesson is supposed to be the other way round,' she said.

'Are you questioning my masculinity?' Cristiano asked. His face was flushed from the cheese and red wine. They'd both indulged a little too freely, resulting in Cesca feeling a rush of drunkenness every time she bent down.

She shook her head, feeling the dizziness again. 'Not at all, I'm just questioning your throwing skills. Didn't you learn to do this when you were a kid?'

'I grew up in the city, there wasn't a lot of opportunity to throw stones,' he told her, reaching out and taking a lock of her hair between his fingers. For some reason the gesture confused her, made her feel uncomfortable. She shuffled her feet, kicking at the shingle beneath her sandals.

She laughed again, but this time to disguise her embarrassment. 'I grew up in the city, too. But throwing stones is a rite of passage. I feel as though you've missed out on an important development milestone.' She stepped back, her hair pulling away from his hold. She sensed his frown, but couldn't quite bring herself to meet his eyes. Cesca had never been very good at flirting, not even after a few glasses of the red stuff. She always felt slightly awkward whenever she sensed a man's interest in her, as if she couldn't work out what they wanted.

'You have a very beautiful laugh,' he told her. Though he kept his distance this time, Cesca felt a shot of warmth in her veins. Who didn't like being told something like that?

'You've been drinking too much.'

'Not at all.' He smiled again. 'You're not very good at accepting compliments, are you? I've found that with English women before. It's as though you're brought up believing the worst about yourself.'

She tipped her head to the side, pondering his words. 'Are Italian girls brought up any differently?'

It was his turn to laugh, deep and low. 'Being a man, I can't say from experience. But I can tell you my sister was always complimented, always loved. Girls in this country grow up

99

knowing there's beauty in every size, every shape, and every shade of hair. Women are worshipped here in Italy, not criticised.' His voice was soft as he spoke, his stare intense. Cesca could feel her heart start to race.

'That sounds like a lovely way to grow up.'

'I was taught from the earliest age to show women respect and adoration. It begins with our mothers, of course, but then we learn to appreciate the femininity that surrounds us as we get older. It makes me sad when women don't understand their beauty and power. Especially one as lovely as you.'

Was it possible to be seduced by words alone? Cesca wasn't sure. Maybe it was the wine again, sending shivers down her spine. Making her skin fizz and pop as if she'd just been doused in soda.

Her voice was raw when she spoke again. 'That's very kind of you.' That was the best she could do. After a lifetime of turning away from compliments about her looks, she couldn't change overnight.

'It's a start.' He gave her a soft smile. 'But if you're going to spend time with me, you'll have to learn to accept compliments all the time. A girl like you deserves them.' His blue-eyed stare seemed to pierce her, and again she could feel the embarrassment suffusing her. He poured another glass of red and she accepted it gratefully, pleased to have something to do other than try to hide her red cheeks.

'Shall we change the subject?' he asked, clearly noticing her self-consciousness. 'Why don't you tell me what brought you to Italy? You said you were here on a working holiday.' He took her hand, helping her to sit down on the soft shingle. He climbed down beside her, stretching his feet out until his bare toes touched the softly lapping water. Cesca did the same, though her legs were shorter, and the lake was still almost a foot away from her pink painted toenails.

'I was offered a job. The people who own the villa – the Carltons – they're friends of my godfather.'

'That was nice of them to give you a job. Have you known them long?'

'I've never met them,' she told him. 'Hugh, that's my godfather, he's in the theatre industry, just like Mr Carlton. They've run in the same circles for years, I think. And when I lost my job Hugh suggested this one, he thought I needed to get out of London.'

'Because of the weather?' Cristiano asked.

His question made her laugh. 'No, not the weather. In fact it was very nice the last time I was there. It's just I'd been having a bit of a bad time and he thought getting away would be good for me.' Way to play things down. 'A bit of a bad time' didn't really capture the lows of the last six years.

His features softened with concern. 'I'm sorry to hear that. Would it be wrong of me to ask what sort of bad time?'

Cesca was torn. This wasn't the sort of conversation she had with just anybody. 'I used to be a writer,' she finally said, her voice quiet. 'But then something happened and I had this terrible block. It made me get very low and depressed, and I couldn't snap out of it.' If this had been a real first date, and not some holiday conversation with a handsome neighbour, maybe she'd have glossed over her problems, and pretend to be all sweetness and light.

Thank goodness this wasn't a first date then.

'I knew there was something about you.' He leaned closer. She could smell the woody fragrance of his cologne. 'You have this lost look about you that makes me want to know more. It's very enticing.'

He was close enough for Cesca to feel his breath against her cheek. Her heart almost stopped beating in her chest. She felt frozen to the ground. Was he going to kiss her? More importantly, did she want him to? He was very handsome, after all, and wasn't afraid to show his interest in her. Something was missing, though, something she couldn't quite put her finger on.

'Can I kiss you?' She felt his words brush against her skin. He cupped her neck with his hand, his fingers curling around her nape. It was only when she felt the softness of his lips brushing hers that she realised it wasn't a question. It was a statement of intent.

Cesca closed her eyes, feeling his hand pulling her closer, his lips pressing harder against her mouth. She waited for that familiar warmth, for the butterflies, for that desperate need to kiss him back. Waited and waited.

But it didn't come.

Feeling her lips pull down into a frown, Cristiano pulled away, releasing his hold on her neck. He was frowning, too, still staring at her, his mouth red from her lipstick and the red wine.

'Was that too much?' he asked, concerned. 'Too soon? I'm sorry that I read you wrong.'

She shook her head, still confused by her own reaction. 'No ... I mean yes ... I don't know. I'm so sorry, you took me by surprise.'

What had he been expecting – for Cesca to throw herself at him?

'It's OK,' he reassured her. 'You need more time, I understand that. The best things in life don't need to be rushed.'

In spite of his words, she still felt embarrassed, and found herself scrambling to her feet, standing up on the pebbled ground. 'I think I'm just tired. It's been a long day, and I should get some sleep.'

Cristiano followed suit, standing beside her. His smile remained painted on. 'Of course. Can I walk you to your villa?'

A flash of alarm shot through her. She could only imagine what Sam would say if she rocked up to the house with Cristiano. 'Oh no, I can go on my own. It's too far for you.'

His brows knitted together. 'It's only next door.'

'Honestly, I'll be fine. The owners, they're very private, they don't like strangers coming onto the property.' Seeing his expression, she began to backtrack. 'Not that you're a stranger, of course. Well, not to me. But they don't know you, and I've promised to take good care of the house.'

Cristiano chuckled. 'Please don't worry, I get it. People guard their privacy very closely here, I can understand that. But I would like to ask a favour, if I can. Will you meet with me again soon? Perhaps we can go out for dinner together. There are a few restaurants around here I'd like to try.'

A long, slow breath escaped from Cesca's lips. 'That sounds nice.'

His smile was big. 'Perfect. I'll make some plans and let you know.'

Cesca nodded her agreement. 'Good night, Cristiano.' She turned, walking along the private beach to the fence that separated Cristiano's side from the Carltons', putting her foot on the lowest rung to climb over the top.

It was only when she fell flat on her face on the other side that she realised just how drunk she was.

*

Sam had forgotten how much he loved to read. It was the first time in years he'd held any written document in his hand that wasn't a movie script, a contract or one of those goddamned magazines, and he had to admit it felt good. This was why he'd come here, after all, to find solitude and space, enough time to breathe, to think, to be someone other than the man Hollywood expected him to be.

He closed his eyes, letting the old, leather-bound copy of *A Room With a View* fall back against his chest, dust rising from its pages and tickling his nose. The warm night air caressed his skin as it breezed through the open window, as gentle as a lover's touch. It had been a long time since he'd been able to doze in silence, without the sounds of LA, or the buzzing of his thoughts constantly interrupting his dreams, but for those few minutes something strangely akin to peace seemed to drift over him.

Gone were the voices in his head telling him he was all wrong. Even the loudest of them – Foster's voice – stayed silent for a while. And for one blissful hour he managed to sleep deeply, his body relaxed and loose as he dreamed on the library chair.

A loud crash woke him, and it was as though all his circuits were switched on at once. He half stood, the book falling onto the floor, trying to work out the origin of the noise.

It was dark in the library. He must have switched off the side lamp before drifting off, and only the faraway lights from the other side of the lake were left to do battle with the blackness. He blinked a few times, his eyes adjusting to the gloom. There was a scratching coming from the hallway, like a cat running its claws down a wall. Not that there were any cats in the villa, Foster couldn't stand them. He wasn't a man for being at one with nature.

The noise started again, echoing through the library. Stretching his muscles, Sam cocked his head to one side. It really did sound like an animal.

It was only a few steps to the doorway. A few more until he made it into the hall, the murkiness of night following him in, though a lamp glowing in the living room tinted the air with a pale yellow glow. Cesca was kneeling in front of him, her bare knees and feet bracing her against the floor as she desperately tried to scoop up the contents of the hall table, which lay crookedly on the marble tiles.

'Need some help?' he asked drily.

Cesca's eyes were wide, her face was flushed pink. Biting her lip, she shook her head, resuming her desperate tidying. The way she kept missing the papers and pens as she swiped reminded him of a toddler learning fine motor skills.

Sam knelt down next to her, taking the papers from her hands. 'It's late,' he told her. 'You can tidy this tomorrow when the light is better.' He wasn't sure why he was being easy on her, not after everything that had happened in the past few days. Maybe it was the way her hands were shaking, or the shallow breaths that had to fight to escape her lips.

'Are you OK?' he asked, more worried this time. It wasn't like Cesca not to have an immediate snarky reply. 'Are you in pain?' He reached out for her arm, scanning her body for signs of injury. It must have hurt like hell if the heavy table had fallen on any part of her.

Cesca glanced up, her eyes glassy. She frowned, not quite able to focus on his face. Trying to scramble up from her knees, she managed to fall forward, arms outstretched as she tumbled against him. She was surprisingly strong for such a petite girl, the force of her full weight winding him. Instinctively he wrapped his arms around her, his hands pressed against her back, as he tried to stop the both of them tumbling to the ground.

For a moment she was still. He could feel her chest hitching against his. Her lips were close to his neck, her warm breath fanning his skin. Only a few inches more and her soft mouth would be pressing against him.

Her palms pushed against his chest as she tried to lever herself away. Looking down, he could see the expression on her face, her pure shock mirroring his own.

'Get off me,' she muttered. It was as though she had no strength. A moment after trying to move out of his embrace, she gave up, collapsing back onto his chest.

'I think you'll find you're the one on me.' He couldn't disguise the amusement in his voice. 'You keep throwing yourself at me. Literally.' All the anger he'd felt earlier was forgotten. Replaced by a kind of *schadenfreude* at her predicament. 'You're drunk, aren't you?'

She struggled in his arms again. This time she managed to dig an elbow into his ribs. It was surprisingly painful, and he instinctively released her in order to grab at his chest, making Cesca once again fall to her knees.

'Shit,' she muttered, her hair falling over her face. Through the blonde veil he could see her eyes still shining, her cheeks still flushed. 'You dropped me, you arse.'

A rumble of a laugh formed deep in his abdomen. The absurdity of the situation was going a long way to take his mind off the pain in his ribs. There was something so comical about the way she was sprawled on the floor, yet still as feral as a cornered animal.

'Are you laughing at me?' she demanded. The cadence of her voice had been slowed by the wine. 'Because there's nothing funny about this.'

But there was. Here was Sam, hiding away from the world in his parents' villa, towering over the tiny spitfire who unabashedly hated his guts. It was almost Shakespearian in its drama, making Sam the fallen hero who was finally having to deal with his nemesis, in the form of Cesca Shakespeare, the pretty, furious, playwright who just couldn't write.

The laughter that erupted from his lips sounded almost alien to him. He cocked his head, frowning, attempting to work out why it sounded so different. It was only after he pondered on it for a minute that he realised the answer: he hadn't laughed so genuinely in a long, long while.

When he was a small child, giggles were as easy as breathing. There were no expectations, no judgements, and no revelations to muffle the sound. Of course he'd laughed in the past six years, he was an actor after all, but even the act of smiling when he was in LA had a control that was lacking here in Varenna.

Right now, he was Sam the boy who grew up in this villa. Not Sam the adult who had failed so completely in living up to everybody's expectations.

'Oh, it's funny,' he managed to say between paroxysms. 'In fact it's goddamn hilarious.'

The corner of her lip twitched. It was the smallest of movements, but it caught his eye all the same. He could see the struggle behind her gaze as she tried to stop the amusement from rising, her attempts at stifling it slowly losing out.

Then she was laughing, too. A giggly-hiccupy sort of laugh that made her whole torso double over. She collapsed back on the floor, her bottom hitting the marble tiles, as she hid her face behind her tanned hands.

'This is all your fault,' she spluttered. 'You mojo-stealing, house-invading, good-looking bastard.'

Even her insults were backhandedly amusing. Her eyes were screwed up, her chest rising and falling with every gulp of laughter, her arms flailing as she once again attempted to scramble to her feet.

It hadn't escaped his notice that she'd told him he was good-looking. Wisely, he decided not to comment on it at that moment. Something to store up and use later, when the time was right.

Cesca slipped as she rose to her feet, the alcohol stealing any sense of balance, and Sam automatically reached out to steady her. This time she let him, failing to pull away from his hold, her body pressing heavily against his.

'Let's get you to your room, OK?' he whispered, the laughter disappearing as suddenly as it arrived. 'You can sleep it off, that's the best thing.'

Cesca didn't protest. Instead she let him half-carry her to the staircase, and carefully lead her up the steps. He had to pause more than once when the effort got too much for her and she became unsteady on her feet. When they reached the top, he breathed a sigh of relief, leading her through the door to her bedroom, where she collapsed onto the king-size bed. It seemed as though she was asleep before her body hit the mattress. Sam stood there, looking at her in her skirt and top, wondering if he should just leave her like that, or take away the hazard that the layers of fabric could impose.

He hesitated. Cesca already hated his guts. If she woke up in the morning wearing only a bra and panties, God only knew what kind of fury she would unleash. He was in enough trouble already, he really didn't need any more.

Even unconscious, Cesca was definitely trouble.

Pulling the covers across her still-clothed body, he took a final look at her face. An expression of peacefulness had stolen the derision that usually crafted her features whenever he was around, and it transformed her appearance completely. For the first time he could see a resemblance to that eighteen-year-old kid he could barely remember, the one whose face lit up whenever she talked about her play. The memory constricted his chest, a strange taste of regret coating his tongue, and he had to swallow hard to take it away.

Had he done this? Been the one to steal away her happiness, her hopes, and her big dream? The thought was like a black cloud in his mind. No wonder she hated him so much.

Turning away, he left her bedroom, walking down the hallway until he reached his own. And as he readied himself for bed he had to fight the urge to stare at himself in the mirror, to berate the man who was staring back. He was a fuck-up, pure and simple. A Midas in negative. The need to make amends took hold of his mind. But what on earth could he do?

There was no point in entertaining the idea of saving her. He couldn't even save himself.

11

*All the world's a stage, and all the men
and women merely players*
– As You Like It

Oh. My. God.

She was never drinking again. Not even the gorgeous red wine that the Carltons kept in the pantry, the one that tasted more like heaven than anything she'd ever come across. The pounding in her head was like a thousand tiny men using pickaxes against her skull, digging, digging, digging until tears formed in her eyes.

As for the nausea, well that was almost unbearable. The cheese and wine she'd eaten last night seemed to have joined forces, mixing together in her stomach to form an evil cocktail. Cesca lay back on the pillow and closed her eyes to the morning light, wishing she'd turned down the final bottle when Cristiano had opened it.

She licked her dry lips, trying to remember what happened after she left the beach. Cracking open her left eye, she took in enough of her surroundings to realise she had at least made it back to her own bedroom, and was thankfully alone.

Yep, definitely never drinking again.

The problem was, she barely drank any alcohol when she was living back in London. She couldn't afford it, and whenever she had any money the thought of a packet of tea bags and a chocolate bar always seemed more enticing than the rows of bottles stacked up on the shelves. Even when Gabi and Alessandro were here, she barely drank more than a third of a bottle of wine. Slow and steady had been her way for the first few weeks.

Not any more, apparently.

Rolling onto her side, she put her hand on her belly in an attempt to soothe it. Her abdomen felt hard and distended, her muscles aching from the constant cramping. Cesca took a deep breath, her thoughts returning to the previous night. She remembered falling over on the sand, then walking back up to the house. Did she go straight to bed after that, or did she hang around downstairs? Oh Jesus, Sam didn't see her in that state, did he?

The memory of her encounter with Sam rose up from the depths of her brain, image by embarrassing image. Had she really thrown herself at him, multiple times? Ugh. The arrogant bastard.

If she could bear to move her hands from her stomach, she'd be burying her face in them right now. Especially when she remembered him almost carrying her upstairs and putting her to bed. Gingerly lifting up the bedcovers, she looked at her body underneath, breathing a sigh of relief when she noted she was still fully clothed. At least she had that final scrap of dignity to hold onto, shredded as it was.

There was a loud buzz in the hallway, as somebody called the villa from the entrance gate. Cesca froze, remembering it was cleaning day, and the crew would be waiting for her to let them in to blitz the house. It took a force of will to push herself out of the bed and stand up without wanting to double over in pain. She reached out and leaned on the whitewashed walls, closing her eyes and taking in small gulps of air.

She could do this. All it needed was to walk downstairs and press the button to open the gate. The crew knew what they were doing, she could just let them have the run of the place. She shuffled out of her bedroom, careful not to make any sudden movements that might end in a pool of vomit.

The stairs were the hardest part. She managed to slowly walk down them, only having to pause once to steady herself, and swallow down the pain. By the time she made it to the security box in the hallway, it felt as though she was almost in control of herself.

'Yes?' she asked through the intercom, her voice cracked.

The gabbled Italian reply, coupled with the video screen of the cleaning van, told her all she needed to know. Cesca buzzed the cleaners in, then sat down heavily on the hall chair, dropping her head into her hands.

'I thought you might want this.'

Sam was standing in front of her, holding a glass of water. In his other hand was a packet of Advil. He gave her the glass, then popped out two pills. Cesca was too surprised to do anything other than take them from him, swallowing them one at a time.

'Thank you?' It came out as a question. If she'd been feeling more like herself she'd probably interrogate him, or accuse him of trying to poison her. Instead she felt a warmth in her chest, one that seemed to pacify her swirling stomach.

'We've all been there,' Sam said, taking the empty glass

of water from her. 'Why don't you go back to bed? You look like hell.'

'Thanks.' Once she was feeling better, she really needed to work on her repartee.

'It wasn't really a compliment.'

'I didn't take it as one. I know I look terrible. I should. It's my own fault anyway.'

Sam wrinkled his nose. 'Nah, we can blame the wine.'

'Yeah, because it jumped right out of the bottle and into my mouth.' In spite of her headache, she felt the corners of her mouth turn up.

'That damn Chianti, it's got a mind of its own. Should be banned, it's a dangerous substance.'

'Shouldn't you be lording it over me?' she asked. 'After all, you don't like me, and you have every right to tell me off for getting drunk and then being hung-over on the job.'

'You're not an equal adversary right now. I'll wait until you're feeling better to make you feel bad.'

'That's very gentlemanly of you.'

'I aim to please.' He flashed her an unexpected smile. 'Now get back to bed, you look awful and you stink.'

'I can't, the cleaners are here. I need to supervise them.'

'I'll do it. Please go back to bed.'

She would have narrowed her eyes, but it hurt too much. 'Why are you being so kind?'

Sam sighed. 'Look, I know we got off to the worst start, and I know we're never going to get along, but the fact of the matter is, for at least the next few weeks we have to find a way to live together. You're not well, and I'm here with nothing much to do, and it makes sense for me to take over. So please go back to bed and sleep it off.'

'I owe you one,' she replied. 'If I ever feel better I'll try and make it up to you.'

That made the corner of his lip twitch, but he ignored her offer anyway. 'Go on, get off with you. If you're not up by this evening I'll come in and check on you. Otherwise, get some sleep, have a shower, and smarten yourself up.'

'Yes, sir.' If she had more than a basic control of her muscles she would have curtsied. Instead she used the small amount of energy she had to climb up the stairs to her bedroom.

Maybe when she was feeling better she'd try to work out Sam's motivations, why he'd been so accommodating to her. For now, though, she'd just be grateful for them, wherever they came from.

It was early afternoon when Cesca made it out of bed the second time. She stepped under the rainfall shower, letting the stream of water soothe her aching muscles. Though a trace of her headache remained, the incessant nausea had disappeared, replaced by a nagging hunger that demanded to be fed. She ignored it, instead concentrating on getting dressed, styling her hair and putting on a dash of make-up. Scrutinising herself in the mirror, she was surprised at how healthy she looked after what she'd managed to put her body through the previous night.

She'd let herself down. Again. That's what it all came down to in the end. As with her life in London, she'd let herself be carried away, not bothering to take control of her own decisions. It had to stop. She'd thought it already had. That was what coming here was about, after all. And even if things at the villa had been slightly set awry by the arrival of Sam Carlton, that didn't mean she needed to deviate from her plans.

That's how she found herself sitting in the silent library that afternoon, in front of the old computer there, staring at the blank screen. The cursor was winking at her from behind the glass, taunting, or maybe hoping.

Writing used to be so easy. The pads of her fingers would move almost instinctively from key to key, forming words without her having to really think them. Like a pianist playing by ear, she would let her movements do the talking.

But now, it was as if she was tone deaf.

She looked at the handwritten notes beside her. Character sketches and plot ideas. They were all there, waiting as patiently as the cursor. She had the bones, she just needed to add the flesh.

'What if it's no good?' she whispered to herself. But no, that wasn't it at all. Her biggest fear was the opposite. What if it was too good? What if it was the best thing she'd ever write? Could she bear to lose it again, to see all her hard work turn to nothing, like it did six years ago?

Glancing up, she saw a photograph of Sam on the library wall. He was laughing with two young girls – his sisters – looking as gloriously handsome as ever. She waited for the familiar anger to hit, but nothing came. Instead all she felt was peace.

It had never been Sam's fault, not really. Deep down she'd always known that. Plays folded all the time, it was the chance everybody took when they gave their heart to the theatre. The only person stopping Cesca writing was herself. And she'd been doing it for six years.

She closed her eyes to take a deep breath in. Her heart

115

was speeding in her chest. And with her eyes still firmly shut, she let her fingers drift across the keyboard, pressing down in a rhythm only she seemed to know. Then, still holding her breath, she slowly opened her eyes to see the words written on the screen before her.

```
ACT 1
SCENE 1
Opens on the interior of a run-down but
wealthy house. Four sisters are sitting in a
kitchen, all wearing mourning clothes.
```

Cesca's breathing was laboured as she added in the first lines. Through their dialogue, the four sisters slowly came to life, each word like a breath, inflating their lungs. And then her fingers were flying, like a musician approaching the crescendo, as the long-dormant part of her brain took over.

Though she was hungry, and still a little weak from the morning's hangover, she found herself typing furiously, stopping occasionally to scribble down ideas on the pad beside the computer. When the ideas refused to surface, she carried on typing anyway, putting in nonsense that no doubt she'd need to cut out when she did her first run of edits. But the process of writing, of actually placing the pads of her fingers on the keys and tapping them, of watching the words form in front of her eyes, it was enticing. Addictive even.

Cesca was exhilarated. It was as though she had been transported from that pretty villa in Varenna back to London, to an old, dusty theatre, with huge red stage curtains and threadbare velvet seats. She was watching her characters interact, jibe, fall in love, and it was beautiful.

As the day wore out its welcome, and the evening slipped its backdrop down over the sky, she carried on typing, breathless and inspired. If she'd stopped to think, maybe she'd have marvelled at how things had changed so much in a few hours. How a day that had started out so badly had turned into something quite wonderful. But she was far too absorbed for that.

Sam waved the cleaners off at lunchtime. They were supremely efficient, removing every piece of dust from the floors and furniture. A couple of them recognised him, two young girls who stood in the corner, unashamedly gossiping until their boss shouted at them to get back to work. Sam tried to ignore it; he was used to interested speculation after all, but this time he felt a tug in his gut as he wondered whether they'd heard about him and Serena Sloane. Thank God Cesca couldn't speak Italian; the last thing he needed was for her to discover the sordid details of his affair. She wouldn't let him hear the end of it.

While the cleaners buffed and polished the inside of the villa, and the gardeners cut and tidied the grounds, Sam grabbed his copy of E.M. Forster and headed out into the gardens, lying in the beautiful Italian sun while he read about early-twentieth-century lives.

Naturally, his mind drifted to Cesca, and to her reaction to him. He and Cesca were both in Italy for different reasons, yet they'd been thrown together in the same house, coming into contact with each other again and again. Wary housemates, tiptoeing around until the summer ended.

And then what? Sam wasn't really sure. There was no doubt about it, he was hiding here, and had no real game plan after that. All he could hope was that after the summer he would have disappeared from the headlines, and he could get on with acting, instead of dodging paparazzi. It wasn't too much to ask, was it? To just be left alone to get on with his job. He tried to ignore the voice in his head – the one that sounded suspiciously like his recently fired agent – telling him that wasn't how the movie industry worked. Deep inside he knew the truth of that. Good acting didn't sell movies, as much as he'd like to believe it, but publicity did. People would only swarm to see a movie if they'd heard of it, and having his face out there was guaranteed to ensure people came to see Sam.

It was a game he was tired of playing, though, especially since he'd been burned.

Just after four, he wandered back into the house, grabbing an ice-cold can from the refrigerator. Gulping it down, he went back into the hallway and up the stairs, deciding to check that Cesca hadn't somehow choked on her own vomit or died in her sleep. Pushing open her bedroom door, he was surprised to see her bed was empty, the covers pushed down at the end of the bed, crumpled and creased. Tilting his head he listened out for her shower, but that, too, lay silent.

She was up then. He hadn't seen her when he walked through the living room and hallway, and into the kitchen, but he couldn't believe she was well enough to go out. Not unless somebody had helped her. He thought about that guy living in the villa next door, the one who had made her laugh then made her drunk, and his stomach contracted. Sam hoped to hell she hadn't disappeared with him, not after the way he'd treated her last night.

When he made it back downstairs, Sam checked all the rooms again, scratching his head when they were devoid of her presence. He was about to wander down to the beach to see if she really was with the guy next door, when he heard some noise coming from his father's study. The door was slightly ajar, and when he looked through the gap Sam breathed out softly. There was Cesca, sitting at his father's desk in front of the computer, her reading glasses slipping down her nose as she typed furiously. She had a distant expression, as if her thoughts were miles from here. She was so intent on whatever she was writing that she didn't even notice Sam standing there.

He noticed her, though. She looked nothing like the hung-over, bedraggled girl of this morning, or the screaming woman he'd first encountered that night at the gate. This Cesca looked altogether different; more composed and yet softer. Even the sunlight seemed to agree, bouncing off her blonde hair like a halo, illuminating her as she worked.

It was hard to ignore her energy and fervency. She was like a magnet, and he felt drawn to her excitement, as though their magnetic poles had switched and were now dragging him in.

Sam curled his fingers around the door jamb. He wasn't sure if it was to steady himself or to stop himself walking in. There was no way he wanted to disturb her, not when she was deep within whatever zone she'd managed to find, but there was something inside him that ached to feel that same powerful emotion. It reminded him of when he was acting, and the character inside him took on a life of its own. Like a butterfly emerging from a chrysalis, you just had to stand back, admire, and wonder where it came from.

Cesca paused for a moment, picking up a pen and tapping it against her lips. Sam held his breath, still not wanting to be spotted, or destroy the mojo she claimed he'd destroyed before. Whatever she was writing about was captivating her, and a part of him ached to know what it was. The moment passed, and she returned to typing, as Sam quietly turned around and left the hallway, his thoughts still with the girl at his father's desk.

He knew the password to that computer. It was his mother's birthday followed by *Varenna*. Something simple that nobody would forget. Perhaps he'd use the computer himself that night, and if he happened to stumble across Cesca's document, that would be a real coincidence, wouldn't it?

At least, that was the lie he was telling himself.

12

To sleep, perchance to dream

– Hamlet

Cesca barely slept that night. Her thoughts were consumed by her play. Every time she closed her eyes she could hear her characters talking, see them moving, and her inner voice started adding in stage directions until all restfulness disappeared. She'd forgotten about this part of writing. The way you couldn't switch off, and how the characters demanded you listen, even when your body was exhausted. If she'd remembered she might have brought a notepad to bed with her, ready to scribble any ideas that came in the night. Instead she only had a glass of water and a battered old romance novel she'd been trying to read ever since she'd arrived in Italy.

Every time one of the characters spoke, it was as though she was hearing her sisters' voices. For a moment she was back in that draughty Hampstead house, the four of them flying around the echoing corridors, shouting at each other when they couldn't find their homework, or their favourite lipstick.

The nostalgia tasted like metal in her mouth. She yearned

for them all, missed being constantly surrounded by her family. Though it was years since Lucy and Juliet left home, quickly followed by Cesca herself, she found herself longing to be back in the kitchen, boiling the kettle for a brew.

Maybe that's why her characters were shouting so loudly in her brain.

There was nothing else she could do; she was going to have to get up and go downstairs to grab her notebook. Clambering out of bed, she snatched a robe to cover up her bare limbs; in this weather wearing only shorts and a vest top was the best way to get some sleep. Knotting the belt around her waist, she made her way out of her bedroom, her bare feet padding across the marble floor. The villa felt eerily quiet, even more so than usual. As she walked downstairs, her eyes adjusting to the darkness, Cesca found herself wrapping her arms around her torso.

There was a pale yellow light coming from the library, forming a rectangular halo around the closed door. Cesca frowned, stopping just shy of the entrance, cocking her head to see if she could hear sounds coming from within. Was Sam still up? For some reason that made Cesca's heart stutter. She hadn't bothered password protecting her play, she didn't think anybody else was going to be using the computer. Until a few days ago, she was the only one in the house anyway.

Not that she could imagine Sam would be interested in her play. After all, he'd shown such little regard for her last one that he'd walked out on opening night. He was too self-absorbed to care about what anybody else was doing, too caught up in being a movie star. The writings of some nobody from London wouldn't even register on his radar.

She took a deep breath. She should just go in there, grab her notebook, and check on what he was up to. He was probably just playing around, Googling himself or something.

With a burst of energy she managed to push the door open and step inside the library, but that's where she stopped. Sam was sitting at the desk, wearing only pyjama bottoms, his torso bare and glinting in the moonlight. It was impossible to ignore the sculpted lines of his chest, or the way his bicep muscles bulged as his fingers hit the keypad. Cesca felt her mouth turn dry as she stared at him, unable to tear her eyes away.

Out of principle she'd never watched any of his movies, and when he'd been rehearsing for her play he'd remained fully dressed. Even since they'd been here together in Varenna, he'd been wearing T-shirts and shirts. She'd never imagined what lay beneath his clothes was quite so ... beautiful.

Damn, was there no end to his outward perfection?

When he looked up, Cesca quickly dragged her gaze away, fiddling at her robe with busy fingers. 'I came to get my notebook.' She spotted it on the desk next to him. All she needed to do was walk forward and grab it, but for some reason her muscles refused to comply.

Sam turned the screen off. Was it Cesca's imagination, or did he have a guilty expression on his face?

'You couldn't sleep either?' he asked. When she finally met his gaze she could see the warmth of his face where the desk lamp lit it, and the softness of his eyes. The easy arrogance she was so used to was gone.

'Not really,' she said. 'I've never been that good at sleeping. I can doze off OK, but then I wake up in the middle of the night with a thousand things on my mind. It's like somebody forgot to flick the off switch.' Why was she telling him this?

'I know that feeling.'

'I thought if I could just write things on my notepad, then maybe I could wind down enough to drift off again.'

Sam nodded. 'That's a good idea. My therapist always suggested keeping a journal and a pen by my bed.'

She wasn't sure what was more surprising: the fact he had a therapist, or him actually admitting to it. It wasn't a very British thing to do. But then, Sam wasn't very British, was he?

'Did you follow his suggestion?'

'I did for a while. But I'm OK now.'

'OK is good.'

'Sometimes it is.' The corner of his lips arched into a smile.

Their conversation was making Cesca feel uncomfortable yet warm at the same time.

'I've never had therapy,' she told him. 'A few people suggested it after my mother died. But I didn't want to go there. And then when the play bombed, I thought about it again but couldn't afford it.'

Sam's smile faltered, the guilty look returning again. 'Couldn't you get it paid for by the government?'

She shook her head. 'I wasn't in a bad enough way. My godfather offered to pay, but by then I wasn't easily persuaded. I thought I could handle things all by myself.'

'You must have done something right,' Sam said. 'Because here you are.'

'Here I am.' She decided not to go deeper. 'And now I

really should go back to bed.' Though Cesca wanted to stay, to grill him about his therapy and find out what the hell he had to talk about with a counsellor, she knew she shouldn't. Every encounter, every conversation, was making her doubt what she'd believed for the past six years. That Sam Carlton was a bastard, someone who only cared about himself.

'Sounds sensible. I won't be far behind you.' She could almost feel him pulling away from her.

Cesca nodded, then turned around to leave.

'Don't forget your notebook.' He held it out to her.

'I need my pen, too.'

'Of course you do.' Sam grabbed it from the desk, then offered them both to her. For a moment, when she took it, he still held on to the other end. There was only an inch between their fingertips. His hand was so much bigger than hers, the tendons beneath his skin defined and sinewy. She tried not to remember how he'd caught her and held on tight the night before.

'Good night, Sam.'

'Sweet dreams.'

'Chance would be a fine thing.'

Sam switched the screen back on. He was only halfway through her script, but what he'd read was engrossing, enough for him to want to see the rest. There were thirty pages in there, full of elegant dialogue and descriptive stage directions, all leading up to the end of the first act.

He'd read plays before, of course, acted in them at drama school. And for the past six years he was rarely without at least a couple of movie scripts, weighing up the offers, working out which ones to go for. He knew a good story when he read it, one that kept you coming back for more, one that made you desperate to play the lead character. Cesca's first play had been like that, the role of Daniel grabbing him from the first scene, and when he'd been cast in the play Sam had been ecstatic.

That was all before Foster's revelation, of course. The rest, sadly, was his messed-up history.

The play was good. Really good. Full of emotion and drama, and almost perfect dialogue. Some of the stage directions needed polishing, and he could see typos and some areas to clean up, but apart from that, her talent shone through. How had she managed to hide it away for six years? There weren't many people who managed to write such a beautiful first draft. In Hollywood most scripts he'd seen had been written over months or years, and by a team of writers, not a single person. Sam breathed out softly, wondering if what she'd said was true, if Cesca's writer's block really had come because of his thoughtless actions.

His eye was caught by a silver-framed photograph of Sam and his sisters. They were playing down at the private beach, laughing their heads off as their mother emerged bedraggled from the water. He could remember that moment so well. They'd spent the day by the lake with his mother and her best friend. For some reason he couldn't remember now, Sam had decided it would be fun to throw his mother in the water, his growing teenage body able to lift her up without much struggle.

But it wasn't that moment that stayed in his mind, it was what happened afterwards. His body tensed at the memory, before he chased it out of his mind. He wasn't going to think about that now.

Looking up, he reached for the mouse, highlighting a badly written stage direction and correcting the words. Tracked changes were on, revealing his interference, but at that point he didn't care. He'd save it in another file. She'd never have to know he read it. Not unless she wanted to.

He was a fucked up mess, but he knew what read well, and Cesca's play could be almost perfect, with a little polish.

Maybe it was a kind of atonement to help her achieve that.

13

The lady doth protest too much

– Hamlet

'It's a baby girl.' Gabi's voice was joyful as it echoed down the telephone line. 'She's so beautiful, Cesca, like a tiny doll. She has ten perfect toes and ten lovely fingers, and everything about her is wonderful.'

Cesca smiled, standing in the telephone box and staring out through the dirty, scratched glass. After yesterday's hangover, she'd decided to get out of the villa this morning and take a refreshing walk up to the village square. It would give her the opportunity to call Gabi as she'd promised to once a week, and then to catch up on her emails to her family and Hugh.

Putting distance between herself and Sam was also a factor, though not one she admitted to herself. But ever since last night, and their discussion about therapy, she'd felt a wave of discomfort come over her. As though it was the middle of winter and somebody had stolen her blanket, leaving her to freeze on a hard mattress. It made her want to curl into a ball.

'That's fantastic, congratulations to you all. I'm so happy

for you.' The news of Alessandro's sister's new baby was an antidote to all the angst of the previous few days. Selfishly, it also meant that Gabi and Alessandro would be able to return home in a couple of weeks, which could put an end to the stifled closeness of living with Sam Carlton. 'What's her name?'

'She is called Vittoria, after Alessandro's mother. Such a pretty name for a pretty girl.'

'And is she sleeping much?'

'Not at all.' Gabi sounded insanely happy about that. 'So we are all doing our bit at nights. I get the two a.m. to ten a.m. shift.'

'And you like that?'

'What's not to like about cuddling a baby? Especially a beautiful one like Vittoria.' Gabi's sigh was full of contentment. 'Anyway, enough about our wonderful news, tell me how things are going at the villa?'

Where to start? 'Well, Sam Carlton arrived unexpectedly.'

'Sam is there?' Gabi's voice rose two octaves. 'Oh my goodness, we didn't know he was coming. Oh Cesca, we should come home right away, he will need looking after.'

Was there anybody who didn't run around him, fulfilling his every need? Apart from Cesca, that was. What was it about him, anyway?

She thought about the way he looked in the moonlight last night and rolled her eyes. Even she wasn't immune to his charms.

'He's fine, he doesn't need looking after. I've bought him some food and he wants to be quiet and left alone. He even supervised the cleaning staff for me yesterday.'

She could almost hear Gabi's smile in her voice. 'He's always been such a lovely man. So kind and helpful.'

'Um, yeah.'

'But are you sure we shouldn't come back? When Mrs Carlton said we could have some time off, she didn't tell me about Sam coming to Varenna.'

'I don't think she knows,' Cesca said. 'He wants to keep his presence here a secret. Said he wants to get away from everything for a few days.'

'Well that's understandable after everything he's been through.'

'Like what?'

'I'm not one to gossip,' Gabi said, 'but it must be so hard for him being followed by photographers all the time. And the lies they make up about him, well it's terrible.'

'What lies?' She held the phone closer to her ear.

Gabi's reply was drowned out by the loud wail of a baby. 'I'm so sorry, Cesca, the baby has just woken up. I need to change her. Can you call me back another time?'

The piercing wails were making Cesca wince. 'OK, I'll call you again on Friday.' She had to shout to be heard over the cries. 'Take care of yourself, and try to get some sleep.'

'Oh I will.' Still sounding absurdly happy, Gabi bade her farewell.

Cesca hung the phone back on its cradle, and leaned her head on the glass, thinking about Gabi's words. What lies was she talking about? For a moment, she thought about going back into the café and Googling him, but somehow it felt dirty. She'd been on the receiving end of gossip a few times herself – she knew how much it hurt.

And anyway, she wouldn't give him the satisfaction of her Googling him. She really wasn't that bothered. It would only add to his smugness levels if he ever found out.

Shaking her head, she pulled the door open and stepped out of the telephone box. There were only a few more weeks until Gabi and Sandro got back. She could make it until then, couldn't she?

It was the afternoon before Cesca got the chance to sit down in the library, turning on the computer and flexing her fingers, ready to type. She had her notebook beside her, the white paper covered in scrawls only she could decipher, with pieces of dialogue and stage directions for the next scene.

There'd been no sign of Sam when she'd returned. The dishwasher held the evidence of his breakfast, so he'd at least been up that morning. Cesca assumed he was somewhere in the gardens, continuing his reading sprint. It was easy to get lost among the lush greenery and trees, and if you wanted to you could probably hide out for a while.

The first thing that hit her when she opened up her play was the amount of red covering the screen. The usually black and white document was covered in lines. Red down the left side of the document where changes had been made, comments on the right in speech bubbles, and bold words where things had been deleted, the sentences underlined to emphasise the fact.

There were tracked changes on her document. Changes she hadn't made.

Her stomach churned as she stared at the screen. She felt invaded, as though something precious had been stolen from her, and it took her breath away.

A moment later, the anger arrived. Her whole body tensed as the explosion started deep inside her, rising up until even her face was bright red with ire.

How bloody dare he? Because there was only one suspect in Cesca's mind. Only one person who would think it was OK to go into somebody's private document and not only read it, but actually make comments on it. She should have password protected it from the beginning, or stored it somewhere other than in the documents, but God, what a bloody ego that man had if he thought she would want him in her private thoughts.

Cesca punched the off button. It was as though a red veil had descended, clouding her thoughts, making her see everything through a wrathful light. She stomped out of the library, determined to find him and give him a piece of her mind, even if it meant she was fired from her job.

He wasn't in his bedroom or the living room, or any part of the villa, so she swung open the glass doors that led to the garden, stalking out onto the patio in her sandalled feet. Standing there, she looked left and right, trying to work out which way to go first.

'Sam?' she shouted out, a frown pulling the corner of her lips down. 'Where are you?' She didn't care that nobody was supposed to know he was here. Didn't care if the entire neighbourhood heard. As far as she was concerned, his need for privacy came very low on her list of priorities.

No response. Either he wasn't close enough to hear, or he was ignoring her. She wouldn't put that past him.

Huffing loudly, she stormed off in the direction of the trees. It was so typical of him to put her to even more inconvenience. 'Sam? I need to talk to you.'

She climbed uphill, heading to the top boundary of the estate. Built on a cliff, the gradient was surprisingly steep, and the exertion, coupled with the warmth of the afternoon, was making her overheat. Rivulets of perspiration ran down her chest.

When she found him, she was going to kill him. It was best for all concerned to put them all out of their misery. Just a little squeeze of her hands and pouf! he would disappear. Nobody could blame her for that.

'Sam?' She was almost screaming now, the frustration of not being able to locate him making her words loud and shrill. 'For God's sake show yourself!'

A rustle of the trees in front of her alerted her to his presence. Sam stepped out of the lush vegetation, rubbing his face, his brow wrinkled with what looked like confusion. 'Are you OK?' he asked. 'Are you hurt?'

Hurt? She was mortally injured, and it was all thanks to him.

'No, I'm not all right. I'm the very bloody opposite of all right.'

He stood there open-mouthed, staring at her, tipping his head to the side as if to try and make her out. 'What's happened?' He reached out for her with one hand, the other rubbing his brow. 'Can I help you?'

She cringed away from his touch. 'Let go of me.'

'So we're back to that again.'

'Back to what?' she asked. 'To me realising what a complete and utter prick you are? To you behaving like you always do – as though you're more important than anyone else?'

Sam blinked. 'I don't know what you're talking about. I've been up here all morning, reading. I haven't done anything.' He smiled at her, as though he expected her to take his word for it.

'Oh yes you have! You interfered with my play, you bastard.

How could you? Didn't you break me enough the first time? Or are you just so bored you'd rather mess everybody else's lives up just for the hell of it?'

Emotions passed over his face. First understanding, then shock, followed by what looked almost like shame. He frowned.

'How did you see that?'

'Because you left comments all over it.'

He rubbed his hand across his face. 'But I saved it somewhere else. You weren't supposed to see that.'

Her eyes widened. 'That's your excuse?' she bit out. 'It's my fault for seeing it, not your fault for interfering?'

'I didn't say that.' He shook his head. 'It's just you weren't supposed to see.'

Cesca rolled her eyes. 'Is this some kind of retaliation? Are you still trying to push me out? You must think I'm a terrible writer to want to screw me over twice.'

'You're being irrational.'

She let out an exasperated shriek. 'There's nothing irrational about me. You're the one behaving like a shit.'

His eyes narrowed. There was a tic in his jaw. 'I'm not a shit.'

'You interfered with my play. You wrote all over it.'

'It was good.' His voice was low. 'I just wanted to make it better.'

'I don't care what you think,' she shouted back. 'I don't care about your opinion at all. I just want you to leave me alone.'

His lips twisted as he stared at her. 'Are you finished?' he asked, the words whistling through his teeth.

She wasn't, not by a long chalk, but she was starting to feel light-headed. It wasn't from relief or a sense of righteousness or any of the things she'd thought she'd have once she'd got everything off her chest. More likely a combination of the heat and the long walk.

'Yes.'

He was like an animal waiting to pounce. She held her breath, anticipating his response. But instead of the fury she'd expected, what he gave her was an icy control.

'Then so am I.'

14

There is no following her in this fierce vein
– A Midsummer Night's Dream

Sam made it back to the villa in record time. He couldn't even remember the walk, or the way he'd muttered to himself, or even how his hands had curled into fists at regular intervals. The need to hit something was becoming a compulsion, as if slamming his hands against a surface would rid him of his rage.

Was she right? he wondered. Did everybody really think of him that way? He was used to being disliked by some – it came with the territory when you were made out to be some kind of Hollywood heart-throb – but for the majority of his life love and admiration had come easily to him. His father excluded, of course.

Cesca's anger conjured up memories of Foster. He and Cesca both seemed to hate Sam's guts. If he could bring out such a strong reaction in people, then maybe there was some truth in what she had to say. Was he really that much of a shit?

Sam walked into his bathroom, splashing cold water onto his heated face. He'd been an idiot for coming here. An even bigger fool for staying after Cesca had made it clear how much she hated him.

He stared into the mirror above the basin, his eyes narrowing as he took in the image reflected back at him. Dark wavy hair, inherited from his mother, as well as her clear blue eyes and Roman nose. His tan he got from mother nature, but the rest of his face must have come from his father. The high cheekbones and sensual lips that people raved about online, the sharp jaw that always seemed to grow a five o'clock shadow no matter how hard he shaved. A face loved by millions, but hated by those who were important to him. He could barely stand to look at it himself.

When Cesca had stood in front of him, her face glowing with anger, he'd felt an urge to touch her. To hold her. To take away the pain in her eyes. His therapist had once told him that anger was only pain trying to fight against itself. If it were true, that would mean he'd caused her to feel that way, and that thought made his chest ache.

More and more he was remembering that girl from six years ago. The one who almost bounced into the theatre with excitement each morning. The one who had explained Daniel's motivations to him, talked him through each scene, and unabashedly encouraged him to show all the emotion he could.

He didn't like the way that memory made him feel. Like that kid he had been, all vulnerable and hurt. His relationships were like a walking time bomb, and it was only a matter of time before this one exploded, too. He didn't need a friend, and he definitely didn't need to be attracted to her. He just needed to lie low until the fallout from his last fuck-up disappeared.

For as long as it took.

*

Cesca spent an hour aimlessly wandering the grounds, feeling the sun beating down on her bare skin. She hadn't put any sunscreen on in her haste to give Sam a piece of her mind, and she could already feel herself pinking up. Not that she cared. What was a little sunburn compared to everything else? If anything it was helping to ease the guilt she was feeling at blowing up at Sam so much.

She'd gone a little over the top. OK, more than a little. She'd reacted purely from anger, not bothering to temper her words, saying things so unkind they made her blush. Cesca wasn't a horrible person, not really. Wherever possible she tried to treat people with friendliness and respect. But there was something in Sam's actions that had triggered her anger once again, taking her back to those awful days when her world came crashing around her feet.

Eventually she made it back into the villa, still unable to shake off the uncomfortable feeling from her shoulders. Grabbing a glass of water from the kitchen, she found her way to the library, trying to ignore the way her skin was stinging from exposure to the afternoon sun.

The computer was where she'd left it, the screen was black but the light still flashing. She switched it on, the first page of her play blinking back to life in front of her.

For the next hour she sat and read every comment, her eyes taking in each change he'd made.

Seeing his words took her back to when she was in English class at school. Every term the teacher would hand out the required texts, old dog-eared books that had been in the department for years. Some of them for longer than Cesca had been alive. Yet each time she'd felt a shiver of anticipation slide down her spine, knowing that when she opened up the book it was more than the author's text she would see.

Each schoolgirl who held that book in their hands would leave a little piece of themselves behind in there. It wasn't just the bookplate they had to sign at the front – with their names, their form and the year they held it – but also in the illicit scribblings they'd leave in pen or pencil in each page, saying what they thought of the passage, what they thought of the book. No two people ever read the same story, because they each brought with them their own view of the world.

And as she sat in front of her own text, seeing it through Sam's eyes, the same feeling was rushing through her veins.

With each word she read, Cesca could feel herself becoming more and more ashamed. Of her actions, of her words, of the way Sam had looked at her with such shock before he stalked away from her and back to the villa. Because his suggestions were good. No, that wasn't enough. They were excellent. He was seeing things so differently to her. Adding comments to make the characters rounder, more real. And all those things that had been holding her back from making the play work were slowly melting away.

She'd expected him to be critical, disparaging even. Instead he was kind, succinct and hit the nail on the head every time. He hadn't bothered disguising how much he liked the story, and he was making her see it from a different angle. A clearer one. One that she could actually see working. She felt herself sink lower and lower, until her lip started to wobble as she read his final comment.

This is brilliant. She needs to write more. It's one of the best scripts I've read in a long time, and I've read a lot.

Her hand shook as she covered her mouth. Cesca couldn't remember when she'd felt more ashamed of herself. She'd accused him of breaking her, of messing up her life, and all the while he'd left such lovely comments. No wonder he'd looked at her as if she was some kind of screaming harridan. She was like a lion who, when offered an olive branch, simply ate the dove for breakfast.

'I'm sorry,' she whispered into her hands. 'I'm so sorry, Sam.'

What on earth was she supposed to do next? Cesca wasn't really sure. All she knew was she'd managed to mess things up, and it was up to her to untangle them again.

Sam didn't come out of his bedroom all afternoon. By evening, Cesca's stomach was grumbling, reminding her she hadn't eaten since that morning, and she decided she'd cook enough food for two. Grabbing some pancetta and wild mushrooms, she put a griddle pan onto the range, igniting the flame to heat it up. While the food sautéed – spreading a gorgeous aroma throughout the kitchen – she boiled up a pan of pasta, watching the water bubble over, occasionally glancing to her left to see if Sam was anywhere to be seen.

The previous nights that he'd been here, Cesca's cooking had never failed to attract his attention. He'd watched with envy as she'd made a quick sauce for some golden strips of tagliatelle, or deftly rolled out some pizza dough before topping it with fresh ingredients. Not tonight, though. This evening there was no sign of him at all. Even when she splashed some wine into the pan and cooked it off before adding the cream.

She'd made enough for two. More than enough, probably,

but from her observations Sam had a pretty big appetite. Placing the pasta-laden plates on the wooden kitchen table, Cesca poured out two glasses of iced water and grabbed some cutlery. Then she wandered out of the kitchen into the hallway, making her way to the grand staircase.

'Sam?' Her voice was tentative. She didn't want to sound angry, the way she had in the gardens. Maybe if she was softer, more cajoling, he might actually answer.

Except he didn't. Cesca stood at the base of the staircase, her ears full of the sound of silence.

'Are you hungry?'

Still no response. Cesca reached for the banister, her movement stopping so her hand was in mid-air. Should she go up, see if he was OK? Maybe he wanted to be left alone, and for her to disappear back into the hole she'd managed to crawl up from. She couldn't blame him, either.

'I've made pasta,' she called again. 'Enough for both of us. Would you like to join me?'

She waited for another minute. The hallway was silent, save for the sound of her breathing and the low hum of the air conditioning as it attempted to fight the Italian heat.

'I'll put it in the refrigerator, then,' she said, as much to herself as to him. 'Come and help yourself if you're hungry.'

Her shoulders felt heavy as she walked back to the kitchen. Once inside, she sat at the table, trying to ignore the empty seat opposite her, and the plate of food that would almost certainly never be eaten. Cesca couldn't understand why she was so upset by their argument – or rather her rant – and his subsequent reaction. The Cesca of a few weeks ago would have been happy with that outcome, of finally seeing the golden boy brought to his knees. Wasn't that what she'd wanted, the opportunity to really tell Sam Carlton what she thought of him? The problem was, she didn't feel satisfied, or vindicated, or any of those emotions she'd thought she have. Instead she felt sick and guilty, and more than a little disgusted with herself.

It was clear Sam wasn't coming downstairs. It was obvious he hated her more than ever, and there was nothing she could really say to make things better.

At times like these, the only thing left to do was write.

15

Mistress, you know yourself,
down on your knees

– As You Like It

Sam had slept in this room since he was a young boy. Though it had been redecorated since that time, not much else had changed. It still had pale blue walls, an oversized bed with an embroidered quilt, and antique furniture that had been in the Palladino family for centuries. Strong and hardy to the touch, yet delicate to look at. Like everything else in his mother's home, he treated it with respect.

Everything except the person pottering in the room below him, that was.

An only child, Sam's mother Lucia had inherited everything when her parents both died in a car crash. That was when Sam was a tiny baby, and they were living in New York, where Foster was an up-and-coming theatre producer. Every summer since then, Lucia had brought her family home, to spend the warm days frolicking in the sun. Villa Palladino had become an anchor in Sam's life, even if he'd avoided it in the past few years. It was here, where there was no phone or Wi-Fi, that he felt most like himself. The pre-Hollywood Sam who loved to read, to play, to spend time with his family. The Sam who could never please his father, but couldn't understand why.

He lay back in his bed, the mattress groaning beneath him. It was ironic that he'd come to Italy to escape his problems, yet had only managed to make more for himself. He should go back to LA, face his self-inflicted demons, and forget that Cesca Shakespeare ever existed. Yet somehow he found that difficult to do. Even when he closed his eyes she was there, staring back at him, her anger and ire somehow only enhancing her beauty.

Because she *was* beautiful. That was impossible to ignore. But more than that she was talented, strong, and not afraid of speaking her mind. There was a wildness to her that enticed him, made him want to know more. That was why he'd been so absorbed by her play. Seeing her intelligence laid out in black and white, in the dialogue between the characters she'd so carefully crafted, had been an eye-opener. Giving him an insight to the woman beneath the hard exterior. Last night, when he was reading her words and adding in comments, it felt like a dialogue between him and Cesca, even though neither of them had said a word.

It was a conversation she hadn't wanted, though. One she'd openly rejected, and it felt like a swift, sharp kick to the gut. It had wounded his pride – of course it had – but it had also made him want to curl up into a ball.

Because he liked her. Damn it, he more than liked her. Somehow, since that first night when she'd screamed at him in the driveway, he'd become more intrigued by Cesca than any girl he'd met in his life. By her straight way of talking, by her refusal to take any bullshit, and by the quiet way she managed to slide into his consciousness.

He liked her, and it only made him feel worse.

It was his stomach that made him climb out of bed. The hunger pangs that made him put one foot in front of the other and walk out of his room. Sam wasn't sure what time it was – his phone was dead and he wasn't wearing a watch – but the stillness of the air told him it was some time after midnight.

Walking past Cesca's bedroom, he felt an urge to push open the door. To see the girl lying there, her hair fanned out across her pillow, her body curled up the way it was the night he carried her to bed. His empty stomach lurched at the memory of her soft skin, the way her breath had breezed across his cheek. Even then, the protectiveness he'd convinced himself he felt had been something more. Something deeper.

In the kitchen, there was a plate of food in the refrigerator just as Cesca had promised. He inhaled deeply when he took it over to the microwave, lifting up the clingfilm to allow the air to circulate. A different man would have eaten this food when it was fresh, sat opposite the pretty girl and talked until he made her smile. Maybe he would have poured her a glass of wine, made her mellow, seduced her with stories, until he could see the thrum of her heartbeat reflected in her gaze. He might have moved a little closer, until he could feel the body heat radiating from her, let his arm rest against hers, until their fingers began to entwine.

Sam knew how to seduce. He'd done it before, with women he could barely remember. But he didn't want to seduce Cesca, he didn't want to give her sweet words that meant nothing.

The microwave pinged and Sam pulled the plate from inside, using a fork to swirl the pasta in the creamy sauce. It was a little thick from being in the cold for hours, but apart from that it smelled delicious. He grabbed a beer from the refrigerator door, popping the cap open and taking a long, slow drink. After hours of fasting it was like a balm to his rough lips.

He was halfway through eating when the sound disturbed him. As ravenous as he was, he barely noticed it at first, but when he paused to take a breath, the mechanical whirring made its way through his consciousness, registering in his brain.

It was so familiar, yet out of place in the middle of the night. It took him a while to realise it was his father's old printer, creaking and bitching as it spewed out paper. It had been in the office for years, brought in by Foster when he was trying to work from the villa, until Lucia had chastised him and said that vacations were for relaxing.

When he finished eating, Sam tidied up, then walked out into the hallway where he stopped for a moment. The library was directly opposite, only fifteen feet away, and yet he hesitated, waiting for a sign.

She was behind that carved oak door. Separated from her only by air and wood, Sam tried to imagine what kind of mood Cesca was in. She'd made him dinner, after all, and left it for him to eat later. Hadn't even poisoned it, he didn't think. Yet it didn't tally with her response earlier, or the vitriol that had poured out of her mouth. It was that memory that stopped him from closing the gap that lay between them. Stopped him from doing anything at all, apart from stand there. Because he was drawn to her, in spite of her anger. Like a kid picking at a scab he couldn't help but want to see her again. To tell her how much he loved her writing, and he was sorry as hell for what he'd done to her.

But his feet remained stuck. He stood there for the longest of minutes, watching, waiting, wishing. And when he finally made his mind up to go back to bed, and sleep off whatever madness had stolen hold of him, the door to the library creaked open. Cesca walked out, coming to a complete stop as soon as she saw him. She was holding a whole pile of papers in her arms, white A4 pages printed with black. Her mouth dropped open, her brow dipping as she stared back at him, neither of them saying a word.

Then the pile of paper fell out of her arms, the sheaves falling to the marble floor, spreading out until the cream and brown marble was covered by a sea of white.

Before he knew it, Sam was at her feet.

She hadn't expected to see him there, that's why her heart was racing. That and the fact she'd managed to drop her entire script across the floor. There was nothing more to it than that, Cesca told herself. Simply a reaction to the unexpected shock.

'Oh shit,' she breathed. 'And the bloody ink cartridge dried up, too. I can't even reprint it.'

Sam chuckled as he surveyed the mess, scooping up the sheets of paper, frowning as he looked at the typed words printed across them.

'There are no numbers,' he said.

'What?' She'd felt surprised to hear his voice. As if she hadn't spoken to him for an age.

'The pages aren't numbered. How are we going to get it in the right order?'

Cesca blinked. 'I don't know ...' She shook her head. 'I hadn't thought to add any. There must be a hundred pages here.'

'The acts and scenes are numbered, though?'

Cesca felt as though she'd just woken up, her thoughts clouded by the treacle in her mind. 'Yes, they're numbered.'

'Then we'll have to read through it. Make sure we have it ordered in the right way. I'll just pick it all up for now, and we can take it back into the library. Lay them out.'

'It's OK, I can do it,' Cesca said, dropping down to help Sam pick up the papers. 'It's my fault anyway.'

'I'd like to help.'

Well, that shut her up. Cesca couldn't think of anything to say to that. Instead she nodded, moving back to allow Sam to scoop up the papers that were left. Once he had them all, he neatened the pile with a shuffle of his hands, then tucked them under his arm as he offered his other hand to Cesca.

Wordlessly, she took his proffered palm. Let him curl his fingers around her hand. Allowed him to pull until her legs were straightening, and they were both standing, a little too close to each other.

'Thank you.' When her words came, they were breathless. A smile curled at the corner of her lips, and he grinned back in reflection, his eyes crinkling as he stared down at her.

He was still holding her hand.

For some reason that sent a shiver down her spine. An electrical pulse that kept bouncing up and down, unwilling to unleash its hold on her nerve endings. A gift that kept on giving.

'It's really good, you know.'

She licked her dry lips. Was it only a few hours ago that she was screaming at him? Now she was pretty much lost for words, unable to come up with any of the repartee she used to be so lauded for. 'It is?'

'You must know how good it is. You can't write something like this and not see how it will affect people. It's amazing.'

It had been a long time since she'd received praise for her writing.

'It's only a first draft,' she said softly. 'Well, a second if you count the changes I made.'

'Changes?' Sam pulled her into the library, his large hand still enveloping her own. When they reached the large rug in the middle of the room he finally released her, kneeling down to place the pile of papers on the floor. Without being asked, Cesca knelt next to him, her skin still tingling from his touch. Her body was flushed in spite of the huge wicker fan that was circling on the ceiling above them.

'Your suggestions ... they were good.' Her voice was quieter still. 'I added them in.'

'But you hated them.' Sam frowned. 'You were furious about them.'

Cesca couldn't meet his gaze. 'I didn't read them before I came to find you.' She was talking as much to the floor as she was to him. 'I wish I had, I'm so sorry. I never should have said those things.'

She sensed rather than saw Sam's frown. It was in the way his breathing changed, in the movement of his body when he shifted next to her. More than that, it was in the way the air thickened between them, crackling and spitting like a freshly lit fire.

'It wasn't your fault,' he said. 'I shouldn't have read your play. It was like reading somebody's diary or something. I'm sorry I upset you, it was wrong.'

'You didn't mean to upset me.'

Sam shook his head slowly. 'No I didn't, but I managed to do it anyway. It's something I do a lot, and let's face it, it's not the first time I've behaved like an asshole to you. I'll try to make it the last, though.'

She pulled her lip between her teeth, sharp edges digging into the skin there. 'I was an asshole, too. I didn't even give you a chance to explain, I just screamed like some kind of harpy. People must have heard me for miles around.'

'You were only saying the truth. Getting it off your chest. That's a good thing, isn't it?'

'No.' She was certain of that. The churning in her stomach was enough evidence of her mistake. 'I could have waited to hear you out, and explained why I felt so violated. Instead I just launched at you, without giving you a chance to explain.'

'Maybe I didn't deserve a chance.'

She blinked rapidly. 'Doesn't everybody deserve to be heard?'

It was Sam's turn to look down at the floor. He was staring at the pile of papers, his forehead wrinkled. 'When I read your play last night, it was like hearing you speak. I wanted to know those characters, know what happens to them. They felt real already.'

Her throat felt scratchy, her voice hoarse. 'I guess they are real to me. I based it on my family.'

'You did?' Sam asked. 'Just like your last play.'

It felt as though her heart was stopping. 'You remember that?'

'I can remember hearing about your mother and putting two and two together. Her death was a big thing in the theatre world. And those four sisters – they're your sisters, right?'

His eyes were shining when he looked at her, reflecting the soft light glowing from the desk lamp.

'My sisters and me, yes.'

'It's heartbreaking to read about their story. I'm so sorry you had to go through that. And I'm desperate to see them all get to happier times. That's if you'll let me read more of it.'

His smile didn't reach his eyes. It barely reached his lips, really. She wanted to touch his face, rub the sadness from his expression. Take his pain away, so hers could go, too. And it was such a strange feeling, in stark contrast to her emotions earlier. Where she'd wanted to hurt him only hours ago, she now wanted to comfort.

'Of course you can read it. I'd love that. All your suggestions, your edits, they were really helpful.' She bit her lip again. 'I should have read them before I reacted.'

'You don't need to keep apologising. If anybody should be sorry, it's me.' He reached out for her hand, taking it in his. She was getting accustomed to the feel of his skin. 'And I am sorry, so fucking sorry for ruining your dreams. For hurting you. If I could go back and change it all I would.' He blew out a mouthful of air. 'You must really miss your mom.'

A lump formed in her throat. 'Yes,' she said quietly.

'It must have been horrible losing her so young.'

She wiped the budding tears away with the back of her hand. 'It was.' She wanted to say more, but the words seized up in her throat.

'When the play folded, it must have felt like you were losing her all over again.'

The tears spilled out. She tried to swallow the emotion back down. 'It felt exactly like that,' she whispered. 'Nobody's ever described it that way before. But yes, writing the play had been cathartic, and seeing it staged was beyond my wildest imagination. When it all went wrong, it almost killed me.'

'I was such an asshole.'

'Whatever you did, you must have had your reasons.'

'I thought I did ... I was ...' He faded out, staring at her. 'Yeah, they seemed important at the time.'

'And now? Are they still important?'

His expression changed. He stared over her shoulder, his eyes cloudy. She wanted to reach out and smooth out his worry lines. 'It's boring,' he said, his voice cracking. 'Family stuff.'

'But as you said, it must have been important at the time.' Her stomach twisted. There was something about the way his eyes were watering that made her feel anxious.

'It was,' he whispered. He exhaled loudly, then rubbed his eyes with the heels of his hands. 'But it's boring. Nothing to write a play about.' He refused to meet her stare.

'It doesn't sound like nothing,' she said softly. 'You know, sometimes it's good to talk about things.'

Sam still stared at the floor, his body as still as a statue. His jaw was twitching, as though he was grinding his teeth. When he finally looked up at her, his expression was blank.

'There's nothing to talk about,' he told her. 'And even if there was, I don't go around spilling my guts left, right and centre. Unless it's written in a script.'

It felt like a verbal slap. 'I was only trying to be nice. I'm not as interested in you as you think I am,' she snapped.

'What?' He frowned. 'Where did that come from?'

She felt hurt that he'd thrown her sympathy back in her face. Did he really believe his own hype? But then, why wouldn't he: he was gorgeous, successful, and had everything he'd ever wanted. Why would he even care what she thought?

She shrugged. 'From you. Look at you: everything about you is perfection. You've got it all, haven't you? The looks, the career, more money than you know what to do with. It's all come so easily to you.'

His eyes narrowed. 'You don't know anything about me.' His tone was a warning.

'I know what everybody else knows,' she told him. 'It's hard to avoid you. You're in every magazine.'

'And you believe that shit?' he asked, his hands clenching and unclenching. 'You believe everything you read? Well maybe you should grow up, Cesca. You know nothing about me. Nothing at all.'

He stood there, his expression furious, staring at her, awaiting a response. She opened and closed her mouth three times, trying to find the words, but failing miserably.

In the end, only two would do.

'I'm sorry,' she said softly.

He blinked a couple of times, his thick lashes sweeping down. He looked as lost as she felt.

'I shouldn't have said that,' she continued, wanting to kick herself. 'I know the papers lie, I've seen it enough times. It must be awful being on the receiving end, and knowing that people are judging you. I should just keep my mouth shut.'

The anger dissolved from his face. 'It's OK.'

'No it isn't. But thank you for being gracious.'

'I'm as much to blame. You were only trying to help. It's

just that ... ' He trailed off, rubbing his face with the palms of his hands. 'I've learned that talking about things doesn't always help.'

'OK.' She didn't know what else to say.

He gave her one of his trademark grins. Easy, sexy, completely false. 'We've probably argued enough for today,' he said. 'How about we get to work on your play instead? It's going to take us all night as it is.'

He reached for the papers, shuffling them in his hands. This time his smile felt genuine.

She wanted to call him out on his bullshit. For a moment there he'd allowed himself to be vulnerable, and she'd felt drawn to him. But the moment had passed, and he was clearly in no mood to talk.

'Sounds good to me.' And though she was full of questions that kept knocking at her brain, she swallowed them down, grateful they'd reached some kind of understanding.

They had time enough for talking another day. Tonight she needed to work on her play.

16

He hath eaten me out of house and home

– Henry IV Part I

By the time they'd finished, they could hardly keep their eyes open. Cesca glanced over at Sam who was trying to swallow a yawn.

'You know, we did this all wrong,' she said. 'It would have been so much easier if I'd printed it out again. I could even have added in the page numbers this time.'

Sam started to laugh, the tiredness making him almost giddy. 'If you hadn't used up all the ink the first time, that would have been a great idea. But unless you want to wait a week for a replacement, then we don't have a choice. A better idea would've been for you to read it out from the computer. We would have got it in the right order in half the time.'

'I'm such an idiot, I'm so sorry.'

'Don't be sorry.' The truth was he couldn't remember a time when he'd enjoyed himself this much. Reading out the lines, taking on different accents. Letting his voice rise in a horrible falsetto whenever he read out a woman's words. His antics had made Cesca chuckle, and hearing her laughter had been a miraculous thing, especially after the awkwardness of their confrontation.

'But you're exhausted. You have bags under your eyes.'

'So do you,' he pointed out.

She pretended to look affronted. 'Well that's not nice.'

'What's sauce for the goose is sauce for the gander.'

'Shouldn't it be the other way round?' Cesca asked. Her voice sounded softer somehow, in spite of her amusement.

'In what way?' Sam frowned.

'Well in this case if I took your saying literally, I'd be the goose and you'd be the gander. So it should be "What's sauce for the gander is sauce for the goose",' she explained.

He shook his head. 'I've no idea what you're talking about.'

This time she laughed. 'Nor have I really. I think I'm delirious. I should probably get some sleep.'

'We both should.' But he didn't want to. Not at all. There was something different between them, different and miraculous. What was it they said about there being a thin line between love and hate? No, not love, Sam told himself. Friendship. That's what was growing in this room, some kind of tentative camaraderie that he didn't want to let go of. As though they were taking tiny footsteps towards each other, trying to shrug off the anger and the disappointment that had come before.

It didn't mean anything else. Didn't mean he had to confide in her or tell her his secrets. He could handle this.

Finally, when neither of them could hold back the yawns any longer, they made their way up the stairs, and he whispered a quick good night to Cesca before she disappeared into her bedroom.

He was half asleep before he'd even climbed into bed, and by the time he sank into the mattress, all sense of consciousness was gone. He must have slept restfully, because when the late morning sun stole through his curtains, he woke up in the same position he'd fallen asleep in. He practically jumped onto the wooden floor, pulling on the first pair of shorts he could find, and dragging a freshly ironed T-shirt over his messy hair, not bothering to attempt to calm it.

Cesca was already awake. He could hear her typing away in the library. A rhythmic tapping that occasionally stopped, long enough for him to imagine her taking a sip of water, or scribbling something on that notepad she always had near. Sam walked into the kitchen, grabbing the coffee pot and filling it up. It was a rare day that he could face the morning without a caffeine injection. The pot had just started hissing when the library door opened and Cesca walked out. As soon as she saw him leaning against the kitchen counter she smiled, and Sam felt himself relax.

So she didn't still hate him. That was a good thing. He was planning to keep it that way.

'Morning.' He smiled back at her.

'Is it?' Cesca asked, her voice teasing. 'I thought it must be afternoon. Some of us have been up for hours, you know. Sorting out the house, talking to the gardeners. Writing a play.'

He liked the lightness in her tone, enough to match it in his own. 'I believe you're getting paid for most of that.'

'Not by you.'

'True enough.'

'Though there's something you could do for me.' Cesca reached across him, grabbing a couple of cups from the shelf.

Sam leaned back, but her arm still brushed his chest, making him grab hold of the counter, when his first urge was to steady her.

'Apart from make you a coffee?'

She offered him the cups and he took them from her. 'Well that, too, of course. But I've finished the second act, well, the first draft of it. Do you think you'll have time to take a look at it later?' She gave him a tentative smile. 'No rush, of course. But I'd really like to get your opinion. Some of the dialogue was really tricky to write.'

'I'd love to.'

She blinked, although the sun was shining nowhere near her eyes. 'Really?'

Her hesitance did something to him. Turned whatever strength was left inside him into mush. 'Really,' he said solemnly. 'The first part of that act was amazing. I can't wait to see where you've taken it. I love the way you've woven the two stories together. Made it so that the modern-day couple are acting the story of the older ones. There's something so elegant about it.'

'I don't know what to say.' She grabbed the milk from the refrigerator. 'Thank you.'

'I'm only telling the truth.'

'Even so, it's lovely to hear it. Being a writer, it's such a lonely job. You spend all day staring at a blank screen, the voices in your head clamouring to get out. And half the time whatever you write is so terrible you have no choice but to trash it. But then sometimes, every once in a while, you manage to craft a piece of dialogue that's so exciting it makes it all worthwhile. Even then, you're scared to show it to somebody else, in case they burst your bubble.'

'It's not a bubble.'

'It feels like it though. And I know it will never be perfect at the first draft. Not even at the second or third. But unless it has good bones, it's impossible to flesh it out. That's why your feedback is so important.' She took his arm. 'But, Sam, you have to promise to be honest. Don't be kind. Tell me where it works and where it doesn't, please. Even if you've no idea why you don't like it, or why some of the speech jars, tell me anyway, OK?'

His throat was aching. He knew how hard it was to put yourself out there, to request the kind of open response that could leave you feeling so low. It was a part of their jobs – his and hers – to allow themselves to be critiqued, but to invite it so openly took a lot of guts. He didn't know anybody in the business who hadn't read a bad review and had it slaughter them. Even after six years, a few unkind words had the ability to sting like a bitch.

'Of course.' His voice was hoarse from the lump in his throat. 'But if today's work is anything like the rest of your words, I already know it's going to be good.'

She was still holding his arm, and he could feel the warmth from her hand covering his skin. 'Thank you,' she said.

'It's a pleasure.'

After he poured them both a coffee, Sam followed Cesca into the library, taking the printout of her work and grabbing the old pen he'd found the day before. While Cesca sat back at the desk, resuming her pattern of typing and stopping, with long sections of deletes, Sam sat back on the old velvet sofa, squinting as he read her words.

That's where they stayed for the rest of the day, one of them writing, the other editing. By the time the afternoon

159

sun began to fall, they were completely worn out and hungry. Neither of them had eaten much all day, and from the sounds of gurgling coming from both their stomachs, they were paying for it now.

Laying his wad of paper on the desk, Sam waited until Cesca looked up from her writing, not wanting to interrupt her flow.

'Come on, it's time for dinner,' he said, gesturing at her to close down the computer. 'This time it's on me.'

Cesca trailed him into the kitchen, carrying the empty coffee cups and glasses they'd accumulated throughout the afternoon. Her body was stiff, muscles aching from hours of sitting in the old leather captain's chair, and from the way Sam was rolling his shoulders, she suspected he felt the same way. Leaning down to put the dirty cups into the dishwasher, she glanced at him from the corner of her eyes.

'Can you even cook?' she asked.

His head tipped to the side. 'What do you mean "Can I even cook?" I'm Italian, of course I can cook.'

The injured expression on his face made her want to laugh. Instead, she swallowed down her amusement and turned on the tap, washing her hands in the basin. 'That doesn't mean anything. The other half of you is American. Your dad's from the States, right?' Her voice trailed off, memories of the previous night stealing her breath away. Was she being nosy again?

Sam's voice was soft as he replied. His eyes even softer. 'Italian. I'm all Italian.'

She nodded. 'OK.'

'I have a complicated family, Cesca. It would take too long

to explain.' He turned around, rifling through the cupboards again.

She wanted to say something to break the quiet, but nothing sprang to mind. She wasn't exactly an expert on families, after all; Cesca had been the master of keeping her own secrets, hiding them away in case her family thought less of her.

When he finally looked back, Sam's expression had regained an equilibrium. A hint of a smile played on his lips, though it hadn't yet made it up to his eyes. 'Well I guess I should concede defeat. Even I can't make a meal out of thin air.'

She could feel the tension disappearing. It made her a little giddy. 'But I thought you were totally Italian. What a let-down.'

This time his smile creased the skin around his eyes. 'Sorry to disappoint you. Maybe if the housekeeper kept the refrigerator stocked we wouldn't be in this position.' His wink was enough to tell her he was teasing. It also made her chest feel tight.

'You obviously don't pay her enough. I'd give her the push if I were you.'

'I've tried, she just won't leave.'

Cesca raised an eyebrow. 'Maybe you haven't pushed hard enough,' she told him. The space between them seemed to be narrowing, less than two foot now. It meant she had to look up, her petite frame dominated by his tall, muscled body. His proximity made her feel anxious and yet ... safe?

'Maybe I don't want to,' he said softly.

Another hesitation, this time even more loaded than before. From her vantage point, she studied him, taking in the sharp, chiselled jaw that was already shadowed with a day's growth of beard, and the full lips that so many Italian men seemed to wear so well. She had to clench her hands into fists to stop herself from touching him, to feel that stubble. What on earth was wrong with her?

When she looked down at Sam's own hands, she saw they were also bunched. His knuckles were bleached white. She was completely confused by the easy banter between them, and the way it was making her feel inside. Like a volcano filled with molten lava.

She squeezed her eyes shut, but the loaded moment followed her in. Instead of seeing him, she could feel him, smell him, hear his rhythmic breaths. If she breathed in hard enough, she could probably taste him, too.

The next minute, it was as though a thread was being broken. She opened her eyes to see Sam standing a few feet away, far enough to remove the aching connection that had existed between them only moments before. She wasn't sure if it was relief she was feeling or something else. Whatever it was, it made her nerves buzz and her head feel full of cotton wool.

'Dinner, then,' Sam reminded her. He looked strangely calm.

'Or lack of it.' Cesca moistened her dry lips. 'I guess we could eat bread and cheese again.'

Sam frowned. 'No, I promised I'd get you dinner, and that won't do. We'll have to go out and get some.'

'But you can't go out. People will recognise you.' Since he'd arrived he hadn't so much as left the gates. 'Make a list and I'll go and buy the food.'

'The grocery store will be shut. We'll have to find somewhere to eat.' Another dazzling smile. 'I'll go incognito.'

A deep breath restored some of her equilibrium. Enough for her to start thinking straight. 'Seriously? You won't make it five minutes up the road. Even if you're not surrounded by photographers you'll have a thousand predatory women sidling up to you. Why don't we just order some food to be delivered or something?'

He shook his head. 'I want to take you out to dinner.'

Oh.

'We can take the rental car. I know a little place that's completely out of the way. No tourists, only locals. We'll drive there, have some food and then drive home again. It's dark, nobody will see us.'

He'd knocked the wind out of her sails again. She frowned. Her whole body was telling her this was a bad idea, but for the life of her she couldn't articulate why. 'Are you sure?'

'It's just dinner, Cesca. Two friends – or at least I think we're friends – sharing some food and looking out over the lake. What's wrong with that?'

So it wasn't a date. Just friends. She could cope with that, couldn't she? A few weeks ago she'd hated this man's guts, and the only way she'd eat dinner with him would be if she could sneak a bit of arsenic into his pasta. But now things were different. Friends went out to dinner together all the time.

'OK,' she said. 'But I'm only going if you drive.'

He reached out for her hand, folding his palm around it as he shook. 'It's a deal.'

Letting out a long exhale, Cesca tried to let her body relax. A night-time lakeside drive followed by dinner at a local restaurant was the perfect way to spend an evening. It was exactly the sort of thing people dreamed of, when they made plans to vacation at Lake Como. Though her inner-girl was excited at the thought of it, it was almost impossible to ignore her inner doubts.

Sam released her hand. 'Let's go and get ready.'

She nodded. Game on, then.

17

If music be the food of love, play on
— Twelfth Night

The drive to the restaurant did nothing to ease Cesca's nerves. An awkward silence had filled the car as Sam deftly manoeuvred around the lakeside road, his bicep muscles flexing every time he changed gear. His other arm was resting on the door, where the window was wound down, letting in the cool night air drifting in from the water.

Sam was right, wherever they were going was really off the beaten track. He drove further up into the Grigna mountains, the lake receding into the distance, and she could feel her ears start to pop with the change in air pressure as they ascended. Finally, when it felt as if they were in the middle of nowhere, he turned a corner and they stopped beside a cliff-side cave.

'This is it?' There were a few cars parked along the grass, but nothing else. She wasn't sure what she'd been expecting, really. Something more glitzy? Swankier? More Hollywood?

'It looks better from the other side,' Sam told her,

climbing out of the car. Before she'd had time to open her door, he was doing it for her, offering his free hand to help her out.

'Thank you,' she murmured, still staring at the cliff top ahead. Holding her hand, Sam led her towards the edge. It was only when they reached it that she realised just how high up they were. The lake below looked so far away, the lights from the villages surrounding it twinkling like tiny fireflies. To the right were some stone steps, and they climbed down them, Cesca grasping the old, rusty rail that had been put there years before. Sam walked ahead, the steps only wide enough for one, but he kept looking behind him, asking her if she was OK.

They reached the bottom, which led to a stone floor, and in front of them was a wide cave. The exterior was festooned with lights and colourful flowering plants, while inside there were a few chairs and tables, as well as a bar at the back of the cave.

'This is Grotto Maria,' Sam said. 'My parents used to come here when I was a kid.'

'It's beautiful.' She looked all around. Cesca wasn't sure she'd ever even heard of a restaurant in a cave before, but she could see why it was already so full of people. Candles flickered on the tables, making the jagged rock walls change in colour as the light hit them. A low murmur of conversation echoed in the cave, accompanied by soft music emanating from the speakers set into the ceiling.

A waiter came over, his face splitting into a smile when he saw Sam. They shook hands, exchanging a barrage of words in Italian that Cesca couldn't understand.

'This is Cesca, a friend.' Sam finally reverted to English

when he introduced her to the waiter. 'And this is Alfredo, he's worked here ever since I can remember.'

'*Bella, bella*,' Alfredo said, extending a hand to Cesca. 'Have you ever eaten here before?'

She shook her head 'No, it's my first visit.'

'Oh, then we will treat you like a queen. Please follow me, we can get you seated and bring you an *aperitivo*.' With that Alfredo led them around the edge of the restaurant. Cesca glanced at the customers, trying to see if they'd noticed Sam. From the way they were all so deep in conversation, she didn't think so.

At the far end of the bar there was a small, natural doorway that led out onto another cliff. This one was narrower than the one at the main entrance, but had a guardrail all around it. In the middle of the space was a single table and two chairs, both positioned to overlook the amazing view below.

'*Signorina*?' Alfredo pulled a chair out for Cesca. Sam took the chair opposite her, waving Alfredo off when he tried to help.

There was the usual shuffle of menus and drinks, the pouring of water and the offering of a glass filled with pink liquid and a slice of orange.

'This is a negroni,' Alfredo told her. 'It is gin, vermouth and Campari. Designed to open your palate for the food.'

She noticed that Sam turned down his own drink, preferring to pour some water from the carafe. Cesca was pleased about that, she didn't really want him driving them home half-cut. It was strange, learning all these things about a man she'd thought she detested. He was responsible, kind. Words she'd never thought she'd use to describe Sam Carlton.

When the waiters left, it was just the two of them again, and Cesca glanced up from the menu, catching Sam's eye.

'Do you see anything you like?' Sam asked.

Cesca bit her lip. 'I don't understand it all. I mean, I can read some of it, the pastas are fairly simple, and I can translate some of the seafood. But the rest I can't read at all.'

'Would you like me to translate for you?'

She smiled at his kind offer. 'I've got a better idea, why don't you just order for me? You've been here before, you must know what's good.'

Sam laughed. 'I usually just let Alfredo order for me. I pretty much eat anything.'

'Me, too.' She tried not to think of her skip-diving days. 'So let's allow Alfredo to order for both of us.'

'Sounds good to me.'

Cesca took a sip of her negroni. It was cool and sweet, the orange peel adding a citrusy edge. 'This is delicious. And probably very intoxicating.' She couldn't even taste the alcohol, that was always a bad sign. 'Remind me to only have one.'

'They wouldn't let you have another,' Sam told her. A smile was still playing around his lips. 'Next they'll be plying you with different wines to accompany each course.'

Her eyes widened with alarm. 'How many courses?'

'Usually six or seven.' He was grinning now.

'I can't drink six or seven glasses of wine. I'll collapse at your feet.' Her cheeks were starting to heat up.

'I know. I remember the last time you drank red wine. I had to carry you to bed.'

Oh God, the mortification. She'd hoped he'd forgotten about that.

'Well I won't be drinking that much again. Especially if you're driving. It's no fun drinking on your own.'

'It's fun for me.'

'I can imagine,' she said drily. 'Hefting me up some stairs while I mutter unintelligibly must have been a whole barrel of laughs.'

'You weren't muttering unintelligibly,' Sam told her. 'You were quite clear.'

Now her face was flaming. How had this conversation even come up? 'I was?'

He nodded slowly. 'Oh yes. You wanted me to know how much of a bastard I was.'

Cesca grimaced, burying her face in her hands. 'Oh God, I'm so sorry. I can't believe I said that.' A small lie. Of course she'd said it. It was nothing more than she'd been thinking since he arrived at the villa.

From the tone of his voice, Sam was enjoying making her blush. 'Yep, to quote you, I'm a "mojo-stealing, house-invading, good-looking bastard"'.

Cesca couldn't look at him, not when mortification was stealing over her like a shroud. Had she really described him that way? It sounded like something she would say.

Pushing her half-full glass of negroni away from her, she sighed. 'I'm never drinking again.'

'But you're cute when you drink.' He reached out, gently taking her hands in his. 'And you're truthful, too. I like that.'

'You like being called a bastard?'

He shrugged. 'At least I'm a good-looking bastard.'

She groaned again. 'I need to be gagged. Or have a nil by mouth sign tattooed on my forehead.'

'If it makes you feel any better I've been called much worse.' He was still holding her hands.

169

'If it makes you feel any better I'm sure I've called you much worse, too.'

'I'll bet you have.'

But not any more though. She couldn't think of a single bad word to describe him. Not with his amusement at her verbal diarrhoea, and his kindness at her embarrassment.

'Either way, I think I'd better stay off the wine.'

Sam rubbed the pads of his thumbs across her palms, making her jump. 'I won't let you get drunk,' he said softly. 'But the wine here really is good. Just have a mouthful or two.'

When their first course came out, the '*primo*' as Alfredo described it, Cesca accepted a small glass of white wine to accompany the small plate of seafood risotto. Raising the glass to her lips, she swallowed a mouthful of the cool Frascati, letting the crisp, dry flavour cut through the richness of the food. Sam was watching her with interest. His own food was untouched.

'Is it good?' he asked, gesturing at the wine.

'Delicious. Too good to be ignored, really. This must be costing a fortune.'

Sam shrugged. 'It's on me, you should enjoy it.'

That brought her back to earth. It must be so obvious to Sam that she'd never eaten anywhere as decadent as this before. Even on the rare occasion she allowed Hugh to treat her to lunch, they would end up in a small, reasonably priced restaurant, where she'd take great pains to choose the cheapest thing on the menu. Somehow she'd let herself be carried away by the beauty of the night, and the magnificence of the setting. The realisation she was eating a meal that would probably cost more than she earned in a month was shocking.

'I'll never be able to repay you. The menu didn't even

have a price on it. I'm sorry, I should have thought before we ordered.'

Sam looked affronted. 'I told you I was taking you out for dinner, didn't I? That means I get to pay. There's no way I'd accept your money.'

An awkward silence followed. The risotto that had been nectar to her lips only moments ago turned to ash inside her mouth. She pushed the rice around her plate with her fork, watching it slide, torn between her sudden lack of appetite and her frugal ways. The old Cesca never would leave anything on her plate. Not when she didn't know where her next meal was coming from.

Sam still said nothing. He finished his risotto and laid the cutlery onto the fine china, picking up his glass of water to cleanse his palate. When he leaned back in his chair and cleared his throat, Cesca found herself brought out of her thoughts.

'I'm sorry.' Her voice was quiet. 'I'm not used to this sort of thing. Back in London a trip out to McDonald's would have been a treat. And even then I probably wouldn't have been able to go Dutch.'

Sam winced. 'What happened to you back then?' Concern pulled at his brow. 'The last time I saw you, you were riding high. I know I left and I ... ' He stumbled on his words, 'I fucked everything up, but that doesn't usually make someone give up on life. You were so young, you had everything in front of you.' He looked at her, tipping his head to the side. 'Why did you give up on writing?'

When the tears stung at her eyes, she squeezed them shut, willing the salty water to disappear. 'I don't know, it just felt as though I'd lost everything. And every time I tried to pull myself out of the hole I'd fallen into, it just seemed to get deeper.'

'But the play was excellent. And so is the one you're writing now. It's clear you were never a one-hit wonder.'

A sharp retort lingered at the tip of her tongue. She swallowed it down, trying to ignore the bitter taste. 'I couldn't write any more. I tried and I tried, but I could barely type a sentence. Even those I did manage to write I ended up deleting. They were complete tripe.' That was back in the early days, when her sisters had urged her to get back into the saddle. When hope wasn't simply a four-letter word. 'I stopped trying in the end. Every time I failed I just got more and more depressed, it was exhausting. And on top of that I was trying to hold down a job, and that didn't work out any better.'

'What sort of job did you have?'

'How long have you got? There were too many to list.'

Sam started to laugh. 'I'm sorry, I know it's not funny. I just can't imagine you flitting from job to job. Not when the girl I knew was so intent on being a playwright.'

'That's what my uncle Hugh says. He reckons the reason I kept getting sacked was because I was born to do one thing. As though my subconscious was sabotaging me or something.'

As they talked, the waiters cleared the table in front of them. Without a word, Cesca's wine was taken away, to be replaced by another when their second course came out.

'It all sounds very dramatic,' Sam observed.

'Well, I'm a writer. As you know, drama's kind of my thing. And anyway, you can't tell me that you've not had a similar experience, unable to play a role well because you just can't get into it.'

172

He shrugged, gesturing at her wine. 'That one's my favourite. You should drink it all.' Then, going back to the subject, he said, 'Some roles are easier than others, that's true. But I can usually find a way to climb into the skin. It's a matter of empathy, trying to put yourself in their position. Seeing the world through their eyes for a while.'

Cesca smiled tightly. 'I think I stopped seeing much of anything at all. The only thing I could think of was how much I'd failed and let everybody down. The producers, the actors, my godfather, my mother . . .' Her voice broke on her final word.

'But you didn't let them down. I did. I'm the one who left you all in the lurch. I'm the one who got on a plane and flew thousands of miles without looking back. It wasn't your fault.'

The second glass of wine was a Chianti, accompanying their *secondo* of succulent lamb with vegetables. When Cesca lifted the glass she could smell the aroma of cherries, and as the wine passed over her tongue it tasted heavenly. 'This is so good,' she told him, offering a smile as if it was an olive branch. 'You should at least have a taste.'

'I'm enjoying watching you.'

The way he said it made Cesca's chest feel tight. As though she was being squeezed right across her ribcage. She took another sip, aware of his scrutiny. Enjoying it, even.

'It doesn't really matter whose fault it was that the play folded,' she said, all too aware of the atmosphere growing between them. 'What happened afterwards was all my fault.'

'What did happen afterwards?' His brows knitted together as he frowned.

'I let myself wallow,' she admitted. 'It's understandable at first, allowing yourself to mourn the success you thought you'd have. But not for as long as I did. I'd wanted to be part of the theatre for so long, that when it was taken away from me I just gave up. I had no Plan B.'

'What about your family? Didn't they try to help?'

'They didn't know. They just think I'm a bit flighty, a bit weird. None of them have seen where I live or know how many different jobs I've done. And they definitely didn't know how poor I was.'

'How could they not know? You're close to them, aren't you? I hardly see my family, but they seem to know everything about me. I can't get them out of my business.'

'For a start, my life isn't splashed across a dozen gossip websites.' She noticed Sam grimace when she said that. 'And though we're close, none of my sisters live in London any more. My dad wouldn't know what day it is, let alone begin to wonder how I can afford to live in London when I barely have a penny to my name.'

'You've got three sisters, right? There's four of you, like in your play?'

'That's right,' Cesca told him. 'Two older, one younger.'

He raised his eyebrows. 'I thought two sisters were bad enough.'

'Yours are both younger, right?' Cesca's smile was genuine. It was a relief to turn the subject away from her own woes.

'Yes. I was nine when Izzy was born, then Sienna came two years later. I'd been an only child for so long, it was a relief to finally have some company.'

'You get on well with them, then?'

She loved the way Sam's face turned softer as he thought of his siblings. 'They're great. And for some reason they think the sun shines out of my ass. Though I have to admit I think the same about them.'

'I hero-worshipped my older sisters, too. Still do, really. Lucy was more of a mother than a sister when we were growing up, after our own mum died. And Juliet – she's the second oldest – well, she was always the beautiful and glamorous one.'

'What about your younger sister?'

'Kitty? She's a bit like me. Everybody says we look similar, at least, though she's never shown any interest in writing. She lives in LA now, you might even have passed her in the street.' She winked.

'I think I'd remember bumping into someone who was as beautiful as you are.'

His words took her breath away. They seemed to slide off his tongue so naturally, yet their impact was like a shot of adrenalin, making the blood speed through her veins.

'So is Kitty an actress?' Sam carried on, as if he hadn't just given her the sweetest compliment.

'No, she's a student and a nanny. She loves children and she loves LA. She's living the dream.'

Sam grinned at her. 'You look very happy about that.'

'Well it's not often you hear about somebody getting what they wish for, is it? Kitty's always been searching for something more. I just hope it all works out for her.'

Sam scooped a forkful of lamb from his plate. 'So do I.'

By the time the meal was over, Cesca was uncomfortably full. After the lamb they'd eaten a salad, and then a delicious plate of local cheese and fruit, followed by dessert. With each course she'd tried a different wine, and though she'd tried to limit herself, her head was feeling fuzzy, her body relaxed and soft. Even the pungent cup of espresso Alfredo brought out to end the meal did nothing to sober her up. So when

175

Sam pulled out her chair and offered her his hand, she took it gratefully, letting him lead her back around the edges of the restaurant.

It was only when they reached the car that she realised that at some point he'd put his arm around her waist, his hand resting lightly on her hip. She leaned into him, liking the way he felt so strong, so sturdy, trying not to notice the warm aroma of cologne that made him smell so masculine.

'Thank you for such a lovely meal,' she told him, still resting against his chest. Sam tightened his hold on her, fingers digging into her skin.

'It was a pleasure.'

'I definitely had a bit too much wine.'

'You hardly drank at all,' Sam told her. 'I promised I'd keep an eye on you. In all you've had the equivalent of two glasses.'

'Oh, I was sure I'd had more than that.'

'Not unless you were downing it under the table.' He sounded amused. 'I'd say you drank the perfect amount.'

'What is the perfect amount?'

'Enough to relax you without losing all control of your faculties.' She could see his mouth twitch. 'Somewhere in between lucid and being carried up to bed.'

'I thought we'd agreed not to mention that again?'

'I don't remember agreeing to anything of the sort. I kind of like mentioning it, because it makes you blush. And you're very pretty when you blush.'

There he was again with the compliments, and of course they made her cheeks redden even more. She searched in vain for the perfect retort. 'Well, you're so much more handsome when you call me pretty.'

He laughed loudly. 'In that case I'll call you pretty more often.'

'You should.'

'All the time.'

'Steady on, nobody can be pretty all the time. Or handsome, for that matter.'

'That's true. You were singularly unpretty the morning after I carried you to bed.'

'It's hard to look pretty with your head halfway down the toilet.' It was so easy, this back and forth banter. She marvelled at how comfortable she felt talking to him.

'Well, if anybody can pull it off, you can.'

'It was a once in a lifetime show, I'm afraid.' She looked up at him, smiling. God, he really was handsome, even when he wasn't shooting compliments at her. Not that she intended to tell him that. 'You'll have to be content with the memories.'

Sam inclined his head, pressing his lips to her ear. 'Don't get big-headed, but you're also easy on the eye when you're not throwing up.'

The way his breath fanned against her skin sent a thrill straight through her. Her toes curled up in delight.

'You have a wonderful way of complimenting a woman.' She raised a single eyebrow. 'I don't think anybody's ever told me that before.'

He smirked. 'Glad to be of service.'

Staring up at him, Cesca wondered if he was going to kiss her. She tried to imagine how his lips would feel against hers, if they would feel as silky soft as they looked. Whether he would push his hands through her hair, coiling it around his fingers. There was a hint of hair growth on his jaw, dark and shadowy. Would it scrape her skin as they embraced? Her own lips opened, a soft breath escaping, and Sam lowered his face until it was inches from hers.

That's when the flash went off, transforming the air around them from a mellow darkness to a bright white flood. Sam moved back, dropping his arms from her waist, and the warm night air flooded between them. Cesca's eyes flew open and she looked to her left, where a young girl was holding a cellphone in front of her, a wide-eyed look of wonder on her face. The next minute she was joined by three others, all pointing at Sam and staring, saying his name over and over again as if he could ever forget it.

'You should get in the car.' The way he said it, low and short, invited no conversation. He almost pushed her inside, closing the passenger door behind her. Walking towards the girls holding their phones, he began to talk in rapid Italian.

The first girl – a pretty teenager – nodded rapidly, and grabbed something from her bag. Was it a magazine? Cesca couldn't tell from there. Whatever it was, Sam was frowning at it.

The next minute he was talking to the girls again, flashing that smile she'd seen before. Beating his eyelashes and flirting like crazy. Cesca felt her stomach contract, all that food she'd eaten making her feel bloated.

Sam took the first girl's phone and stepped between the four of them, letting them wrap their arms around his waist as he took a selfie of them all. Then he kissed them on the cheek, leading to high-pitched giggles, waving as he walked away.

As soon as he climbed back into the car, his flirty façade crumbled. His face looked like thunder.

'They deleted the photos of us,' he said shortly. 'So you don't have to worry about being seen with me.'

'I wasn't worried.' She was more concerned about his mood. It had spun on a dime.

'Well you should be. The last thing you need is your face all over the tabloids.'

Cesca swallowed, though her mouth was dry. His expression of anger was enough to silence her for the whole of the journey home.

Back at the villa, Sam parked the car in the garage as Cesca opened up the house, and the two of them walked into the hallway. Cesca opened her mouth, wanting to ask him why he'd reacted so strangely. Why a fan taking a photograph had soured his mood so much. But before she could form the words, Sam was already halfway towards the staircase.

'Good night, Cesca,' he said quietly, then turning until his back was to her, he climbed the stairs.

'Good night, Sam.' She stared at his retreating body. It *had* been a good night, right until that girl took the photograph. The way he'd looked at her had been exhilarating, and she'd been so sure he was about to kiss her. Even stranger, she'd wanted him to.

And now he was gone, and she was standing here in the hallway all alone.

It felt like the story of her life.

18

For where thou art, there is the world itself . . .
And where thou art not, desolation

– Henry VI Part II

Sam slammed the bedroom door behind him, barely slowing down as he stalked across the marble floor to the bathroom on the far side. Wrenching on the tap, he cupped his palms beneath the stream, lifting them to splash the ice-cold water on his face. It was only after he'd done this three times that he finally lifted his eyes to the mirror, seeing the damp-faced, dark-eyed stranger staring back at him.

What the hell had he been thinking? It was like Serena Sloane all over again. He'd let his libido do the talking, taking a pretty girl out to dinner, practically kissing her in front of a camera before he finally came to his senses. And all his plans to stay in Varenna out of the public eye would disappear with one touch of an Instagram button.

To hell with fame. To hell with photographs splashed across tabloids. He didn't like that game any more.

Running his wet hands through his hair, he slicked it back, but the water did nothing to cool his fevered skin. He was too het up for that, too riled, too full of the memory of Cesca and that almost-kiss.

It was impossible not to think about it. Even with his eyes open the image of Cesca staring up at him was branded in his mind. The way her eyes had widened and her mouth fell open as he leaned down towards her, leaving him in no doubt that she felt exactly the same way he did.

But how did he feel? That was the question, and he wasn't sure he was willing to answer it. Because there was no future in this, he wouldn't let there be.

He'd learned his lesson after Serena Sloane. He'd let their friendship cloud his judgement, believing he could trust her. And now here was Cesca, with her pretty smile and probing questions. He was in danger of making a fool of himself all over again. Pushing himself away from the basin, he grabbed a towel, drying his face before throwing it in the hamper.

He should leave. Get on the next flight to Hollywood and face the crap he'd left behind, before he managed to mess things up more than he ever had. Before Foster and his mom got wind of where he was, and got hold of him to tell him just how much he'd embarrassed the family.

But the thought of getting on a plane and leaving Cesca here in Varenna made his head hurt. In spite of their confrontations, he felt alive for the first time in for ever. He enjoyed being with her, reading her play, watching her cook. He'd told her he was her friend.

There was another thing, too. Something deeper. Something he wasn't sure he was really ready to admit to himself. Because he liked her, as well. *Really* liked her. And Sam wasn't sure how he was supposed to deal with that.

He splashed his face again, as if the first time wasn't enough. The water clung to his skin, and he shook it, droplets flying into the basin. He couldn't let himself give in to his feelings for her. Friends, that's all they were. And he could handle that, couldn't he? A superficial summer friendship he left behind at the end of the season, brushing it off like sand from his shoulders.

In a few weeks he'd leave Varenna, and leave Cesca Shakespeare far behind him.

It was as simple as that.

Every time Cesca looked down at the screen she could feel Sam's scrutiny warming her face. If she glanced up, he'd be deeply absorbed in the paper in front of him, scribbling across her typed words, making suggestions or corrections to her grammar. But as soon as she looked away, she could hear him stop writing, and the minute shuffles in his seat, as he resumed his intense study of her once again.

It was both perplexing and exhilarating. And if she was being honest, Cesca was irritated by his pretence at a lack of interest in her, at least whenever she was looking. Because she wanted him to be interested, had wanted it ever since that night they went out to Grotto Maria, when he'd come within a breath of pressing his lips against hers.

How strange it was that the man she'd hated had become the one she desired. And yet there seemed to be an inevitability to it that soothed her dramatic heart, a closing of the circle, a righting of a wrong. It was as though she had finally opened her eyes for the first time, and was seeing him as he really was, not the devil-in-disguise her brain had imagined him to be.

'Sam?' She stared at him over the edge of the screen. He frowned momentarily before looking up. Even their eye contact was enough to give her a jolt.

'Yes?'

'How long are you planning to stay here?' She'd been wondering that for a while. When he'd arrived he'd made it seem as though he was just passing through, but he wasn't showing any signs of leaving yet.

He shrugged. 'I'm not sure. I think I'll see out the summer, then fly back to LA after that. I haven't got any work pencilled in until the fall, so the world's my oyster until then.'

Cesca nodded, used to the feast-or-famine nature of the entertainment industry. 'But aren't you bored? I mean there's only me here, and really nothing much to do. You must be going crazy without the Wi-Fi or connectivity.'

Sam tapped the lid of his pen against his lips. 'I'm not bored at all,' he told her. 'To be honest it's a relief not being able to be contacted. I don't get to spend time alone very much in Hollywood. I'm either working or networking, and my phone is constantly ringing. I'd kinda forgotten what silence sounded like.'

'And do you like it? The sound of silence, I mean.'

He tapped his lips again. 'I do, very much.'

The past few days had been just like this. Mornings and afternoons in the library together, Cesca writing and printing out pages while Sam wrote the corrections in red pen in the margins. Then they'd cook, eat dinner, before Sam would disappear, telling her he was tired, and that he wanted to have an early night. The first day she'd been amused by his disappearance, the second she'd been confused. By the third night – last night – she'd started to get angry. Why was he ignoring her after that perfect evening in the restaurant?

'What about your family?' she asked. 'Wouldn't you like to visit them while you have some free time?'

'It's more that I don't think they particularly want to see me,' he told her.

'What do you mean?' She frowned. 'Why wouldn't they want to see you? I can tell they're proud of you, your photograph is on nearly every wall of this place.' He was being evasive again. Maybe she should have Googled him after all.

'My mother loves me.'

'And your father?'

'That's more complicated.' Sam gently placed the pen down on the pile of paper in front of him. 'Foster and I, well as I hinted before, we don't see eye to eye. He's an asshole.'

'It's hard to see eye to eye with an asshole,' she agreed. 'And Foster sounds like the king of them.'

Sam burst out laughing. It made his whole face light up. 'That's true. And what's worse is that he'd love that description.'

'Well, when I see him, I'll tell him exactly what I think.'

She watched as Sam's face fell. 'Jesus, don't go anywhere near him. I shouldn't have mentioned him.'

'I can look after myself, you know,' she said crossly. 'I've dealt with enough assholes in my time. He doesn't frighten me.'

'But he frightens me,' Sam said, rubbing his face with his palms. 'Or at least the thought of him near you does.'

She tipped her head to the side. 'What is it about him? What hold does he have on you that makes you like this?'

It was a shock to see Sam stand up and walk over to her. She was so used to him keeping his distance these past few days. She could feel her pulse start to speed as he came closer, leaning over the desk where she was sitting.

'It's not about him,' Sam said. 'It's about you. He's poison, Cesca, and the worst kind, too. The kind that looks good, tastes good, so you take a big swallow. And it's great, right up until it starts to sting at your gut.'

She pushed the chair away from the desk, standing up, but still he towered above her. She reached out, cupping his jaw with her hand, feeling the warmth of his skin against hers.

'I promised not to ask about him,' Cesca said. 'But I can tell you this. Whatever he did, he can't hurt you any more. You're a grown man, a success. The world's at your feet.'

There was a haunted look in his eyes that cut right through her, making her want to envelop him in her arms.

'You don't know him like I do,' Sam whispered. 'No one does. They'd laugh at me if I told them the truth.'

'What truth?' she asked him. 'Shit, sorry, I promised not to pry. I'm going to shut up now.'

He winced. 'Don't worry. It doesn't matter anyway.'

'Of course it matters. I don't get what hold he can still have on you. You're better than him. When we first met I just thought you were some big-headed actor who sold me out. But that's not who you are.'

'Who am I then?' he asked with a whisper.

'You're Sam Carlton. The boy who walks into a theatre and makes jaws drop open. The man who sets Hollywood on fire. You're the person who can sell a movie just with a smile and a wink.' She leaned into him. 'You must know who you are, Sam.'

'And yet in his eyes I'm nothing.'

'Then he's blind.'

'I've spent my life trying to make Foster Carlton like me. But he can't even stand to look at me. And now I've embarrassed them all . . . ' Sam went suddenly silent.

'How have you embarrassed them?'

'It doesn't matter, none of it does. Because I don't want to see Foster, or my mother, and I definitely don't want to see my sisters. I'm going to see out the summer here, then I'll fly back to Hollywood, and you can forget you ever met me.'

Cesca stepped back, as if she'd been stung. Even touched her face with her hand to check it didn't hurt.

Sam shook his head. 'Look, I'm sorry, I know I sound crazy, but I promise it's better this way.' His face softened as he reached out and tucked a stray lock of hair behind her ears. 'Why don't I go and get us a drink? All this talk about Foster has left a bad taste in my mouth.'

With that he left the library, making his way across the hallway to the kitchen. Cesca stared after him for a moment, frowning.

Sam Carlton was an enigma, and clearly the master of avoidance. For some reason that only made her want to know him even more.

19

A ministering angel shall my sister be
– Hamlet

'We've missed you on our video calls,' Lucy told her. 'It hasn't been the same without you.'

'I've missed you, too.' Cesca leaned her head on the glass of the telephone box. 'But there's no way to join in. There's no Wi-Fi at the house, and the Internet café closes on Sunday afternoons.'

'We could change the day?' Lucy sounded hopeful.

'It's not worth it,' Cesca said. 'I'll be coming home, soon. In the meantime I'll keep emailing.'

'How are things over there?' Lucy asked, her tone sympathetic. 'Is that actor giving you any trouble?' Cesca had told her sisters about Sam's arrival at the villa, appreciating their sympathy at her past colliding with her present.

'He's behaving for the most part,' Cesca replied, not wanting to go into all the details. She wasn't even sure how to explain it to herself. 'Anyway, enough about me. How are the others?'

'Juliet's OK,' her sister told her. 'She's busy setting up the flower shop, and running after Poppy. Thomas hasn't changed at all, more's the pity. And Kitty's good. Enjoying life in LA, I think. But more importantly, how are you? I hear you've been writing again.' Lucy sounded intrigued.

'I've been trying.' Cesca didn't want to get her sister's hopes up. 'It's early days so we'll see. Who told you anyway?'

'I spoke to Hugh last week. Dad got locked out of the house and I had to track down the spare keys. Easier said than done when you're three hundred miles away.'

'That doesn't sound like Dad.'

'He's getting older, it's natural for him to be a bit forgetful,' Lucy said. 'It was fine, all's well that ends well.'

'Very Shakespearian.'

'That's us all over.'

Cesca glanced at the display in front of her. 'I guess I should go. This will be costing a fortune.'

'OK then, but keep in touch. Email me when you can. Oh, and Poppy got your postcard, she was really excited apparently. She says she wants to visit Italy when she grows up.'

Cesca softened at the mention of her niece. Juliet was the only one of the sisters who'd had a child, and none of them saw Poppy as often as they'd have liked to. Another reason to dislike Thomas.

'Give her my love the next time you guys Skype.'

'I will. Oh, and Cesca?'

'Yes?'

'Keep writing, OK?'

She smiled. 'Yes, ma'am.' Her lips were still curled up with good humour when she gently placed the phone back in its cradle, and pulled her card from the slot. She'd forgotten how much she missed talking with her sisters. Maybe that was one thing to look forward to when she got back to London.

She couldn't think of much else left for her there.

Later that evening she was sitting in front of the desktop, her fingers flying across the keyboard as she finished the second act. Every now and then she glanced over at the sofa where Sam had been so many nights that week. It was empty now.

A noise from the kitchen made her look up. She heard a cupboard slam and then the sound of running water. She stood up and walked across the library. The need to see him was overwhelming.

'Hey.' He saw her before she even walked into the kitchen. 'I was just getting a glass of water to take up to bed.'

'Are you avoiding me?' she asked him.

'Avoiding you?' His brows knitted together. 'What makes you think that?'

'I haven't seen you all day. Every time I looked for you, you were gone.'

'Are you stalking me?' He smiled, but it didn't quite reach his eyes.

'I miss you,' she said softly. 'Did I say something wrong yesterday? Was it talking about Foster that made you angry?'

'I'm not angry.' Sam's voice was low. 'What makes you think I'm angry?'

'Because the last time I made you angry you avoided me for days.' She looked up at him through her lashes. 'It's getting to be a habit.'

His smile disappeared. 'You didn't make me angry,' he said. 'I just wasn't feeling well today. I took myself off for a walk, that's all.' He stepped towards her, reaching out to touch her face. The sensation of his fingers against her skin made her gasp. 'I'm not avoiding you, Cesca.'

A mouthful of air escaped from her lips. He took another step closer, until there were only inches between them. Her whole body was rigid at his proximity.

She inclined her head to look at him. Two small vertical lines formed between his brows. He licked his lips, still staring at her.

'Then what are you doing?' she asked him.

'I don't know,' he whispered, more to himself than her. 'I've no fucking idea at all.'

He reached his other hand out, cupping her cheek with his curled palm. She stood as still as a statue, waiting to see what he would do. Her breath caught in her throat as she willed him to dip his head down, press his warm lips against hers. She could almost taste the sweetness of his kiss.

But he didn't move at all. Just stared at her with those conflicted eyes, as though he was looking for all the answers she didn't have. For half a minute she stood there, gazing straight back at him, unwilling to step back, but unable to move forward.

'Sam?' she finally said, her voice tentative.

He stepped back as though she'd slapped him, dropping his hands from her face. His arms hung limply by his side as he took another step away from her. 'Yes?' His voice was terse.

She blinked rapidly.

'Are you . . . did you . . . ' Her words tangled on her tongue. 'Are you OK?'

He laughed, though it sounded a little off. 'I'm fine.'

A wave of frustration rushed over her. 'You don't look fine.'

'How do I look?' he asked.

As if you were about to kiss me.

'You look shocked,' she told him. 'Was it something I said?'

Another laugh. Just as false as the last one. 'I'm fine, honestly. Why don't we go back into the library? You can work on your play, and I can finish reading that damn book. That way you won't think I'm avoiding you any more.'

She nodded. Her jaw was starting to ache from the way she was grinding her teeth together. 'Yeah, I should get back to it, I guess.' She turned around and headed back to the office, feeling him following close behind. Not too close though. It was as though even the distance between them was a measured decision.

By the time she sat back down at the desk her whole body was tense. He was lying, that much was clear. He *was* avoiding her.

Maybe it was time for her to show him what he was missing.

20

She's beautiful, and therefore to be wooed; She is
a woman, and therefore to be won

– Henry VI Part I

'I'm going out tonight.'

At first he didn't hear the words. Or at least they didn't go in. They were out in the gardens, taking a rare moment off to sit beside the ornate fountain that sat at the centre of the patio.

'What?' He turned to look at her. She was lying back on the sunbed, her hair fashioned into a messy topknot. Though the swimsuit she was wearing was modest – at least by Hollywood standards – he couldn't help but let his eyes linger on the way the red fabric clung to her skin. He swallowed, his mouth suddenly dry, as he realised exactly what she'd just said.

'You're going out? Where, who with?' He frowned, sitting up. Like Cesca he was dressed for the sun, wearing a pair of trunks and not much else. His skin had already taken on a deep colour, his ability to tan quickly an inheritance from his Italian mother.

'With Cristiano,' Cesca said quietly. 'He wants to take me out to dinner. I bumped into him in the village this morning. Apparently there's a restaurant he'd like to look at.'

'The guy next door? What restaurant is he taking you to?'

Cesca shrugged, flinging an arm over her eyes to block out the sun. 'I don't know, some place on the lake. I'm not even sure if I want to go.'

'Then don't.' The words slipped from his mouth before he could stop them. The thought of her going on a date with that smooth bastard from next door made him feel physically sick. Sam wondered if it was simply protectiveness, the same sort of emotion he'd get at the thought of one of his sisters dating. That had to be it, didn't it?

'I already said yes. And he's been nothing but kind to me, it would be rude to turn him down now.'

'And last time you went out, he got you drunk,' Sam pointed out. He was trying to keep his voice even, but it was getting increasingly difficult. 'What if he does it again and . . . takes advantage of you?' He spat out the last words. 'Jesus, Cesca, don't you even know how to take care of yourself?'

She sat up suddenly. Her face was screwed up, turning a deep shade of red. 'Of course I know how to take care of myself. I've been doing it for years. And for your information I wasn't intending to drink at all. Not that it's any of your business.'

'Of course it's my business.'

She swung her legs around. He tried to ignore their lean-ness, the way her skin glowed beneath the scrutiny of the sun. 'Seriously,' she said. 'What's it got to do with you?'

'We're friends, aren't we?'

'Are we?' She looked confused.

'Well, after spending weeks cooped up here together, I thought we were more than acquaintances.' For some reason her denial of their friendship cut him deep.

'I know that . . . ' She trailed off, looking down at her feet. Her nails were painted an eye-catching pink. 'It's just I never really know what we are. Boss and employee, combatants, friends. You seem to swing from one to the other without giving me any kind of advance notice.'

'I do?' His voice was softer now.

She shrugged. 'It feels like it.' A piece of hair had escaped from her topknot and was curling around her neck, reflecting the sun. 'Maybe I'm not sure how I see you, either. It's not that long ago that I hated your guts. Every time I heard your name mentioned I wanted to throw something.'

He laughed. 'That's understandable. I wasn't that impressed by you the night we met, either. It's not the first time somebody's been disappointed I'm not my father, but it was the first time it annoyed the hell out of me.'

'I wasn't disappointed you weren't your father. I wasn't exactly keen on meeting him either. And now I'm even less inclined to make his acquaintance.'

Sam turned until he was sitting opposite her. Their knees were almost touching. 'I thought we weren't talking about that.'

She smiled. 'I'm not talking about it,' she pointed out. 'You are. You're the one who brought him up.'

He frowned. She was right. What was it about this girl?

'Stop changing the subject,' he said, his face flushing. 'We were talking about your date. This guy, Cristiano. I don't trust him.'

'Why not? He's a respectable businessman. And even if he wasn't, I *can* look after myself.'

He allowed himself to breathe. 'Yes you can. And that's the only reason I'm not stopping you from going on this goddamned date tonight.'

She looked affronted. 'Who do you think you are, my dad? I'm going on this date because I've decided to. What you think about it is completely irrelevant.' Her tone wasn't quite as angry as her words suggested.

'If I didn't want you to go, you wouldn't.' He was playing with her now. Enjoying her response, and the frisson of something dangerous between them. It lit him up, like a bonfire crackling in the night-time. He shouldn't be doing this, but he couldn't help himself.

'How would you stop me?' she breathed. Her eyes were sparkling, her lips full and open. She was a challenge waiting to be met.

'I could use my charm.'

She shook her head. 'It has no effect on me.'

He licked his lips, feeling the parched skin beneath his tongue. 'There are other ways.'

'What other ways?' Her knees were touching his. He could feel the smoothness of her skin, the warmth of her body. It was tantalising.

'I could stop you physically.'

He was aware of her gaze on his body. She was sizing him up, looking him up and down. It took everything he had not to start flexing his muscles.

She quirked an eyebrow. 'Physically? How?' Her toes brushed his. It shot a spike of excitement through his veins.

'I could lock you in your bedroom.'

'I'd climb out of the window. It's nothing I haven't done before. It's amazing how agile you can be when the landlord comes calling for his rent.' She was teasing him. He could tell it from the mischievous expression on her face.

'Then I'd have to tie you up.' He looked her straight in the eyes. He saw them widen at his suggestion, then her chest hitched with a deep breath. Her eyes, so excited before, became heavy-lidded. It took a moment for her to formulate a reply.

'That might work,' she said slowly. The words lingered in the air long after she closed her lips. The idea was like an invisible thread, weaving between them, pulling them together. He pictured her lying on her bed, half-naked, her body bound and trussed.

Jesus, what was going on here?

Her flush deepened, spreading down her neck and to her chest. His eyes followed its progress, lingering on the swell of her breasts. The fabric of her swimsuit was so thin he could see almost everything through it. Including the way her nipples hardened.

'Would you like me to tie you up, Cesca?' His voice was as gritty as an unmade road. He was playing with fire. She knew it and he knew it, yet Sam couldn't help himself. He kept stretching out his fingers until they burned.

'I'd like to see you try.' There she was, feisty as hell, staring up at him through half-closed lids. 'I'm not the sort to get caught very easily.'

'I bet you're not.'

She lifted the stray piece of hair, tucking it back into her topknot. The gesture pulled at her chest, making her breasts rise, coming tantalisingly close to escaping from her swimsuit. Sam couldn't tear his gaze away.

'I'm up here, you know.'

Finally he looked up, smirking. 'Oh, I know exactly where you are.'

She tipped her head to the side. Her lips held the hint of a smile, but there was more to her expression than that. She was interested, fascinated, even. The way she was looking at him made Sam want to drag her straight up to the house and to his room.

'And where's that?'

'Sitting opposite me, staring up at me, talking to me when you should be thinking about your date.'

She pulled her lip between her teeth, chewing on it. 'What makes you think I'm not thinking about my date?'

'Because you haven't mentioned his name in the last ten minutes.'

'You've been talking non-stop for the last ten minutes. I haven't had a chance to form a thought.'

Her sass made Sam laugh. 'If you were really into him you wouldn't be sitting here flirting with me.'

'What makes you say that? A little flirting is harmless, isn't it? It doesn't mean anything, not really. Just a way to pass the afternoon.'

Her denial made his hands curl into fists. Of course flirting meant something, or at least it did right then. 'I can't imagine you flirting with that guy next door like this.'

Her lips curled up. 'You think I won't? He's handsome, he's funny, and he speaks with the most glorious Italian accent. And he's rich. There's that, too.'

'I'm rich.'

That made her laugh loudly. Her body shook as she chuckled, until Sam found himself joining in. 'Hey, I can do an Italian accent, too.' He said it with a New Jersey twang.

'And you're funny, don't forget that.'

He flashed her a sour smile. 'It's just the handsome thing, then. He wins.'

'Oh, as if you don't know how pretty you are,' she scoffed. 'You're the face that launched a thousand teenage fantasies.'

It was his turn to sneer. 'Oh come on.'

'Don't try to deny it, pretty boy. I've heard about the MTV awards.'

He grimaced. 'The less said about that, the better. And anyway, who wants to be pretty? It's not exactly masculine, is it?'

'What would you rather be? Handsome, beautiful, drop-dead gorgeous? I can use those if you like. Either way, you're a good-looking bastard and you know it.'

'They're only looks.'

'Easy to say when you have them.'

'Well you're not exactly hard on the eye,' he told her. 'After all, Don Juan next door has asked you out on a second date.'

'It's not exactly a date.' Her eyes narrowed. 'Anyway, why do you care so much?'

'About what?' He sat back, feeling like he was being found out.

'About whether I go out on a date or not.'

'I don't care.' He shrugged, feigning nonchalance. 'I just don't want to see you getting taken advantage of.'

'So you offer to tie me up instead?' She looked up at him. 'Because that's not taking advantage of me at all.'

'I'm not going to tie you up,' he said quietly, though the image in his brain was still too alluring to ignore. 'I only want you to be safe.'

Lies, all lies, and he knew it. Cesca probably knew it, too.

It wasn't protectiveness that was making him want to grab her and hide her away. More an intense jealousy that made him want to curl up beside her and hold her until the night was out.

'I will be safe, honestly.' She gave him a reassuring smile. 'It's only a night out. I'll probably be back before midnight.'

Sam nodded, but the movement was tight. So she was going on the date, regardless of how he felt. The stupid thing was, he couldn't blame her. She'd already told him he was blowing hot and cold, like some kind of out-of-control air-con system, and their conversation now had only underscored her point.

He liked her. Christ, he liked her, but he hated himself for doing so. He was like a schoolboy, pulling pigtails, afraid to put himself out there. What was wrong with him?

He pushed, she pulled, she pulled, he pushed, and still he found himself standing on the same, lonely spot. He was losing something that wasn't even his, and the fact it hurt him was laughable. 'Enjoy yourself.' The worst thing was, he meant it. He wanted her to be happy. Just not *too* happy.

With that he stood up, grabbing his empty glass and the book he'd barely been able to read.

'I will. Don't wait up.'

She said it with a laugh, but it still riled him. He turned away so she couldn't see his expression. 'I won't.' Another lie. He scattered them amongst the truths. Because there wasn't a chance in hell that he was going to sleep without making sure she was home. And if she wasn't then he'd just march next door and drag her home if he had to. He'd probably enjoy doing it, and if Cesca's flirting was anything to go by, she would, too.

Then he was back full circle. Face to face with the realisation that he was falling for Cesca Shakespeare, when every synapse in his brain was telling him not to. When history had told him that every time he got close to somebody, they let him down.

He wasn't sure how long good sense would prevail.

It was strange, going through the motions of getting ready. A long, cool shower followed by a heated wrangle with the hair-dryer. Then the anxious surveying of her clothes, wondering what she would wear, what *he* would like. Whether *he* would think she looked pretty.

But it was the wrong *he*. Sam, not Cristiano. God, she was such a loser.

It was sinful to be dressing for one man, while getting ready to go on a date with another. Yet she couldn't help but think of Sam as she slicked her lips with gloss, and ran her mascara wand through her lashes.

She didn't recognise the girl looking back at her from the mirror. So removed from the Cesca who had closed in on herself, the Cesca who had fallen and couldn't climb back up. If she could go back to London and tell that girl that not only would she be living in the same house as Sam Carlton, but that she'd actually like him, she'd probably have been told where to go. Yet it was all true.

Their flirting this afternoon had sent a shockwave through her body, and the after-effects were still buzzing in her cells. She felt energised, alive, as if she'd woken up after a long, deep sleep, and now all she wanted to do was run around and laugh.

It wasn't a laughing matter, though, was it? Not least

because she was completely confused by Sam's constant vacillations. It was like watching a tennis match, her neck was aching from the back and forth, and she wasn't sure who was winning any more.

Wasn't certain there could be a winner.

She'd arranged to meet Cristiano at the gate at eight that evening. He'd protested, explaining it was wrong for him not to pick her up at the house, that she was hurting his masculinity. She'd laughed it away, because the last thing she'd wanted was him meeting Sam. Not when he was in the kind of mood he was. She wouldn't put it past him to say something to embarrass her, or to embarrass Cristiano, but if she was really honest, part of her wanted to see her housemate fighting for her.

But it would do her good to leave the house, to talk to somebody other than Sam. To see the real world out there untainted by his close proximity. She had to be suffering from some kind of Stockholm syndrome, didn't she? She blushed as she remembered their conversation again and how he'd looked when he'd threatened to tie her up. The mere suggestion had been enough to make her breathless and overheated, the slickness between her legs the evidence of how he'd made her excited.

Yes, she definitely needed to get out of here. Before she did something she might not regret.

Sam was nowhere to be seen when she walked down the stairs and into the hallway, one hand clutching her bag, the other holding the thin wrap she'd slung across her shoulders. Her hair was loose, tumbling in natural waves to her shoulders. It tickled the skin there, bare except for two spaghetti straps, her dress clinging to her torso then flaring out across her hips. Printed with small blue flowers, the fabric came to a stop at mid-thigh, showing off the glowing tan she'd acquired.

Just after eight she left the villa and walked up the driveway, making her way to the main gate. She could see Cristiano's car there, the man himself leaning on the hood. A pang of guilt hit her for making him wait up there. Still, the alternative was too awkward to contemplate.

Cristiano pushed himself off the car and was watching her, a big smile plastered across his face. In his hand he held the most glorious bunch of flowers, with pale calla lilies surrounded by cascading amaranths. Hand-tied with twine, she could tell simply by looking at them that they'd cost a fortune.

'You look wonderful,' he said, as soon as she walked through the gates. Inclining his head, he pressed his soft lips to her cheek. She could feel his gaze as he looked her up and down. 'These are for you.'

Surprised, she took the proffered bouquet. As much as she'd enjoyed teasing Sam this was a date, she'd really believed it to be a night out with a friend. 'Thank you, they're beautiful,' she said. 'I should put them in water or something. I can run inside and put them in the basin. I won't be a minute.'

'Let me at least drive you,' Cristiano suggested. 'Or escort you.'

Cesca was torn. She couldn't just leave him waiting here again . . . but then what alternative did she have? It would be churlish to simply let the flowers die, and in this weather they were bound to wilt before they'd even left the village.

'Um, well, OK. But can you wait in the car before I run the flowers in?'

He was unruffled. 'Of course.'

That's how she found herself returning to the house within a few minutes, driven by the one man she'd tried to keep away from the villa. Taking a deep breath she ran up the steps, looking back at Cristiano, half afraid he would follow her in. Instead he gave her a wave and a smile, leaning his arm on the open window, his arm hairs bleached from the sun.

Cesca grabbed the hem of her dress, afraid the wind would lift it, her other hand clutching the flowers. She made it into the kitchen before she noticed him. Was already halfway to the basin before he cleared his throat. She came to an abrupt stop, releasing her dress and putting her hand to her chest.

'I didn't see you there,' she said, willing her heart to stop going crazy.

'Clearly.' Sam's voice was dry. 'You almost ran me over.' His gaze flashed over the bouquet. 'That must have been the shortest date in history. What happened, did he make a pass before you even made it through the gates?'

She tried to ignore his mocking tone. 'For your information, I'm just putting these flowers in water. And then I'll be going back to my date.'

His smile got wider. 'He's here?'

'No. He's outside, waiting for me in his car.'

'What sort of car?' Sam sounded genuinely interested.

'I don't know.' She felt cross, though she couldn't understand why. 'A convertible of some sort. Silver. Nice.' Leaning down, she grabbed a glass vase from the cupboard beneath the sink.

'That's such a typical girl thing to say. I wasn't asking about the colour.'

She rolled her eyes. Was he deliberately trying to bait her? She took a deep breath, there was no way she wanted to start an argument with him while Cristiano was outside. Running the tap, she poured the cold water until the vase was half full. 'Does it matter? It's a good car, and I'm about to leave in it. That's all you need to know.'

'Is he waiting outside?' Sam asked, his voice even.

'Yes ... no ... why do you want to know?'

'I want to see what car he has for myself.'

'Oh no you don't.'

His face was the picture of innocence. 'Do you have a problem with that?'

Cesca sighed. 'Look, you're the one who wants to hide away from the world and doesn't want anybody to know you're here. And now you want to come out and introduce yourself to my date?' Her voice was as exasperated as she felt. 'What are you trying to do here?'

'I just want to make sure his car's roadworthy. And that he's Cesca-worthy.'

'For goodness sake.' She shoved the flowers into the vase, not bothering to arrange them. 'I'm leaving now. Goodbye, Sam.'

It was only when she made it to the hallway that she realised he was following her. Shaking her head, she pretended to ignore him. He shadowed her through the front door and down the steps. From her vantage point on the driveway she could see Cristiano's look of shock.

'Are you satisfied?' she asked Sam through gritted teeth. 'Is the car good enough for you?'

'It's a Ferrari Spider.' Sam's voice was so quiet she could barely hear him. 'Nice.'

Something in his tone made her turn to look at him. The expression on his face was unfathomable. It made her want to reach out, to touch him, to smooth the lines away. It took everything she had to walk away, leaving him standing on the steps.

Too bad he didn't get the memo. He followed her to the car, walking over to Cristiano and holding out a hand. 'Hi, I'm Sam Carlton.'

Cristiano stared at him for a moment, before taking Sam's proffered palm. 'Cristiano Gatto. It's a pleasure to meet you.'

'Are you two going anywhere nice tonight?' Sam had a conversational tone. His mercurial mood swings were driving Cesca crazy.

'Just a little restaurant I know along the coast.'

Sam's smile split his face. 'Cesca has a thing for restaurants along the coast.' He glanced at her from the side of his eyes. 'She prefers risotto to pasta, though.'

Cristiano frowned. 'OK ... '

'If you buy wine, she really likes the Valpolicella. Not a 2002 one though. That was a terrible year.'

'Cristiano is a restaurateur,' Cesca told him tartly. 'I don't think he needs your advice on food and drink.'

Sam shrugged. 'Just trying to help. Oh, and she promised to be back by midnight, so I'll see you before twelve.'

She whipped around to look at him, furious. 'Sam!'

He threw his hands up in the air. 'What? I'm just repeating what you already said.'

Cristiano's frown deepened. 'Is there a problem with me taking her out? Something I should know about?'

'Um, excuse me, I'm still here,' Cesca pointed out. 'And there's no problem with taking me out, I'm a free agent.'

'Of course you are,' Sam agreed, sounding insanely cheerful. 'Now go and enjoy yourself. Nice to meet you, Cristiano.'

'You too.' Cristiano started to get out of the car, ready to walk around and open her door, Cesca supposed.

'No need to get out, I can do it.' Sam flashed another smile before opening the passenger door. He held his hand out for Cesca. She shook her head, ignoring it altogether, settling herself into the low passenger seat.

'I'll see you at twelve. Have a good time.' Before she could stop him, he leaned down and pressed a kiss to the side of her face, just below her ear. His breath on her skin made Cesca shiver. After lingering there a moment longer than was polite, he stood up and slapped the side of the car twice.

'Goodbye then.'

'Goodbye,' Cristiano said, the look of confusion still morphing his features. Cesca said nothing. Instead she shot Sam a dirty look, hoping it conveyed everything she was thinking right then.

Cristiano started the engine, expertly turning the car so that they were facing up the driveway, then slowly pressing his foot on the accelerator to cover the distance to the gate. When Cesca looked back, Sam was still standing at the bottom of the steps, arms folded across his chest.

For some reason that gave her no satisfaction at all.

21

Love is a smoke raised with the fume of sighs
– Romeo and Juliet

A night out with Cristiano was like watching a movie for the second time but seeing all its imperfections. They were driving on the same road, alongside the same lake, yet even the view seemed less magnificent than it did when she was with Sam. Cristiano tried his hardest, of course, and his natural charm did much to distract her from her thoughts. But every time there was silence, they kept going back to the villa.

To Sam.

She'd pretended to be cross when he'd accompanied her down to Cristiano's car, and if she was really honest part of her was annoyed at his presumption. But that part was dwarfed by the warmth that was licking at her insides, as she remembered just how put out Sam had been earlier.

Cesca had liked that angry glint in his eyes. She'd enjoyed his controlled sarcasm. Most of all she'd loved the way he'd stared at her as Cristiano had navigated the car up the driveway, as if his favourite toy was being stolen by his arch enemy.

Not that she was a toy. But she liked the analogy anyway.

'The lake is beautiful, is it not?' Cristiano's voice broke through her musings. When she turned to look at him he was smiling, his eyes on the road as he steered with one hand on the wheel, the other tapping out a rhythm on the car door. Though he shared a heritage with Sam – and both of them sported the same dark good looks, they had so little else in common. Not in her eyes, anyway. And it was a disappointment to be driving along this beautiful road with a man who wasn't sparking any feeling in her at all. It felt even worse that she was wishing he was somebody else. Somebody altogether more annoying.

'It really is. I love the way the boats all light up at night. They look like fireflies dancing on the surface of the water.'

'The view next to me is beautiful, too.' This time he turned his smile on her. His teeth glinted in the moonlight. 'I'm sorry if we upset your friend. He didn't seem very happy that you were leaving.'

He was the master of the understatement. 'He's just being awkward,' she told him. 'He likes to wind me up.'

'Like a clock?' Cristiano frowned.

'No, I mean he likes to annoy me. Make me angry. It's an English expression. Though I guess it could come from winding up a clock. Making things tighter and all that.'

'Are you angry now?'

Cesca considered his question. She wasn't exactly angry, but she wasn't relaxed either. There was an edge to her that made her skin hurt. 'Not right now,' she said, aware that she was on a date with another man. 'But I'll be having words with him when I get back. There was no need for him to be so . . . ' She screwed her face up, trying to think of a good word to describe Sam's behaviour. It hadn't exactly been rude, but he hadn't been gracious either.

Possessive. That's what he'd been. The child and toy analogy came to mind again.

'Whatever.' She waved her hand. 'Let's not talk about Sam any more. Why don't you tell me about this restaurant. You're thinking of buying it, right?'

So the drive continued, with Cristiano happily filling her in on the local restaurant scene, explaining the different cuisines, and how he'd been trying out the local competition. Before she knew it they were coming to a stop, parking in a lot right outside a large, modern building.

Inside, it was as different from Sam's restaurant as night and day, all glitzy and new, full of beautiful people who wanted to be seen.

'Do you like it?' Cristiano asked. 'It's very similar to my restaurants in Roma. We are so sick of the old-fashioned mama and papa places. It's all about glamour and modernity.'

'It's ... ' Cesca took a deep breath. 'I can see why it's so successful. Everybody seems to be enjoying themselves.'

'If I could, I would have flown you to Rome to see my restaurants.'

She could imagine what Sam would have said to that.

'This is perfect.' She looked up as what looked like the owner came over to Cristiano and shook his hand. The two exchanged pleasantries for a moment, and though she didn't understand the words she could tell Cristiano was asking a lot of questions. Eventually, he turned back to her.

'Would you mind if I join Mario for a quick tour of the kitchens? The head chef is an old friend and it would be good to get his thoughts on this place.'

Cesca gave him a smile, trying to swallow down the feeling of relief. Cristiano was obviously more interested in the restaurant than he was in her. Somehow that put her at her ease. 'Please, go ahead.'

'I will ask Dino to take you to your seat,' Mario said. 'And get you an *aperitivo*, of course.'

'Something non-alcoholic please,' Cesca said, she wanted a clear head.

As the night progressed she couldn't help but feel the same way as she had earlier. That this almost-date was like a photocopy; the quality was so much worse than the original. Vibrant colour turned into blurred black and white. Even the food, as beautifully presented as it was, tasted less real to her palate.

After their dessert was cleared away, the waiter brought over a small porcelain cup of espresso, and a glass of something deeply bronze. Cristiano lifted it up, inhaling the flavour, then inclined the glass to her.

'Just a small brandy,' he said. 'To toast our evening together.'

She could smell the alcohol wafting up from the table. Brandy had never been her favourite drink, and the aroma wasn't changing her mind. Not wanting to be rude, she lifted the glass to her lips, trying not to screw up her nose. 'Of course.'

A sip of the fiery liquid burned as it slid down her throat. The heat radiated through her stomach, warming her from the inside. Cristiano smiled approvingly at her.

'You've seemed very nervous tonight,' he observed. 'As if you aren't really here with me.'

'I have? I'm so sorry.' She felt her cheeks heat up. How

rude she must have seemed. 'I'm just a little tired. It's been a long week.' The smile she offered him was genuine. It wasn't his fault she was a hotbed of contrary emotions; after all, the last time she'd seen him Cesca had hated Sam.

Now ... not so much.

'Was it the way I picked you up?' Cristiano asked. 'Maybe I shouldn't have brought the flowers. But when I saw them, they reminded me of you. Classical. Beautiful.'

She shook her head. 'Of course not. The flowers were lovely, and so is the restaurant. I'm so sorry I've not been on top form.' Bloody Sam. Lovely Sam. Gah, either way it was all his fault. And the truth was no matter how good the food, or the company, or anything else here in the restaurant, it was all for nothing. Because Sam wasn't there.

'Thank you for taking me out tonight,' Cesca said to Cristiano as he drove them back home along the lakeside road. 'I hope you managed to relax with all that talk about work.' He'd disappeared more than a few times, not just to the kitchen but also to the office where he'd spent at least half an hour talking with the owner. By that time Cesca had moved to the terrace and drunk her espresso alone overlooking the lake. She'd squinted as she gazed to her right, trying to make out which building could be the villa.

'I'm so sorry.' Cristiano looked suitably apologetic. 'Mario confessed he's already had a lot of interest in this place. I don't want to lose out on it, but I know how rude I've been. He wanted me to see the kitchens and the books, to meet the chef. It was too good an opportunity to turn down.'

'It's not a problem.' She could hardly complain to him when her mind had been elsewhere, too. It had been more than a relief than anything, getting to spend some time on her own. Giving her the space to try and untangle her fevered thoughts.

'It was very ungallant of me. I apologise.'

'There's no need to, honestly. Work comes first, I get that.' She smiled at him. 'We had a nice evening, and hopefully you managed to make some decisions about the restaurant.'

Cristiano's smile was sad. 'I'll be returning to Rome next week, to talk to my bank. By the time I close on the restaurant if I decide to buy it, well, you'll probably be gone.'

Cesca's stomach dropped. It had nothing to do with the thought of not seeing Cristiano again, though. 'I probably will.' Back to dreary London. To her lack of job, her lack of home, her lack of opportunities.

A lack of Sam, too.

When they pulled up to the gates, Cesca didn't argue with him about driving her right up to the villa. Instead she hopped out of the car, keying the number into the pad, thanking God that Sam hadn't turned on the evening lockdown code. As the gates creaked open, she climbed back into the car, letting Cristiano pull forward until he came to a stop at the foot of the steps.

'There's no need to get out,' she said, noticing his hand on the door.

'Not at all.' Ignoring her protestations, Cristiano got out and walked around to her side of the car, opening the door for her. 'I may not have given you the best date tonight, but I'm still a man. Let me see you to the door.'

Cesca let him take her hand and lead her up the steps, coming to a stop in front of the large front door. The security light was shining down from the porch, illuminating them both. She looked up, her mouth suddenly dry as she stared up at the handsome Italian.

'Thank you again.' Her voice was quiet. 'I'm sorry I wasn't much of a companion.'

'I think you had a lot on your mind, too.' Cristiano's tone was gentle. 'Am I right in thinking you're a little ... ah ... confused about your feelings?'

Cesca's eyes widened. 'My feelings?'

He laughed. 'Oh, not for me. From the moment I picked you up tonight I got the impression I'd been, what do you call it, friend-zoned. Is that the right expression?'

The words sounded funny coming from the suave Italian. She couldn't help but laugh. 'I'm sorry,' she said again, knowing how true it was.

'It's OK. As I said, I'll be leaving for Rome soon. I just wanted to spend some time in the company of a beautiful lady, and I got my wish.'

'I'm glad.' She really was. For the first time in an age, Cristiano had made her feel attractive. Wanted. But he was also kind enough to see that she wasn't looking for anything more than a casual friendship. 'It's been lovely spending time with you. At the café, on the beach ... thank you for making me smile again.'

'At first I wanted to do more than make you smile,' he confessed. 'But I'll settle for that.'

She didn't tell him that at first she might have wanted more, too. Because that seemed like ages ago now. Before she'd found herself again. Before she'd found her writing. Before Sam had made her feel more confused than she'd ever felt. Instead she gave him another beaming smile, hoping it was enough.

213

'Good night, Cristiano. And if I don't see you again before you leave, have a safe journey.' She put her hand out for him to shake. Instead he folded it in his own, pulling her towards him. Using his other hand he tipped her head up, pressing his lips to hers. They were warm, full, and softer than she had imagined.

'Good night, Cesca,' he whispered against her lips. Then he pulled back, offering her a regretful smile. 'And at least I got my kiss.' With that he turned and walked down the steps, offering her a brief wave before he climbed back into his car. She watched as he pulled away, dust and gravel kicking up beneath the rubber as his tyres spun on the driveway.

She let herself in, flipping up the deadlocks behind her to secure the house. Pulling off her heels, she padded through the hallway, the floor cool against her feet as she walked. It was as though the awkwardness of the date had followed her in along with the night-time air, blanketing her, reminding her that she didn't belong here. Didn't belong anywhere. And yet she was aching to find somewhere that she fitted into.

When she walked into the kitchen the first thing she saw were the flowers. A large antique vase full of pelargoniums and geraniums. She recognised the blooms. She'd seen them throughout the gardens. Sam must have picked them himself, and arranged them. She closed her eyes for a moment, breathing in the scent.

But why? That was the question dominating her mind. Why had he done this? She tried to remember his expression when she'd brought Cristiano's flowers in. His attitude was confusing, almost nonchalant, when she'd put the flowers into a vase. And when he'd walked her out to the car he'd been amused. So what had changed between her leaving the house and coming back again?

He had all the answers and she had none. Somehow that seemed as wrong as her date had. Like walking through a crooked house and slipping to the side of the room every time.

'Sam?' She called his name quietly.

There was no response. She could feel her heart pounding against her ribcage.

'Sam?' A little louder this time, though her voice was still tremulous. Her hands curled into fists, her nails digging into her palms.

'Sam?' Almost a scream. A need to be heard, to find him.

There was a clattering of feet as he ran down the stairs. The drumbeat of his footsteps as he made his way down the hall. Then he was there, standing in front of her. His brow furrowed as he opened his mouth.

'Are you OK?' He was breathless. 'Has something happened?'

She blinked back the tears, not sure why they were there. 'You picked some flowers.' She was finding it hard to breathe. As if the air was too thick and viscous to be inhaled.

'I did.' He took a step towards her. 'I wanted to say sorry.'

It was her turn to frown. She stared at him through watery eyes. 'Why?'

'Because I was an asshole. I threw your flowers away.'

'Cristiano's flowers? Why?'

'I didn't like them in here. I don't want you getting flowers from another man. So I put them in the trash.'

'Oh.'

'And then I thought about you coming home and seeing they were gone, and it made me feel like a bastard. So I went and picked some more.' He looked as confused as he felt. 'I'm a dick, right?'

She shook her head. 'No, they're beautiful.'

Sam looked over at the vase, the furrows still deep in his brow. 'They're not enough.'

'They're not?' She was trying to read him and failing miserably. Where was the man whose sarcasm had fuelled Cristiano's car down the driveway only a few hours ago? It was hard to equate him with the one standing in front of her, so unsure of himself. And yet, like two sides of the same coin, somehow they formed part of a whole. A multifaceted man, one who could be strong yet fragile, and completely overwhelming. Her own little mystery wrapped in an enigma.

'They're just flowers, Cesca. They'll be here for a while and then they'll die.'

She licked her dry lips. 'Then we can pick some more.'

Sam didn't reply, though it felt to Cesca that his body and his expression was telling her all she needed to know. He was still staring at her, his eyes wide, his mouth open, and it was as if his body was being drawn to hers. Like a magnet, she could feel his pull, and from the way his muscles tensed she felt he could feel hers, too. The air between them seemed to shimmer, as if the strength of their longing was changing the very molecules there.

'And when those ones die?' he finally said.

'We just keep on picking.'

She wasn't sure what they were talking about any more. Not flowers, that was for sure. Whatever the stupid words escaping from her lips were, Sam seemed to be finding them fascinating.

'We just keep on picking,' he repeated. 'I like that.'

Cesca tipped her head to the side, scrutinising him. Sam took a step forward, clearing half the space between them. When he spoke, his voice was like gravel. 'How was your date?'

'A flop.'

A chuckle escaped his lips. 'Should I be sorry?'

'I don't know, should you?'

He looked stronger. More certain. 'I'm not sorry.'

'I didn't think you would be. Strangely enough, I'm not sorry, either.'

'That's like fucking music to my ears.' He cleared the final distance between them before she could say another word. Not that any came to mind. Her thoughts were too full of him, of his proximity, the smell of his aftershave, the way his hair fell over his forehead. She reached up, her fingers brushing his hairline as her thumb smoothed the furrows on his brow. Her action only made him frown harder. He looked at her as if she was a puzzle waiting to be solved.

'Cesca . . . ' He breathed her name as if it was oxygen. But she didn't want to hear his words, she wanted to taste them. To savour them as they tipped from his mouth into hers. To feel them form on his tongue.

'The way you look at me.' He shook his head. 'It's fucking entrancing.'

Sam dipped down until his eyes were level with hers. She felt his breath on her face, fanning her skin. He blinked and his lashes tangled against hers. Soft, like a snowflake drifting down. Then his hand cupped her chin, his fingers digging into her cheek as he angled her face to the left. The next moment he was closer still, his nose sliding against hers, his lips pressed against the corner of her mouth.

'Is this OK? Tell me this is OK.'

She was too mesmerised for a moment to answer. But then she felt him hesitate, his lips frozen against hers. 'It's OK,' she said hurriedly, desperate for him to move them. 'It's more than OK.'

That was all it took for him to cradle her head in his hands, his lips sliding across hers as if it was the most natural thing on earth. Then their mouths were moving against each other, softly at first, then firmer, until the need he created was like a drumbeat in Cesca's veins.

It was deafening, but she never wanted it to stop.

22

You have witchcraft in your lips

– Henry V

Sam slid his hand down from Cesca's face, fingers feathering her neck as his lips moved roughly against hers. His other hand tangled into her hair, against her scalp, all the while kissing her hard, fast, as if he couldn't get enough. Then he opened his mouth, his tongue teasing her bottom lip, begging silently for her to open hers, too.

'Christ, you taste good.'

She moaned softly against him. The sound went straight to his groin, making him hard in a matter of seconds. His senses were overflowing, with her taste, her scent, her touch. His body was vibrating to the sound of her sighs.

'You're so fucking beautiful,' he whispered.

'You're the beautiful one.'

It was like music to his ears. The girl he wanted, wanting him back.

Cesca arched into him, looping her arms around his neck, linking her fingers as she caressed his skin there. He could feel the warm softness of her body pressed against him. She tasted sweet, her mouth warm, wet and everything he'd hoped for. Sam wanted to pinch himself, see if he was still awake, or if this was another one of those dreams that had been plaguing him for days. The ones that woke him up with a confused mind and a hard dick. The ones where she was always out of reach.

He'd thought she was out of reach in reality, too. He'd placed her there, after all. In his collection of things to admire but not touch, she was number one on the list.

Yet here he was, touching her all over, and it was god-damned amazing.

'Sam.' Her words formed against his mouth. He could feel them vibrating there.

'Mmm.' He wasn't willing to stop kissing her. Not yet. Instead he dipped her back, angling her head further still, sliding his lips down to kiss and nip at her neck. Her skin still held a memory of perfume there. Something classy and floral. He could smell it, inhale it, practically taste it.

'God, Sam.' Her words were little more than air. Gasped and strangled. 'Don't stop.'

'Wasn't going to.' He moved his hand up from her waist, cupping her breasts, feeling the shape of them against his palm. Her nipples were hard, pressing against the fabric there. He pinched one between his thumb and forefinger, rolling her flesh until he could feel her fingers dig into his neck. Her nails scraped his skin, a harsh, scratching pain that only made him want more.

'Did he touch you like this?'

'No.' She shook her head rapidly.

'Did he make you feel like this?'

'Never.'

'I can't stand to think about it.'

'Then don't. Nothing happened. He hardly talked to me, he was busy all night. And even if he had I would have bored him to death. You're the only subject I wanted to talk about, anyway.'

'You wanted to talk about me?'

'Everything about tonight was about you. Even the clothes I'm wearing.'

'In that case, I appreciate them.'

Sam slid his hand beneath the neckline of her dress, the thin fabric giving way beneath his touch. He could feel the lace of her bra, barely covering her breasts, a sudden roughness in contrast to her silky-soft skin. When he brushed his thumb against her nipple it made Cesca jump. A quiet 'oh' escaped from her lips. Sam glanced up from his vantage point at her neck, catching her eyes. They were wide, expressive, reflecting the light of the hallway. He wanted to lose himself in their warm depths. There was a wonder there, a shock at the way the evening had turned, but also a desire that he could feel touching him deep inside.

He pulled back, lifting his head to hers. 'I've been thinking about doing this for days.'

'You have?' She frowned. 'I didn't notice.'

'You didn't notice me following you around the house? You didn't see me stalking you out to the car tonight, and pretty much warning off your date?'

A chuckle rumbled from her throat. 'I did wonder why you were so angry.'

'I was furious,' he told her, reaching out a finger to trace along the swell of her breasts. He stopped in the middle, where the flesh dipped against her ribcage. There was a line of tiny buttons there and he unfastened them one by one, until the fabric fell open, revealing her pale blue bra. 'You were going out with another man. And all I could think of was that you were going to have a better time with him than me.'

'I didn't.' Her voice cut off as he pushed his fingers beneath the lace edge of her bra. 'Have a better time, that is. I barely saw him, if you want to know. He spent more time talking to the owner than he did with me.'

It was Sam's turn to frown. 'What an asshole.' His fingers slid completely inside. She gasped as she felt the tips slide against her. 'I wouldn't ignore you on a date.'

'I know you wouldn't.'

'I wouldn't want to.' He looked up again. 'Because the only thing I'd want to talk about would be you.'

'That's a very boring conversation.'

Sam laughed. 'You're so fucking cute.'

She wrinkled her nose. 'You know I don't like that word.'

He stopped his hand movements. In a flash her own hand moved to join his, pressing him against her breast. 'I thought I told you not to stop.'

Chastened, he cupped her again, feeling the weight of her in his palm. 'Why don't you like being called cute?'

'Because I'm five foot nothing and it makes me feel like a kid.'

He squeezed hard. 'You don't feel like a kid to me.' Roughly, he dragged the fabric cup down, below her breast. Exposing her. The wire beneath it pushed her up, her nipple high and proud.

'Can I kiss you here?' He ran a finger over the rosy peak.

Her eyes flickered down. A look of uncertainty flashed across them.

'I don't have to . . .' Sam voiced his concern. 'Not if you don't want to.'

'I want you to.'

'But?' he prompted.

She was silent for a moment. Had he gone too far? Sam didn't think so. In his experience – and if you made him, he would admit it was fairly extensive – getting to second base was rarely a reason to stop. Yet Cesca was so far removed from the girls he'd been used to he wasn't even sure what she was thinking.

'But it's been a while,' she finally admitted. 'Since I've done this kind of thing, I mean. A long while.'

He wasn't sure why that thought excited him so much. It was as wrong as wanting a girl to be a virgin when the guy was a player. Such disparity in power wasn't ever something he'd looked for in a relationship. But being the one to ignite this feeling inside her . . . well that was like a shot of adrenalin to the heart.

'We don't have to do anything you don't want to.'

She was alarmed. 'I want to, I do. Believe me.' She looked down at her still-erect nipple. 'And if you don't believe me, maybe my body can persuade you.'

'Sweetheart, your body could persuade me of anything right now.'

She grabbed his thumb, moving it gently across her skin. The peak of her breasts dug into the pad. 'Do I need to persuade you?'

'Does it look like I need persuading?' Surely she could feel the ridge of his cock against her leg? He wasn't exactly pulling it away from her. 'Does it feel like I do?'

'Not exactly.'

'Then don't worry about my motivations, Cesca. I can promise you I'm all in here.'

She swallowed nervously. He watched the delicate skin of her neck undulate as she did. 'You are?'

'Yes, I am.' He said it loudly. Resolutely. Unsure of whether he was trying to persuade her or himself. But the truth of the words was so apparent, so obvious, it was amazing to him that she couldn't see that too.

'OK then.'

'OK?' He wasn't quite sure what she meant. There was no way he wanted to go further than she was ready for. Not after dancing around her for so long. But after the night he'd had – one spent pacing furiously, worried about what she was up to with that Italian asshole – it was hard to restrain himself.

'OK then, don't stop,' she told him. 'Keep doing what you're doing, but do it a bit quicker.'

He couldn't help but laugh at her petulant tone. 'Don't get angry at me. I don't like it when you're angry.'

She arched an eyebrow. 'When have you seen me angry?' Not waiting for his answer, she threaded her fingers through his hair, pushing him down, until his lips were only a breath away from her nipple.

Sam waited, tasting the anticipation, feeling the warmth radiating from her. 'How about when I edited your work without asking you first?'

'That was different. That was ... oh ...'

He silenced her with a sweep of his lips. Then, capturing her nipple between them, he pulled her in, teasing her softly with his tongue. He felt her harden still more, the blood rushing to the peak, making her sensitive and achy.

Then he sucked at her, his mouth closing around her flesh, the delighted gasp escaping her lips sounding like music to his ears.

His next few minutes were spent worshipping at her breasts, kissing first one then the other until she was a hot mess of sighs. The throbbing between his legs increased, becoming almost painful, and he was certain that if he carried on for much longer he was likely to explode.

'Cesca?' It was his turn to whisper against her skin. He licked her then blew softly, the cold air making her skin tighter still.

'Mmm?'

'Can we go up to my room?'

'Mmm.'

It wasn't a no, and that was all he needed to hear.

Twenty steps. Nineteen. Only eighteen steps until they got there. Cesca seemed as impatient as him, half-running up the stairs as his fingers rested on the swell of her behind. When they reached his room he felt the slightest hesitation. Not because he didn't want her in there, but because he wanted her in there too much. It wasn't a feeling he was used to.

Pushing the door open, he gestured for her to go in. 'Can I get you a drink?'

She looked at him, amused. 'No thank you.'

'Then take a seat.'

That made her burst out laughing. 'You're making this sound like a job interview.'

He couldn't help but join in, seeing the truth of her words. 'I'm sorry, it just feels a bit weird.'

'Bringing me to your room?'

'No, not at all. Bringing a girl to my room. It's like being a teenager all over again. Except I never brought a girl to my room when I was a teenager.'

Cesca was disbelieving. 'Never?'

'Not this room.' He shook his head, looking around. Of course the room was different to when he was a kid. Cooler, more sophisticated. But the bare bones were still the same – the walls, the shape, the layout of the furniture. There was something else, too. Something he wasn't quite able to put into words yet. The feeling that for the first time in six years the real him was coming out. Not the Hollywood Sam who attracted women like a jar of honey attracted flies, but the kid who was still deep inside him. The one he'd tried to shield for too long.

If he thought about it too much it would mess his mind. He shook his head to get rid of the voice inside. He didn't want to think about anything else but *her*.

Cesca sat down on his bed, the covers dipping beneath her. 'In that case I'm honoured.' Her eyes met his. 'And relieved.'

'Why relieved?' There was too much distance between them. He walked over to the bed, sitting down next to her. Without thinking he took her hand between his, running the pad of his thumb across her palm. That simple connection soothed him, locked away the anxiety that only a few minutes apart had created. When their bodies connected, it seemed as though their minds did, too.

'I had images of you being rampant in here,' she admitted. 'I don't think I could live up to that.'

'Oh, I was rampant. It was just a party for one, that's all.' He lay back on the bed, pulling her with him so she was curled up at his side, her head resting on his chest.

'You don't strike me as the sort to want for female company.'

He swallowed hard. 'I don't want to talk about female company.'

'No?' She propped herself up on her elbow, surveying him carefully. 'Why not?'

'Because I'm with you. And you're the only female I'm interested in.'

He could sense the insecurity wafting from her in waves. Didn't she know how much he wanted her? It was a shock to him that she couldn't see how much he liked her, admired her, wanted to possess her.

She let out a lungful of air. He reached out to trace her lips, his finger following the line where pink fullness gave way to flesh. She pursed her mouth, kissing it, then her tongue peeked out to taste him. The gesture sent the blood straight to his cock. He allowed himself to fantasise for a moment, picturing those full lips enveloping him, as her hair trailed down his thighs. It was electric.

'Do that again and I won't answer for my actions.'

She stared at him, her eyes wide. Then, deliberately, she grabbed his hand, bringing his finger back to her mouth. This time she sucked him inside. It was like sliding against velvet. Warm and wet. Jesus Christ, did she know what she was doing to him?

He flipped her over on the bed, her back landing on the mattress. Straddling her hips, his knees either side of her, he grabbed her hands, lifting them over her head. The movement made her chest rise up, her bra visible beneath the open buttons of her dress. Her skin glowed in the soft light of his bedroom.

When he looked at her he half expected to see shock in her eyes. Instead there was a strength that surprised and gratified him. His action hadn't surprised her at all, he'd done exactly what she'd wanted him to.

What he'd wanted, as well.

She was the one pinned on the bed, but she was the one in control, too. Just one word and he'd let her go. A different kind of word and he'd hold her so close she wouldn't be able to breathe.

'I'm going to take your dress off now.' Starting with the hem, he slowly lifted it over her body, revealing first her legs, then her stomach, and finally her chest. She shifted on the mattress to free up the fabric, until he lifted it over her head. Then she was lying there in front of him, in her bra and panties.

Slowly, he allowed his eyes to roam her body, taking her all in. From the mole on her upper thigh to the soft undulation of her belly. The way her nipples were pushing against the lace of her bra. Just above the waistline of her panties her skin turned from pale to golden. He ran a finger along the divide, marvelling at her smoothness. Then he was touching her all over, allowing his hands to roam, across taut skin and muscle, then to the softer, warmer parts.

Reaching behind her, he unclasped her bra. She was shaking beneath his touch. Not afraid though, no, definitely not that. Or no more fearful than he was about where this was going.

'I'm not going to have sex with you tonight,' he told her. The way she winced gratified him. Knowing this girl – this beautiful, clever girl – wanted him, was like a shot of adrenalin to the veins. But this thing growing between them was too delicate right now. He wasn't willing to break it by moving too fast.

'You're not?'

'I am going to touch you, though. All over.'

'What if I want to touch you, too?'

She ran her palm down his bulging jeans, curving her fingers to squeeze him. He bucked against her involuntarily, her touch taking him to the chasm between pleasure and pain. It was a relief when she unfastened his jeans, allowing his cock to escape the denim. Then she grabbed him again, this time circling her fingers around him, and it brought stars to his eyes.

'Be my guest.' His voice was guttural against her breast. Then he sucked her in and she cried out. He slid his hand inside her panties, and she was wet, so wet. His fingers sought her out, his thumb circling her until she started to moan. Her own hand fluttered on him, moving up and down erratically, squeezing his tip as she did. But even without rhythm the pleasure was almost unbearable. It took everything he had not to grab her hand and force it into his shorts.

Her hips were circling now, moving in time to his thumb. He slid a finger inside her, then two, noticing how warm she was, how tight.

'Don't stop, please don't stop.'

'I'm not stopping, baby.' He lifted his head from her chest. She looked fucking glorious, her head tipped back, her lips full and open. Still moving his fingers inside her, he pressed his mouth against hers. She kissed him back feverishly, her tongue curling against his, her breath warm and short when they parted.

'I'm going to come.'

She didn't need to tell him, he could already feel her tightening around him. He flicked his thumb harder, moved his fingers faster, tasting her pleasure as he kissed her again.

Her mouth dropped open as she lifted her hips up, her eyes wide as she stared at him. She convulsed around his fingers, her tightness only making him harder, and tiny little breaths escaped from her lips. He curled them inside her, wanting to prolong her pleasure. It was only when her body dropped back onto the mattress that he slowly slid them out.

She was still holding his cock, though.

'You're fucking gorgeous,' he whispered against her mouth. Seeing her explode with pleasure was the hottest thing he'd ever seen. Before he could say anything else Cesca reached inside his shorts, her hand enveloping his cock as she started to move it up and down.

Sam squeezed his eyes shut, seeing lights dancing behind the lids. The pleasure she was creating caused him to fall back on the bed, allowing her better access to him, as she pulled him free of the jersey fabric.

The next moment the soft warmth of her mouth slid over him. For a second he felt as if he was going to explode right there. Then she moved her lips down, enveloping him, and he thought if heaven involved sex, then he was already there.

Sam cupped the back of her head, feeling her move up and down as she bobbed her mouth on him. It wasn't going to take much to finish him, not when he was already so tightly wound by her, by the night, by the sight of her pleasure as it stole her breath.

She cupped his balls, and he felt them tighten. Everything about him was narrowing into a single point. Then she slid her tongue up his shaft, circling his tip, and all he could think was 'now, now, now ...'

'I'm going ...' The words died on his tongue. He tugged at her urgently, trying to signal his impending orgasm. She batted him off, refusing to move her mouth, instead she was sucking, licking, tasting ...

Behind the screen of his eyelids the pleasure exploded, turning his vision into a kaleidoscope of colours. He exploded in her mouth, too, the joy flooding out of him, as she swallowed it down. Then she pulled away, wiping her mouth with the back of her hand, collapsing to the mattress where she lay next to him.

It felt as though every bone in his body had turned to rubber. A really heavy, exhausted kind of rubber. All the frustrations of the night, his fears as she left for an evening with another man, his worry that she wouldn't return his admiration – they all disappeared with a single breath.

It was Cesca who broke the silence that followed. 'Well I don't usually do that on a first date. Especially with a guy who didn't even go on the date.'

The corner of his mouth twitched. 'I'm glad to hear it.' He reached out for her, gathering her into the crook of his arm. Like him, her movements were slow, weighed down by satiation. She curled into him again, one of her thighs sliding between his.

'Stay for a while.' Like his body, his words were heavy with fatigue.

'OK,' she mumbled into him. 'Just for a bit.'

Before he could protest, her breathing turned heavy and rhythmic, as sleep began to steal its way across her. He closed his eyes, letting it take him, too, still holding her against him.

23

*This bud of love, by summer's ripening breath, may
prove a beauteous flower when next we meet*

– Romeo and Juliet

'We should be able to leave early next week.' Gabi's voice
crackled down the telephone line. 'I just want to make sure
the baby is sleeping a little better before we go. The poor
little thing is waking up every two hours.'

'Next week? That's very soon.' Cesca's thoughts turned to
Sam, who she'd left back at the villa an hour earlier. 'I thought
you'd be gone for longer.'

Gabi laughed. 'What happened to the girl who wanted to
go back to England? Has Varenna made you fall in love with
it? That happens, you know.'

Staring out at the village square, Cesca saw how easily it
could. The village had a character of its own. Traditional yet
welcoming, a little piece of old Italy along the banks of Lake
Como. 'It's a beautiful place to stay,' she admitted. 'I'll miss
it when I have to leave.' The thought of returning to London
made her chest hurt. She couldn't bear to go back to that old

life, not that it was any kind of existence, really. Living hand to mouth, dodging landlords and cosying up to bosses. Not able to write a single word . . .

'Your contract is to stay until the end of the summer, right?' Gabi asked. 'And it would give me and Sandro the chance to check on his sister a few more times if you stayed around. You don't have to leave on our account.'

'We'll see,' Cesca replied, her mind still on London. 'I don't want to outstay my welcome. I'm here to do a job, after all, and once that's done I won't be needed here any more.' There was that tight feeling around her ribs, again.

After Gabi hung up, Cesca stayed in the telephone box to call Hugh. Since that first week in Varenna, she'd only spoken to him a couple of times.

'How lovely to hear from you,' Hugh said, after she identified herself. 'Would you like me to call you back? I know how expensive these long distance phone calls can be.'

'It's OK,' she told him. 'I've bought an international calling card with the money the Carltons paid me in advance.' She didn't want to be *that* girl any more.

'Very wise. So how are you doing, poppet? Have you managed to get much writing done?'

'As a matter of fact I have.' Her voice was full of smiles. 'I'm three quarters of the way through the first draft. I can't tell you how good it feels.' What a difference a few weeks made. She was happy to give him a positive answer.

'That's wonderful, I can't wait to read it. I don't suppose you can send it over to me, can you?'

She laughed. 'It's on the computer at the villa, and there's no internet access there. Besides, I'd like to wait until it's finished if that's OK.'

'I suppose I'll have to wait then. It won't be that long until you come back, will it?'

Another reminder of the limited nature of her stay here in Varenna. An unwelcome one, too. Why couldn't she just stay here for ever, in her lovely cocoon with her writing and Sam?

Oh, Sam. She didn't want to think about leaving him right now. Not after the past few days.

'A couple of weeks, possibly,' she told him. 'I spoke to Gabi earlier – she's the housekeeper – and they're talking about returning to Varenna next week. I'll need to hand everything over to them and make sure it's all shipshape.'

'I thought you'd be rushing back just as soon as they arrived. Not that long ago you wanted to leave straight away.'

'Yeah, well, I may have been a little precipitate,' she admitted. 'Uncle Hugh, I'm so glad you found me this job. It's changed everything.' It wasn't hyperbole either. When she looked in the mirror this morning after cleaning her teeth she wasn't sure she recognised the girl looking back at her. In such a good way, too. She looked healthier, stronger, and so much more in control. For the first time in years she was taking life by the horns. And the ride was starting to feel amazing.

'I can't tell you how happy that makes me, my darling.' Hugh's voice cracked as he replied. The closest he came to admitting to emotion. 'Now you have to keep it up when you get home. We can look into grants, competitions, the opportunities are out there. You just need to take them.'

She didn't want to talk about that. Not that she wasn't grateful for his support – she knew how lucky she was to have him. It was more that she didn't want to face the reality of going home.

It was like she'd been in rehab and now had to see if she could keep her sobriety back in the real world. It was scary.

'That sounds good.' She hoped he didn't notice how quiet her voice was.

'Are you OK?' Of course he noticed. 'I thought you'd be happier about that. My God, if you could write the way you did when you were eighteen, I can only imagine what you can produce now. All the emotion, the angst you've been through. It's perfect training for a writer.'

'I'm fine.' She tried to sound resolute. 'Honestly, you don't need to worry about me.' It was such a familiar refrain, but this time – for the first time in six years – it was true.

Hugh was quiet for a moment. She tried to picture him in his London apartment, sitting on one of his antique chairs. In her mind she could see rain pebbling against the window, obscuring the grey clouds outside. 'Well, let me know when you're ready to come home. I can arrange for you to be picked up at the airport. Do you know where you're planning to live? I could clear out my spare bedroom.'

'I'll find somewhere,' she said. 'If the worst comes to the worst I can stay with my father for a few days. And you don't need to pick me up, I can use the Underground. I can afford it now.' Not for long, though. Not without a job or benefits.

'Well, the offer's always open. I'm looking forward to seeing you. And to reading your play.'

'I'm looking forward to it, too.' A tiny lie. Because she loved him, and at any other time it would be true.

When she arrived back at the villa, arms laden with food, Sam was waiting for her at the gate. He'd taken a chair out there and was editing her work in the sun, crossing through her words. He looked up when he heard her approaching, a smile breaking out on his face. She wanted him to lift his sunglasses, too, so she could see his eyes. She hated it when she couldn't see them.

'I hope you're wearing sunscreen,' she said, as he took the bags from her hands. 'It's almost midday.'

'I hope you are, too,' he said pointedly. 'Especially with your pale skin.'

She looked down at her arms. 'I'm not pale. Well, not any more, anyway.'

He raised his eyebrows. 'Parts of you are.' She sensed his gaze sweeping down over her body. Was it wrong that she liked his appreciation?

'You don't exactly have an all-over tan,' she said, as they crunched their way along the gravelled driveway.

'No I don't.' His smile was slow, but devastating. 'But I don't think sunbathing naked would do a whole lot for my public profile.'

She raised her eyebrows. 'Oh, I think you're wrong. Imagine the girls' reactions when they see how ... um ... impressive you are.'

Sam chuckled. 'You think I'm impressive?'

How did she manage to get herself into these conversations? For a girl who was supposed to be good at words, she managed to get tied up in knots whenever she was talking to Sam.

'As I told you, I don't have that much experience.' She grinned, running lightly up the steps to the front door.

The corner of his mouth twitched. 'You did tell me that.' Was it her imagination or had his voice become lower and thicker? Much like the atmosphere between them.

'I wonder if it's possible for us to talk without innuendos,' Cesca said.

'That would be very boring,' he replied. 'I like talking to you in innuendos.'

'You do?'

He laughed again. Everything he did only heightened her attraction to him. She hated that. She loved it too.

'It'd be boring if we just talked about the weather. And pretty unsexy if we used all the anatomical words. Innuendos seem like a good compromise to me.'

'In that case, I found your, ah, flashlight very impressive.'

Sam spluttered. 'My flashlight? Wow, I'm not sure if that's an innuendo or just an insult.'

'Is it too small?' she asked. 'Too big? Is there a better way of describing it?'

'How about my cock?'

Cesca gasped. 'I can't believe you just said that. Cock isn't an innuendo. It's a real description, and a rude one at that.'

'You think cock's rude?'

'Sam!' Her cheeks were flaming. She must look so much like a prude. Shaking her head, she walked into the kitchen, with him following closely behind.

'You didn't seem to think it was rude last night when you were kissing it.'

Wow, she really hadn't expected him to be so direct. And it wasn't as if she was completely innocent. After all, she'd had sex before, she'd read dirty books, and she knew all the words she needed to. But hearing them come from his mouth was dirty and exciting and made her light up inside.

'Say it,' he said, taking a step towards her, sliding his sunglasses over his head.

'What?'

'Cock. I want to hear you say it.'

'No way.'

'Say it.' Another step towards her. 'Or are you too scared?'

'I'm not scared of you.' Except she was, just a little bit. Scared of the way he made her feel.

'Then I want to hear it come from your mouth. Just four little letters, Cesca. C. O. C. K. Now say it.'

Sam moved closer still, until their legs were touching, their torsos only inches apart. He leaned forward, his hands flat on the work surface, until he was caging her in. A thrill shot through her at his proximity. She could smell the woody fragrance of his cologne, and it made her want to run her nose up and down his throat until she got more.

The look of amusement on his face mixed with desire. 'Come on, baby.'

'There's not a rat's chance in hell that I'll say it.'

'Then I'll have to make you.'

Her eyebrows rose up in challenge. 'Try it.'

He leaned forward, taking her chin into his hand. There was a heat in his eyes that she could feel burning at her, too. He pressed his lips to the corner of her mouth, and she felt their softness, their warmth.

'Say it, baby.' He kissed his way along her bottom lip, until it started to tremble. 'Say it, and I'll make it worth your while.'

His tongue slid along the seam between her lips, dipping inside. Without a conscious thought she opened for him, kissing him back as he pushed inside, his hand still cupping her face. Cesca's eyes fluttered closed, her breathing stilted as Sam's body pressed against hers. She could feel it all; the hard planes of his chest and stomach, the thick muscles of his arms. The way he grew hard against her as she pushed herself into him, giving herself up to his passionate embrace.

Sam was the first to break the kiss. Cesca let out a little whimper before he moved his lips to her neck, kissing the sensitive skin there.

'Say it,' he whispered against her.

'No.'

'Say it or I'll stop.'

'You wouldn't.' Her words were a gasp. He'd paid attention, learning which parts of her to target, and he was applying his knowledge with vigour.

'Try me.' She could feel his lips curving into a smile against her skin as he stole her words. Then he pulled back, the sudden rush of air against her skin underscoring his absence. Her eyes flew open, and she went to grab his head, wanting him back there.

'Sam, please.' Her cheeks were bright red.

'Cock,' he teased. 'Cock, cock, cock.'

'OK!' She threw her hands up. 'You want me to embarrass myself?'

'I want you to set yourself free. There's nothing embarrassing about words. Only the meaning you attach to them.' He traced her lips with his finger. 'If we were talking about chickens you'd say it with abandon.'

Cesca rolled her eyes. 'Cock. There I said it. Are you happy?'

'Your voice dropped when you did it. You need to own the word. Try again.'

'Cock.' She was a little surer this time.

239

'Not loud enough.'

'Oh, for God's sake. COCK. COCKCOCKCOCKCOCK.' She shouted the words, the sound reverberating through the kitchen. Sam started to laugh, his serious expression dissolving away. He took a step back, putting a hand on his stomach, bending over as the laughter exploded from him.

'You should have seen your face, Cesca,' he spluttered.

'I just don't see the point of saying words simply for shock effect.'

'I swear I'm going to have it tripping off your tongue by the time I'm through with you. You'll be "cock this" and "cock that" and you won't even blink an eyelid.'

'I certainly won't. And you can cock off.'

That only made him laugh harder.

'It's just over here.' Sam grabbed her hand and led her around the side of the house, where the gardens gave way to the steep slopes up the mountain. Though evening had arrived, the heat of the day still clung onto the air around them, reddening their faces as they crossed the grass. Eventually they came to a stop, beside a wooden door that led into the hill itself. He slid an old-fashioned iron key into the lock. The mechanism creaked as he released it, then he pulled the door open to reveal a brick tunnel.

'Wow.' The cool air escaped from the doorway, hitting their skin. 'I never even knew this was here.'

'It's Foster's favourite part of the villa,' Sam said. 'He's been stocking it for years.'

She couldn't help but notice the way he almost spat out his father's name. Curiosity piqued her. What was it about that man?

They walked inside the tunnel, and Sam pulled the door closed behind them. 'To keep the temperature even,' he told Cesca, when she looked alarmed.

He flipped a switch to illuminate the darkness, and the wall-mounted lamps flickered on. Leading her deeper still, they finally came to the cave itself, a large, rectangular cavern lined with wooden shelves. Lying on those shelves, covered in a layer of dust, was a myriad of bottles. So many she couldn't count them. All angled slightly down, so the corks keeping in the wine wouldn't dry out.

'I've never seen anything like it,' she admitted, still looking around with wonder.

'According to my mother, it was built by my great-grandfather to impress his wife. She came from a family of wine growers and in wooing her he decided to fill the cave with her wine to impress her. Apparently that's the only reason she agreed to marry him.'

Cesca laughed, running a finger down the nearest bottle. The dust wiped off onto her finger, revealing a deep green glass below. 'Sensible woman. Even if he wasn't very good-looking, at least she could drown her sorrows.'

'Hey, of course he was good-looking. I'm related to him, after all.'

'Is that where you get your modesty, too?'

Sam flashed her a smile. 'Nah, that's all my own hard work.' He inspected the bottles, lifting a couple of them up to look at the labels. Finally he pulled one from the shelf, blowing on it to disperse the dust. 'This one's my favourite. Foster bought a crate about fifteen years ago, but we're down to the last few now.'

'Won't he mind if we drink it?'

Sam rolled his eyes. 'He won't even notice. And it's not as though he's short of wine in here.' He waved at the shelves. 'Plus I buy him a crate of wine every year for Christmas. He's the hardest person to find gifts for.'

As soon as they walked back outside the heat hit them. Sam quickly locked up the cave and they headed into the villa, both seeking the relief of the air conditioning. In the kitchen a lasagne was bubbling in the oven, and on the work surface was a board full of cheeses and crusty bread. Another thing she'd miss about Italy when she left it – over here they knew how to make an evening meal into an event.

'It'll be another ten minutes,' Cesca told him, after checking the dish.

'Perfect. Enough time for us to have an *aperitivo*.' Sam grabbed a bottle of gin. 'I'll make us a negroni.'

'I thought you warned me against drinking with strange men,' she teased, watching as he poured the gin and Campari into a shaker. 'You said I couldn't be trusted when I'm drunk.'

'That's what I'm banking on.' He winked at her before pouring the cocktail into two small tumblers. 'And anyway, the better the drinks, the more you're likely to savour them.'

'I've never had such good wine before I came here,' she admitted. 'Well, I never had much wine at all.' She was struck by how different their lives were. He'd told her on their way back from the cave that the bottle he'd chosen was probably worth a few hundred euros. Spending that much on wine made her feel a little faint. It was so out of her league.

The rich movie star and the impoverished writer. It would make a good story.

'When you finish your play we'll crack open the champagne,' he said, handing her her glass. 'Cheers.'

'Cheers.' They clinked their glasses together, then Cesca took a sip. Just like at Grotto Maria, the negroni was delicious. 'Anyway, what makes you think I'll finish my play here? I may not complete the first draft until I'm back in London.'

'That's not going to happen.' Sam was looking at her over the rim of his glass. 'I won't let you leave until it's done.'

'What if it takes me months?'

'I'd be OK with that.' He leaned forward again, brushing his lips just below the shell of her ear. 'In fact I'd be delighted. Whatever it takes.'

'Try explaining that to your rabid fans,' Cesca said. 'It's not that long before you'll be back in LA. You must have commitments.' Though she kept her voice light, there was an edge to her words. Like earlier, when she spoke with her godfather about returning to London, she could feel the unease deep inside her.

Sam took another sip of his negroni. She could see it glistening on his lips. 'I'm a free man until the fall.'

Cesca grabbed a couple of plates from the cupboard, and proceeded to lay the salad out on them. Sam was leaning on the counter next to her, watching as she chopped the juicy tomatoes.

'What are you filming next?' She didn't like the idea of him being away on location, surrounded by beautiful women. It was hard to picture this Sam – her Sam – in a Hollywood setting. And yet she should, because that was his life. Somehow the thought made her feel a little nauseous.

'The final *Summer Breeze* movie.' He sounded anything but enthusiastic. 'It's the last one I'm contracted to. After that

I'm hoping to do some more edgy roles. Maybe even get out of Hollywood for a while. I'm kind of sick of being the dumb heart-throb.'

Cesca bit down a smile. 'Must be hard to be typecast.'

'Hey, I resent that.' The oven timer went off and he silenced the alarm, then took the lasagne out of the stove. 'Anyway, most of the people I meet actually think I'm Tyler Graham. I get called that more often than I'm called Sam in the streets.'

She laughed. 'That must be annoying.'

'You could say that.' Sam wrinkled his nose. 'And I know it sounds ungrateful because it was my big break. But when you're permanently typecast as a nineteen-year-old surfer it can get a little stale. Especially at the age of twenty-seven. I guess that's Hollywood. You either play the game or you get out of town.'

Cesca handed him the knife and he cut the lasagne into portions, steam rising up from the dish. The smell of fresh pasta mixed with Bolognese sauce filled the kitchen.

'I can imagine,' Cesca said. 'It's kind of ironic that neither of us really grew up after you left for Hollywood. You because your audience wouldn't let you, and me because I refused to accept my failure.'

'You look grown up to me,' Sam told her. He carried their plates over to the table, then pulled out her chair. It was strange how she was already taking his gallantry for granted. It wasn't as if every guy their age treated women that way. Maybe it was his upbringing, being raised by an Italian mother. Whatever the reason, she found herself liking it very much.

Sam poured the wine he'd found earlier into their glasses.

It was so dark it almost looked black. 'This one smells almost as good as it tastes,' he told her, lifting his wine glass to his face. He inhaled deeply, and Cesca followed suit.

'It smells delicious,' she agreed, swirling the glass so the wine sloshed around it. 'I still feel bad that it's so expensive, though.'

Sam looked her straight in the eye. 'You shouldn't.'

'Says the man who probably earns double the cost of that bottle for every minute he works.'

'I haven't worked out how much I earn a minute,' Sam laughed. 'But I can tell you I earn enough to cover the cost of the wine.'

'But I don't.'

He angled his head to look at her. 'That bothers you, doesn't it?'

'The fact I couldn't normally afford to drink wine like this?' she clarified. 'Not really. It's lovely but I'm just as happy with a six pound special from the grocery store.'

'No, I'm not talking about the wine. I'm talking about the fact I can afford it and you can't. I saw the same thing when we went out for dinner – you didn't like me picking up the check.'

She didn't like where this conversation was heading. It was touching a nerve and she felt it all over her body. 'I like things equal. If I go out for dinner with somebody I like to pay my way. It feels awkward to rely on somebody else, as if I'm beholden to them.'

'What about if the other person *wants* to buy you things?' Sam asked. 'What if that brings them happiness? I mean I could sit and drink this wine alone, and I could have gone out to Grotto Maria and had dinner for one, but that would have been sad. Having you share those things with me adds to my enjoyment. You can't put a price on that.'

'I've always wanted to be independent,' she told him. 'And having somebody buy me dinner doesn't really make me feel as if I'm succeeding on my own. I don't like accepting things if I can't give something back in return.'

Sam tipped his head to the side, scrutinising her. 'Did Cristiano pay for your dinner?'

Cesca blinked twice. There was a jealous tone to his question, that she couldn't help but notice. And it warmed her from the inside out. 'I don't think he was charged,' she admitted. 'I didn't see a bill, and I suspect it was a freebie because he was thinking of buying the place.'

Sam looked gratified. 'Cheap bastard.'

A shocked giggle tumbled from Cesca's lips. 'That's rude. And anyway you're the one stealing wine from your father. What does that make you?'

He winked. 'Messed up and full of issues.'

There he went again. This time she couldn't swallow down her interest. 'What do you mean by that?'

Sam shrugged. 'Nothing.'

She sighed. 'You keep bringing this up and shooting me down. I don't get it. It makes me feel . . . ' She trailed off, her face screwed up as she tried to find the right word. 'Like I'm not good enough.'

He looked shocked. 'What do you mean? Of course you're good enough. Too good, if I'm being honest.'

Cesca twisted the napkin between her fingers, looking down at her empty plate. 'I've opened myself up to you, I've let you read my play. I've told you all about my problems and my issues and my family. But every time things get personal you just pull away.' She looked up at him through her lashes. 'And I get it, I think. This is just casual to you, and that's OK.'

Sam's expression was pinched. 'It's not casual,' he said quietly.

For some reason that made her chest ache. 'Then why won't you talk to me?'

He reached out for his empty wine glass, running his finger around the rim. A soft hum echoed from the crystal. 'It's old news.'

'No it isn't.' She pushed her plate out of the way and leaned across the table. 'I can tell by your face it's still important.'

He blinked, looking at her with heavy-lidded eyes. For a moment he looked like a child. Young. Lost.

'I'm sorry,' she whispered. 'I've done it again. It has nothing to do with me.'

He was still looking at her, and his expression was breaking her heart. She stared back, her lips firmly closed, feeling the electricity buzzing in the air. For a moment neither of them spoke, the only sound in the room the tinny ring from his crystal glass.

Eventually, he leaned back on his chair, his eyes still on hers. 'Actually, it has everything to do with you.'

She frowned. 'It does?'

He nodded slowly. 'You asked me before why I left the play so suddenly. I think I said some bullshit about family stuff. I guess that much was true.'

Goose pimples broke out on her flesh, in spite of the warmth in the kitchen. She felt as though she'd smashed through an invisible barrier.

'The night before we opened, I got into an argument

with Foster. Not that it was unusual in those days. It felt like every time we saw each other we almost came to blows. I could never do anything right as far as he was concerned.' Sam paused for long enough to refill both their glasses, then took a long sip of wine. 'He'd been drinking. He was a nasty drunk – still is, I guess. But that night he took it to a whole new level.'

Cesca's hands curled into fists, her nails digging into her palms. Sam's face took on a faraway look, as though he was reliving that moment with his father.

'I was a bit of a punk, too,' Sam told her. 'You'd probably agree with that. I was cocky, arrogant, thought I could rule the world. I didn't miss an opportunity to rub it in Foster's face, either. I'd call him an old man, tell him his time was over, told him to make way for the younger generation. Stupid stuff like that. But that night, I tipped him over the edge. Told him he wasn't good enough for Mom, that he never was. That she'd have been better off never marrying him.'

'And then?' Cesca was full of trepidation.

'Then he grabbed me by the collar and shoved me against the wall, hard enough for my head to bang against the plaster. The next minute he was screaming at me that I was a little bastard, that I was no son of his, that if he hadn't married my mom the two of us would be rotting somewhere.'

'Your dad called you a bastard?' she asked, wide-eyed.

Sam looked down at his hands. 'Funny thing was, he was right.'

'Why?'

He swallowed hard, still not looking up. It took everything she had not to reach across and touch him, tip his chin up, make him look her in the eye again.

248

'Sam?' she prompted.

'That night, he told me he wasn't my father. Told me in no uncertain terms that my mom was pregnant when he met her, that my dad was some kind of asshole who'd walked out on her. That he'd adopted me when they got married.' He squeezed her hand tighter. 'The way he said it though, Cesca, as if he wished he hadn't bothered. It gutted me.'

'Of course it did.' A tear rolled down her left cheek. 'That's a disgusting way to tell you about it. What did your mum say when he told you?'

'She doesn't know I know. None of them do. Just me and Foster.' He frowned, as though he was remembering something. 'And ... '

'And me?' she said.

'Yeah.'

So he'd confided in her. For some reason that touched her deeply. It hurt to see this man – this handsome, strong, talented man – brought low by memories he somehow couldn't escape.

'He never liked me,' he whispered. 'And for twenty-one years I had no idea why.'

'But he adopted you,' she said. 'Why would he have done that if he didn't like you?'

'I came as a package deal, I guess. He wanted my mom, and she was pregnant with me. He didn't exactly get a choice.' His eyes glinted in the flickering light of the candle. She grabbed his hand, folding it in her own.

'What made you think he didn't like you?'

Sam finally looked up at her, his face impassive. His eyes were piercing. It was as though they were digging through her, searching, looking. They made her ache.

'Little things,' Sam finally said. 'And big things. Words, jibes, telling me I wasn't good enough. My grades weren't good enough, my acting was terrible, I was a terrible son to my mother. He actually smiled when he told me the truth about my father. Like he enjoyed inflicting the pain.'

Her face softened. 'He's a rat bastard.'

'Anyway, that's enough about my messed-up family.' He looked straight at her. 'I'd rather finish our dinner and get to bed.'

There was a heat behind his stare that sent her heart racing. The promise behind his words was enough to take her breath away. Everything inside urged her to take him upstairs, to comfort him, to hold him until the bad guys went away.

They could talk about his parents another day.

24

This is the very ecstasy of love

– Hamlet

'Are you almost done?'

Cesca jumped at the unexpected question. She was at the spitting stage of her tooth brushing, the paste foaming out over her lips. She put her brush down and turned around, wiping her mouth with the back of her hand. Last night they'd fallen asleep together almost as soon as they'd got into his room, their naked limbs tangled together. Today, though, he seemed brighter, more like his old self. She'd spent most of the day writing, while they talked about silly things. His favourite book, her favourite meal, whether she liked blue better than green.

And now dinner was over, he'd suggested they get an early night. The way he'd said it had sent an army of shivers down her spine.

'You scared me.' Her voice was mangled by the fact her mouth was still full of paste. A little more escaped from the corner of her lips.

Sam smiled, leaning his shoulder on the doorjamb. 'You missed a bit.' He gestured at her mouth.

'Can't a girl get a bit of privacy?' They were doing this all backwards. She hadn't even made love with him yet and he was already seeing her at her worst. OK, so technically she'd fallen asleep with him, but apart from that they'd only fooled around.

Whatever 'fooled around' meant. Because it didn't seem foolish at all to her.

'You were taking too long.' He sounded petulant. 'And I wanted to see you.'

She frowned. 'And I want to see you, too. But not right now.' More spittle found its way out. 'Just go outside for a minute, let me finish up in here.'

Sam threw his hands up as if in surrender. 'Hey, don't blame me if you brush your teeth like a two-year-old.'

She picked up her toothbrush and held it in front of her, wielding it as if it was a weapon. 'Get out!'

When she finally emerged from the bathroom, teeth cleaned and face scrubbed, Sam was sitting on her bed, thumbing through a book on writing he'd found on her table. Cesca felt strangely naked. It wasn't the fact she was wearing sleep shorts and a vest top, nor the fact she was make-up free. No, it was her soul that felt exposed and vulnerable.

'Hey.' He looked up as she walked in, a smile on his face. 'You look pretty.'

Cesca frowned. 'Liar.'

'Why do girls always doubt a guy when he says that? What's not to like when you've washed off your make-up and put your hair in a bun? It's cute, it's sexy. It's real.' He reached out for her. 'And when you do that funny little twisty thing with your mouth, it's even sexier.'

'What funny little twisty thing?' She allowed herself to be pulled to the bed, grimacing.

'That one.' He reached out to touch her lips. 'It's cute.'

'I thought we'd talked about cute. I hate that word.'

Sam placed the briefest of kisses on her lips. 'It doesn't mean the same in America as it does in England. It's a compliment.'

'If you say so.'

'I do.' He brushed the hair from her shoulder and kissed her neck. 'Cute means wholesome yet sexy. The kind of girl you want to take home to your mom just as soon as you can bear for her to get dressed.'

Cesca coughed out a laugh. 'At least you don't take them to meet your mum naked.'

'I've never taken a girl to meet my mom.' The expression on his face told her he was serious. 'Never wanted to.'

'What about that girl ... oh God, I can't remember her name. The one who plays the shop girl in *Summer Breeze*?'

'Katya? We were never an item.'

'But the newspapers said you were,' Cesca said. Then, noticing his incredulous expression, she hastily added, 'And I know you shouldn't believe everything you read, but it seemed like a done deal, if you know what I mean.'

'I thought you avoided all mention of me for six years. Anyway, I try to avoid getting too close to anybody in the business.' His voice was thick. 'Most of the girls over there only want you for one thing.'

She raised her eyebrows. 'One thing?'

'You've got a dirty mind.' He laughed, though it sounded hollow. 'No, they want you to help their careers. Everybody in Hollywood is a user. It's almost impossible to have a normal relationship there.'

Her face fell. 'Not everybody. My sister's there, remember?'

'But she's not an actress, right?'

She shook her head. 'No.'

'Then maybe she's different.' He smiled. 'Like you.'

Sam's eyes flashed as he stared at her, his pupils dilating. He blinked twice, his long lashes sweeping down, and Cesca's chest started to ache from holding her breath.

'You're very beautiful, Cesca Shakespeare.'

'I am?' Her breath, once released from her lungs, came out in short puffs. She felt like an old wreck of a car stop-starting down the street.

'You really are.' Sam cradled her face between his hands. She closed her eyes for a moment, letting his touch consume her. Then his breath was warming her lips, his mouth barely touching hers. This time his kiss was soft, gentle, the tip of his tongue dancing along the seam of her mouth, and Cesca found herself rising to it, kissing him back, inviting him for more.

Sam pushed her back on the bed and they were a tangle of limbs, their bodies pressed together as their kisses became more urgent. And for long minutes they lay together, hands tangled in each other's hair as they continued to embrace.

Cesca wrapped her bare legs around Sam's hips. She could feel his hardness straining against her, the friction heating her up. He was moving his hips now, a soft gyration that was making Cesca sigh. Her hands feathered down his back, her fingers stroking his spine. Then they were grabbing his arse, digging in, pulling him against her until she moaned.

Sliding her hands beneath the waistband of his pyjamas, Cesca pressed her palms against his skin. Encouraging him, pushing him, whispering words of desire. Sam's own hands were pulling down the straps of her vest top, pushing the fabric to her waist. Then their bare chests pressed together, flesh on flesh, and the sensation made them both frantic.

Sam's thumb hooked around her flannel shorts. He slipped them under the elastic waistband, his knuckles nudging her hips. 'Is this OK?' He stopped kissing her long enough for their eyes to meet. His expression was rapt, his mouth swollen from their embrace. Cesca nodded rapidly, lifting up her hips in encouragement.

He knelt back, running his hands down her body. His lips followed them, kissing and teasing, spending long moments on her nipples until they were so hard they were almost pain-ful. Then he moved down, his lips creating a trail of desire down her chest then her stomach, little kisses and licks that drove her crazy. His fingers dipped further, grazing against her core, his thumb rolling and rubbing in circles until she felt as though her whole body was humming. Then his mouth was there, soft brushes of his lips at first, then a deeper, teasing, lick. She started to lift her hips in time, his hands holding onto her behind, supporting her as she bucked.

'Sam.' Her voice was a sigh. 'Oh God, Sam.'

She was getting closer now. Her whole body was pulled tight, like an over-tuned instrument. Taut and highly strung, ready to unravel. Sam played her hard, getting ready for the crescendo, and she felt her thighs tense at the oncoming wave.

'I want you to make love to me,' she whispered, not sure if he could hear. She tugged at his hair and Sam lay his head on her thigh, looking up at her.

'Are you sure?'

She liked the way he kept asking. He was handing her the

reins, telling her they'd move at whatever speed she wanted. 'I'm certain.'

'I need to get a condom. Don't move, OK?'

'I'm not going anywhere.' She closed her eyes and waited for him, her toes curling at the feeling of desire that kept shooting down her legs. Her thighs ached from wanting him between them. He was back in less than a minute, settling between her legs, and she found herself curling her own around his hips.

There was that moment, that desperate pause, when he pressed his tip against her, waiting for her body to acquiesce. She breathed it in, tasted their desire, waiting desperately for him to slide inside.

'You're beautiful.' Sam kissed her, still waiting to make the final move. He was teasing her, making her crazy with desire, and she loved it.

'So are you.' She moved her hips, encouraging him in. Sam smiled against her mouth. He moved a hand down to her side, stilling her, circling his cock around until she was almost begging.

'Sam . . . '

He was enjoying this too much. But then so was she. He kissed her again, digging his fingers into her hipbone as he slowly slid inside.

Cesca moaned into his lips as the pleasure hit her deep inside. The warmth was spreading, from her stomach, radiating out to her breasts, her thighs, her toes. Then he was moving, thrusting into her, and she clung onto him, feeling everything start to rise. Her hands were shaking, her head falling back, Sam's name escaping from her mouth like a litany.

'Sam, Sam, Sam . . .'

'Yes, baby.' He was breathless, still moving inside her. Every time he withdrew he slid deliciously against her, drawing her pleasure out inch by inch.

'I can't . . . I'm going . . . I . . . I . . .'

Her words disappeared as she tensed beneath him, her hips rising up so her back was arched away from the mattress. It was as though every muscle in her body was clenching, moving to the rhythm of her orgasm, drawing out the intensity as fireworks sparked beneath her eyes. When she opened them Sam was staring at her, an unfathomable look on his face. She stared back at him, wondering if for him this was merely physical. Or was he feeling the emotional connection as much as she was? From the way he was looking at her, she had to believe he did.

Then he was falling, too, letting out a deep moan as he spilled inside her. His head dropped to her shoulder, his teeth digging into her flesh, as her skin tingled beneath his lips. She liked his weight on her, his firmness, the way he had given as much of himself to her as she had to him.

She closed her eyes, feeling tears pricking at them. She didn't know where the emotion had come from. Swallowing it down, she willed the tears to go away, to dry up before Sam could see them.

There was being vulnerable, and there was cutting your chest open and letting someone else tear your heart out. She could do the first one. The second? It remained to be seen.

She'd fallen asleep almost as soon as he'd cleaned himself up, disposing of the condom and washing himself in her bathroom. He'd climbed back into bed with her, feeling her body soft and pliant against his as she curled into him, her head nestling against his shoulder.

He wasn't used to spending the night with somebody. It had never really been his thing. He liked his own space, his own bed, having room enough to spread out. But it felt right, having her here.

For now.

Cesca sighed in her sleep, moving closer into him. He put his arm around her shoulder, feeling the softness of her skin beneath his. She was warm and supple against his naked body, and he glanced at the clock, wondering how long he would be able to hold off wanting her again.

Sam hadn't come into her room with the intention of making love to her. Like last night, having her body curled around his would have been enough. But she was like a drug, one taste and he wanted more. The problem was, drugs were bad for him.

And so were women.

Since his confessions yesterday, Cesca had tried a few times to mention his family, and he'd cut her off. Made a joke, changed the subject, pressed his lips to hers. Anything to quieten the incessant thoughts in his brain. Reminding him that making himself vulnerable only led to pain.

In Hollywood, vipers wore pretty clothes, and whispered sweet things until you spilled all your secrets. Here in Italy? He didn't think so. But it didn't stop him panicking every time she mentioned his family.

Cesca's eyes fluttered open. She caught his gaze, a slow smile breaking out across her lips. Her hand brushed against his chest. 'Did I fall asleep?'

He took a deep breath, returning her smile. 'You did.'

'I'm sorry. That was rude of me.'

Sam raised an eyebrow. 'That was the least rude thing you did all night.'

She coughed out a laugh. 'Sam!'

He liked this part. It was as easy as the sun rising in the morning. They talked, they laughed, they made love, and it all felt so natural. It was the thinking he didn't like, the analysing. Having to face things he'd long since tried to ignore.

The answer was simple, really. He wouldn't do it. Better to concentrate on the here and now. To kiss those luscious lips that were curled up in front of him. To ravish Cesca's naked body as she curled against his own.

Her hand fluttered down from his chest, along his abdomen and between his thighs. Sam closed his eyes as she wrapped her palm around him, her thumb caressing his tip as he hardened in her grasp.

Letting the excitement wash over him, Sam reached for Cesca, drawing her to him so he could kiss her hard. The worries of a few moments before washed out of his mind on a tide of lust, replaced by a need that pulsed through his body.

He wanted her. Now. Everything else could wait.

25

And summer's lease hath all too short a date

– Sonnet XVIII

Cesca stopped typing, sat back and stared at the screen. A shiver snaked its way down her spine, lingering at the base, making her shift in her chair.

The End.

She'd done it. OK, so it was only a first draft, and more than anybody else she knew it needed a lot of work, even with Sam's editing. But to see those words written on the screen was almost impossible to take in. She'd never thought she'd type them again.

She blinked a couple of times, her eyes watering with emotion. She didn't like crying – she never had – and to do it over a play seemed stupid. And yet still they formed, little droplets pooling at the rim of her eyes, threatening to spill over any moment.

'Are you OK?' Sam asked, alerted no doubt by the silence from her lack of typing. 'Shall we take a break?'

Shaking her head, Cesca swallowed the lump in her throat before answering him. 'I'm OK, I think. I just . . . ' She trailed off, needing to check the screen again, to persuade herself she'd really written those words. 'I just finished the first draft.'

His laughter sounded relieved. 'I thought something terrible had happened.' He squatted beside her, reading the words out loud. '*The End*. That's fantastic.'

'Thank you.'

'So did the main couple get together?'

Cesca tipped her head to the side. 'Wouldn't you like to know?'

'Yes I would, and I'm going to find out. And if you ended up tearing them apart just for the sake of dramatic impact, I may have to rewrite it for you.'

She grinned. 'You old romantic. Who would have thought the hard-nosed Hollywood actor wanted a happy-ever-after?'

'I've got a vested interest in this,' he reminded her.

'You have?' She was teasing him, her eyes dancing as her gaze caught his.

'Yeah. We've been working on this story together. And that guy, he deserves to make the heroine happy. Not break her heart.' He eyed her carefully. 'If he did, I'd have to beat him up or something.'

'That's very gallant of you,' she murmured. 'Threatening to beat up a make-believe character. I should be swooning or something.'

Sam flexed his bicep muscles, a grin lingering at his mouth. 'I'll always fight off fictional characters for you, babe.'

'And there I was thinking you'd run for the hills.'

'Just because I did it once before, doesn't mean I'd abandon you again.'

'No?'

'No. I'm not an asshole. Not any more.'

She closed her eyes as his mouth moved from her hair to her neck, lips sliding across her skin. Goose pimples broke out as his hands brushed their way down her shoulders, caressing her arms before moving around to her chest.

'We're supposed to be working,' she murmured.

'You've finished,' Sam whispered into her neck. 'And I can't think of a better way to celebrate than this, can you?'

No, she really couldn't. Cesca closed her eyes as Sam slid his hands beneath her vest top. It had been like this for the past week, ever since she'd woken up in his arms the morning after they'd first made love. When they weren't talking, sharing stories, their hands were all over each other. It was as though they could never get enough, but they were going to try anyway.

It was like being in a perpetual state of bliss. Light-bulb moments when you discovered something new, followed by the bonding that only mutual understanding could bring. They had so much in common, both being brought up in the theatre, and nearly everybody that one of them mentioned had connections with the other.

In the past week they'd had long days, talking about plays and exchanging stories, as Cesca worked at the computer. And at night they'd eaten well, then curled up together, sharing hopes and dreams before they shared their naked bodies. With each day that passed, she found herself falling a little further, letting Sam catch her in his willing arms.

And she was falling, that was for certain.

In the end, it was her body that made the decision. She turned in her chair, letting him take her into his embrace. His lips sought hers out immediately, kissing, touching, tasting. They couldn't get enough of each other, their bodies saying what their words couldn't. Cesca abandoned herself to the need, just like she did in the bedroom, the shower, the living room, at the beach ... anywhere he touched her, her body would start to sing.

'Tell me they have a happily-ever-after,' Sam whispered into her lips. He pushed the straps of her top down her shoulders, revealing her tanned skin. 'Or I'll have to rewrite it.'

She laughed again. 'OK, they got a happily-ever-after. Are you happy now?'

He moved his lips down, kissing the swell of her breasts. 'Fucking ecstatic.'

Later, after their lovemaking turned into a nap, Cesca found herself waking in Sam's bed, his arms wrapped around her in a muscle-bound clinch. The room smelled of sex and Sam, a combination that made her feel warm and turned-on at the same time. For once, he was fast asleep, his mouth open as he snored quietly. Another thing she'd discovered about him; he was a terrible sleeper.

There was a breeze coming up from the lake. It lifted the white gauze curtains covering the windows in Sam's room, making them dance in its wake. Along with the air it brought the sounds of the lake, of the water lapping the shore, and the distant calls of people on boats. She sighed in contentment, turning in Sam's arms to get comfortable. Another hour of sleeping, and then they would get up, and either lie in the sun or swim in the lake.

She'd almost fallen back to sleep when the noise woke her up. The sound of an approaching engine, and the crackle of tyres on gravel. Then there was the banging of car doors, and a low hum of conversation replaced the engine. Cesca's eyes flew open in alarm.

'Sam?' She turned, shaking his shoulders to wake him up. 'Sam, Gabi and Sandro are here.'

Lazily, he cracked open an eye. 'They're a day early. They're not supposed to be here until tomorrow.'

'Exactly.' She escaped his hold, sitting up in his bed. The thin sheet fell from her, revealing her naked chest. 'And they're about to walk into the house. We need to get dressed.'

He was so much calmer than she was. 'Relax, they're used to us taking naps. We can go down and say hi in a minute.'

'But they're not used to us taking naps in the nude, Sam. And the last thing either of us want is to be found in bed together.'

'Baby, calm down. Gabi and Sandro are loyal, they're not going to say anything. And anyway, they're not going to walk into my room, are they?' He pulled her back into his arms.

'Hello?' A voice called up from the hall. Female and Italian. 'Is anybody here?'

Sam sat up immediately, horror etched across his face. 'Fuck. That's my mom. What the hell's she doing here? Jesus, we need to get up.' He scrambled out of bed, searching for his clothes. 'We need to get dressed, right now.'

Cesca laughed nervously. She could almost feel him withdrawing from her, as he pulled on his trousers. 'What happened to being calm?'

He turned to look at her, frowning. 'This isn't funny.'

It felt like a slap. She wanted to recoil from the shock of it. 'I'm sorry . . . ' The humour drained out of her face as she looked around for her clothes, locating them strewn across his bedroom floor.

'Miss Shakespeare? Are you around here?' A male voice. Distinctly American. Just the sound of it turned Sam's face

264

pale. And it was close, nearer the door than before, definitely not in the hall where his mom's voice was coming from.

'What do I do?' Cesca asked Sam, the panic rising inside her. 'Should I tell him I'm here?'

He shook his head furiously. 'Get in the bathroom.' He practically shoved her towards the en suite. 'I'll distract them, take them outside. When it's clear you can come down. Tell them you were listening to music while cleaning or something.'

With only a few words he dismissed her as anything except a servant. She walked into the bathroom, pulling the door closed behind her, trying to catch her breath. An indignant anger suffused her body at his dismissal, and at the way the intimacy between them had disappeared without even a kind word. But then she really was the hired help, and in Sam's parents' eyes she'd like to keep it that way. At least until they could work out what the hell was going on.

Shit shit shit.

Sam tugged at his hair as he looked at himself in the bedroom mirror. He could hear his stepfather pacing up the corridor, his size twelve feet stomping on the wood. A sense of unease passed over him, his stomach twisting as the echo got closer.

'You can do this,' he told himself. He was an actor, after all. He could plaster on a smile and pretend everything was OK. He ran a hand through his hair, vainly attempting to tame it, not wanting to give Foster yet more ammunition to use against him. Hair like his father's, or so Foster had said. Sam was a walking, talking symbol of everything his stepfather hated.

Taking a deep breath that did nothing to calm him, he pulled the bedroom door open and walked out.

'Hey.' He practically barrelled into Foster, who was standing on the landing. 'I didn't know you were coming.'

Foster frowned. 'So you *are* here. When I spoke to Gabi this morning, she told me you'd turned up. You could have asked, Sam, or given us some notice.'

'It's good to see you, too.' Sam tried to walk past his stepfather, aware that Cesca was still in his bedroom. It made him sick to the stomach to think of Foster discovering her in there. But his stepfather didn't move, and his tank-like body blocked the way.

'You've got a lot to answer for,' Foster hissed. 'Your mother's been in a complete state. And your sisters have been in tears. You just disappeared without a word.'

Sam's hackles rose. He'd barely been talking to his stepfather for a minute, and he already wanted to hit him. 'I needed a break.'

'So you came here, to your mother's home? What if the paparazzi find you? You know how much your mom values our privacy here. It's the same as always, you fuck things up and then you come and expect us to clear them up for you. You're twenty-seven years old, Sam. When are you going to grow up?'

His stepfather was poison. Sam could feel the little kid he used to be wanting to cower away. But he wasn't a little kid any more. He was a man, and he needed to act like one.

'It's private and remote. The paps aren't going to find me here, and even if they did, what could they do?' he asked. 'I've kept a low profile, I'm not exactly flaunting myself here.'

'There's a first time for everything.'

'What's that supposed to mean?'

Foster looked shocked at Sam's response. And maybe he

should. It was the only time in years that he'd stood up to him, and had looked him in the eye man to man.

'It means you have no fucking sense at all. What were you doing running around with a married woman anyway? I told your mother, you have the morals of a fucking alley cat. The apple never falls far from the tree, Mr fucking Jackhammer.'

'I'm my mother's son, too,' Sam said. 'And I think she brought me up pretty well.' No mention of Foster's influence. He didn't deserve it.

'Of course you are, darling.' His mother's voice made them both jump. They'd been so intent on each other, squaring up like fighting dogs, that they hadn't heard her approach. 'And I'm very angry with you, why didn't you return my calls?' She took Sam's cheeks in her hands, kissing him on both sides. 'I've been worried sick about you.'

Sam shrugged. As always his mother's intervention calmed the waters. 'You're the one who insisted on cutting this place off,' he reminded her. 'No Wi-Fi, no phones, remember?'

Lucia pouted. Her face held few signs of her age. 'You could have sent word. Or gone into town to call me.'

He grimaced. 'I'm trying to keep a low profile.'

'Oh, Samuel, you'll never make a spy.' She laughed, hugging him again. 'We spoke to Gabi and she told us exactly where you were. She was so worried that she couldn't be here to look after you, and that she'd left ... oh, what's her name ... to do all the work.'

'Cesca,' Sam said quietly. 'Her name is Cesca.'

Lucia hooked her arm through her son's, leading him towards the stairs. 'That's right, Cesca. It's a lovely name. How has she been getting on? Has she looked after you?'

Lucia kept up a steady stream of questions as she led him

downstairs, asking him about his time in Italy and the movies he had planned when he returned to LA. Finally, when they made it into the kitchen, with Foster trailing behind, she paused long enough for him to answer.

'So who is this girl, anyway?'

Sam's stomach dropped. 'What girl?'

'The one in the papers. Serena Sloane. Is it serious between you?'

'No, not at all. It's all been exaggerated. I didn't even know she was still married.' He searched for a way to change the subject.

'It wouldn't have been difficult to find out,' Foster interjected.

'Yeah, well. I didn't.' Sam looked down. 'I'm not that kind of guy, you know, I wouldn't steal somebody's wife.'

'Of course you aren't,' Lucia said, squeezing his arm. 'Foster, stop making him feel bad.'

Her husband raised an eyebrow but said nothing – he saved the worst of his insults for when it was just him and Sam. He'd done it for years.

'Anyway, she's obviously fame hungry,' Lucia added. 'Horrible woman, using you to get some notoriety. You need to be more careful about the people you hang around with, Sam. You know not everybody has your best interests at heart.'

She didn't know the half of it. 'I know that. And yeah, some people haven't proved to be the friends I thought they were. I've fired my agent.'

'You have?'

'Turns out he represented Serena, too. I've left it in my lawyer's hands.'

268

'Oh, darling, that's awful.'

'You need to get some better business judgement,' Foster remarked. 'You always trust the wrong people, Sam. I could put you in touch with a good agent.'

'Of course your father could help,' Lucia said, always trying to be the bridge between them. 'Why don't you let him make a few calls?'

'He can't do anything while he's here, not without a phone signal,' Sam pointed out. There was no way he was going to let Foster have anything to do with his career, but, as always, he wanted to protect his mom.

'When we get back to Paris, then,' Lucia said, smiling at him. 'It would be lovely to see you working more closely. I keep telling Foster how wonderful it would be if you were in a play he produced. I'd love to have my two men in the same city for once.'

Sam caught Foster's gaze for a brief moment. His stepfather looked as excited by that prospect as Sam felt.

'When are you going back to Paris, anyway?' Sam asked. 'I thought you were going to be there all summer.'

'In a few days, maybe a week,' his mother said. 'We all needed a break. As wonderful as Paris is, in the middle of the summer it can be stifling. All those people . . . ' She grimaced.

'A week?' Sam couldn't help but raise his eyebrows. A whole goddamned week? It was bad enough when they thought Gabi and Sandro were coming back, knowing he and Cesca were going to have to cool things down, at least in front of them. But now his mom and Foster were here, that put everything up in the air. He couldn't even begin to think about the fallout.

'And the girls?'

269

'They ran straight down to the lake, of course.' Foster smiled indulgently. 'They didn't know you were here.'

'All my family together at last, it's like a dream come true,' Lucia said, hugging him yet again. 'We're going to have a wonderful time.'

Holding his mother in his arms, Sam closed his eyes, wishing he could agree with her. From where he was standing, the dream was turning into a nightmare.

'We'd like dinner at seven, on the terrace. Foster is wheat intolerant, so Gabi usually does risotto,' Lucia said. 'And Izzy has decided to become a pescatarian, so something with fish would be lovely.'

Cesca nodded, trying to keep busy so she didn't have to look at Lucia for too long. Every time she did, a sense of shame washed over her. The woman had been paying her to do practically nothing, apart from writing her play and sleeping with her son. That knowledge made Cesca blush.

'Of course. I'll go into town to stock up. Let me know if there's anything else you need. I'm so sorry everything wasn't ready for you. It was inexcusable.'

Lucia laughed, and it sounded just like Sam. 'Not at all. You weren't to know we were coming. And if I'd thought about it we could have waited until tomorrow, when Gabi and Sandro come back. But I was so desperate to get out of Paris, we just upped and left this morning. The heat in the city was so oppressive, I longed for the lake.'

Cesca smiled, placing glasses on the silver tray she'd found in the cupboard. 'If you'd like to go back outside I'll bring your drinks out. Your rooms are made up now, too, if any of you would like an afternoon nap.'

'A *riposo*,' Lucia said. 'We used to have those when I was a little girl. Foster doesn't like napping, though. He says it wastes the day.'

Even the mention of Foster's name was enough to rile Cesca. She'd heard his exchange with Sam while she was hiding in the bedroom, and she'd wanted to run outside, to tell him what she thought of a man who enjoyed hurting his son. But deep down she knew she'd only make things worse for Sam. If they could get any worse.

When she took the tray of drinks out to the terrace, the whole family was there. Sam, his mother, the older, silver-haired man she recognised to be Foster, and two teenage girls who were lying on loungers, letting the afternoon sun warm their bodies.

'Let me help you with that.' Sam jumped up to take the tray from her. His hands covered hers, and for a moment everything felt right. Until she looked into his eyes, and couldn't see anything at all. Just a blankness that made her stomach contract.

'Thank you,' she murmured, letting Sam hold the tray while she handed the drinks out. When there was only one glass left, they attempted to swap, Cesca taking the tray while Sam took the glass.

'Actually, I think I'll have a beer,' Sam said. 'I'll run in with you and get one.'

'I can bring you one out.'

'It's fine, I could do with some cooler air, anyway.'

'Stay here, Sam,' his youngest sister called out. Cesca tried to remember her name from their conversations, but couldn't recall if she was Izzy or Sienna. 'I want you to tell me about your new movie.'

271

'Yes, stay. Cesca can bring you a beer out, can't you, Cesca?'

'Of course I can.' Her smile was tight. She didn't know why she was feeling so put upon. She'd had enough waiting jobs, she knew the score. Waitresses were meant to be seen and not heard, silent bringers of food and drink who then disappeared into the background. But in the weeks she'd been here, she'd shrugged off that persona. Let go of the Cesca she'd been, the one who was talked down to by patrons and managers alike. She'd come to see this beautiful villa in Varenna as a haven, a home, not a place of work.

That had been her first mistake. A big one, too. She should have known better than that.

She carried the empty tray back into the kitchen, wiping it clean before storing it away. Then she pulled the refrigerator open, reaching inside for a bottle of beer. The glass was cold and damp, rivulets wetting her hand.

'You don't need to ignore me, you know.'

Cesca whipped around to see Sam standing behind her. 'I wasn't ignoring you. I was doing my job.'

He blinked a couple of times, looking confused. 'Are you angry at me?'

'No.' She leaned back against the worktop, still holding the bottle. 'I'm angry at myself more than anything. I got too comfortable, I'd forgotten why I was here. It feels as though everything I've done has been so disrespectful to your parents. They're paying me, after all.'

'Disrespectful?' Sam frowned. 'How have you been disrespectful?'

She looked around him, to confirm they were alone. 'Sam, you know how. I was lying in bed with you when they arrived. That's not exactly star employee material, is it?'

272

His face relaxed as he laughed. 'Did you want to be a star employee?'

Cesca sighed. 'They were good enough to give me a job when I needed one. If they find out about us it's going to look terrible.'

He took a step towards her, reaching out to grab her by the arms. 'There's nothing terrible about us.' The next moment she was in his arms. She stiffened for a moment, still afraid of being discovered, but then her emotions got the better of her. She melted into him.

'I just want to go home,' she whispered. 'I feel really out of place here.'

'Hey.' He brushed his lips against hers. 'What happened to that girl who was celebrating finishing her play? You don't need to feel out of place. You're as good as any of them out there. Better. And I hate seeing you serving us all like some fucking maid.'

'I hate it, too,' she confessed.

'The sooner Sandro and Gabi get here the better,' Sam said.

Cesca looked up at him. 'But I'll be leaving after that. And I won't see you again.'

'Of course you'll see me. I'll fly over, you can fly to see me. This doesn't mean it's the end of us.'

His words made her heart feel light, as though a burst of helium had been let loose in her chest. 'It doesn't?'

'Do you want it to be over?' For the first time, he faltered.

'I want—'

The sound of the glass door sliding open silenced her. Sam jumped back, releasing her arms, and she busied herself at the refrigerator, pulling ingredients out to check their sell-by dates.

'Sam, I thought you were coming straight back out.'

'Hey, Izz, I was. I just needed to talk to Cesca about something.'

His sister turned to look at her. 'What about?'

Cesca cleared her throat. 'He was telling me you're a pescatarian.'

'Did Mom tell you?' Izzy asked her brother. She flipped her dark, curly hair over her shoulder. She was the older sister – Cesca remembered that now – and at eighteen she was a real beauty. Looking at her, Cesca could imagine Lucia at the same age. A peach ripe for the picking, ready to be used by Sam's father. Then discarded when things got tough.

Sam glanced at Cesca. 'Yeah, she did. How long's that been going on?'

Izzy screwed up her nose. 'For the first two weeks we were in Paris, Dad took us out for a steak every night. I got sick of the things, so told them I wanted to be a vegetarian. Mom said I couldn't so eventually we compromised.'

She could see Sam trying to stifle a grin. 'So fish don't count?'

Izzy looked guilty. 'Of course they count, but I only eat responsibly farmed fish. I'm doing my bit, Sam.'

'I'll make sure you get some for dinner tonight,' Cesca interjected.

Izzy shot her a grateful look. 'Thank you.' Then, grabbing Sam by the arm, she pulled him away, telling him to come back outside. This time, Sam let himself be pulled, only pausing one moment to glance back at Cesca.

'Later,' he mouthed.

She wasn't sure if that was a threat or a promise.

26

Love is blind, and lovers cannot see,
The pretty follies that themselves commit
— The Merchant of Venice

'Cesca?' Sam opened the door to her bedroom, tiptoeing in. 'You awake?'

She sat up, rubbing at her eyes with tight fists. 'I am now. What time is it?' She leaned across and flicked on her bedside lamp. The glow illuminated her face, casting a soft yellow across her skin.

'It's about two,' Sam whispered, sitting down on the edge of her mattress. 'Sorry I didn't come earlier. Foster's only just gone to sleep. Oh, and here.' He put a rectangular metal stick on her desk.

'A memory stick?'

'I remembered your play was still on Foster's computer. I downloaded it for you, didn't want him to delete it or something.'

Cesca was touched. She picked up the memory stick, tracing the words on it with her fingers. 'Thank you.'

'It's nothing.'

'It's something.' She felt a lump in her throat. 'Even I'd forgotten about that play. I hadn't thought of it all day. Well, not since everybody arrived.'

'You haven't had a chance.' Sam looked thoughtful again. 'You've been running around like crazy. I never realised how demanding my family was until I put myself in your shoes.'

'It was fine. To be honest, it was nice to keep busy, not to have to think about things for too long.'

'Not to think about me, you mean?'

There was a strange expression on his face. A mixture of wistfulness and regret. She reached out to cup his jaw. 'Don't be silly, of course I wanted to think about you.'

'You did?'

She clambered onto her knees, crawling close enough to him to press her lips to his. 'I missed this.'

He cupped the back of her head with his hand, deepening the kiss, and she felt herself relax in his embrace. All day she'd been on high alert, overthinking everything she did. Unsure if she was simply looking after the family, or trying to win some kind of approval from them.

Sam slung his arm around her, laying her back down on the bed. He propped himself above her, arms caging her in on either side. 'My family have the worst fucking sense of timing.'

Her smile was weak. 'Story of my life.' The last time Foster interfered, Sam had disappeared to America. That sense of foreboding returned again. 'I should leave, Sam. This isn't right.'

He frowned. 'What isn't right?'

'You and me. Here. All the stuff that's been happening between us.'

'What if it's the only thing that's right?' he asked. 'What if it's the only thing that I can think about, day or night?'

Her mouth was dry. 'What if it was?'

'Then I'd be pretty fucking annoyed that you don't think it's right.'

'Sam . . . ' She screwed her face up, trying to find the right words. It should be easy for a writer, shouldn't it? But every time she tried to put her feelings into sentences, it was as though she got writer's block. In the end, she had to settle for honesty. 'What if it's the right thing, but the wrong timing?' she asked him. 'Because everything feels so out of time right now.'

'What are you saying?' He rolled to the side, his expression closing up.

'I don't know. It's just that it was all so good, then as soon as your family arrived I felt so bad. Now all I want to do is get out of here.'

'You want to leave?' he whispered.

'I don't even know what I'd be leaving,' she told him.

'Me. You'd be leaving me.'

She tried to swallow the emotion down. Sam's expression wasn't helping. He looked bereft. 'I don't want to leave you,' she said.

'Then don't.'

'But I can't stay anyway. Gabi and Sandro arrive back in the morning. I'll be surplus to requirements.'

'Then stay as my guest.'

'As your guest?' She wasn't sure what shocked her most: his offer, or her visceral response to it. Being described as his guest felt like a kick in the gut. 'Is that what I am, *your guest*?'

He looked confused at her vehemence. 'Of course you're

not just my guest. But you're the one who wants to hide everything from my parents. You're the one who wants to pretend to be a servant and look after us without even looking me in the eye.'

'So if I told you I wanted you to come clean to them you would?'

He looked almost panicked. 'I don't know ... I ... God, Cesca. Everything was so easy, so uncomplicated, you know. It's not a good time right now. Foster and I ... well, our relationship's complicated. I don't want to make it any worse.'

'I know.' She felt her heart breaking, piece by tiny piece. 'And I can understand if you don't want to introduce me as your ... whatever it is we are. But I can't just stay here and pretend to be something I'm not, either.'

'I'm not asking you to do that.'

'Yes you are,' she pointed out. 'You're asking me to pretend to be a friend, or an acquaintance or something.'

'You want me to tell them we're lovers?'

She shook her head. 'I don't want you to tell them anything at all.' Tears pricked at her eyes. 'I just want to go home.'

'But you don't have a home.'

'Thanks for reminding me.'

'Cesca, I don't know what you want me to say or do. I'm trying to find a solution here, but you keep knocking me down. What is it you want from me?'

His question stunned her. In the embarrassment of the day, all she could think about was wanting things to go back to the way they were. When she and Sam spent their days writing and editing, and their nights tangled between the sheets. But that option was void, and accepting that the best had already been and gone was heartbreaking.

Was there anything else she wanted? Cesca wasn't sure. All she did know was that the pain in her chest was unbearable. As though she was losing something she wasn't even aware she had.

'I don't know what I want,' she said. 'It's so late, and I'm tired, and it will be another day tomorrow. We should both get some sleep.' Alone. She didn't say the final word, yet it rang out anyway in the half-light of her bedroom.

'You want me to leave?' There was that closed expression again on his face. She was getting used to that.

She nodded. 'It would be awful if someone found you here.'

'Fine.' He stood up, running a hand through his messy hair. 'I'll see you tomorrow.' He didn't bother to kiss her before he left. She didn't bother to ask him to. Instead she switched off the lamp and stared out into the darkness.

'Are you OK? We can take a rest if you need one,' Gabi suggested, giving Cesca a brief smile. Since Gabi and Sandro had arrived mid-morning, they'd spent the hours deep-cleaning the kitchen and dining room, and they were both flagging in the heat. Sandro was outside, working with the gardeners. Every now and then he'd put his head around the back door, and Gabi would pass him a glass of iced water, which he'd swallow down in seconds before he disappeared again.

'I'm fine, it's you I'm worried about. You shouldn't have to work so hard after travelling all day. I could have done this while you recovered.'

'Not at all, we've had weeks of relaxation. And you've done a great job of keeping everything going on your own. I feel like I'm taking advantage of you, but this takes half as long with two of us doing it, so while you're here . . .'

'It's not a problem,' Cesca told her. And really, it wasn't. She was happy hiding away in here, scrubbing at the tiles. For one it kept her mind occupied, especially as Gabi was talking enough for both of them. It also kept her away from Sam's family.

And from Sam.

'I'll be out of your hair soon enough,' Cesca told her. 'I was planning to walk into town tomorrow to organise my flight home. I can't imagine Mrs Carlton wants to pay two lots of wages for us.'

Gabi's face fell. 'Oh no, you shouldn't leave so soon. Please stay. There's so much we can use you to do, all the things that are too much for me, especially when Sandro is so busy with the garden work.'

'I need to get home. I was only ever meant to be here while you were away. Anyway, I'm pretty sure you can employ some women from the village to help you.'

'It's not the same.' Gabi pouted. 'And I want to hear all about your stay. Did you get a chance to explore Varenna, did you make any friends? You need to be here for long enough so I can get all the gossip from you.'

Cesca laughed lightly, hoping Gabi couldn't see through her nonchalance. 'What gossip? It's been very quiet here.'

'What about Sam?' Gabi lowered her voice. 'Did you read what the papers said about him? Do you believe that he did all those things with that woman?'

Cesca stopped scrubbing. She could feel her pulse start to speed. 'What woman?'

'The actress, that blonde one. Serena Sloane. She's very beautiful, but according to the papers also very married.'

Serena Sloane? Cesca had heard of her before. The gorgeous blonde actress was on another level altogether. She and Sam must have made a stunning couple.

The image in her brain made her feel sick.

'No, he didn't tell me about that.' She kept her voice as level as she could.

'I'm sure it's not true anyway,' Gabi said hastily, interpreting Cesca's quietness for a refusal to gossip. 'He's too nice a boy for that.'

'Yes, much too nice.' Cesca leaned forward and started scrubbing harder, until her fingers felt raw.

'You know, if you really do need to go home, can we at least agree that you stay until the weekend?' Gabi asked. 'Signor Carlton is having a small party, and I'll need your help to organise everything.'

'A party?' Cesca asked, weakly. 'Does Sam know about that? I thought he wanted to keep his whereabouts quiet.'

'Oh, there's always a party at this time of year. It's the festival, you see. Signora Carlton loves to entertain, and then take her guests down to the beach and watch the fireworks on the lake.'

'I see.' It sounded beautiful. A few days ago she would have been excited at the prospect. But now it felt as flat as everything else surrounding her.

'Please tell me you'll stay. Sandro can drive you to the airport the very next day, I promise. But it will be so useful to have your help, and I'd be so grateful for it.'

Gabi took Cesca's hand, squeezing it tightly, as her face lit up with expectation.

'I guess it might take that long to book the flight any way ...'

'Yes!!' Gabi gave her a hug. 'Thank you so much. You're a lifesaver, you really are. I'll let Signora Carlton know that you're going to help.'

Giving her a small smile, Cesca went back to her work, scrubbing the floor with a vengeance.

A few more days, and then she could fly home. She could make it that long, couldn't she?

'So what's your next project?' Foster's voice boomed across the table. They were all sitting around on the wooden deck overlooking the beach. As the family ate the feast Gabi had prepared for them, Sandro walked around topping up their wine glasses.

'The last *Summer Breeze* movie,' Sam replied. 'We start filming in October.'

'That's a strange time to film a summer movie,' Izzy said. 'Shouldn't you be doing it now?'

'It's pretty warm in LA in October,' Sam pointed out. 'And it's amazing what they can do with effects. The main challenge will be for me not to shiver every time I run out of the ocean. If I can do that, we should be good.'

Izzy and Sienna giggled, and he shot them a wink.

'I expect you'll be pleased those films are over,' Foster remarked. 'It wasn't your best idea, signing up for those. They're not exactly art, are they?'

Sam felt himself bristle. 'A lot of people enjoy them,' he replied. 'And who are we to say what art is, anyway?'

'I can tell you what it isn't,' Foster replied, with a laugh. 'It's not staring at some topless guy in the sea, which is all your fans want to do.'

Sam took another mouthful of risotto. It was tasteless

and gloopy now. For a moment he longed to be sitting in the kitchen, scooping up pasta as he talked with Cesca. Was it really only a couple of days since they did that?

'Stop it, Foster,' Lucia chided. 'Sam did wonderfully well to get that role. You know he hates it when you tease him.'

Sam stayed silent, not wanting to rob his mother of her innocence. If Foster only teased him, Sam could have quite happily taken it.

'What's on the plan after that?' Izzy asked.

'I'm not sure yet. I might leave Hollywood for a while. I'm getting sick of the circus there.'

Her face lit up. 'Maybe you could come home to London, we've missed you so much. You could stay with us for a while.'

There followed a moment of pleading from all the Carlton females. Sam shivered at the thought of moving back home. At least he had his independence – he could thank *Summer Breeze* for that.

'I don't know, Izz. I'll have to see what happens. It's always easier to be in America when there are auditions and stuff.' Plus it was thousands of miles from Foster. That was another bonus.

'We'll get him back somehow, won't we, Mama?' Izzy said. 'Even if we have to use our female persuasion.'

'Of course we will, darling,' Lucia replied. 'He's been away for far too long.'

Later that evening, after Foster had holed himself up in the library, and his sisters were watching a movie, Sam went looking for Cesca. He hadn't seen her all day, and had the distinct impression she was avoiding him after their discussion the previous night.

He found her in her bedroom. She was wearing sleep

shorts and a vest top, her hair tied up into a high ponytail. She was writing, a notepad propped up on her knees, her face screwed up in concentration. Her absorption stopped her from noticing him at first, allowing Sam a minute of observation that somehow soothed his soul. In here, without the presence of his family or Gabi and Sandro, they could be just Sam and Cesca.

Why couldn't it always be like that?

'Hey.' In the end he broke the silence, unable to watch her any longer without seeing those pretty eyes. Cesca looked up, started, then slid the pencil behind her ear.

Christ, could she get any cuter?

'I didn't see you there.'

'Clearly.' Sam was amused by her deer-in-the-headlights expression. 'Are you hiding from me?'

'No.' Cesca, on the other hand, didn't seem amused. 'It's been a long day and I was ready for bed. I assumed you'd be busy with your family.'

There was a brittleness to her voice he didn't recognise. For a moment she seemed more like the Cesca who had screamed at him through the gate than the girl who had melted in his arms.

'I guess we were both a little busy today. I hated watching you serving them – serving us, I guess. It seemed wrong letting you clear the tables without eating with us.'

'That's what I'm paid for, Sam,' she reminded him. There was still no give in her expression.

'There isn't enough money in the world to put up with my stepfather.'

Cesca looked at him, her voice quiet when she spoke. 'He's poisonous.'

284

'Yes, he is.' Sam took a step closer, until he was standing over her bed. His fingers itched to touch her, to run a finger down her silky thigh. It felt wrong to be in here with her and not be holding her. 'But I don't want to talk about him.'

Her mouth twitched. 'What do you want to talk about?'

Sam sat down on the mattress, and Cesca moved away from him. For some reason that made him want to drag her across the bed. He wasn't going to let her draw away, not now.

'Us.'

For the first time she laughed. 'What "us", Sam? There is no us. There was just two lonely people who were looking for a bit of fun on holiday.'

His stomach contracted at her words. 'That's not true.'

'Oh come on,' she said. 'We both know I was just a distraction, after you split up with Serena Sloane. Or at least we do now,' she said, pointedly. 'It would have been nice if you'd have informed me before I opened my legs for you though.'

'How did you know about her?' His voice took on an icy tone.

'Were you trying to hide it?' she asked. 'Or maybe you couldn't care less that I knew. What am I, the next Mrs Jackhammer? Just another notch on your belt?' Not even a very pretty notch compared to the beautiful Serena.

'You were never just a notch on my belt.' His hands curled into fists.

'Of course I was. You don't just jump out of bed with one girl then into one with the next unless you're trying to get over her. And I understand, I do. You never offered me anything other than friendship, and I certainly never asked you where we stood. So let's just take it for what it was.'

Sam's jaw was tight. 'What was it then?'

'A friendship that went a bit too far. We're chalk and cheese. You're some massive Hollywood star and I'm a writer who can't even get a job. It would never work, and if I'm being honest I don't think we should try. Let's just leave it as it was, a wonderful holiday fling between friends.'

'You want to just be friends?' It felt as though every muscle in his body had turned to steel.

'I want us to stay friends,' she told him. 'And I don't think we'll do that if we keep doing this ... thing, or whatever you want to call it.'

'Making love?' he suggested.

'Sex, Sam. We had sex.'

'It was more than sex.'

'Oh, come on, we both know that's not true. You should at least, you've had enough of it, after all. Go ask Serena Sloane.'

'That's a bit fucking low. I'm a twenty-something single guy. What do you expect?' The corner of his mouth rose in a sneer. What the hell was wrong with her?

'Nothing,' she replied. 'I expect nothing at all. And that's what I usually get. You didn't promise me anything, and I didn't expect anything. Just some fun in the sun.'

'Fun in the sun ... ' Sam repeated.

'That's right.'

'That's all it was to you?'

'To us,' she said. 'We distracted each other. You took me away from my loneliness, and I took your mind off Serena Sloane.' Was it his imagination, or did Cesca spit out that name? 'And now it's time to leave and we can go home without any regrets. You to LA, and me to London.'

'Is that what you want?' He narrowed his eyes. Maybe he'd been wrong about her after all. Weren't all women the same?

'It's what you want, isn't it?' she asked him. 'You've made it perfectly clear you don't want to introduce me to your family.'

He shifted on her bed. 'That's not what I meant.'

'Then what did you mean?'

Sighing, he ran a hand through his wavy hair. 'I don't know ... it's not the right time. There's a lot going on in my life right now. You want me to explain exactly what we are to my parents, but I don't even know myself.' He frowned, staring at her. 'What do you want me to say?'

'How about Mom, Dad, this is my girlfriend?'

He blanched. 'Jesus, Cesca.'

Her eyes looked watery in the moonlight. 'It doesn't matter,' she said, biting her lip. 'You've made your position perfectly clear.'

'I have?'

'Yes. I'm perfectly good enough to lie in your bed every night, but not good enough to bring home to your mum. I guess we both know where we stand.'

A surge of anger washed through him. 'That's not fucking true and you know it. I like you, Cesca. And I thought you liked me. It's just ... complicated. You know that.'

'It's always going to be complicated,' she told him. 'This is meant to be the easy bit. Every time I try to get closer to you, you cut me off. You don't want anything more than a surface relationship.'

'So what do you want?' he asked.

She blinked a couple of times. Was that a tear in the corner of her eye? 'More. I want more.' She sounded almost torn by her admission.

'I can't give you more.'

'I know.'

287

He squeezed his eyes shut for a moment, seeing stars beneath his lids. 'You deserve more,' he told her. 'You deserve everything.'

'Don't go there, Sam,' she warned him. 'Don't say it's not me, it's you. Don't tell me you don't deserve me. Spare me all the crap, I've heard it before.'

He leaned closer, until their faces were almost touching. 'So that's it? I can't give you everything you want, so it's over?'

'It is. So I'd like you to leave now.'

'Leave where?'

'My bedroom. I'm tired and I need to sleep. We've got a party to get ready for.'

Ah, the party. Another wonderful Foster idea. Sam grimaced at the thought of being surrounded by his stepfather's friends, but he'd promised his mother he'd stay for it. The delighted expression on her face had been almost worth it.

'I guess I'll go then.' He was half expecting her to start laughing, to tell him it was a joke. And maybe if he had a little less pride, he would have begged her to let him stay. But after a day filled with emotions, followed by a night hearing exactly what his stepfather thought of him, Sam was exhausted. He was all out of energy.

'Good night.' He didn't wait for her to reply. Instead he simply walked out of her room, making sure the corridor was clear, and then tiptoed to his own room, collapsing on his bed.

Squeezing his eyes shut, he tried to ignore the incessant voice in his head, telling him he was fucking everything up all over again.

It had been a hell of a day.

*

'Good night, Sam.' She was aware she was talking to the darkness, and that he had long since gone out of earshot. It seemed important to say it anyway, if only to remind her own heart that he was gone.

Gone.

At least she'd done it on her terms this time. She hadn't woken up to find out that Sam had left for LA and turned her world upside down. After all the progress she'd made – on herself as well as her play – she couldn't let him sabotage it for her again.

Curling up on her bed, she pushed her notepad to the floor, hearing the thud as it dropped onto the wooden boards. She wrapped her arms around her legs, hugging them to her chest, trying to ignore the pain that was emanating from deep inside.

She'd done the right thing, she told herself again. And of course it was going to hurt. But she'd get through it, she always had. She was a survivor, wasn't she?

27

Doubt truth to be a liar,
but never doubt I love

– Hamlet

Cesca took one last look in the mirror before heading downstairs. Her hair was perfectly coiled into a French plait, her white shirt pristinely ironed. It was tucked into the tight black skirt that Gabi had loaned her. One size too small but what choice did she have? It stopped high above her knees, revealing her toned, tanned thighs.

'You'll have to do,' she whispered at her reflection. Just one more day, and she could leave this all behind. She was booked on an early flight to London the following morning, which meant she and Sandro would have to leave for the airport at the crack of dawn. But it was necessary – she clearly wasn't needed here any more, now that Sandro and Gabi had come back. There was no point in her staying for Sam, either.

As soon as she made her way downstairs, she was hit by the frantic commotion. The staff had spent most of the day preparing for this – after they'd risen at the ungodly hour of six to take delivery of the food and drink – but it didn't cease to amaze her how much work there was to do for one little party.

No, not even a party. Lucia was insisting on calling it a soirée. Not that Cesca understood the difference.

She found Gabi in the kitchen, talking rapidly to the chef and cooking staff who'd been brought in for the occasion. They'd already split the duties, agreeing that Gabi would supervise the kitchen, while Cesca and Sandro took control of the waiting staff. He would be in charge of the drinks, while Cesca would direct the food. With her experience in waitressing – as sketchy as it was – it seemed like the best idea.

'Everything on track?' Cesca was breathless with nervous anticipation. 'Do you need me to do anything?'

Gabi shook her head. 'It is, as you call it, the calm before the storm. The waiting staff are ready for you, as soon as the guests start to arrive.'

'OK then.' Cesca straightened her shoulders, rolling her neck from side to side to loosen the muscles. 'Good luck in the kitchen.'

'Ah, this is my happy place. More importantly, good luck to you out there.'

She'd probably need all the luck she could get. Cesca rounded up the waiting staff – comprised of local students looking for some extra cash – and tried to give them some orders using a mixture of English and pidgin Italian. Luckily one of the older boys took pity on her and started to translate, leading to the others nodding in agreement.

'Thank you,' Cesca whispered.

'You're very welcome.'

The next hour passed in a blur of final preparations, as

291

she sent the staff in and out of the kitchen with trays of food. They were dispersed throughout the public rooms of the villa, ready to provide canapés along with the glasses of Prosecco and Chianti being readied by Sandro's team. There was no sign of the family, thankfully, apart from a brief glimpse of Foster as he emerged from the library to grab a glass of red wine, but then he was gone again, ensconced in his office.

Just before eight, the guests started to arrive. Impossibly glamorous and expensively clothed, Cesca felt dull and dowdy in comparison to them. They didn't notice her, anyway, too intent on gossiping and drinking glasses of wine to see who was handing the food and the drink out. It was amazing how invisible you could be when dressed in black and white.

The chatter silenced for a moment, before the furious whispering began. The guests were all looking out on the terrace, pointing and nodding at each other. Cesca followed their gazes, already knowing what she was going to see. And there he was, in glorious, beautiful splendour. Not her Sam, though. No, this was definitely Hollywood Sam who was standing before them, drawing everybody's gaze in a way that was as natural as breathing.

She tried to see him as they would. As a famous actor, one whose presence commanded every stage, even the one on his family's terrace. He was almost too beautiful to look at, his face freshly shaved, revealing the strong jaw she liked to run her lips across. Then there was the hair, falling over his eyes, so he had to brush it away, as she had done so many times.

He was wearing a pair of grey suit trousers and a blue shirt, open at the collar to reveal a dusting of chest hair. The material was thin enough for her to make out the muscles beneath, and she could feel her hands twitch as she remembered what it felt like to touch him there.

'Shall we refill the trays?' one of the waiters asked, tearing her concentration from the scene on the terrace. Flustered, Cesca turned to him. 'Yes, please. Gabi should have some more antipasti in there for you.'

He must have heard her voice cutting through the living room, because the next moment Sam was turning to look at her. Cesca caught his gaze, standing glued to the spot, feeling goose pimples breaking out on her skin in spite of the evening warmth.

Her breath caught in her throat. She wasn't sure if she was imagining the longing she could see on his face. She was sure it was on hers anyway. The visceral need to touch him, to be held, to feel safe within the confines of his muscled arms.

Stop it, she told herself. Stop it right now. He's not yours.

Before she could turn around, Sam broke her gaze, laughing at something somebody had said. She watched as a woman leaned up to whisper in his ear. Cesca's stomach lurched like a drunk man when he laughed again. That flirtatious bastard. She was doing the right thing leaving tomorrow. There was no way she could take much more of that.

Tomorrow. She just needed to make it through until tomorrow. Then perhaps the mess in her head might somehow disappear.

By ten the party was in full swing. Cesca's staff had less to do, as Sandro's staff bore the brunt of the work, with the guests more interested in drinking wine than eating the delicacies Gabi had prepared. So she filled their trays with drinks, directing them through the crowds of people mingling on the terrace. The air was warm and fragrant out here, from the scented candles burning on every counter and table top. Cesca was just making her way back into the house, her tray empty of glasses, when she felt a hand encircle her wrist.

Her heart sped when she looked up to the see the owner of it. Then disappointment suffused her when she saw who it was. She quickly bit the feeling down, trying to hide it with a welcoming smile. 'Cristiano,' she said. 'I didn't realise you were back.'

'I'm only here for two nights,' he told her. 'I've come to sign the papers for that restaurant we visited. The Carltons were kind enough to invite me to their party.'

Cristiano looked at home among this crowd. As comfortable as she was awkward. What was it with Italian men, how were they able to own any room or terrace they walked into?

'Well it's lovely to see you. I'm afraid I'm working so I should go back in.'

His grip tightened. 'Please stay with me. I don't know anybody here. I was about to run down to the beach and climb over the fence to get back home.'

His wide-eyed expression made her laugh. 'Let's hope you have more luck than I did.' She blushed when she remembered falling over, when she drank too much wine with him by the lake.

Cristiano laughed. 'Oh I was very lucky that night. I got to spend time with a beautiful lady. Plus she was kind enough to flash me her knickers.'

Now her cheeks were burning. 'That was an accident.'

His laughter was louder than before. 'I know, that's why I enjoyed it so much.' He lowered his voice. 'I'm so sorry about the night at the restaurant. It was too good an opportunity to turn down. I promise I didn't take you there with ulterior motives. I really did want to take you on a date.'

She shook her head. 'It doesn't matter, really it doesn't. We had a nice time anyway.'

'Yes we did,' he said. 'But still, it was a terrible way to treat such a beautiful lady. I would like to make it up to you.'

'There's no need. And even if there was, you couldn't. I'm flying back to London tomorrow.'

His face fell. 'Such a shame. You'll always remember me as the Italian who ignored you on a date.'

'Of course I won't. I'll remember you as the kind person who took pity on a poor English girl and made her laugh. Plus you bought me lots of coffee in the piazza.'

She smiled at him, and he returned her grin. Cesca was starting to get that end-of-a-holiday feeling. The one where you felt sad to say goodbye to things, knowing you wouldn't be seeing them again.

With his lips still curled up, Cristiano reached out to stroke her cheek. 'You really are very lovely, *tesoro*. It's been a pleasure meeting you.'

He was going to kiss her. Cesca could see it in his eyes, as heavy lidded as they were. She opened her mouth to say something, but then his lips were soft and warm against hers.

'Can I have a word, please?' Someone grabbed her by the shoulder, pulling her away from Cristiano's grasp. Shocked, Cesca turned to Sam, surprised by the look of anger on his face.

'Sam. It's a pleasure to see you again,' Cristiano said.

Sam completely ignored him, pulling Cesca through the crowd. As they made it to the corner of the house, the fireworks began to explode over the lake, turning the sky a myriad of colours. Cesca tried to shout at him, to tell him he was hurting her, to ask him where they were going. But it wasn't until they'd made it past the secluded garden beyond Foster's wine cave that he even slowed down.

'Sam, what is it?'

He stood for a moment to catch his breath. She watched him close his eyes, squeezing the muscles as though he was trying to get control of himself. 'You were kissing another guy.'

'I wasn't.'

'In front of me. You were flirting and laughing and kissing him, and I wanted to knock his fucking teeth out.'

'It's none of your business.'

He threw his hands up. 'Of course it's my goddamned business. You're mine, Cesca.'

She shook her head violently. 'No I'm not.'

'Are you his then?' Sam's voice was incredulous. 'You want to be with that asshole?'

There was something about his jealousy that made her feel afraid and turned on in equal measure.

'No, I'm not his and I'm not yours. I'm mine, Sam, mine. Nobody owns me.'

'I can see that.'

Cesca frowned. 'What's that supposed to mean?' The fireworks overhead were turning Sam's face from vermilion to a golden colour.

'I've been watching you all night.'

The way he said it sent a shiver down her spine. 'That must have been very boring for you.'

It was his turn to shake his head. 'It was fascinating. And enraging. Do you know how many men were checking out your legs? I had to watch them leering every time you walked past. I wanted to kill every last one of them.'

'Sam.' Her voice was gentler, more cajoling. 'I can't stop people from doing whatever they want to.'

'That fucking skirt though ...'

'It isn't even mine,' she protested. 'I had to borrow it from Gabi. I didn't bring any waitressing clothes out with me.'

He tugged his hair impatiently out of his eyes. 'I can't stand looking at you and not being able to touch you. I can't stand hearing your voice and knowing you're not talking to me. I can't stand seeing you laugh and know that it isn't me who made you happy. I can't fucking stand any of it, Cesca.' His voice lowered to a whisper. 'It's killing me.'

'I'm leaving tomorrow,' she told him. 'Then you won't have to see me at all.' It was obvious he didn't like her the way she liked him. Why would he? He was so far out of her league it wasn't funny. No, it wasn't funny at all. It was heartbreaking.

'You're not leaving.'

'Yes I am.'

He reached out and tucked a strand of hair behind her ear. The shock of his touch made her jump. But he didn't let go. Instead he moved his fingers down her cheek, along her jaw-bone, drawing a line of heat hotter than any of the fireworks exploding above them.

He leaned down, pressing his lips where his fingers were only moments ago. 'Tell me this doesn't feel right, Cesca. Tell me this doesn't feel good.'

She opened her mouth but nothing came out. It couldn't, because to deny his words would have been a lie. Instead she

297

let him kiss her throat, his hands brushing up and down her sides, until he moved his lips up, sliding them back towards her mouth.

Then she was kissing him back, her lips greedy and demanding. He circled his hands around her waist, pulling her closer, and it felt so right she thought she might explode.

'Cesca,' he murmured against her mouth. 'Tell me you want me.'

He slid his hand beneath her blouse, trailing his fingers up her spine.

'Of course I want you,' she sighed.

'Then why are you fighting me? Babe, something that feels this right can't be wrong, can it?' He was kissing her again, deeply, passionately. She closed her eyes, the explosions in the sky turning her lids different colours. Every part of her wanted to hold him, to be held. It was the first time in days she'd felt happiness.

'Sam!' A female voice called from around the corner. 'Sam, we need you.'

He took a step back from Cesca. 'That's Izz,' he told her, his expression turning to confusion. 'What the hell?'

Then his sister was running around the corner, her blonde hair swinging out behind her. 'Sam, Mum needs you. Dad's fallen on the beach and she can't pick him up.'

Sam looked alarmed. 'Is he OK? Is it his heart?'

Izzy shook her head, still looking frantic. 'No, he's drunk too much. But he's being really horrible and she doesn't want people to see him like that. She wants you to help him up to the house.'

Cesca watched as Sam listened to his sister's words, his expression morphing into anger. 'He's drunk?'

'Like a bloody newt. Seriously, the things he's saying, I'm surprised Mum hasn't slapped him.'

'Like what?'

Izzy's voice dropped. 'Things about you. He's such an arsehole, Sam. Honestly, anybody would think he hates his own son.'

'Ah, fuck . . .' Sam turned to look at Cesca, who by now had straightened her skirt and sorted her hair out. 'I need to go, OK?'

Cesca nodded.

Sam glanced at his sister, as if he was worried about revealing anything in front of her.

'Can we talk about this later?'

She nodded again. 'Of course. But you should go and help your dad. It sounds as though your mum needs you.'

'She does,' Izzy agreed, shooting Cesca a curious look. 'Come on, Sam.'

With that, the two of them left, heading for the beach at the side of the lake. Cesca waited until they disappeared around the corner of the house before she stepped out of the shadows. Her entire encounter with Sam couldn't have lasted for more than a few minutes, yet it seemed like hours had passed since she'd last held a tray in her hands.

It was time to get back to work. To pretend nothing had just happened.

Waiting and waitressing. They were the stories of her life.

28

It is a wise father that knows his own child

– The Merchant of Venice

The party was still thronging as Sam circled his way around the guests, heading down to the lakeside beach. Izzy held his hand, her face anxious as they neared the steps that led down to the sand. 'He's over there.'

'Who else is here? Have any of the guests seen him like this?'

'Just Mum and Sienna. Sandro and the waiters managed to lure the rest of the guests up to the villa once the fireworks ended. It's amazing what people will do for a glass of champagne.' Izzy's words were much too world-weary for a girl of eighteen.

As soon as they were on the sand, Lucia looked over at them, her face ashen in the glow of the moon. 'Over here,' she said, pointing at a dark shadow. 'We've managed to get him out of sight.'

'Is he unconscious?' Sam asked. He hated seeing his mother looking so lost.

'Not quite. He's still saying the occasional word. Talking

about . . . things,' she replied. 'I don't know what to do, Sam, how to get him up to the house without everybody seeing him. It's such a mess.'

The way she looked at him, as if he could solve everything, made Sam feel helpless. He might have been strong, with gym-honed muscles, but he had no chance in hell of carrying Foster's three hundred pound frame.

'Who's that?' Foster's voice was little more than a slur. Whisky thickened his vowels and hacked at his consonants.

'It's Sam.' Lucia knelt next to her husband. 'He's come to help you.'

Foster struggled on the shale, attempting to sit up. There was a thud as his body hit the ground again, followed by a curse. 'What the hell's he doing here?'

Sam could make out his stepfather's question even though the words ran into each other like bumper cars at the funfair. He didn't feel the usual lurch of rejection, though. Instead he could taste the disgust in his mouth.

'He's come to help you, Foster,' Lucia said, still crouched next to him. 'We need to get you back to the house. There are guests here, we don't want them to see you.'

'Don't fuckin' need his help. He's no good anyway.'

'Why are you being so horrible?' Izzy asked, blinking hard as if to hold back the tears. 'You're always nasty to him.'

It hadn't escaped her notice, then. Sam hesitated for a moment, before turning to her. 'You need to get Sienna and go back up to the villa. Keep the guests busy, we don't want them coming back down here.'

There was no way Sam wanted his sisters hearing Foster's drunken rants. Especially as he was skirting so close to telling them things they didn't need to know.

'I don't want to leave you here,' Izzy whispered. Her protectiveness made him melt. How a hundred and twenty pound girl thought she could look after him, he had no idea.

But then his mind turned back to another day on this beach, with Foster showing them his dark side. That day he'd held Sam's head under the surface until he was practically drowning. His sisters – young as they had been – had run out to help him. Christ, even the memory brought tears to his eyes. The bastard had been drunk as a skunk that day, too.

'You'll be helping us if you go up there,' Sam said. 'Let me and Mom take care of him, and we'll talk later, OK? Can you do that for me?'

Silently, Izzy nodded. Tears were pouring down her cheeks. She gestured at Sienna, who was sitting on the deck, her knees tucked under her chin. 'Come on, Sienna, let's go.'

'Oh no, don't leave, let's all be one happy family. Right, Sam?'

'Foster, be quiet.' For the first time there was a hint of anger in Lucia's voice.

'But, baby, that's what we are. Me, you, the girls, and that little ... bastard.'

'Foster!' She clapped a hand over her mouth. 'Stop it please.'

'Izz, go now,' Sam whispered urgently. 'Please get Sienna out of here.'

'You don't have to listen to him, he's not really your brother.'

For a minute everybody went quiet on the beach. All they could hear was the gentle sounds of the party carrying on the breeze. The soft murmur of conversation, the occasional tinkle of laughter, juxtaposed against the lapping of the lake waters against the shore.

'What does he mean?' Izzy asked.

A wave of nausea squeezed at Sam's stomach, bile scratching against his throat. 'Nothing,' Sam said. 'He's just drunk. Go on, Izz, I'll explain later, OK?'

'Don't you tell her what to do. She's not your sister.' Foster started coughing, a deep, choking noise.

'Of course I'm his sister.' Tears were streaming down her face. She grabbed Sam's hand, squeezing tight. 'Why are you saying that, Daddy? Stop it, stop being horrible.'

Sam pulled her into him, hugging her tight. Then Sienna joined them, her face pale as the moon. 'Just ignore him,' Sam said. 'I promise it's going to be OK. If you guys can hold it together and get up to the villa, I'll talk to you later. I just need to help Mom down here first.'

He could feel Izzy's chest hitching as she tried to get control of her sobs. Sienna was altogether more silent, controlled. 'What's he talking about?' she asked. 'I don't understand.'

'Nothing, he's talking shit. He's drunk too much and he's being stupid. Please go back to the house.'

'Sam's right,' Lucia said. 'Your father, he's not well. Please, darlings, let us take care of this.'

'You are my brother, aren't you?' Izzy was crying hard, now. 'Sam, tell me he's lying.'

Was it possible for a heart to break? Sam thought it could be. 'Of course I'm your brother, Izz. There's no doubt about that. We're family, you can't get rid of me. But right now, we've got a situation. I need your help to solve it. Please can you go up to the villa and wait for me there?'

She nodded, still sobbing. Then, grabbing Sienna's hand,

the two of them headed for the villa, leaving Sam alone with his parents.

As soon as they were out of earshot, Sam turned back to the beach, heading towards where his stepfather lay. But it wasn't his stepfather he was looking at, it was his mother, who was kneeling there, devastated.

'You knew?' she asked through her fingers, which were still clamped over her mouth. 'You knew, Sam?'

'That Foster isn't my father? Yes, I knew.'

Lucia shook her head. Her expression was broken. 'You weren't meant to know. I didn't want you to know. How did you find out?'

Sam glanced at Foster. The efforts of shouting and moving must have been overwhelming. He was lying silently on the beach, his dinner jacket covered with gravel and sand.

'He told me.'

'No.' She started to cry. 'Oh no, Sam, no. He should never have told you. I'm so sorry, baby, so sorry.'

Sam crouched down, gently taking his mother into his arms. 'Hey, it's OK, it's OK.'

'How could he do that? How could he tell you without my permission? He promised me we wouldn't say anything, he promised me it would stay a secret. You must hate me right now.'

'I don't hate you.' He harboured no anger for his mother at all. It was his stepfather who attracted his ire.

'I'm furious with him, I can't believe he did that. How long have you known?'

He couldn't lie. That's what had got them here. Secrets and lies, all wrapped up in protection.

'About six years. Foster told me the night before I flew to LA.'

'Six years?' It was almost a shout. 'Sam, you've known that long and not told me? Didn't you have questions, didn't you want to talk to me? I can't believe you didn't say anything.'

He shrugged. 'There was nothing to say. He told me and I left, that was pretty much it. I didn't want to upset you. Not when you were so fragile.'

'I'm not fragile,' she told him. 'I'm fine now. OK, so I went a bit downhill after I had the girls, but that was PND, darling. The therapy helped.'

Sam licked his dry lips. 'Foster told me it was my fault.'

Tears filled her eyes. 'Oh no, darling, no. It wasn't your fault. None of it was. It happens to a lot of women. I got better, didn't I?'

'You did,' he agreed. 'But I was scared this would send you back to that place again. I couldn't do it, not when Izzy and Sienna needed you.'

It seemed stupid now, seeing how upset she was. It was bound to come out at some point. But Sam had been too shaken up to think about that.

Lucia pulled back, looking him straight in the eye. 'I'm upset because you didn't tell me. Because he didn't tell me. And I'm upset at myself for letting you find out without me telling you.'

Sam smiled. 'There's a lot of upset about not telling.'

'Lies,' she said. 'They always find you out.'

He nodded. 'They do.'

'Will you ever forgive me? I wanted to protect you. I didn't want you to carry the stigma of being *illegittimo*. I thought this would make things right.'

'There's nothing to forgive. You did what you thought was best at the time. And you tried to give me a happy childhood. It wasn't your choice to tell me, that's all on him.' He took her hand, squeezing it tight. 'You're my mother and I love you.'

A fresh flood of tears ran down her cheeks. She lifted his hand to her face, kissing his palm. 'You were my first born. My beautiful boy. I've always been so proud of you, of the man you've become.'

'I'm not perfect.' Sam's voice cracked.

'You're perfect to me,' she whispered. 'Every child is perfect to their mother. We bring you into this world and we try to protect you, even though we know it's impossible to do. And we watch you grow and flourish, and make mistakes, knowing that you'll be hurt and we can't do anything to stop it. Still we love you and think you're wonderful, simply for being you.'

He wasn't going to cry. Not here on a beach with his stepfather unconscious next to them. But that didn't mean he didn't feel the tears inside, threatening to spill out. It took a force of will to keep his eyes dry.

'Izzy and Sienna will want an explanation,' Sam said tentatively, afraid to make things worse. 'We'll need to talk to them.'

'We can do that. Right after we decide what to do with him.' She spat the words out – gesturing at her husband, a beached whale on the sandy shingle. 'I'm half inclined to leave him here. Let him wake up to his hangover in the morning.'

The temptation was almost too delicious. But the wrath of Foster Carlton wasn't something he wanted his mother to suffer. Or his sisters.

'Let's try and wind the party down,' he suggested. 'Then

306

Sandro and I can grab a couple of the stronger staff to help bring him back up to the villa.'

She squeezed his hand tighter. 'You would do this for him, after everything he said?'

'No, I'd do it for you. For Izzy and Sienna. Not for him.' Never for him. Not after everything that had happened. 'Why don't you stay here with him and I'll go back to the party? See if I can find Sandro and Gabi. Once everybody's gone we can sort this out.'

His mother nodded, gesturing for him to leave. 'Thank you,' she whispered. 'You're a good boy.'

Sam raised an eyebrow. 'I wouldn't go that far. The only reason I'm suggesting I go up is if you leave me with him I wouldn't trust myself.'

'Fair point. But thank you anyway. For being a good son to me.'

'Any time,' Sam whispered. As he left the beach, he could hear his mother whisper-shouting at Foster, berating him for everything he'd done. Sam's lips twitched as he half listened, remembering how scary Lucia Carlton could be when crossed. It wasn't karma, nowhere near it, but there was something pleasant about knowing Foster was going to be uncomfortable for quite a while.

It was an hour before the final guest left, and the villa was empty save for the family and the staff. Sam had gone crazy, trying to usher people out, explaining there was an unexpected illness that they had to attend to. And all the time he was looking out for Cesca, but she was nowhere to be seen. He could feel himself becoming agitated, losing control. Everything was so messed up.

After they managed to haul Foster up from the beach and put him in the guest room on the ground floor, he resumed his search, wandering from room to room in agitation. It was only when he wandered outside to the terrace that he saw her, on all fours, scrubbing red wine stains from the pale stone slabs. A flash of anger took hold of him as he saw the state of her knees, the skin red and raw from being scraped against the rough floor.

'What are you doing?' He stalked straight over, grabbing at her arm to pull her up. A look of shock came over Cesca's face as she scrambled to her feet, shrugging his hand away from her bicep.

'I'm cleaning, what does it look like?'

'You don't need to do that, the garden crew can do it tomorrow.' He scowled at her scraped knees. 'Do they hurt?'

Cesca brushed the dirt from her skirt. 'Not really. And I can't leave it – if I don't scrub it now the stain will set, and then the whole slab will have to be replaced.'

'Can't one of the staff do it?' Sam looked around at the bustle of activity surrounding them. The team of waiting staff had somehow morphed into the cleaning crew. Not one of them was standing around doing nothing.

'I *am* the staff, remember?' Cesca said pointedly. 'This is what I'm being paid to do.' Her voice turned gentle as she looked at him. 'How's your family doing?'

Sam swallowed. 'Not great. It's a mess, Foster ended up blurting out everything. Now everyone knows he's not my father. He's lying in bed comatose, my mother is in pieces, and my sisters can't understand what the hell's going on.'

'I'm so sorry. It's everything you didn't want to happen, isn't it? How are you feeling?'

'I don't know. I think I'm in crisis control mode at the moment. I've left my sisters on their own for a minute, but I'll have to get back to them. They deserve some kind of explanation, but they keep crying.'

'Of course they do. They're your sisters and they love you. This must have come as such a shock to them, no wonder they're so upset.'

'I need to see you before you leave.' He glanced around, looking at all the people surrounding them. The terrace wasn't exactly the most private of places right then. 'Can I catch up with you later?'

Her face fell. 'Oh, yeah, OK.'

'Are you sure? It's just that I said I'd go and talk to Izzy again in a minute. And my mom, she's started on the wine, I want to make sure she doesn't do anything stupid.'

'Of course, family comes first, always. You should go to them, they must need you.'

But he needed her, too. Not that it was the time to say it. He was already uncomfortable enough, whispering family secrets among the local staff. 'I'll catch you later, OK?'

'Of course.'

There was an expression on her face he couldn't quite put his finger on. Her breath was fast, and her fingers were grabbing tightly onto the cloth she'd been cleaning the stone with. But what really got him was the way she wouldn't quite meet his gaze. Her eyes kept darting to the left, as if she was waiting for something, though what it was he didn't understand.

Whatever it was, it felt as though he was losing control. Again.

Sam didn't like that feeling one little bit.

*

309

'They've all gone.' Sandro walked into the kitchen, a look of weariness weighing down his features. 'I've locked everything up. Time for bed, I think.'

Cesca glanced up from the sink, where she was washing the plates that wouldn't fit into the already-full dishwasher. Gabi was next to her, drying the crockery with a thin towel before gently piling them in the cupboards. 'We're almost done. Cesca, why don't you go to bed now? I can finish here. You and Sandro have an early start in the morning if you want to get to the airport in time for check-in.'

Her stomach dropped at the thought of her flight home, only hours away from now. Upstairs in her bedroom, her case was packed, with only her night and travelling clothes left hanging in the closet. She glanced around the kitchen, trying not to let the tears come to her eyes. Somewhere, somehow, in the past couple of months, this Italian villa had come to feel like home.

And then there was Sam. That was way too messed up to think about.

'Yes, please go,' Sandro agreed, when Cesca didn't reply. 'We won't be long here.'

The kitchen door opened, and Lucia Carlton walked in. Though her face was perfectly made up, there was no disguising the red rims around her eyes, or the bereft expression on her face.

'Gabi, Sandro, I wanted to thank you.' Her eyes alighted on Cesca. 'And you, too, Cesca. Thank you for all you did tonight. I don't just mean the party either. Sandro, thank you for helping Sam with my husband. I know it can't have been pleasant.'

Cesca had never seen anybody look so awkward. Her heart

went out to the beautiful Italian lady, standing in the middle of the kitchen and wringing her hands.

'It's always my pleasure to help,' Sandro murmured.

'We'd do anything for your family, you know that, Signora Carlton.'

Lucia nodded, her lips thin with worry. 'And I can count on your discretion?' she asked. 'If word got out that Foster was like that. Or if people starting gossiping about the nonsense he'd been saying ... we'd all be so embarrassed.'

'We would never talk to anybody about this. What happens here remains here, I promise you that,' Gabi said, looking downwards. 'Is there anything we can do to help you with Signor Carlton this evening?'

'I think we'll leave in him the downstairs guest room. Thank you for making it up so quickly, Gabi. I don't want to move him when he's still so very intoxicated, but I'll stay with him tonight to make sure he doesn't get any worse.' She didn't look at all happy at that prospect. 'Cesca, you're leaving tomorrow, is that right?'

'I ... I think so.'

'That's for the best. We'll be leaving ourselves as soon as Foster's feeling better. And I'm absolutely certain Sam will be on his way to LA as soon as he can get on the next flight.'

Was it possible for Cesca to feel any worse than she already did?

'Sandro will drive her first thing in the morning.' Gabi smiled reassuringly. 'And of course you can count on our complete discretion, can't she, Cesca?'

'Of course,' Cesca agreed, her face red. 'I wouldn't talk to anybody about this. I promise.'

Lucia sighed. 'Thank you all, you don't know how much of

a relief that is to me ... well, to all of us, really. My husband said some terrible things, and a lot of them weren't true. I hope he didn't say too much when you were helping him up from the beach, Sandro?'

'He said nothing at all,' Sandro replied. 'He was pretty much unconscious. Sam and I had to practically carry him all the way to the villa.'

Cesca hadn't seen that, she'd been too busy with the guests, taking over while Sandro and Gabi were helping the family. They'd all been engaged in damage control by that point. Her heart ached for Sam having to see his stepfather like that. And though she had no idea what Foster had said to him, Sam had told her enough about the man to know it hadn't been pleasant. What a mess everything had become.

'I'll say good night, then,' Lucia said, filling a glass with ice cold water. 'Have a safe journey home, Cesca. I'll see you tomorrow, Gabi and Sandro.'

With that she left the kitchen, pulling the door gently closed behind her.

This time, when Gabi suggested Cesca go to bed, she agreed readily. Even though she knew there was no possible way she could sleep.

She was getting used to that.

29

Adieu! I have too grieved a heart
to take a tedious leave

– The Merchant of Venice

Cesca tossed and turned in her bed, checking the dial on her watch every five minutes, wondering whether Sam was still planning to see her. When he'd told her he'd 'talk to her later', Cesca had assumed it was a promise of sorts. Especially after their encounter in the gardens. But that was before Foster messed everything up. Now it was almost three in the morning – only two hours before she was due to leave – and she was wondering if she'd taken it completely the wrong way.

Maybe he'd meant it as a goodbye.

The thought made her hands shake as she reached out to put her watch back on the bedside table. He couldn't have meant that, could he? After everything that had happened, he wouldn't just let her walk away without even a proper farewell? He'd told her she was his in the gardens, as he'd plundered her mouth with his kisses. Was that real, or just something he'd said in the heat of the moment? Was it possible his words were fuelled by jealousy more than desire?

Her mind went back to the nights they'd spent apart since his family had arrived at the villa. Though it had been Cesca who had initiated their separation, Sam hadn't exactly fought against her. He might have liked her, but not enough to want to keep her.

The thought made her want to cry.

Cesca glanced over at the case up by the door, waiting for Sandro to carry it down to the car in the morning. She was leaving exactly as she'd arrived; alone. She could live with that, couldn't she?

Another half-hour passed, slower than molasses, and Cesca tossed and turned until the sheets were a wrinkled mess at the bottom of her bed. Her agitation was increasing, thinking about him, wondering why he still hadn't made an appearance at her door.

It brought back old memories. Dark ones of her falling so far after he left. So hard to push out of her mind.

Sighing, she sat up, swinging her legs around to hit the floor. It was the inaction that was killing her. The waiting for somebody who clearly wasn't coming. She'd been waiting for too long – for six years – this time she wasn't willing to hang around any more.

The landing was quiet as she stepped out of her bedroom, her bare soles padding against the warm wood floor. It took seconds for her to reach Sam's door, not long enough for her to think of her next move. Should she knock? Just barge her way in? Cesca hesitated for a moment, resting her hand on the thick oak panel.

That's when she heard the voices. A low and deep one, followed by one distinctly feminine. Her mouth went dry as she realised he wasn't alone.

'I don't understand, how could he lie to us for so long? How could you?' It sounded like one of his sisters, though she couldn't make out if it was Izzy or Sienna.

'I didn't want to upset you.' That was Sam's voice. 'I wanted to protect you. It doesn't mean anything anyway, I'm still your big brother.'

Another soft sob. 'But all the things he said about you, Sam. I hate him, I really do. I'm never going to talk to him again.'

'Of course you will, he's your father, after all.'

'He's a liar and I don't want anything to do with him. I don't even want to see him, not ever again. He's such an arse.'

Cesca thought she heard Sam's low chuckle. Its familiarity stabbed her like a knife. 'You don't have to do anything you don't want to, sweetheart. Just take it easy, OK? You've had a big shock, and it's a lot to take in. I know when I found out it sent me reeling.'

'And then you left us all without a word. I never really understood until now. I thought you were just being a typical bratty older brother, and didn't care about us at all.'

'I'll always care.' Sam's voice sounded like warm sunlight. 'I always did. I just couldn't stand being near him.'

'Nor can I.' A small silence followed, punctuated by the occasional sob. Cesca closed her eyes, imagining Izzy crying into her brother's chest. Sam was probably stroking her hair, whispering quietly to his sister. Listening to such a private discussion was making her feel uncomfortable. Cesca was about to turn around and walk back to her room when Izzy spoke again.

'I keep thinking about how mean he always was to you. No wonder you left for Hollywood.'

'Yeah, I guess that was one of the reasons,' he agreed. 'But not the only one. I think I was looking for an excuse to leave.'

315

Oh, Cesca remembered.

'Please can you come back and live in London with us?' Izzy pleaded. 'I can't stand the thought of being there with Mum and Dad. I hated it when you went away, please come home.'

'Izz . . .'

'Sam, please.' Her voice was plaintive. It made Cesca want to cry.

'I can't.' Sam sounded half broken. 'I wish I could, but I can't live in London. I've got a life in LA, friends, a job. I can't move back there for you.'

Another silence. Another sob. Cesca felt as though her heart was breaking alongside his sister's.

It was clear there was no space for her in his world. He'd made that obvious enough when he'd refused to introduce her to his parents. And now his family had imploded, there was no hope at all. As much as it hurt to accept that, she would have to. Even if she'd fallen in love with him.

He'd liked her enough to help her with her play, but not enough to call her his girlfriend. She'd been a convenient distraction, especially at night. What else had there been for him to do apart from that? He'd been hiding away for a few weeks, taking a break from the Hollywood rat race. If Cesca hadn't been here, it would have been somebody else.

She could feel her heart starting to pound against her chest, a drumbeat of misery. She bit her lip in an attempt not to cry. Standing there, on the other side of the door to him, she realised it wasn't simply two inches of oak that was coming between them.

It was life. His life. And it didn't include her.

*

'Maybe I can come and live with you, then,' Izzy said, wiping her tears away with a curled fist. 'Because I'm not living with that bastard any more.'

'Izz, you don't have a choice. Anyway, you're off to university soon. You'll only have to go home for the holidays.'

Sam looked down at his sister, taking in her watery eyes and red cheeks. The tears had turned her irises a cerulean blue, so like her father's it was uncanny.

'I won't let you ignore us any more, Sam,' she told him. He tried not to smile at her stubbornness. Her eyes might have been like Foster's but her attitude was all Lucia's.

'I wasn't planning on ignoring you. And now that everything's out in the open, I won't have an excuse, will I?'

'So I can come and stay with you?'

Sam sighed. He was such a sucker. 'Or I'll come and visit you, OK?'

'I thought you hated London.'

'I don't hate it, I just wasn't that happy there. But I'm older now. If I have a break between movies I'll come over. I'll never live there, but I can visit if you like.'

Izzy sniffed. 'That sounds lovely. I just want us to be all together. You me and Sienna, like we used to be.'

Sam smiled into her hair. 'That sounds good to me.' Though he'd never forgive his stepfather for revealing his secret in such a way, Sam couldn't help but think there were some silver linings to his intoxication.

'You know, Izz, it's really late. You should go and get some sleep. We can talk about this some more in the morning.'

She squeezed his shoulders, as if afraid to let go. 'I don't want to be alone. Can I sleep here tonight?'

'With me?' Sam asked, surprised. 'Um . . . I guess.'

'Not that I can sleep anyway,' she told him. 'But I promise not to disturb you too much.'

He raised his eyebrows. 'You've always been disturbing.'

Izzy hit him, though her heart wasn't really in it. 'Stop it. I already hate one Carlton man, don't make me angry at you, too.'

Sam softened. 'I'd never make you angry at me, at least not again. Try to get some rest, OK?'

She was still clinging on to him. 'Don't leave me.'

Taking a deep breath, Sam lay down on the mattress, letting his little sister curl into him. Her face was wet against his arm. From the corner of his eye he could see the door, still closed.

He swallowed, though his mouth was dry. As much as he wanted to go to Cesca, there was no way he could leave his sister like this. No way he could take her with him, either. He was stuck, having to choose his family above the girl he'd messed around.

Izzy finally fell asleep a few hours later, her face screwed up as if in concentration as she dozed. Sam gently disentangled himself from her hold, freezing as she muttered quietly, before he slowly rolled across the bed and onto the floor. He waited for a moment, staring at her slumbering form. It was only when her breathing became rhythmic and her body relaxed that he finally allowed himself to walk out into the hallway.

Cesca's door was ajar when he got there, the pale light of the early dawn escaping through the crack. Sam frowned, grabbing the edge of the oak to slip inside her bedroom, not wanting to wake her if she'd managed to fall asleep.

It was the emptiness that struck him as he pulled the door

closed behind him. The emptiness and the silence. As he looked around, he realised exactly what had happened.

She was gone, and so were her things. Even the bed had been stripped, leaving a bare mattress and duvet where sheets and covers had previously been. And though the room still smelled like her, that was the only part of Cesca that remained.

'Is everything OK?'

Sam turned around to see Gabi behind him, a dusting cloth in her hand. 'Has she gone?' he asked urgently.

'Cesca?' Gabi asked. 'Yes, Sandro's taken her to the airport. She's booked on the early flight to Heathrow.'

Sam glanced at his watch. It was almost seven o'clock. The early flight always left at seven-thirty. Even if he jumped into the Ferrari and put his foot down all the way, there was no way he could catch her.

'She didn't say goodbye,' he whispered, as much to himself as Gabi.

'She wanted to leave quietly. She had a lot on her mind,' Gabi said.

Sam looked at her, trying to work out if she knew more than she was saying. 'Did she ... did she leave anything?'

Gabi shook her head. 'She came like she arrived, with one suitcase and not much else. It's such a shame, we'll miss her. She was like a ray of sunshine around here.'

Sam swallowed, torn between opening up and hiding away. 'She was,' he agreed.

'I think you'll miss her too,' Gabi said. 'After all, it was just the two of you for a long time. You must have become close to each other.'

'We were friends,' Sam said. He was feeling light-headed, and had to lean on the wall for support. 'Until I upset her.'

'You did?' Gabi raised her eyebrows.

Sam moistened his lips with the tip of his tongue. The ache at her leaving was a nagging pain in his gut. How the hell had he managed to mess everything up again? 'I didn't treat her very well.'

'Why not?' Gabi looked almost embarrassed at her question. 'Oh, I'm sorry, Signor Carlton, that was very rude of me.'

Sam sighed, rubbing his face with his hand. 'Don't be sorry. You sound exactly like her. Apologising for something that's not your fault. It isn't your problem I'm all messed up, and it isn't your problem I shut down every time somebody gets close. It's mine.'

Gabi looked more confused than ever. And he didn't blame her, he must have sounded like a crazy man. But there was this need to talk, to confess, to work out how the hell he managed to get so tangled up. Gabi just happened to be there to listen.

'I liked her,' he said, his voice quiet. 'No, that's wrong. I fell in love with her. But I panicked, got scared, and pushed her away. It's all my fault.'

'You love her?' Gabi asked. 'You love Cesca?'

'Yes.'

She clapped her hands together. 'Well that's wonderful.'

He shook his head. 'No it isn't.'

'Why not?' Gabi asked. 'Love is always wonderful. You're both single, you're both beautiful. It's perfect.'

'Because I messed things up,' he told her. 'And now she's gone and probably never wants to see me again.'

'Of course she does. That's why she looked so sad when

320

she left. I thought it was because she was going to miss Varenna, but now I know it's because she's in love with you.'

'She'll never forgive me,' he said. 'And she shouldn't. I was an asshole to her.'

Gabi's eyes sparkled. 'Girls are more forgiving than you think,' she told him. 'Sandro is always doing things that drive me crazy, and yet I let him make it up to me anyway. It's amazing what a bit of love can do.'

Pushing himself off the wall, Sam turned to look at her. 'So what should I do?'

She smiled. 'You fight for her. You fight for her like you've never fought for a woman before. And if she's kind enough to give you another chance, you make sure you don't mess it up.'

Fight for her. He could do that, couldn't he?

For the first time, he really thought he could.

30

What's gone and what's past help
Should be past grief
— The Winter's Tale

'What can I get for you?' Cesca stood in front of her customers, pencil and pad poised to take down their order. The couple looked at each other for a moment, then the woman nudged the man. He scratched his head, staring at the menu.

'Do you have anything other than cereal?'

Cesca bit her lip. It was a question she was asked every day, by practically everybody who came into the café. Taking a deep breath, she blinked twice before answering them. 'I'm afraid not.'

What was it about the name of the café that the patrons didn't understand? It was written in bright blue paint above the entrance. *Cereal*. Simple, right?

'Not even some toast?' the man asked.

'I'm sorry, no toast. We have a hundred different kinds of cereal, though,' she replied, trying to keep her tone cheery. 'If you're allergic to anything, we can offer you gluten free cereal, and rice milk?'

'I'm not allergic,' the woman leaned forward to tell her. 'I just don't want cereal for dinner.'

Cesca gave her a look. It was somewhere between understanding and exasperation. 'I'm afraid that's all we have. It's a concept café. Cereal for breakfast, lunch and dinner.'

'That's just silly,' the woman protested. 'Who eats cereal for dinner? Especially at seven pounds for a bowl of Cheerios. I could buy three boxes in the supermarket for that.'

Biting her lip to stop herself from suggesting the woman did just that, she gave her another sympathetic smile. It wasn't the first time she'd heard the complaints – far from it – but honestly, what did they expect from a café called Cereal?

'We have ten different types of milk,' she told them, as if it was going to help at all.

In the week she'd been working here, Cesca had seen it all. Sharp-suited men slurping their Frosties while discussing business, rich mothers dragging their children in and stuffing Coco Pops into their complaining mouths. Even first dates that must have seemed a good idea at the time. She wondered if any of them made it to second dates.

Of course, that turned her thoughts to Sam. Nearly everything did. Right now she was thinking about that perfect first date – the one in the grotto where he'd taken her secretly. They hadn't even kissed then, though she'd been thinking about it a lot. Now she'd never kiss him again.

The thought made her feel sick.

'Do you want to leave?' the man asked his companion. 'We can go somewhere else if you'd like?'

'I just want to go home,' his date replied. 'I don't think we're really compatible.'

It was a paraphrase of the words she'd said to Sam eighteen

days ago, but close enough to make her heart clench. God, was she ever going to get over him?

She wandered into the kitchen where Simon, the owner, was making up orders. 'Table fifteen have left without ordering,' she told him. 'They were upset they couldn't have toast.'

He raised his eyebrows. 'Did you run another customer off? I'm going to have to deduct the lost profits from your wage.'

'Piss off,' she said lightly. 'They don't leave because of me. They leave because your menu's stupid.'

'It's a concept café,' he sighed. 'Why can't people understand that?'

'Because it's a crazy idea. You're going to go bankrupt within a year.'

He folded his arms across his chest. 'I could sack you for that.'

'Feel free. I'm only working here as a favour to you. And I'll be leaving anyway just as soon as my script goes into production. So if you want me to go now . . . '

'No!' He stepped in front of her. 'I didn't mean it. We need you, Cesca.'

Wasn't that the truth? He couldn't keep the staff for love nor money. 'In that case, feel free to up my wages.'

'If you promise to stay for six months, I'll double them.'

She shook her head. 'No can do. I'll be busy working in the West End by then.' Her voice was filled with confidence. 'I told you from the start I'd help out until I sell the script. After that, you're on your own.'

She felt like a different person, being able to stand in a kitchen and hold her own. Such a contrast to the girl who'd been fired from the Cat Café only months before. And even though her heart was achy and tender from losing Sam, it still felt good.

Cesca was still mulling that over when her shift finished, and she clambered on the bus to Hampstead, heading for her dad's house where she'd been staying since she'd arrived back in London. He'd been almost shocked when she'd finally taken him up on his offer of some temporary shelter, but had hidden the surprise well, leading her to her old bedroom, nodding sagely as she babbled an explanation that it was only until she got herself straight.

Everything was temporary, really. The job, the house. A means to an end, a roof over her head and a source of sustenance while she touted her play around. She'd have to get used to it again, she supposed. To not knowing where her next pay cheque was coming from, or whether she'd be able to afford the rent that month. But somehow it seemed different to before. In the past six years this had been her life because she thought she had no other option. Now it was a necessity while she was pursuing her dream.

And boy, was she pursuing it.

Another thing she'd learned in Italy: it wasn't your circumstances that made you happy but your attitude. And hers had taken a 180-degree turn.

'Good evening.' Her father looked up from his book as she walked into the living room. It was one of those rare occasions when he wasn't hiding in his office. 'Did you manage to avoid being sacked?'

'Just about,' she said. 'It was a close thing, though. Apparently telling the owner his whole café is stupid isn't the best way to keep a job.'

Her father smiled. 'You always did lack diplomacy, my dear.' He checked his watch. 'Oh, and your sister called an hour ago.'

'Lucy?'

'No, it was Kitty. She's having a whale of a time in LA, apparently. Said it was always sunny over there. When I told her it was raining here she began to laugh hysterically.'

'That sounds like Kitty.' It was funny, almost painfully so, to think her sister was living in the same city as Sam. Everywhere Cesca looked there were reminders. 'I'll turn the laptop on and Skype her.' Much cheaper than phoning. Plus seeing her sister on the screen was so much better than just hearing her voice. 'Do you mind if I borrow it?'

'You silly girl, I already told you it was yours. Now go and call your sister.'

Taking a pit stop in the kitchen to pour a glass of water, Cesca headed for the tiny bedroom at the top of the stairs. She flicked the computer on, watching it blink to life, then clicked on Skype. Kitty was in the favourites, along with her other sisters. She smiled when she saw their names.

It only took a couple of rings for Kitty to pick up. Then her face came on the screen. She was smiling, her face glowing in the light of her computer. 'Hey, lovely.'

There was something about talking to her sisters that felt like coming home. Of course they'd had their differences – and over the years she may have hidden the worst of her plight from them – but they were as familiar to her as an old coat. Warming, cosy, and comfortable to wear. 'Hey yourself. How's LA treating you?'

'Never mind that, we have girl talk to do.'

'We do?' Cesca's brow rose up.

'Yes, we do. This guy, this Sam, what are you going to do about him?'

Cesca groaned. 'Ugh, word gets around fast. Have you

been talking to Lucy?' On her arrival back in London, Cesca had spent over an hour on the phone to her eldest sister in Scotland, pouring her heart out. She should have known word would spread.

'No, she told Juliet, who told me. Anyway, that doesn't matter, does it? You know as well as I do if you tell one of us you tell us all.'

That was all too true.

'Well if you've been talking to them, I hope they've told you it's as over as quickly as it began. I was nothing more than a holiday fling to him. And I've accepted that now.' Lies, all lies. She was nowhere near acceptance. 'So there really isn't much to tell you.'

'We're talking about Sam Carlton, right? The one who ruined your play and then ran off to Hollywood? The one who turned up in Italy and tried to ruin your summer, too?' There was a smile in Kitty's voice. 'Except he didn't ruin it, did he, you little minx? From what I've heard he rather made it. So I think there's quite a lot to tell.'

Cesca groaned. 'I don't know what you mean.' She avoided Kitty's gaze across the video connection, not knowing where to begin. It all sounded so stupid, she barely understood it herself.

'He was on the *Mary Jane Landers* show this afternoon.' Kitty sounded like the cat who got the cream.

Cesca looked up straight away. Didn't her sister know how bad she was making Cesca feel? The conversation felt like death by a thousand bruises. Why on earth was she talking about some celebrity chat show with her, while Cesca's heart was breaking?

'Was he?'

'He was. And I think you should watch it.'

Now she was going too far. Why was Kitty looking so smug? 'It's not on over here.'

'It's already on the Internet. You can watch it on YouTube, I'll send you the link. It's only ten minutes long.' She'd barely finished speaking before the URL came up in the chat box. 'Go on, click on it.'

Cesca's eyes widened. 'Now?'

Kitty gave a little chuckle. 'Why not?'

Because she didn't want her sister seeing her break down. Because she wasn't sure she could see Sam's face without wanting to throw something at the laptop screen. Because everything felt too raw and painful.

'Just watch, it, Cesca.' Kitty's tone turned cajoling. 'I promise it's not that bad.'

She clicked the link, which took her straight to the YouTube channel. After five seconds of adverts, the clip came on. Mary Jane Landers was talking to camera, making a joke about the audience needing a 'Summer Breeze' because it was getting hot in there. And then she was introducing Sam, to the whooping and catcalls of the audience, who from the camera shot were all thirty-something women.

Was it wrong to hate an entire age demographic?

And then Sam walked in, and it was like the past two weeks had never happened. As though he was walking into the library, giving her a smile before grabbing her for a kiss. Except this time the smile wasn't for her. It was for Mary Jane and a hundred goddamn women.

Cesca could feel her heart pounding against her ribcage as she watched Sam take a seat, and say hello to Mary Jane. Then he was running a hand through his hair, pulling it out of his eyes, and Cesca could almost feel those coarse strands in her palms.

'So, Sam, I hear you've been a bit of a naughty boy,' Mary Jane said. More giggles and catcalls came from the audience. Sam turned to camera, an awkward smile on his face.

'I've been a bit of an idiot, yes.'

'Is it true what they've been saying?'

He raised his brows. 'What have they been saying?'

'That you're like a jackhammer.' She turned to the camera and made a silly face. 'We all want to know if you really are.'

Sam laughed and rolled his eyes. 'I can think of better ways of describing me.'

It was strange, watching him on the screen. He was Hollywood Sam, all perfectly groomed, yet there was still a hint of the other Sam, too. Her Sam. It made her heart ache.

Mary Jane asked him another question, but Cesca was too busy staring at Sam to hear. It was only when Kitty shouted, 'This is the bit,' that Cesca really started listening.

'So what's the deal with you and Serena Sloane?'

Sam grimaced. 'There is no deal. It was practically over before it began. If I'd have known she was married it wouldn't even have got that far. You know what Hollywood's like. Why tell the truth when you can tell a thousand lies?'

'So you're available?' Mary Jane waggled her eyebrows. The audience laughed.

'I didn't say that.'

Cesca leaned forward, intent on hearing every word. Somebody could have thrown a million pounds into her bedroom and she still wouldn't have moved an inch.

'Well this is interesting. Tell us more, please, but try not to break all our hearts, OK?' Mary Jane said, leaning forward.

Cesca wasn't sure whether she wanted to slap her or hug her for asking.

'There's not too much to tell, yet.' Sam smiled as he started to talk. 'But I met a girl this summer and she was . . . really special. I don't think she understands how special, but I'm determined to let her know somehow.'

'Will she be watching now?' Mary Jane looked excited at the prospect of a live exclusive. 'You could tell her on air.'

He shook his head, grinning. 'She lives in London. And she's probably busy working or doing something important. She's a writer.'

'Is she a screenwriter? Will we have heard of her?' Mary Jane asked. 'And more importantly, where did you meet her?'

He could be talking about anybody, couldn't he? OK, so the likelihood of him meeting two writers this summer was small, but it was still a possibility.

'In Italy,' he replied. Cesca's pulse increased. 'At a villa on Lake Como.'

'How beautiful.'

'The scenery is stunning, yes, but compared to her nothing is beautiful.'

It was as if every member of the audience sighed. Cesca found herself joining in.

'He's totally talking about you, right?' Kitty shouted. 'I mean, you're a writer and you were in Italy. Oh my God, Cesca, this is so exciting. I live in LA and I meet actors all the time, but even I'm fangirling a bit right now.'

Cesca didn't know how to feel. She'd walked away from him in Italy, after all. To hear him say on national television that she was special to him made her want to laugh and cry at the same time.

330

So she did. 'Oh God, Kitty. What does this mean?'

'It means you need to call him, you idiot.'

'I don't have his number.'

'You don't?'

Cesca shrugged. 'No. I didn't have a mobile over there, and his didn't work. We communicated the old-fashioned way.'

'Oh I bet you did. The universal language of love.'

'Shut up.'

'Make me.'

It was like they were twelve again. Bitching at each other, in a good-humoured way. Cesca welcomed the break from her emotional turmoil.

'Oh for goodness sake, do I have to do everything?' Kitty asked. 'I'll find his number for you and message it over, OK? But only if you promise to actually call him.'

'How are you going to find his number?' Cesca asked.

Kitty tapped her nose with the tip of her finger. 'Contacts, of course. I know people who know people. Or at least I know nannies who know people. Leave it to me, I'll sort your love life out for you.' With that, Kitty ended the Skype call, no doubt to get a head start on her search. Cesca watched the clip at least five more times before she closed the laptop down and popped her head around the door of the living room to tell her father she was going to bed.

It was midnight by the time Kitty sent a text, with Sam's phone number included. Cesca lay in her bed, surrounded by darkness, staring at the lit screen of her own, cheap, phone.

When she'd left Italy she'd thought her heart was breaking. By the time she landed in London she was sure it had. And for the past two weeks, no matter where she went, he was always the first thought in her mind. She'd serve a customer and wonder what Sam was doing then. She'd walk past an Italian restaurant and remember Sam's obsession with pasta. She'd walk into a newspaper shop and see Sam's face staring out of a magazine.

Her Sam.

That was who he was. Not Sam the boy who ruined her play, or Sam the actor who spoke to her so callously. No, he was Sam, the guy who edited her words, who teased her mercilessly, who kissed her until her lips swelled up. The golden boy who spoke perfect Italian with the sexiest accent, who could seduce her with his words.

Definitely *her* Sam.

Cesca sat up in bed, grabbing her phone, tapping on the number her sister had texted over. A green phone symbol came up and she clicked it, waiting breathlessly as the call tried to connect. It was going to cost her a fortune, one she definitely didn't have, but right at that moment she couldn't care less.

Then there was a click, and the call was diverted straight to voicemail.

Disappointed didn't cover it. She left a stuttered message, telling him she'd seen the show, that she wanted to talk to him, and could he please call her back. Reluctantly she hung up, putting the phone on the table beside her bed, leaving it on in case he called back soon. It was only four in the afternoon in LA, he could call her at any time.

Except he didn't. And as Cesca lay in her bed, watching the hours tick over on her alarm clock, she could feel sadness suffuse her. When morning came, and there was still no call, she was more disappointed than ever.

31

Sam scrawled his name across the contract, passing it back over to the woman on the other side of the desk from him. Marcella Di Bacco took the papers from him, flashing him a brief smile. A fifty-something blonde, she was every inch the professional. Her clothes, her hairstyle, they all added up to somebody who was totally in control.

'Thanks for organising the interview,' Sam said. 'I know it must have taken a lot to get me on there so quickly.'

Marcella nodded. She wasn't one for showing emotions, Sam noticed, but then that wasn't what he was planning to pay her for. One of the biggest publicists in the business, she had connections most people in LA only dreamed of. That's exactly what the dollars were getting him.

'It wasn't easy, but it was necessary. You'll find that's what I'm best at, finding fast solutions to problems. I'll also be sitting down to work out a long-term strategy for you, too. I'll need to work with your agent on that.' She looked up at him. 'Have you signed with one yet?'

'I'm going with Larry Morgan.'

'From the Creative Artists Agency? I thought he wasn't taking anybody on.'

Despite being in the middle of a sprawling city, Hollywood was a small place. Everybody was in everybody's face.

Sam shrugged. 'What can I say? Larry called me as soon as I landed in LAX.'

'Lucky boy. When do you start shooting the next *Summer Breeze* movie?' Marcella asked.

'In a month.'

'And what are your plans after that?'

'I want to take a break for a bit. Maybe do some theatre work. Get out of the Hollywood rat race for a while.' He felt relieved just saying it.

'OK, well leave me with this, and I'll start drawing up some plans. We want to avoid all that speculation about your relationship with your co-star this time, as well as countering the publicity the Serena Sloane incident created. Maybe we can have some print interviews with you and your new girl-friend, use it to dampen down all the speculation.'

'She's not my girlfriend,' Sam pointed out. Not yet, anyway. And possibly never, if the way she left Italy reflected her feelings for him.

'Well, keep my team updated, OK? Let's schedule another meeting for, say, two weeks' time. Then we can make some concrete plans.'

He nodded. 'I'm not sure I'll be in town, but we can Skype, right?'

'Of course. Oh, and just to let you know, Serena Sloane's

publicist has emailed me. Serena isn't at all happy about the backlash she's had. She's planning to set the story straight, to admit there was a lot of fabrication. This should be good for us.'

Sam raised his eyebrows. Even thinking about Serena left a bad taste in his mouth. That's why he paid a publicist – to deal with the people he didn't want to. 'I'll leave it with you, then.'

The sun was beating down on the sidewalk when he emerged into the street. A late heatwave had descended on the city, and the warmth radiated from the pavement as he crossed the road to find the parking lot. As he reached his car, he flicked on his phone, and it rang almost straight away.

There were only a few people he answered immediately. His mother was one of them.

'Hey, Mom.'

'Sam? I just saw your interview, who's this girl you were talking about?'

'Nobody.' Sam's reply was terse. He wasn't quite ready to start talking about his personal life with his mother. Not yet. They were slowly building bridges back towards each other, but he couldn't help but feel a shot of anger at her wanting to know his business when she'd lied about hers for so long.

'Thank you so much for not mentioning your father.' She sounded conciliatory, as though she understood his emotions. 'I really appreciate it.'

He waited for the usual panic to descend at the mention of Foster, but shockingly it didn't. 'I promised you I wouldn't say anything, and luckily she didn't ask. Though I'm not willing to keep it a secret for ever, I'll wait until things have calmed down, OK?' After six years of living a lie, he was ready to climb out of that particular prison. 'How are Izzy and Sienna doing?' Two of the main reasons he was keeping quiet about his parentage – they were still coming to terms with the lies they'd been told for their entire lives. They all were. It was going to take some time for them all to get over it.

'Surprisingly well,' his mother said. 'Though of course neither of them are talking to Foster. Nor am I, come to that.'

'Is he bothering you?' Sam asked, climbing into his car. 'If he's still being an asshole you need to tell me, OK? I'll speak to him if you want.'

'Not really, my darling. He's got his tail between his legs for now. He's still in Paris at the moment, finishing things up there. I guess when he comes home we will talk, but until then I'm quite happy giving him the silent treatment. It's a lot less than he deserves, after everything he did to you. I'm still not sure I can forgive him for that.'

Sam swallowed. He hadn't told her everything, but then she didn't need to know it all. It was in the past. Foster couldn't hurt him any more.

The same day Sam had left Varenna to return to LA, Lucia and her daughters had caught a flight to London. They had left a very hung-over and sheepish Foster to return alone to Paris, where he'd committed to seeing out the season at a theatre there.

He heard whispering coming down the line, followed by a strange scuffling noise. Then silence for a moment, as some kind of argument continued.

'Izzy, let go of the telephone.' His mom sounded fainter now. 'Sam, your sister insists on talking to you,' she managed to say, before the excited voice came on the phone.

'Sam, who's this girl you were talking about?' Izzy was

breathless, from wrestling the phone away from her mother, no doubt. 'You never told me about a new girlfriend?'

'What girl?' He was stalling for time.

'That writer you talked about, the one from London. Why didn't you invite her to the party? Was it because of Dad? You know the party would have been so much better if he wasn't there, the miserable git.' Izzy barely took a breath. 'You're coming over here to see her, right? When are you coming? Will you bring her over then? Sam, does this mean you might move back to London after all? Oh God I hope so.'

He laughed. 'Izz, calm down, take a breath, OK? I'm not going to talk to you about my love life right now. But yes, I'm planning on coming to London soon, to check if you guys are OK more than anything.'

'Oh, that's fantastic, make sure you come for a long time. We've got a lot to catch up on.'

'You start at university next month,' he pointed out.

'Then you can drive me there, can't you? My friends would love to meet you.'

He tried to picture himself turning up at her college, surrounded by paparazzi. It wasn't a pretty image. 'I've got to come back to film the *Summer Breeze* movie,' he reminded her. 'But I promise I'll see you before then.' He was keeping secrets again, but this time with a purpose. He had plans to go to London, but his family would have to wait. There were other things to attend to first.

'OK.' He could almost hear the pout in her voice. 'I guess that will have to do.'

He was still smiling when he said goodbye and rang off, flinging his phone on the passenger seat as he fired the engine up. Switching on the satnav he scrolled through the favourites, coming to LAX in the list. It seemed like he spent half his life in that airport, either departing or arriving, but never before had it sent a pulse of excitement through his veins as soon as he tapped on it.

It was time to go home. To his real home. And it wasn't a city or a town, or even a house on the edge of a lake. Home was where *she* was, wherever that would be. London ... Varenna ... it didn't matter. Because what he'd learned over the past few months was that home was a feeling. It was the thing that relaxed your muscles, that made you breathe a little easier. It was the place that you looked forward to being all through the day.

Home was Cesca Shakespeare. Even if she didn't know it yet.

The rain had been pouring all day without letting up. Every time a customer walked into the restaurant, they left a puddle in front of the doorway, a hazard-in-waiting that Cesca dried with a mop as soon as possible. It was nearing the end of the tourist season, but even that didn't account for the drop in business. Half the tables in Cereal were empty, looking forlorn with their clean china crockery and sparkling glasses all neatly laid out. The novelty was obviously wearing off. Cesca wondered if Simon could keep the place going for much longer.

'Can I have the bill, please?' a man called over to her from the corner. He was sitting opposite two teenage children. They'd barely looked away from their phones for the entire time they'd been there. A single father, Cesca had presumed, taking his kids out for the obligatory Saturday dinner. It didn't look as though any of them were enjoying it much.

A huge flash of lightning lit up the glass front of the

restaurant, and Cesca's eyes blinked in protest. She waited for the clash of thunder to follow – the storm had to be close to be that bright – but her anticipation was in vain. Only silence followed.

Another flash. This time the door to the restaurant opened, and more flashes lit up the outside street. Cesca blinked again, her eyes attempting to adjust to the shock of the light, and refusing to focus on the doorway in front of her. It took a moment to realise the flashes were coming from cameras, not the storm.

The door slammed shut, a dark figure leaning his back on it, his chest hitching as though he were trying to catch his breath. He was dripping with rain, puddles forming at his feet, and Cesca almost turned around to grab her mop and bucket once again.

But then she worked out who it was.

For a moment she was frozen on the spot. Her mouth was ajar, her eyes wide open, but when she tried to talk no words came out. The few patrons still in the café turned around to stare at the newcomer, whispered words of excitement hissing out as soon as they realised who he was. She heard his name, over and over again, like a record on repeat.

'Sam. Sam Carlton. The one from all those films. You know, the one who broke that girl's heart, oh, I don't remember her name.'

If this was a movie, she would be running towards him, throwing herself into his arms and letting him kiss her, as the water from his clothes seeped into her own. She could almost picture it, damn, she could have written it, but somehow, she still couldn't get her feet to move.

'The bill?' the man at the table next to her said. 'Can you get it for us?'

'Shut up, Dad.' The eldest teenager, a girl, finally dragged her eyes away from her phone. 'That's Sam Carlton.' A blush stole over her face, and Cesca wondered if her own cheeks were just as crimson.

She was starting to shake. Staring at this man, this glorious, soaking wet, beautiful man, standing only ten feet in front of her. It was unmistakably Sam – *her* Sam – the boy who could make her laugh and cry almost at the same time.

'Cesca?' He took a step towards her, still dripping wet from the rain. If she cared at all, she might have told him it was a health and safety hazard.

'I think so.'

He smiled. 'Hey.' His voice was soft, low. Beyond him, through the frosted glass, she could see a crowd of people gathering. An audience of a kind, watching the story play out in front of them as the rain poured down. The people in the cheap seats.

'I see you brought your friends with you.'

This time he laughed. Twisting his neck he looked out at the paparazzi and fans who were clustered in front of the window. Some of them were practically pasted to the glass. 'They told me to say hi.'

She lifted a hand up. 'Hi.'

Was this what it was like to be Sam? Living a life bleached by a dozen photographers, your movements feeling like a stop-motion video every time they went off? She felt a fresh flood of sympathy for him. No wonder the villa in Varenna had seemed like a haven to him.

Sam came to a stop in front of her, catching her waving hand in his. He folded his palm around it, his skin warm and wet where he held her.

'Hi,' he said again.

'Hi.' Her voice was soft. 'This is a long way to come for dinner. Even if you like cereal.'

He bit down a smile. 'I'm a big fan of cereal, but that's not why I'm here.'

She raised her eyebrows. 'It's not?'

Sam shook his head. He was still holding her hand. It felt nice ... natural. 'I've heard they've got a gorgeous new waitress. I came to check her out.'

She was aware of the silence in the restaurant. Of the intense scrutiny of everybody in the room. Yet somehow it didn't matter, because standing in front of her was the man she'd spent all night thinking about, the one who had pretty much anchored her thoughts for the past six years. He'd been the villain of her life for so long, yet now he was every inch the hero.

'I saw you on the TV,' she said. 'Something about falling for some English girl?'

'You did?' He looked surprised.

'And I called you.'

Sam frowned, grabbing his phone from his pocket. The screen was black. 'I forgot to turn it back on when I landed,' he said. 'I was too busy thinking about finding you.'

'How did you find me?' she asked. 'Or has word of Cereal spread far and wide?'

He smirked. 'I got my mom to call your godfather.'

Good old Hugh. He might have been her godfather, but he was also a sucker for a good story. She could only imagine the grilling he'd give her when she next saw him.

'And here you are.'

'Yes, I am.' There were only inches between them, but the gap still felt too big. It was overwhelming having him so

341

close. The dampness of his clothes magnified his fragrance, until it felt as though the whole room smelled as good as him.

'You left without saying goodbye,' he said.

She took a deep breath, but it did nothing to calm her down. Her senses were too full of him. 'You were a bit busy. I waited for you that night, but you didn't come.'

'Why didn't you come and find me?' A flash of pain crossed his features.

'I tried,' she told him. 'But you were with your sister, and she sounded so upset. Then she asked you to come to London and . . . ' She trailed off. Was she really strong enough to have this conversation in front of all these people? God, what the hell would everybody say? She wasn't used to being the centre of attention. She liked to write the action, not star in it.

'And you thought I didn't want you.'

She nodded, too shaken up to form words.

Sam closed his eyes for a moment, taking a deep breath. She watched as his full lips parted, the bottom trembling as the air rushed in. She swallowed, remembering the way they'd felt against her mouth every time he'd kissed her. Soft and hard, gentle and deep. It was only the knowledge they were being watched that kept her from tasting him again.

When he opened his eyes, his stare was hot and intense. It took her breath away. 'You were wrong.'

'I was?'

'I wanted to see you more than anything. I wanted to tell you what a stupid asshole I'd been. That I want to kick myself for refusing to open up to you. That what I felt for you – what I feel for you – was so strong, it scared the hell out of me.'

'It scares me, too.' It was all she could do to whisper.

342

Sam leaned closer. She could feel the warmth of his exhalations. 'I can't go back and make up for what I did, but I can fight for you. I'll do whatever it takes, Cesca, to show you how much I care for you. I nearly ruined everything once, because I was scared of being real with you. I won't ruin it again. Please say you'll forgive me?'

The vehemence of his words took her breath away.

'I forgive you,' she whispered. 'How could I not? Your words are so beautiful.'

'They're true. The only thing I want in life is standing right in front of me.'

'But your work is in LA, and I'm thousands of miles away.'

This time he smiled. 'We have the best jobs for being flexible on location. I'm an actor, you're a writer, we can be wherever the hell we want to be. When we're working, of course we'll need to be on set, or in the theatre or wherever. But when we're on a break – and I intend for us to take lots of those – we can be wherever we want to. And I don't care where that is as long as we're together.'

'I don't care, either. You can even bring your friends if you like,' she said, pointing to the ever-growing crowd.

'He really should kiss her now,' the teenage girl next to her whispered. 'Otherwise this is going to get pretty boring.'

They both laughed, the girl's words somehow managing to cut through the tension. 'The director has spoken,' Sam whispered.

Was she ready for her close-up? Cesca had no idea, but she was pretty sure it was going to happen whether she was ready or not. And when Sam took her in his arms, pulling her body tightly against his, she was overwhelmed by the sensations pulsing their way through her body. There was lust

343

there, of course – how could she feel anything else when he was pressing his sinfully gorgeous hips into hers? But there was something else there, too, something deeper and more cerebral. It heated her from the inside out, as the man she'd fallen for pressed his lips against hers. And when she closed her eyes, the camera flashes around them reminded her of the fireworks exploding that last night on Lake Como.

In the screenplay of her life, it felt as though every scene had been working up to this. The rejection, the fall, the long, hard climb back up again. And now she was almost at the summit, only to find the man who had broken her standing up there already, reaching out a hand to help her up the final few feet.

Sam's tongue slid against hers as he pushed his hands into her hair, angling her head to give him better access. She looped her arms around his neck, fingers brushing against his neck, as their bodies pressed closer still.

'We'd better get out of here,' Sam whispered in her ear, as they caught their breath, 'before this becomes something that's definitely not a spectator sport.'

Cesca laughed, then buried her head in his shoulder, wondering what on earth she was doing in front of quite so many people. 'I should ask my boss . . .'

'Yeah, no need.' Simon was only a few feet away from them. 'I think you've probably given us enough publicity for one night.'

'She might need a few days off,' Sam told him, while Cesca pressed her lips against his neck. 'Maybe even a week.'

'No problem at all,' Simon said. 'Take as much time as you need.' When Cesca finally looked up she could see a big smile on his face. He was probably already counting the customers that this free publicity would bring in. 'Let me know when you're coming back, OK?'

She nodded, though deep inside she suspected she might never be back. Sam tugged on her hand, pulling her outside into the pouring rain, and across the road to a waiting taxi. In their haste to leave, she'd forgotten her coat, and her blouse and skirt were soaked by the time they climbed inside. The fabric clung to her body, and the cold air inside the cab made her shiver.

Noticing her discomfort, Sam pulled her close, then leaned forward and tapped on the glass between the back seats and the driver. 'Could you turn the heating up, please?'

'Sure.' The driver turned the dial on the dashboard.

They were alone at last – well almost – and it gave Cesca a chance to really look at Sam. Of course, he was beautiful. All the world knew that. But it was what lay underneath the skin she cared about the most. The man, the one who had left behind the boy she once knew, the one who made her feel as if she was the most treasured prize.

'You look tired.' She traced the dark shadows beneath his eyes. His skin was soft to the touch.

'I've got jetlag on top of my jetlag,' he admitted. 'But it's not just that. I haven't been able to sleep much since I last saw you.'

'I haven't either,' she said. 'I haven't stopped thinking about you.'

An expression of relief crossed his face. 'I wasn't sure if you were. I wondered if you left that night because you were done with me.'

'I'll never be done with you.' It was almost a relief to say it. Sitting there, in the black cab idling at the side of a busy London street, Cesca could feel the emotions inside of her starting to explode.

'I wouldn't let you be.'

'We should probably get out of here,' the driver said through the intercom, as more flashes went off, and the crowd started to surround the cab. 'Where to, guvnor?'

Sam turned to look at her. 'Your place or mine?'

She laughed. 'I haven't got a place.'

'Neither have I,' he admitted. 'Let's just drive for a bit,' he suggested to the driver. 'Head west.'

The cab pulled away, cutting a swathe through the bedraggled onlookers, the tyres splashing water to the left and right. As people jumped out of the way, Sam reached for Cesca, cupping her face with his hands.

'Where are we going?' she asked, breathless from the intense way he was looking at her.

The corner of his lips quirked up. 'I've no idea. But it doesn't really matter. As long as I'm with you we can drive around all night, if you like.'

'It'll cost ya.' The driver's interjection made them both laugh.

'We could go and see my dad in a while,' she suggested. Not that she was in any hurry for that. Not when he was about to kiss her, and it looked as though he was planning to do it for a while.

'But now?'

'Now I'd like you to kiss me again,' she told him.

He ran his thumb along her lip then inclined his head to hers, until their mouths touched. When he dipped her back so that he could really plunder her mouth, Cesca closed her eyes, savouring every moment.

It was time for her fade to black.

346

Epilogue

Journeys end in lovers meeting
– Twelfth Night

'Stop touching your face, you're going to ruin your make-up.' Kitty grabbed Cesca's hand, pulling her fingers away from her cheeks. 'Calm down, honey, it's going to be fine.'

Cesca didn't reply. Nerves had taken away all her words.

Lucy was sitting on her other side. It was strange, being sandwiched by two of her sisters when they'd been apart for so long. But it gave her a glow that outshone the brightener that the make-up artist had used.

'We're nearly there,' Lucy said, squeezing her other hand. 'Another five minutes, OK, Cess? You can make it that far, can't you?'

'I miss Juliet,' Cesca said. 'She should be here.'

'Of course she should. But she can't, not without leaving Poppy, and we know she could never do that.' Lucy's tone was matter-of-fact, but she didn't catch their eye. 'Though if her stupid bastard of a husband knew the meaning of the word compromise, maybe she wouldn't have to dance to his tune all the time.'

347

'Amen,' Kitty agreed. 'I think she's a saint for putting up with him.'

'She doesn't have any other choice,' Cesca murmured. 'Not when they have Poppy in common. That poor kid.'

Her legs had started to shake. As the car snaked through the familiar streets of London, she could feel the nerves practically exploding out of her. If she'd managed to eat anything for the past few days, she might even have been sick.

When the car finally came to a stop outside the theatre, the crowd lining the red carpet turned to look at them, and a dozen camera flashes exploded at once. Then the paps noticed them, and started to surround the car, pressing their camera lenses against the tinted glass of the windows.

'They're going to be very disappointed when they realise Sam isn't in here,' Lucy remarked.

'Not at all, our Cesca's a star in her own right nowadays. She was in *Hello!* last month, and constantly splashed across the Internet. Did you see those pictures of that beach in Hawaii?'

'Shut up.' Cesca gave her sister a mock-annoyed stare. 'We all know they're only after one thing. And it isn't a glimpse of my cleavage.'

'That wasn't just a glimpse,' Kitty pointed out.

The security guy they'd hired for the night climbed out of the passenger seat, talking quietly into his microphone before walking around to open the door for them. She watched him push the paparazzi back with only the smallest amount of pressure. Whoever he was, this guy was good.

'I can't believe this is your life now,' Kitty said. 'Whatever happened to little Cesca who spent her whole time in front of a typewriter? Look at you now, all glamorous and sought-after. I don't know what to make of it, really.'

'It's not always like this,' Cesca said. 'It's not as if we go around in limos every day with some guy in a black suit pushing us along. Most of the time it's boring, we argue over who makes the coffee, I shout at him when he leaves his dirty boxers out. Last week he used up all the hot water and I didn't talk to him for an hour.'

'Well, that's definitely a capital offence,' Kitty agreed. 'No girl should have to shower in cold water.'

The door opened and the security guard reached for Cesca's hand. She turned to narrow her eyes at Kitty. 'Were you trying to take my mind off things?'

'It worked, didn't it?'

It had, at least for a moment. But now that she was climbing out of the car and onto the pavement, reality hit her with full force. There were people shouting, calling her name, asking her where Sam was. She smiled at the cameras, letting the security guard's soft hand on her back guide her forward. They walked past the hoardings on the side of the old building, posters depicting a scene from her play, with beautiful recommendations written by the usually harsh critics. She had to stare at them for a moment to really take them in.

This was her play. Hers. And it was finally being premiered.

'Cesca, is it true you're pregnant with Sam's baby?' somebody shouted as she posed in front of the posters.

'Have you split up with him? Where is he?'

'Does he still go like a jackhammer? Or was that just the Serena Sloane effect?'

Keep smiling, she told herself. Keep smiling and it will all be OK.

After answering a few questions about the play, Cesca found herself walking into the theatre foyer, where a welcoming committee of the staff were waiting. The manager, a man she'd got to know well in the time they'd been in rehearsals, came up and shook her hand vigorously.

'Congratulations. We're delighted for you.'

'Thank you. Is everybody here?' She looked around.

'Everything's fine. The cast are waiting for you backstage. Can I give you a glass of champagne to take with you?' He gestured at one of the girls holding a silver tray of champagne flutes. She was dressed in a white blouse and black skirt, a more familiar uniform than the designer dress Cesca was wearing.

'Thank you.' Cesca took the glass even though she was too hyped up to drink it.

When she arrived backstage she was hit by the commotion. People were running everywhere, orders were being shouted out, a young assistant with a clipboard was counting down the minutes. Cesca took a moment to breathe it in, to absorb the excitement. As a young child sitting in her mother's dressing room she had thought it romantic. Now it felt like so much more.

It was her lifeblood.

She pushed open the door for the dressing room, looking inside to see all the seats taken. The actors sat in front of their mirrors, adding final touches to their make-up, some whispering their first lines to their reflections. Each of them had their own ritual, honed through years of superstitious practice. Another part of this world that made it so unique.

Then there was the leading man. A dark-haired guy making his theatre debut. He had his eyes closed, his lips moving softly as if he was repeating the words over and over again. Though his face was calm, his leg kept shaking, moving up and down in a rhythm of its own. Cesca squashed the urge to touch it, to curl her fingers around his thigh. He was getting in the zone, and she didn't belong there.

Not yet.

'Break a leg, everybody.'

A few of them looked over, waving to acknowledge her. But there was only one person she was looking at. Sam, turned around, his face still impassive but his eyes ablaze. A single look and he had the ability to turn her legs to jelly.

He wasn't her Sam. Not right now. He was too deep in character for that. But when she was at the theatre she wasn't his Cesca, either. Yet somehow they managed to make it work.

And when they got home, they were completely each other's.

'There's some cards for you over there,' one of the cast told her, pointing to the table in the corner filled with flowers and gifts. She walked over, picking up the envelopes with her name on them. She could take the bouquets later.

The first card was from the producer. The man who'd taken the risk to stage her show, in spite of her past history. She read his kind words then propped it on the table, sliding her finger beneath the flap of the next card.

The second was from Sam's mum. Cesca couldn't help but smile as she read her words. *To the talented girl who has lit up my son's life. Your mother would have been proud of you. Kisses, Mama Lucia.*

In the time since Sam had walked back into her life, Cesca had come to know his mother and sisters well. Even when she was in London and he was in LA, they'd still invite her out to lunch, making her feel part of the family. Lucia had filled a void that Cesca hadn't realised she had. A surrogate mother of sorts.

351

'You forgot my card,' Sam said softly. She looked up to see him standing in front of her, a silver envelope in his hand. Still *her* Sam, after all. Cesca took it from him, opening it up to see a postcard of Varenna inside. Her eyes lingered on the beautiful villas that lined the lake, and the lush greenery that grew on the banks.

'Where it all began,' she murmured.

'The play?' His eyes were shining beneath the bright lights of the dressing room.

She shook her head. 'Us.' Her heart was full as he cupped her face with his hand, his palm warm against her skin. She read the back of the card. *Your play captured my imagination, but you captured my heart. Always yours, Sam.*

'Thank you,' she whispered. 'Thank you for always being mine.'

'I always will be. And if I wasn't covered in greasepaint I'd be kissing the hell out of you right now,' he said.

'If you weren't covered in greasepaint, I'd let you. But since this is my play, and my reputation, I'd rather not ravish the leading man before he even gets on the stage.'

Sam laughed. 'We'll save the ravishing for afterwards then.'

'Sounds good to me.' She rolled onto the balls of her feet, lifting herself a couple of inches higher, enough to whisper in his ear. 'Break a leg, Sam.'

He ran the pad of his thumb across her cheekbone. 'You, too, gorgeous.'

Cesca blew him a kiss, then walked out, making her way back to the public areas. Tonight she'd be watching her play from the audience, seeing the action from a different side.

Sliding into the seat between her sisters, she grabbed

each of their hands, squeezing them tight. A moment later the lights went down, and the hum of conversation dwindled to nothing.

She closed her eyes for a moment. This was finally it. After all this time, and all this angst, her play was making its West End debut.

What's Past is Prologue. It couldn't have had a better title.

'It's very different to movie acting, isn't it?' Randall, the older actor who played the father in the play, shot him a smile before turning back to the mirror and wiping off his make-up. 'So much more immediate, so intense. The adrenalin rush, man, there's nothing like it.'

'It's something else.' Sam took a deep breath. Twenty minutes after the final curtain had fallen and his body still hadn't recovered. It was like legal heroin. 'Though I'm not sure if I can take that night after night.'

'Oh, it gets easier. I bet you were just as nervous at your first movie premiere. And then by the second and the third, it's like old hat.'

Sam frowned. 'I wouldn't go that far. At my last premiere poor Cesca was pushed over and pretty much trampled underfoot.'

'Ah, I wondered why she was surrounded by security guards this time.'

'I thought she'd probably prefer to watch the play unbruised.'

Half an hour later Sam was climbing out of a black Mercedes, his own security guard pushing his way through the crowds. Sam walked into the wine bar, where the after-party was being held, and was immediately surrounded by admirers.

There were familiar faces, too. Will Allen, his best friend, had flown in from Hollywood, and was currently flirting with one of the production staff. Izzy and Sienna, looking glamorous in full-length gowns, were arguing with his mother over whether they could have another glass of champagne. And in the corner at a table were Hugh and Cesca's father, being clucked over by Cesca's sisters as they brought them drinks and plates of food.

'Congratulations, Sam.' Hugh shook his hand.

'You were fabulous,' Lucy told him, kissing his cheek. Kitty hugged him tightly and gave him a wink.

'Did you bring Milly with you?' Cesca's father asked. 'I saw her acting with you. Are you in love with her?'

'No, Dad,' Lucy interjected, a harassed expression on her face. 'This is Cesca's boyfriend, remember? And that wasn't Mum on the stage, it was an actress.'

'Of course it was.' Oliver looked annoyed. 'That's what I said. Well done, Sam. You were excellent.'

'Thank you, sir.' He nodded at Cesca's dad, unsure about what just happened.

The only person missing in the room was Foster, and he hadn't received an invitation. He was estranged from Lucia, after all. Not welcome here.

'Have you seen Cesca?' Sam asked the producer, who was surrounded by investors all talking rapidly.

'Last I saw her she was heading for the bathroom. She was looking a bit green.'

Thirty seconds later, Sam was barging his way into the women's bathroom. There were two girls at the sink, gossiping wildly, though their mouths stilled as soon as they caught sight of him in the doorway.

'Oh!' Shock was immediately replaced by interest. The girl nearest him smiled, her eyelashes fluttering. 'I think you may have the wrong room.'

'Can you give me a moment?' Sam inclined his head to the door.

'You want us to leave?'

'My girl isn't feeling well. I want to check if she's OK.'

The woman next to him sighed. 'Isn't that the sweetest? Why can't we find one of those, Marie?'

'Because they only exist on the stage?'

The two of them left, still arguing over whether Sam was real or not. He swallowed a smile, then walked towards the occupied cubicle, pausing to knock on the door.

'Cesca?' He kept his voice quiet. 'Babe, you in there?'

A shuffling came from inside. 'What are you doing in here?'

'I came to find you. David said you weren't feeling well, I wanted to help.'

'You shouldn't be in here. Imagine if anybody gets a photo of this. You'll be splashed all over the tabloids like some kind of sexual deviant. You'll be The Jackhammer all over again.'

Sam laughed. 'It's hardly deviant to be in a bathroom with your girlfriend. Especially when she's not feeling well.'

'In a public loo ...'

'Sweetheart, I really don't care if I'm the lead headline, I'm not going anywhere. So come out and let me take care of you.'

'I'm just being stupid.'

'You and I both know you're anything but stupid. Come out, let me hold you.'

The lock clicked, and the door opened inward. Cesca was sitting on the closed toilet seat, her elbows on her legs, her face propped on her hands.

'You know there's about a billion germs on those things?'

She looked up. 'I'm living life on the edge.'

'Come here.' He held out his hand. She took it, allowing him to pull her up and into his arms. She melted against him, her body soft against his. He ran his palms down her bare shoulders. 'Did I tell you how beautiful you looked tonight?'

'Says the man in the dinner jacket.'

'This dress, it does things to me,' he whispered in her ear. She shivered beneath his touch. 'It will look even better when it's on the floor.'

'Dirty boy.'

'You know it.' He chuckled against her ear. 'So why aren't you out there celebrating? Everything went so well tonight. The reviews are good, the audience loved it. Didn't you see the standing ovation at the end?'

'I was hiding in the foyer by then.'

He stepped back, still holding her shoulders. A quizzical expression formed on his face. 'Is there something wrong? I thought this was all you ever wanted. Did something happen you haven't told me about?'

She licked her dry lips. He followed her movement. 'I'm just . . .' She took a deep breath, refusing to meet his gaze. 'Scared, I guess.'

'About what?'

'That something's going to go wrong. I mean, things like this don't happen to me. I'm the girl who spent six years going back and forth like a ping-pong ball. Now here I am in some obscenely priced dress climbing out of limos, and being photographed everywhere I go. What the hell has happened?'

'You're not happy?'

'No, that's not it.' She covered his hands with hers. 'It's more that I'm too happy. I've got everything I ever wanted. My play, a home, my guy.' There were tears forming in her eyes. 'What if I lose it all again?'

Sam felt every part of her anxiety. It made him want to hold her tight. Of course she was afraid, she'd lost so much in her life. They both had.

'Babe, I can't promise things are going to be easy. I can't promise it's all going to be smooth sailing. But I can promise that whenever things get rough, I'll be right next to you, holding on tight. We could be rich or poor, and I couldn't give a shit as long as we're together.'

She nodded, her eyes wide as she stared at him.

'And if everything goes wrong, then I know a really great girl who can survive on no money. I've even heard she's good at dumpster-diving.'

Was that the tiniest smile playing at her lips?

'She's kick-ass at it,' Cesca whispered.

'And there's nobody I'd rather go dumpster-diving with than you.'

A tear rolled down her cheek. 'In some crazy, messed-up way, that might be the most romantic thing you've ever said to me.'

'Then I'm kicking myself for being totally shit at being romantic,' he told her. 'Because you deserve romance. You deserve everything. Including tonight. You've worked so hard, baby, please come out and enjoy it. If you spend your life worried you're going to lose everything, you're going to miss out. I don't want you to do that.'

Her gaze met his. 'I don't want to do that either.'

'Then let's go out, drink some champagne and talk to our

friends. Then we'll go home, I'll rip this dress off you, and remind you exactly what life's about.'

'It's about sex?' She frowned.

It was his turn to laugh. 'No, about love. Making it, having it, keeping it. I can't think of anything better than that.'

'Nor can I.' She melted into his arms again, her head inclined as he looked down at her. And when he pressed his lips to hers, he could taste the champagne mixed with her tears. It was an intoxicating combination.

'I love you,' she whispered against his mouth. Her breath was as warm as her words.

'I love you too, baby.'

And, really, nothing else really mattered. What was past was prologue, and the future was unwritten. They couldn't ask for any more than that.

Acknowledgments

I know this is the boring bit, but so many people helped me to shape Cesca's and Sam's story into the book you are reading today. Firstly to Meire Dias of the Bookcase Agency – my agent and dear friend. I honestly wouldn't be here without you. And to Flavia Viotti: agent, entrepreneur, and extraordinary woman. You both inspire me.

Thanks also to Anna Boatman for your support and advice, to Dominic Wakeford for your patience, and to the whole team at Piatkus for believing in me.

To Ash, Ella and Oliver – you make everything worthwhile. Thank you for trekking around Italy with me while I made notes and pretended it was a holiday. I promise to set the next book in an equally lovely destination.

To the rest of my family, thank you for your faith in this daughter and sister who sometimes spends more time in her head than in the real world.

I have so many wonderful friends that to name them all would take another book, so I'll try to be brief. Thank you to Claire, Melanie, Gemma and Kate for pre-reading. Thanks also to my RNA friends, to my Enchanted Publications friends, to my online friends, to my Rayleigh girls, and to everybody who has believed in me, and encouraged me in my writing.

Finally, to my readers; thank you for picking up this book. I hope it transported you to a world where dreams come true and love wins out. I always enjoy hearing from you, and can often be found on Twitter or Facebook, or via my website. Come and say hello if you have a few minutes. I have virtual chocolate, and I'm not afraid to share it.

Until the next time,

Carrie x